Her heart was breaking, but she couldn't let on. He'd only feel triumphant that he could affect her this way…

"All alone?" That deep velvety voice caused her heart to thump heavily in her chest.

Maya felt heat prickling on her skin as his gaze moved from her face to her bare shoulders and down the length of her legs. "I needed some fresh air," she said with more coolness than she felt. "That's all."

"That dress suits you," he said softly, his blue eyes electric as they settled back on her face. "It's no wonder he's been drooling over you like a puppy-dog."

"I don't know who or what you're talking about."

"Your latest conquest, who else?" He moved closer and she took a step back, but the balustrade effectively blocked her in. "Did he tell you his father's an Earl? Could be quite a good catch, don't you think?"

"Why, Rajiv, surely you're not jealous," she challenged, leaning back against the balustrade and pasting on a fake smile.

"Maybe I am," he acknowledged tightly. "Or maybe I don't like seeing my brother made a fool of. Touch me," he demanded, as he took her hand in his and drew it down his body, pressing her palm against the heated bulge that strained against his zipper.

Maya could feel the pulsating throb of his erection as her hand began to explore his body of its own accord.

Rajiv shuddered uncontrollably. "God, that feels good," he groaned, his breath hot against her neck. "I want you—I want you now. Let me come to you room later, let me please you. You know you want it, too."

Maya listened to his words with a mixture of pleasure and pain. How many women had he whispered those words to before? she wondered. If only Jay's accusations were not so fresh in her memory, if only Kirti wasn't there in the very next room.

She wants him, but she knows he's going to marry someone else…

When Maya Stewart arrives in London to visit her best friend Jay, she's aware that he's keeping the fact that he's gay a secret from his traditional Indian family. However, deceiving his dangerously good-looking older brother, Rajiv, is something Maya hadn't expected to deal with. The attraction between her and Rajiv is intense and immediate. But after being warned by Jay of Rajiv's reputation as a player and womaniser, Maya tries her utmost to keep her distance from him—although Rajiv doesn't give up easily.

He wants her, but he's sure that she's his brother's lover…

Rajiv Maddox has demons of his own to battle, including a darker side to his tortured soul. Highly suspicious of Maya, he thinks that she could be the reason for Jay's suicidal depression, yet Rajiv can't deny his attraction to this beautiful flame-haired Scottish girl. But one thing he knows for sure—if she finds out what a monster he really is, she'll run fast and hard in the other direction.

Can two people from two different cultures and such dissimilar worlds find any common ground or has fate doomed their love from the beginning?

KUDOS for *Passion & Deceit*

In *Passion & Deceit* by Leela Atherton, Maya Stewart goes to England to visit her friend, who is gay. His family doesn't know, however, and they think she is his lover. So when the chemistry sparks between Maya and her friend's brother Rajiv, he thinks she's cheating on his brother. Maya wants to tell him that his brother is gay and that they are only friends, but she can't bring herself to betray her friend. And besides, Rajiv scares her. He has made it clear that he intends to marry an Indian, since his mother is Indian, and so Maya knows, even as she's falling for him, that they have no future. But when they do finally get together the sparks really fly and the sex is HOT!!! This isn't your grandmother's romance, ladies. It's got lots of steamy love scenes. My kind of book! The characters are well-developed, realistic and three dimensional. The plot is filled with plenty of sexual tension, and even more sexual frustration. If you want a book to turn you on and steam up the windows, *Passion & Deceit* is it. ~ *Taylor Jones, Reviewer*

Passion & Deceit by Leela Atherton is a steamy romance that's pretty darn steamy. It's the story of a Maya Caucasian woman and Rajiv a man who is half-Indian and half Caucasian. He was bullied in school due to his half-breed status and the fact that his father was English, so Rajiv went to school in England. He is determined that his own children will not suffer the same fate and is therefore adamant that he will only marry an Indian woman. But that doesn't stop from making a move on Maya, nor from taking her, even though he thinks she is his brother's lover. It's a bit of a shock for the poor man when he discovers that she is a virgin and his brother is gay. The sex is hot, which, in my opinion, is the only kind of sex worth having, and if this book doesn't turn you on, then you've already been dead a week. The plot is strong and the characters are very real. I felt their frustration even as I enjoyed the sex scenes. This is a book you'll want to read when you have some privacy, trust me. *~ Regan Murphy, Reviewer*

ACKNOWLEDGEMENTS

I wish to thank Black Opal Books for believing in me and my writing, particularly Lauri Wellington and Faith Caminski for all their guidance and support.

A special thanks to Mark Coker and smashwords.com for giving me the opportunity to self-publish my work, making it available to readers all over the world. The amount of downloads and reviews of my work on Smashwords kept me motivated. I will always be indebted to you.

To the author who influenced me most, from my early teens up until today, Ms Anne Mather, a writer way ahead of her time. My work would not be what it is, were it not for her influence. Thank you for bringing excitement to a young teenager's life.

A big thank you to my friend Karin Ades, not just for her knowledge and support, but for recommending smashwords.com.

And my sincere gratitude to my true friends (you know who you are) for your interest and enthusiasm on this journey.

Last and most importantly, with love to my husband Giulio, for always believing in me and my work, and my daughter Nila, for keeping me young.

PASSION & DECEIT

Book 1

Leela Atherton

A Black Opal Books Publication

Black Opal Books

BECAUSE SOME STORIES JUST HAVE TO BE TOLD

GENRE: STEAMY ROMANCE/INTERRACIAL ROMANCE

This is a work of fiction. Names, places, characters and incidents are either the product of the author's imagination or are used fictitiously, and any resemblance to any actual persons, living or dead, businesses, organizations, events or locales is entirely coincidental. All trademarks, service marks, registered trademarks, and registered service marks are the property of their respective owners and are used herein for identification purposes only. The publisher does not have any control over or assume any responsibility for author or third-party websites or their contents.

PASSION & DECEIT ~ BOOK 1
Copyright © 2014 by Leela Atherton
Cover Design by Jackson Cover Designs
All cover art copyright © 2014
All Rights Reserved
Print ISBN: 978-1-626941-91-5

First Publication: OCTOBER 2014

Published by Black Opal Books **http://www.blackopalbooks.com**

DEDICATION

In memory of my mother who may not have approved,
but would be happy for me just the same.

Every time I think of you, that is how I see you, how I see us, frozen for all time on that canvas, immune to the fading of memory. I spend immeasurable moments imagining myself in that scene, until I feel I am entering the space of the photograph and am no longer the man who observes but the man lying beside the woman. Then the quiet symmetry of the picture is broken and I hear voices very close to my ear.

"Tell me a story," I say to you.

"What about?"

"Tell me a story you've never told anyone before. Make it up for me."

~ Rolf Carlé
© 1989 by Isabel Allende

CHAPTER 1

Rajiv exited the Mercedes and made his way reluctantly toward the entrance of the busy train station. The London weather was humid after the cool comfort of the air-conditioned vehicle. He had planned to send one of his staff to meet the girl rather than coming himself, but his concern for his brother had made him change his mind at the last minute. Besides, he was curious to meet her, to find out if she was the reason for his brother's state of mind. He was usually good at judging people. In fact, he believed that this was one of the main reasons for his success in business. His instincts were sharp when it came to people. He would even go so far as to say that he used to analyze people and enjoy figuring out what made them tick. He shoved his hands into his trouser pockets and paused for a moment, *used to*, not anymore. Lately he'd felt a growing sense of boredom seeping into his life, into his soul. He shook himself mentally, aware that his introspective behaviour was drawing some attention from the bustling commuters. Only beggars and the homeless loitered around Kings Cross Station and he was too well dressed to be either.

Maybe it was Sanjay's depression rubbing off on him? But deep down, he knew this feeling of...emptiness...had started quite a while before his brother had returned to London.

An attractive dark-haired woman caught his eye and smiled tentatively. Rajiv smiled back automatically and then moved purposefully toward the main area of the station. Now was not the time for all this introspection. Besides, he didn't want to keep Sanjay's girlfriend waiting.

Rajiv noticed her immediately. She was standing at the station's meeting point, a small suitcase on wheels beside her and an animated expression on her face. It seemed as if she found the rather squalid hustle and bustle of Kings Cross Station quite fascinating.

His brother had said, "Just look for the most beautiful girl in the station and that will be Maya."

At the time, Rajiv had smiled to himself, but it seemed his brother was right, for she was quite striking. He couldn't decide whether she looked like a hippy who'd just stepped out of the 1960s or a nymph from a Pre-Raphaelite painting. Her hair was unusual. He searched for the right word to describe it…Titian, perhaps? A coppery color, streaked with gold, it hung straight down to her waist and could not possibly be natural. He could not make out the color of her eyes yet, but there was no mistaking the beauty in their slanted shape. She was dressed in a lilac cotton top that hugged her slim body and hinted at small, tight breasts. His gaze dropped down to take in the flowing Indian skirt and flat, strappy leather sandals. As his eyes moved slowly back up her long lissom body, he realized that she had become aware of his appraisal.

Her gaze was cool and dismissive, telling him plainly that she was accustomed to being surveyed by the opposite sex and didn't particularly enjoy it. The look she gave him was clearly unfriendly, and Rajiv decided it was time to make her aware of just who he was.

Watching him approach, the expression on her exquisite face would have stopped most men in their tracks and, as he got closer, Rajiv found himself staring into haughty green eyes. Incredible, expressive eyes, that almost stopped him in his tracks. Her skin was smooth and creamy, just a trace of color shading her high cheekbones. His eyes settled on her full inviting mouth and he saw her lips tighten in anger.

"Maya—Maya Stewart?" He kept his tone impersonal and she nodded, her expression clearing. "I'm Rajiv Maddox, Sanjay's brother."

"Oh." She seemed at a loss for words and Raj felt a kick of pleasure. He'd managed to unsettled her cool confidence.

He held out his hand reluctantly. For some reason, he was not keen to touch her. Her palm was cool when his fingers came into contact with her soft skin and he drew away quickly, trying to ignore the shiver of awareness that ran up his arm.

She was quite tall he noticed now. He was used to towering over woman—like Kirti—but this girl was as different from Kirti as it was possible to be.

"It was very kind of you to meet me." Her voice was low, with a subtle lilt that betrayed her Scottish origins. "From what Jay has told me, you're a very busy man."

Rajiv frowned. "It's no problem." He was wondering just how much his younger brother had told her about him. "My driver's waiting just outside the station." He picked up the small suitcase, motioning her toward the exit.

Outside, the sun was shining but the London air still felt humid and polluted. Rajiv squinted his eyes against the sudden brightness, looking for the Mercedes. He saw it parked in a No Parking Zone, and Bijal was climbing out, ready to assist them.

"This way," he said, nodding towards the Mercedes.

He introduced her to Bijal, his driver and head of security, irritated by Bijal's reaction to her warm smile. As she slid gracefully into the vehicle he caught a glimpse of long slim legs, lightly tanned with thin silver chains circling each delicate ankle—Indian style. Rajiv felt a stirring below his belt and scowled, irritated with himself. He handed her suitcase to Bijal and made his way round to the other side of the vehicle, climbing in beside her but keeping as much distance between them as possible.

She turned to him with a smile. "I've heard driving in London can be a nightmare. You're lucky to have someone else do it for you."

Rajiv stared at her, unable to concentrate on what she was saying for a moment. Her smile was devastating, lighting up her beautiful face with a charm that seemed so genuine. He blinked and forced his brain to begin functioning again. He needed to remember who this girl was and that she was strictly out of bounds.

"Yes, driving in London can be either stressful or boring," he managed finally, wondering if there was sarcasm behind her comment on being *lucky* to have someone else do the driving for him. "I much prefer to pay someone else to do it for me," he added dryly. He could smell her perfume now, a subtle floral fragrance that teased at his nostrils and stirred his senses.

"You don't look at all like Jay," she observed, as Rajiv shifted in his seat.

"How do you mean?"

She hesitated. "Well, Jay is sort of quiet and sensitive."

He raised his eyebrows. "And me—I'm not the sensitive type?"

He'd managed to embarrass her. He could see the flush that colored her cheekbones and, for some reason, it pleased him. He wanted her to feel uncomfortable. He wanted her to know that he was not the *quiet, sensitive* pushover that his brother was.

"Well, I hardly know you, but judging from first impressions I would say you seem more the strong, sensible type." She smiled that devastating smile again, her tone almost playful, and Rajiv stared, undecided whether to be insulted or not.

Hell, no wonder Jay imagined himself in love with the girl. She was all too disturbing—so different from the women he usually met, both Indian and Western. But he still didn't trust her. Jay had come back from university in Edinburgh a changed person—a shadow of his old self, and Rajiv was not sure if this girl sitting beside him was to blame.

"How is Jay?" she asked and he turned away, finding it easier to concentrate when he wasn't on the receiving end of those sultry eyes.

"He's…well, since being back in England he's been rather low." There was no point in lying. She'd see it for herself soon enough. "I gather you've spoken to him lately?"

"Yes," she answered, "but Jay was never much good on the phone."

"Well, we're all hoping that your presence will snap him out of it." He turned, watching her reaction to this.

"Depression is not something you just snap out of," she said.

"Ah, yes." He leaned his head back against the soft leather upholstery of the car. "I forgot. You've got a degree in psychology now, right?"

Her eyes flashed at the irony in his voice. "I wasn't talking as a psychologist," she answered tightly. "I was talking as Jay's friend."

Jay's friend, so that's how she was going to play it. This was going to be interesting.

She was looking out of the tinted window now, as they passed through the West End on their way to the house in Knightsbridge. Rajiv had been extremely reluctant to take her home with him. In fact, he'd had an argument with his mother on the phone about it the day before.

"Why can't she just get a train straight from London to Wiltshire?" he'd asked his mother impatiently.

"Because she'd have to get across London to Victoria Station and then wait God knows how long for a connecting train!"

He could hear her voice becoming agitated and, knowing what she'd been through these past few weeks, Rajiv had relented. He would do as his mother asked and drive her to Wiltshire the following day.

Since Sanjay had come back from University, both Rajiv and his mother had become more and more concerned about his mental state. Even being in the peaceful countryside of Wiltshire had made hardly any difference to Jay's general apathy. Rajiv could see the strain it was putting on his mother. Since his father's death four years ago, Rajiv had taken over the running of the company as well as the role of head of the family.

His mother had come to rely on him to deal with any crisis that might arise. Having grown up with an Indian mother and a very English father, Rajiv had always felt Indian.

Now that the family was in trouble, it was up to him, as the male head of the household, to deal with the problem.

This was a crisis, he reminded himself grimly. Seeing his brother wasting away for no apparent reason was tearing the family apart. And if this—Maya—was that really her name? If she could be of any help, he was willing to give it a go, even if his instincts were telling him she could cause complications for the whole family.

"London's certainly changed since I was last here." Her soft accent pulled Rajiv back into the present.

"And when was that?" he asked, trying not to look at her full pink mouth, the bottom lip lush and inviting.

"Oh, years ago." She sighed. "I came on a school trip."

"Well, it couldn't have been that many years," he said dryly. "You look to me like you've barely stepped out of the classroom." He said it to annoy her, but she laughed and Rajiv felt that laugh all the way down to his groin.

"Was that meant to be a compliment?"

He tried not to respond to her impish smile but it was impossible. She was teasing him! Rajiv Maddox was not used to being teased. Being CEO of Maddox Junta Investments meant that the people he came into contact with, male or female, were very much aware of who he was and acted accordingly. He didn't think any of them would even dream of teasing him.

He wanted to make some cutting retort but looking into those twinkling cat eyes he felt at a loss for words—another rarity. His eyes dropped to her mouth and suddenly he caught a tantalizing glimpse of a dainty pink tongue. He could feel his skin prickling, a wave of heat washing over him. This was crazy, he told himself, turning jerkily away, loosening his tie, and unbuttoning his shirt. She might be beautiful, she might be different from any woman he'd ever met, but she was probably a player or an opportunist, or both, and even if she wasn't, she was his brother's girlfriend, for God's sake.

His cell phone buzzed. It was his PA, Joseph, asking where he was. Joseph reminded him of a meeting they had that afternoon.

"Don't panic Joseph," he replied, not wanting to say too much with Maya in the car. Even though she was staring out the tinted windows, she couldn't help but hear his side of the conversation. "I managed to get the meeting moved to tomorrow morning at nine and I'll be in well before then. Just make sure all the documents are in order, okay?"

He ended the call abruptly, not wanting her to know about his earlier decision to meet her himself and taking the afternoon off to find out what he could about her before leaving her with Sanjay.

He stared out at the busy London Street, wishing he hadn't made that last minute decision to pick her up. Wishing he could put as much distance between himself and this girl and yet, at the same time, not wanting to let her out of his sight. His phone buzzed again and, with a sigh, he answered it.

Rajiv noted her expression as they entered the Knightsbridge house. Well, he thought to himself, it would do her good to feel a bit overawed. The girl was far too confident for her own good, *and for my peace of mind*, added a little voice.

"Mrs. Travis." He greeted the housekeeper as she approached them. "This is Miss Maya Stewart, the young lady I told you about. Maya, our housekeeper, Mrs. Travis." He watched her smile as she shook the older woman's hand.

"How nice to meet you."

"Thank you Miss." The housekeeper turned to him. "I have the room ready, Mr. Rajiv, shall I get Bijal to take the luggage up."

"Yes, thank you, Mrs. Travis." He was tempted to disappear into his study, to gather his thoughts, before preparing for tomorrow's meeting. Tempted to send her up to her room with her suitcase. But his mother had instilled her *good Indian manners* in him too well to be ignored. "Shall we go through to the drawing room?"

She followed him through, surprise registering on her face at the size and elegance of the room, and Rajiv wished he could read her thoughts. Was she materialistic? Most— maybe all—of the women he knew were. Was wealth a turn on for her? And did it even matter, as long as she could bring his brother back from that dark place where he seemed to be hiding?

"What can I offer you to drink?" he asked, heading for

the liquor cabinet. "Or would you prefer Mrs. Travis to make you some tea?"

"Tea would be nice," she said, her eyes moving round the room.

He poured himself a stiff whisky and gulped down half a measure before going to order the tea. It might only be five-thirty in the afternoon, but it had been one hell of a long day. And it wasn't over yet.

She was standing by the window when he re-entered the room, the afternoon sun catching traces of gold in her lush coppery hair. It was a most unusual color—*if it is real*. It certainly looked genuine, but nowadays you never knew. His eyes traveled downward.

He could just make out the long, slim, lines of her legs through the thin cotton skirt. Her body was really something. She could easily have been a model. He'd dated a few models in his time, but none of them had had the body, or face to match hers.

Was she aware of the effect she was having on him? he wondered, making his way back to the liquor cabinet and draining the whisky with a feeling of annoyance.

"So what exactly do you know about my brother's situation since he came home from University?" he asked as she turned to face him.

"His situation?" She frowned. "Um, not much, really."

"But you've spoken to him on the phone, right?" he continued, watching her carefully.

"Yes, we've spoken a number of times and he did sound rather subdued, I noticed."

"So, do you have any idea why he's so…subdued or should I say depressed, seeing as that's what the doctors are calling it?"

He knew he was grilling her, but it was time to try and get to the bottom of this. If she knew anything that he didn't, he was determined to get it out of her.

"I—why, no. He—he seemed fine when we were up in Edinburgh together. I really can't say."

She was lying. He could feel it in his gut and his expression told her so.

"I care deeply about my brother, Miss Stewart, and seeing him like this is causing my mother a lot of distress." He walked slowly toward her. "I would hope that if you have any idea what the problem is, you would be kind enough to help us out." He was close enough now to see the faint flush on her cheeks and the way her teeth were biting nervously into her full bottom lip.

"I—I'm sorry, Mr. Maddox, but I really don't know what to say."

She was staring at some point below his chin. Not even a very good liar, he decided.

"Please, call me Rajiv." He spoke softly and had the pleasure of seeing her color deepen before he turned away to pour himself another drink. This time he added ice and water to the whisky. He needed his wits about him if he was going to find out just what it was she was hiding.

"How come do you and Jay have Indian names?" She was trying to change the subject, he was sure of it. "I thought if you were Catholics…"

Rajiv sighed, frustrated. "My first name is James, like my father's." His jaw clenched. How he hated that name. "My mother chose my second name, Rajiv, which is what she's always called me and since my father died I've never answered to the name "James."

She looked genuinely interested, intelligence shining through those green eyes. "And Jay?" she asked. "Everyone in Edinburgh calls him Jay?"

"Jay's first name is actually Jacob—very Catholic," he said. "His second name's Sanjay, once again chosen by my mother. Anymore questions?"

He knew he was being rude and abrupt, but their names seemed unimportant under the circumstances.

She flushed. "I'm sorry, I didn't mean to pry."

He shook his head, feeling petty and mean. "No it's just difficult to focus on anything besides Sanjay's illness at the moment."

"Of course," she said softly and then remained silent, waiting for him to speak.

Rajiv took a deep breath and got straight to the point. "Since returning to England, Jay has spent all of his time moping around Cranthorpe. That's our family's country home." She nodded and he continued. "At first that's all we thought it was, moping around, but he stopped eating and started losing weight, sleeping until two, three in the afternoon. Finally, my mother called in the doctor who diagnosed his depression. Naturally, we were shocked. Jay has always been what you described as a sensitive boy, but he's never in the past suffered from depression. Besides, some Indian people, like my mother, don't really understand depression." He paused, trying to gauge her reaction, but she just nodded sympathetically. "The doctor prescribed antidepressants, which he's been taking for about two weeks now, but unfortunately there hasn't been any noticeable improvement."

The sound of Mrs. Travis approaching silenced him and he waited while she deposited the tea with some Indian cakes on a low table beside one of the sofas.

"Thank you, Mrs. Travis." Rajiv watched Maya seat herself and pour the tea, while sipping slowly at his whisky, the warmth of it easing some of the tension from his gut. Finally he continued. "My mother noticed that the only time Jay seemed even remotely energised was when he was talking about you, or after he'd spoken with you on the phone. So she suggested inviting you over for a visit."

"I see." She nodded her head. "So it was your mother's idea."

"Yes, but it was the first time we'd seen Jay enthusiastic about anything in weeks," Rajiv continued. "What we're hoping for now is that this enthusiasm will continue and that your presence there will somehow draw him out of this state that he's in."

She nodded, not saying anything, and Rajiv felt a sense of irritation, as she sat there demurely sipping her tea.

"I can't help wondering," he added softly. "Do you think his leaving Edinburgh—and you—could have anything to do with his depression?"

This got her attention and the teacup rattled as she set it down. "I really can't say. I mean he might be missing university life and—and all his friends, but it's difficult to know, really."

"And you, do you think he's been missing you—lovesick, perhaps?" He loomed over her, hands pushed into the pockets of his trousers, watching the surprise register on her lovely face. Surprise and…something else. She *was* trying to hide something. Rajiv felt sure of it. But what? If she and Jay had been having an affair, why should she want to hide it? Unless she was no longer interested in continuing the affair.

"I doubt that very much." She stood up. "And now if you don't mind, I'd like to go to my room. It's been a long day."

Damn right, he minded. If she escaped now, he might not get another chance to figure out what she knew. But there was little he could do, short of forcing her to stay where she was.

And somehow, he knew that approach wouldn't work with her. No, perhaps he should try a more subtle approach—try to charm her.

The idea was decidedly enticing. He'd used his charm

on many women in the past, usually to get them into bed. But he wasn't trying to get Maya Stewart into bed, he reminded himself. She was probably his brother's lover, for God's sake.

But inveigling himself to her might still be the best way to get to the truth. After all, he was doing it for his Jay. And didn't the end justify the means?

CHAPTER 2

Maya stared at her reflection in the mirror of the marble-topped dressing table beside her bedroom window. The face that stared back at her looked anxious and flushed, her bottom lip swollen and sensitive. *In other words guilty as charged.* Or so Rajiv Maddox would be thinking. God, the man could terrify you with just one look, and the looks he'd been giving her had been full of scepticism and suspicion.

With a groan of frustration, Maya stood up, unable to face the mirror any longer. This bedroom, in fact the whole house, had come as something of a shock to her. She had known that Jay was from a well-off family, but she had not realized just how affluent they were. Was that why he was finding it so difficult to tell his brother the truth?

She shook her head, unable to get the man's presence out of her mind. Rajiv Maddox was way too disturbing. His face had a harshness about it, which should have detracted from his looks, but somehow, only seemed to add to his attraction. He was attractive. There was no doubt about that. His Indian roots were obvious. Even if his father had been English, he obviously took from his mother's gene pool. Thick black hair, brushing his collar, and those sleek, high cheekbones would turn any woman's head. Only the eyes could give away the fact that he was not fully Indian. Sky blue eyes that seemed to change shades with his mood, becoming darker when he was angry—as he had been not long ago, just before she had run out on him. Those darkened blue eyes had told her clearly that he wasn't finished with her and she shivered at the thought.

He was so different from Jay, whose gentle charm and easy-going manner had given her so much pleasure during their time at university. Jay, with his streaky brown hair and amber eyes. He didn't really look Indian at all. Most of the time she would completely forget that he was half-Indian and, the fact that he was Catholic, like her, only added to that impression.

Maya stared out at the perfectly landscaped garden beneath her window. Everything about the place reeked of taste and wealth.

The bedroom was huge with an attached bathroom that could probably put five star hotels to shame. Her bare feet sank into the cream colored carpet as she made her way through to the marble-tiled bathroom with its sunken bath and turned on the heavy silver taps. An array of expensive-looking toiletries was set up on one of the bathroom shelves and Maya shook her head in wonder, adding some luxurious bubble bath to the water.

Rajiv Maddox had suggested they meet downstairs at seven, so she had about an hour to relax and prepare for the inquisition. For she was sure that was what he had planned. She would have to be strong, as she had no intention of letting Jay down. His secret was safe with her, no matter how formidable his brother turned out to be.

After a luxurious bath, she used one of the soft white towels to dry herself and massaged some of the creamy body lotion from the bathroom into her skin. Her body felt hyper sensitive, as her mind kept drifting to the dark and broodingly attractive man whose eyes seemed to see right through her.

Her wardrobe was limited, to say the least, so in the end she decided on a pair of silky harem pants in a deep rusty color. It was a warm evening, and the light cotton fabrics she preferred were suitable for such weather. On top, she wore a beaded blouse of emerald green, which tied around the waist. Maya knew it was probably not the kind of attire he was used to seeing on a woman, but this was her style of dress and if he didn't like it, then tough for him.

Brushing her long hair until it shone, she added a touch of mascara to her eyelashes and a tinted gloss to her lips. Then, trying to quell the quivering butterflies in her stomach, she made her way downstairs again.

Rajiv was in the process of pouring himself a drink when she entered the drawing room. He too had changed she noticed. The business suit was gone and, in its place, he was wearing a black shirt, opened at the throat, and a pair of black trousers. His hair looked slightly damp and she guessed he had recently stepped out of the shower. Images of him naked in the shower popped into her mind and it took all her self-control to greet him in a cool and confident manner.

"Hi." His gaze traveled down the length of her and slowly up again. "Can I get you something to drink?"

"Um, a dry white wine, if you have it?" Maya replied, sliding her hands into the pockets of her pants.

He raised an eyebrow. "Sure you don't want something stronger? A Gin and tonic or a Martini perhaps?"

"No thanks," she replied. "I don't normally drink spirits."

He smiled wryly and she wished she didn't sound so prim. She seated herself on one of the settees, and then wished she hadn't when he passed her the glass of wine and lowered himself down beside her.

He was close enough for her to smell the clean soapy smell that emanated from his body. She could see the thick lashes that fringed his eyes and the smooth dark skin stretched tautly over his cheekbones.

"Well, aren't you going to try it?" he asked softly, and then seeing her confusion added with a smile, "The wine, is it dry enough? Most Indian people prefer sweeter wine."

"It's lovely," she replied, after taking a small sip.

He was playing with her, trying to unsettle her. Why? And why was her body responding to him in this way? She took a deep steadying breath and stared down at the wine in her glass, a flare of anger beginning inside her. This man was not going to overpower her with his sexual magnetism.

"Is something bothering you," he asked. "You seem nervous?"

"Would it please you if I were?" she asked, giving him one of her coolest looks.

He laughed and her head jerked up to stare at him in shock. God, how different he looked! Their eyes locked. He was still grinning, looking sexy as hell, and Maya's insides turned to mush. She couldn't stop staring at the little laughter lines that fanned his eyes and how the humor had softened his chiselled features.

"You know you're not at all what I expected either," he said finally as the laughter died away.

"I suppose that begs the question—what did you expect?" She kept her tone cool.

He leaned back, observing her through half closed lids. "That's a tricky question to answer," he said softly.

Maya held his gaze with difficulty and waited, not saying anything until finally he continued. "You see I've never met and of Jay's girlfriends before." This did not surprise her, but she refrained from saying so. "I've met a lot of his friends, male and female, but no one special—I don't think. So I wasn't really sure what to expect, but I think perhaps you're..." He paused as if searching for the right words. "...more mature than what I imagined."

Maya smiled. "I get told that a lot, actually."

"I rather guessed you would," he responded ruefully.

Maya tried, but she simply could not drag herself from the lazy intimacy of his gaze.

The sound of footsteps approaching was a heartfelt relief and she turned to smile weakly as the housekeeper came into view.

Mrs. Travis beamed, her affection for the man obvious. "Dinner is ready, Mister Rajiv."

The room they ate in was not the main dining room. It was too small, Maya guessed, and too intimate for her peace of mind. But she needn't have worried. Rajiv Maddox was on his best behavior. The charged and intimate atmosphere she'd sensed before seemed merely a figment of her imagination. He could certainly be a charming and entertaining host when he wanted to, telling her about the places he'd traveled to, sad and funny stories, especially about India, which fascinated her most of all. So, with the delicious Indian cuisine, superb wine, and candlelit atmosphere, Maya found she was enjoying herself more than she ought to.

"Your name, Maya," he observed toward the end of the meal. "It's Indian, is it a nickname?"

"No." She smiled. "My parents spent some time in India before I was born and they obviously liked the name."

"Really? Were they like hippies, traveling round India?" She couldn't help laughing at the picture of her parents being described as hippies, and he stared back at her, his blue eyes darkening. "What?"

She shook her head. "It's just the idea of my parents as hippies. They were teachers, primary school teachers in Calcutta," she said.

"I see, and are they still teaching now?"

"My mother still teaches part-time, though she's visiting her sister in South Africa right now," she said. "But my father died—almost four years ago."

"I'm sorry. He must have been quiet young when he died."

His expression was sympathetic and she wondered if he was remembering his own father.

"Yes it was a difficult time—cancer." She tried to keep the pain from her voice. "I think my mother's only just starting to get over it now."

"Do you have any brothers or sisters?" he asked.

"No, I'm an only child," she answered, trying to lighten her tone. "You're very good at drawing people out you know. Perhaps *you* should have studied psychology."

He frowned. "Is that what I'm doing? I didn't realize. Couldn't it be that I'm just interested in you?"

"You mean in what makes me tick."

"You make it sound calculated, like I've got some kind of hidden agenda?" His eyes held hers. "What is it, Maya? Are you afraid of me?"

She laughed, ignoring her body's response every time he said her name. "Should I be?"

He seemed to take the question quite seriously, pausing for a moment. "No, you shouldn't. As long as your interest in my brother is genuine, you have nothing to fear from me."

"Jay and I have always had each other's best interests at heart," she said carefully.

"We're very worried about him, you know," he murmured, his lean, dark fingers twisting the stem of his wine glass.

He stared across at her and Maya felt a mixture of awareness and guilt as their eyes locked once again. If only he wasn't so damn attractive, she thought, and so dangerous.

This was not a man to fool with and Jay had put her in

a difficult position. It was obvious what the problem was, but it was not her secret to tell.

"You have a very expressive face."

His words startled her. Could he read her mind? She shifted uncomfortably trying not to look alarmed.

"Why do I get the feeling that you're hiding something from me, Maya?" Those dark, blue eyes seemed to penetrate her soul.

"I'm sorry that you feel that way," she said, running the tip of her tongue along her parched upper lip. "All I can say is that I'll do my best as far as Jay is concerned." This at least was true.

Rajiv sighed raking his fingers through his hair and rubbed the back of his neck. Maya experienced the craziest desire to go round and massage his aching muscles, to feel the tension slowly ease from his lean, hard body. "I guess I'm just grasping at straws," he said roughly. "You'll have to forgive me. I don't usually accuse my guests of deceit."

ⱭↃⱭↃ

It was a perfect summer's night and Rajiv wished he was in the right frame of mind to enjoy it, but he wasn't. Normally, he loved sitting out here on the patio overlooking the lush garden in which he and Jay had played as children—at least when their father wasn't around. Had Jay been as unhappy as he had, Rajiv wondered. They had both suffered at the hands of their father, no matter how Rajiv had tried to protect his younger brother from their bullying father. He'd married their mother simply for her family's wealth. Constantly reminding his sons that they were *halfbreeds*, not something to be proud of, in his opinion. His mother had suffered too, his drinking and womanizing well known, and she had suffered the humiliation in dignified silence. Things had been easier since the old man's death.

Or at least it felt that way to Rajiv. Sanjay had been free to drop out of studying law, which his father had insisted he study. Rajiv had encouraged him to work on gaining a degree in the Arts, something Sanjay had always had a passion, and talent for, and his brother had seemed really happy doing what he'd always dreamed of. Yes, Sanjay had always been the more sensitive one, but he'd never been the silent, withdrawn person that he had now become.

Since Maya had gone to bed about an hour ago, Rajiv had been sitting out here trying to figure out what the hell was going on. He could have sworn she was hiding something and, at one moment during dinner, he'd had to stop himself from grabbing and shaking her. He smiled cynically to himself. That would have certainly rattled Little Miss Cool. In fact, it would give him great pleasure to get under her skin, *and under her clothes too*, he admitted ruefully to himself. Yes, the idea of getting beneath those rather bohemian clothes of hers caused a definite throb of excitement in his lower region. But the rapid realization that it was his brother's girlfriend he was lusting over brought his little fantasy to an abrupt end. Instead, his imagination began conjuring up pictures of Jay doing the dirty deed. Rajiv rose abruptly out of the chair. The idea of his brother and Maya making passionate love was not a pleasant one.

It seemed crazy, but he was aware of a distinctly possessive feeling toward her. *Well, you'd better loose it buster*, he told himself. The woman was not his to possess and, besides, he didn't even trust her. Just because she was young and beautiful, with a body to die for, didn't mean there wasn't a devious mind lurking beneath it all. He needed to get Carlton to do a background check on her first thing tomorrow. He should have done it before she'd arrived, but he hadn't expected her to be such an enigma. He needed to know more about her. He had to find out what it was she was hiding.

He walked to the end of the patio and felt his eyes drawn toward her bedroom window. The curtains were closed but there was a sliver of light shining through. So she too was still awake.

What was she thinking about? Pictures of her lying naked in bed entered his wayward mind, her coppery hair spread out on the pillow and her green eyes sensual and inviting…With a groan of impatience, Rajiv made his way back into the house and headed for the liquor cabinet. It was going to be a long night.

℮⁄❀℮⁄❀

Maya was having breakfast the following morning when Jay telephoned. Rajiv had left for the office early that morning, she'd been informed, and was expected back around midday to drive her to Wiltshire.

Mrs Travis brought the cordless phone through to her, and she couldn't help feeling like someone out of a Hollywood movie, sitting in the same room that they'd dined in the night before, with the sun shining through the long windows, a spread of fresh fruit, cereal, crispy bacon, eggs, toast, coffee, *and* fruit juice set out just for her.

"Maya, are you there?" she heard Jay ask anxiously.

"Jay, yes I'm here. How are you, darling?"

"Fine, I got your text yesterday saying that you'd arrived safely." He paused. "Sorry I didn't get back to you, but I've been preoccupied lately, as you can imagine."

"That's okay, Jay," she assured him. "It'll be much easier once we're able to talk face-to-face."

"Oh, Maya, it's so good to hear your voice," he said with some enthusiasm. "I can't wait to see you. I need some normality around me and no one's more normal than you, love."

"I guess I'll have to take that as a compliment." She

laughed, wondering if Rajiv had been exaggerating his brother's state of mind. He sounded quite upbeat to her. "But seriously, Jay, how are you? Your brother seems worried."

"Oh God, him and mother are driving me crazy. Worry, worry, worry. I think Indian people have perfected the art of worrying. I've been a bit low that's all. You know it's not very pleasant being dumped, or maybe you don't know," he added with a bitter laugh. "Bet you've never been dumped before. You're far too beautiful."

Maya sighed, hearing the note of despair beneath his humorous tone, "So you haven't heard from him since leaving Edinburgh?"

"Not even a whisper," he answered tightly. "But stuff him. It's you I can't wait to see. Only problem is we'll have to wait another day."

"But I thought your brother was driving me over today."

"I know, I know, but he's just called us from the office and there's some kind of business meeting that's taking longer than he expected—it's always something with him— so you'll be leaving early tomorrow morning, instead." He paused. "Are you okay with that?"

"Yes, of course, I am," she said quickly, but another evening alone with Rajiv Maddox caused a shiver of nerves, *or was it excitement*, to course through her body.

"So what did you think of my dearly beloved brother then?" asked Jay, as if able to read her mind. "I hope you didn't swoon like all the others. But you're not the type to swoon, are you?"

"Jay! Your brother has been very hospitable." She couldn't think of anything else to say.

"Has he been giving you the third degree—about me, I mean?"

"He's very concerned about you and I—I felt he was

hoping I could help in some way. Oh, Jay, he made me feel so guilty!"

"God, Maya, I'm so sorry. I've put you in a difficult position. Christ, what am I going to do with my life?" His voice was suddenly filled with anguish.

"Jay darling, it's okay," she said hurriedly. "I'll be there tomorrow and we'll talk this through. We'll work it out. You just need someone to talk to that's all. To put things in perspective."

Her words seem to calm him down. "You're right, Maya. I need some company, someone who I can be myself with. God, I can't wait for tomorrow." His tone lightened up a little. "But what about you, what are you going to do with yourself today?"

"Oh gosh, there's so much to see here. Maybe I'll go to the Tate Modern. I've been dying to see it."

After reassuring Jay that she was perfectly able to find her way around London, they ended the call, and Maya stared out of the window, frowning. The sooner the truth was known the better, she couldn't help thinking.

It was turning out to be another beautiful day and, after changing into a violet ankle-length skirt and a white cotton blouse, Maya threw a light cotton sarong into her oversized bag and ran down the marble staircase. It took a good few minutes to locate Mrs Travis in the huge house. When she finally found her, Maya mentioned that she was going sight-seeing and would be back later. She was impatient to get out into the sunshine and enjoy this unexpected day in the big city.

She decided to take the bus rather than the Underground. It would give her a chance to take in the sights of London on her way to the Tate Modern—one of the largest and most popular Museums of Modern Art in the world.

The huge building, positioned right on the South Bank of the Thames, was a renovated Power Station built in the earlier part of the twentieth century and simply beautiful, or at least she thought so. She was not in a hurry to enter the building, quite happy to savor the sunshine and the river and the beauty of the Art Deco brick building towering above her.

Finally, she went inside and lost herself in the world of art. The place was so huge that by four o'clock she had seen perhaps just a quarter of the works on display. There was no way she would get to see all of it in one day, she realized, and, besides, she was feeling hungry. On her way down the escalator, she spotted a café overlooking the river and couldn't resist taking a seat by the window and ordering herself coffee and a sandwich.

Sitting there with the afternoon sun warming her skin, Maya realized how good it had been to allow her mind to escape for a few hours. But now, even with the magnificent view spread out before her, she couldn't prevent her thoughts from straying back to Jay and, of course, Rajiv Maddox. Last night had been unnerving to say the least, and not just because of his suspicions, but also her unexpected reaction to him. She had lain awake for ages pondering on it. Why was she so aware of the man? Normally, she was quite cool and self-contained where men were concerned. It was something she had learned over the years, something that came with having to deal with men and their reactions to her. She was not a vain person. In fact, she sometimes felt her life would be a lot easier without the attention that her looks and height seemed to attract, but she'd learned to live with it.

During her time at secondary school, she'd gone from being a tall, ginger-haired, gawky teenager, who'd been made fun of by her fellow students and had transformed into a slim, shapely young woman who'd attracted too much attention from the male students. And she'd felt more comfortable dealing with the teasing jokes than the sexual attention that followed her physical transition. Things had become easier once she'd gone on to university and especially once she'd met Jay. They had hung out together in a small group of friends and most people had assumed they were a couple, which had suited her just fine. She'd always felt more mature than most of the other rowdy students, except Jay of course, and that was why it was so puzzling that she felt almost like a teenager again with Rajiv Maddox. And keeping secrets from him made things even more complicated.

How would he react to the fact that his brother was gay? Was he the kind of macho-man who despised homosexuality and saw it as unnatural? She certainly hoped not. He didn't come across as macho—masculine certainly—but not macho. She shivered—all too masculine for her peace of mind. Was that what this was all about? Was she just sexually aware of him? Just! She hadn't spent four years studying psychology without learning about the power of sex. It was never *just* sex.

Maya stared out at the river as her fingers fidgeted restlessly with the empty coffee cup. Sometimes she felt she'd read more about the power of sex than she would ever experience. The fact that she was still a virgin at the age of twenty-one was not something she was ashamed of, but it was private. Jay knew and her best friend, Josie, knew she'd never had a serious boyfriend. But then she'd never met anyone who she'd wanted to have sex with. In fact, up until yesterday she would have said that sex was something that didn't really excite her. But now she wasn't so sure.

Finally, she left the Tate Modern and strolled, with all the other tourists, along the riverbank, still lost in her thoughts. After a while, she crossed one of the bridges and made her way toward the West End, enjoying the hustle and bustle of tourists, street vendors, and oblivious office workers. The sun was still shining brightly, so it was with some surprise that she realized it was almost seven o'clock. Not sure which bus to catch, she decided to splurge and hailed a black cab, giving him the address in Knightsbridge.

Even the taxi driver looked impressed as they pulled up outside the elegant white entrance to the house. Maya paid the fare and, taking a deep breath, climbed the steps, wondering if Rajiv was there or not. It didn't take her long to find out.

The front door was flung open by the very man who'd been on her mind for most of the day.

"Where the hell have you been?" His sable hair was ruffled as if he'd been raking his fingers through it and his tie was askew, the top button of his shirt undone.

Too shocked to say anything, Maya just stood there and stared at him.

"Come inside, for God's sake," he muttered, standing back as she entered the house.

"Has something happened to Jay?" she asked with sudden dread.

"No nothing's happened to Jay," he answered as his eyes raked over her. "It was you we were worried about, Goddammit."

Maya's eyes widened in surprise. "Me? Why on earth—"

"Because it's nearly eight o'clock, that's why." He slammed the door shut and stood over her, his face tight with anger. "And as you're not familiar with London we were beginning to think the worst."

"So there you are, miss." Mrs. Travis appeared and Maya was relieved to see her smiling. "I told Mister Rajiv you must have just forgotten the time. It's easily done in the summertime, isn't that right?"

Maya nodded, smiling gratefully back at the older woman.

"You don't know London," he said, ignoring the

housekeeper. "It's a big, dangerous city, I hate to think—"
He broke off, turning away from both of them and making
his way towards the drawing room.

Maya stood there, unsure of what to do next, when Mrs
Travis offered to make her a cup of tea. "You go through
with him," she said softly. "He'll probably calm down now
that he knows you're safe."

Taking a deep, breath Maya turned and followed him
into the drawing room on shaky legs.

CHAPTER 3

So, did you have an enjoyable day?" he asked tersely, after pouring himself a measure of whisky and taking a rather large swig.

Maya stood awkwardly in the middle of the room, feeling like a naughty child, wondering how he managed to drink so much and yet never seem effected by it. "Yes, very enjoyable," she managed. "I guess that's why I didn't realize how late it was."

"And where did you go?" he continued, regarding her with those disturbing, blue eyes.

"To the Tate Modern," she answered, wishing she were not so susceptible to his piercing gaze. "I've wanted to see it for ages, so when Jay called and said we weren't leaving till tomorrow…" She shrugged her slim shoulders. "I'm sorry you were worried. I should have realized the time."

"Forget it. You need to give me your mobile number. I could have called and all this drama would have been avoided," he muttered, setting down the now-empty glass and thrusting his hands into his trouser pockets. "I guess I overreacted. You can obviously take care of yourself, and I'm too old to be playing the anxious nursemaid."

"You're not old!" she blurted without thinking.

His mouth curved sardonically. "I'm thirty one years old, Maya. That must seem ancient to you."

Maya moistened her lips. "Why? Do I make you feel old?" she asked, suddenly breathless.

His eyes narrowed on her full soft mouth. "Yes, you make me feel old, but maybe it's safer that way."

A quiver of nervous excitement overtook her. "What do you mean?"

"Forget it." His voice was unexpectedly harsh and he pushed his fingers through his hair impatiently. "I was going to invite you out for dinner tonight, but I guess you're tired after your eventful day out."

Maya caught her breath. "No, not at all—I mean I'd love to go out for dinner, if you still want to, that is."

He arched a mocking brow. "Of course I do. It's always a pleasure to take a beautiful woman out—even if she does make me feel quite ancient." He smiled wryly. "Shall we meet back here in about an hour then?"

She nodded in agreement, trying to quell the thrill that ran through her at the thought of spending the evening out with him. "Okay."

Upstairs in her room Maya had a quick shower and washed her hair. She found a powerful hairdryer in the bathroom cabinet and finger-dried her hair, while her mind buzzed with nervous excitement. He was just being kind, she told herself soberly, inviting her out for an innocent dinner in the big city. There was no need to react like a naïve schoolgirl out on her first date.

By the time she'd changed into a vintage, ankle length dress edged with lace at the bodice, she felt calmer and more in control of herself. With her hair hanging sleek and loose down her back and some smoky eye-shadow added to her lids, she slipped a soft, black cardigan over her shoulders and made her way downstairs with five minutes to spare.

Rajiv was at the bottom of the staircase, talking to Mrs Travis, and his gaze lifted at the sound of her heeled sandals on the marble tiles. He too had changed into a pair of black trousers and matching jacket with a white shirt opened at his dark brown throat. Maya felt her stomach muscles tighten as his eyes met hers, dark and brooding. This man was far too experienced and dangerous, she realized, and she should stay as far away from him as possible. Her body was telling a different story, though, as her breasts swelled beneath his intent gaze.

"You look lovely, miss!" Mrs Travis exclaimed as Maya reached the bottom of the stairs. "Doesn't she, Mr Rajiv?"

"Quite lovely, Mrs Travis," he replied softly, his eyes locked on her. "Shall we go then?"

It was a warm evening and Maya found herself slowly relaxing, enjoying the drive, staring keenly out the window as they passed the famous hotels along Park Lane and made their way toward the West End. Rajiv instructed Bijal to drive past some of the main tourist attractions, watching indulgently as she expressed her delight at the flashing lights of Piccadilly Circus and the legendary theatres along Shaftsbury Avenue, advertising their celebrated stars.

Eventually, they stopped outside a French restaurant in a narrow side street of Soho, and Rajiv informed Bijal that they would make their own way home by taxi. He seemed to be a considerate employer, she couldn't help thinking, as he led her toward the entrance of what looked like a small but exclusive restaurant. Maya admired the intimate, candlelit atmosphere as the manager greeted Rajiv and showed them to a secluded table.

Although she had been concerned that the evening might be a bit of a strain after the earlier drama, Rajiv proved himself both amusing and quite skilful at getting her to open up and talk about herself. He was an attentive listener, who asked intelligent questions. Maya found herself telling him about the organization she would begin working for in Edinburgh in the autumn and their work with disadvantaged children and youth.

The food was delicious. She had invited Rajiv to choose for her, as her knowledge of French food was minimal. Scallop soufflé, followed by gigot of lamb served with baby vegetables and a lemon mint risotto was what he ordered for both of them. She savored every mouthful, deciding French cuisine came a close second to her favorite, Indian food. Rajiv laughed when she told him this, saying it was impossible to compare the two.

And so, with the warm ambiance, divine food, and Rajiv's flattering interest, Maya found herself relaxing and enjoying the exquisite wines that he'd chosen after a serious conversation with the manager.

ↄↄↄↄ

Rajiv twisted the stem of his wineglass between his fingers in an unconsciously caressing gesture as he watched her spoon the orange-infused panna cotta into her mouth. She had disposed of the black cardigan she'd been wearing earlier and her bare skin glowed like satin in the soft light. He could see the outline of her breasts pressing against the fine lace of her dark green dress. It was obvious that she was wearing nothing beneath it and his fingers itched to push the narrow straps off her shoulders and watch it fall away. His hand tightened around the wineglass as he dragged his eyes away from her breasts. She looked incredibly beautiful in the flickering candlelight, and he was quite aware that he was not the only male in the room to notice this. Even the French waiter had been hovering around like some callow youth until Rajiv had given him a killing look that had sent him on his way.

While he told himself that he was doing this for his brother's sake, he was uncomfortably aware that he was enjoying himself far more than he should. She was interesting—intelligent, besides being beautiful—and totally different from the women he was used to. A part of him was savoring every moment spent with her, while another side of him was greatly relieved that tomorrow he would be handing her over to Sanjay.

Were they lovers? he wondered. He felt a knot beginning in his stomach. Would they be sharing a bed at Cranthorpe? His mother certainly would not approve, but then they could always sneak around after everyone was asleep. God knew, he'd done it often enough himself in his younger days. He forced himself back to the present, not wanting to think about his brother and her together.

"So how did Jay sound to you on the phone today?" he asked, striving to keep his brother's welfare a priority.

"Actually, he sounded quite well," she replied, giving the waiter one of her winning smiles as he discreetly cleared their table.

She was a little tipsy. He could tell by the way her eyes sparkled and the warm flush of color on her cheeks. Rajiv leaned back in his chair, trying to resist the pull of her charisma.

"You're not listening to a word I'm saying, are you?" she accused him with a teasing smile.

Rajiv shook his head. "I'm sorry, I must have drifted. What were you saying?" he shifted restlessly, trying to quell the stirring heat below his belt.

She took another sip of her wine and licked the dark moisture from her lips. "I was saying I'm going to do my best to give Jay a good time while I'm at Cranthorpe."

And what the hell is that supposed to mean? For a second Rajiv thought he'd said the words out loud.

"That sounds...helpful," he responded finally, with a

tight smile, trying to prevent his mind from painting pictures of her and Jay having a "good time" together.

"Tell me about Cranthorpe," she said softly, leaning her elbows on the table and looking deep into his eyes.

Rajiv forced his mind to concentrate on her question and, ignoring the pulsing heat of his body, did his best to answer her.

❧❧❧

It was almost eleven, by the time they left the restaurant and, as Maya lowered herself carefully into the back seat of the taxi, she realized that the wine had gone to her head.

"Are you okay?" Rajiv enquired, once he'd settled himself beside to her.

"I think I drank a bit more than I should have," she said with a sigh, feeling an almost irresistible impulse to rest her head on his broad shoulder.

"I'll make you a coffee when we get home," he stated, a mixture of concern and amusement in his blue eyes as he gazed at her in the dim light.

"Hmm, yes coffee sounds good. Thank you, Rajiv." She yawned and leaned her head back against the seat of the taxi feeling her eyes droop slowly closed.

"Maya, wake up, we're home."

She opened her eyes slowly to find Rajiv bending over her, his fingers stroking her bare shoulder in a gentle caress that sent shivers down her arm and caused her breasts to swell and tighten. She let out a soft moan and saw his expression change to one of concern.

"Are you okay?" he asked tightly.

"Yes, yes. I'm fine," she said, drawing away from him as she tried to bring her heated senses under control.

It had to be the wine, she told herself, for never before

had she experienced such a powerful response to any man's touch. Her nipples felt overly sensitive against the smooth fabric of her dress and there was a warm melting feeling between her thighs. She climbed carefully out of the taxi and waited while he paid the driver, breathing the fresh night air into her lungs as her body slowly cooled.

"Come, let's go inside and make you a strong coffee." He unlocked the door and, placing a firm hand at the small of her back, propelled her gently inside.

Once again, Maya felt her body quiver in response to his touch.

The house was quiet and in semi-darkness as he led her toward the kitchen which was situated at the back of the house. Even in her state of drowsy sensuality, Maya had to admire the large room with its white-tiled floor, solid white cupboards, and stainless-steel accessories. Mrs. Travis must be in her element here, Maya thought, noticing how spotlessly clean everything was from the pristine floor to the marble-topped plinth in the center of the room.

There was a counter with some high stools at one end of the room and Rajiv pulled one out for her. "Can you manage?" he asked, eyeing her cautiously.

"Of course I can," she insisted, stifling a giggle and climbed gingerly onto the high chair.

"I shouldn't have ordered that second bottle of wine," he stated grimly, as he moved with graceful ease and familiarity around the kitchen.

"It's no big deal. I'm just a wee bit tipsy is all," she said softly, her accent more pronounced as she watched him place two cups beneath the large, ultra-modern Gaggia coffee maker.

"Well, I don't want you arriving at Cranthorpe with a king-size hangover," he drawled, his sensual mouth curving into a lazy smile. "My mother would be most unimpressed, I think."

He leaned his hips against the marble counter, and eyed her curiously as he waited for the coffee cups to fill. "You're quite an enigma, aren't you?" he remarked, studying her face. "Cool and confident one minute and all unworldly innocence the next."

Maya let out a throaty laugh. "You make me sound like some kind of femme fatale." The effect of the wine, together with his deeply masculine presence was a heady mix. She felt a crazy impulse to play the femme fatale, to wind her arms around his lean hard body, and make him totally aware of her as a woman. "Surely I'm not that irresistible." She moistened her lips. "Am I?"

His eyes narrowed on her full moist mouth and he straightened up moving slowly toward her. "Don't play games with me Maya," he advised softly, stopping right in front of her, his hands gripping the sides of her stool and effectively trapping her. "You've had too much to drink and you may bite off more than you can chew."

Maya swallowed tightly. "I don't know what you're talking about," she said, heat prickling on her skin. "I think I should go up to bed now."

"Not until you've had your coffee. We need to sober you up first."

His face was only inches away from hers and she could see the thick, black lashes that fringed his blue eyes.

She tried to control her unsteady breathing, but the masculine, faintly musky scent that rose up from him teased her senses, causing a quiver of awareness deep inside her. She had to get away from him, Maya realized, away from the sensations that were threatening to overpower her. She lifted her hands and pressed them against the hard wall of his chest, intending to push him away, but he was even stronger than she had imagined and the warmth of his muscled body beneath her palms felt deliciously exciting. She wanted to feel his bare skin against hers, she realized impulsively, as her hands moved up of their own accord to the opening of his shirt.

"What the hell are you doing," he ground out, but he didn't stop her fingers from reaching inside to explore his smooth brown throat.

"I'm touching you," she murmured huskily, moistening her lips with the tip of her tongue.

"You're completely shameless, aren't you?" he said hoarsely, his breath coming hard and fast as she loosened another button of his shirt and allowed her hand to slide inside and explore the warm skin of his chest.

His body felt hot and slightly moist against her palms. Somewhere in the back of her mind, she knew that what she was doing was crazy. The alcohol had clouded her senses and she would regret this later, but it wasn't enough to stop her.

When his hand moved up her arm to encircle her throat she tilted her head and stared with blatant sensuality into his glittering eyes. She parted her moist, sensitized lips and Rajiv needed no further invitation. With a self-deprecating groan, he lowered his head and covered her mouth with his.

It was not a gentle kiss and there was no slow build up to it. He invaded her mouth and her senses, his tongue penetrating and forcing an immediate response from her. Maya felt as if she were drowning, the blood pounding in her veins as he explored the moist interior of her mouth, drawing the tip of her tongue into his mouth, biting at it, and then suckling greedily on it. Nothing could have prepared her for this sensual onslaught. She had been kissed before, but those vague memories of emotions that had barely scratched the surface could not be compared to the all-consuming desire that engulfed her and left her body crying out for fulfilment.

His fingers moved upward to thread themselves in the silkiness of her hair, twisting it almost painfully into his fist and pulling her head back so he could trail kisses down her throat toward the swell of her breasts. She felt the thin, shoestring straps of her dress being eased off her shoulders and down over her breasts.

"God, but you're beautiful," he whispered, his eyes moving from the glowing passion of her face down to the naked beauty of her swollen breasts, the nipples dusky and tight with desire. His lids were heavy as he grazed his thumb over one pouting tip, watching her arch with pleasure, and then finally he lowered his head and sucked hard at her nipple. A sob escaped her as she dug her fingers into his hair and arched her body up against him.

Maya felt the swollen ridge of his erection when he eased her knees apart and pressed himself intimately against her. A fleeting sense of triumph seized her at his blatant desire. She could feel the hard heat of his erection through the flimsy fabric of her dress, rubbing against her moist flesh and sending ripples of sweet, painful, pleasure through her. A long moan escaped her lips. She wanted to tear the clothes from her body, to feel his naked flesh against hers, easing the ache that was building deep inside her with the urgent bulge of his arousal.

His breathing was ragged as he dragged his mouth back to hers in a long drugging kiss, his hands hot and heavy on her straining breasts. Of their own accord, her fingers trailed down from his neck, over the smooth, slick skin of his muscled chest, her nails scraping against his rigid nipples.

She heard him expel a tormented groan. "My God, I must be out of my mind!" He swore savagely, dragging himself away from the soft inviting warmth of her body. "I almost forgot who you are!"

Maya felt her blood turn cold. He was staring at her with a look of loathing on his drawn features and, with trembling fingers, she pulled the slim traps of her top back over her shoulders, shame and devastation washing over her. "How do you think Jay would feel about this?" he demanded, raking unsteady fingers through his hair, his eyes filled with grim accusation.

"This has nothing to do with Jay!"

"Nothing to do with Jay?" He shook his head in disbelief. "You're really something, you know that? What are you saying—that you and Jay have some kind of 'open relationship' and it's okay to screw his brother? Is that right?"

Maya opened her mouth to disabuse him, but then quickly closed it again. It was not for her to say and, anyway, she could see he had already made up his mind about her. With a cold shiver of despair she climbed off the stool, collected her bag, and her cardigan with hands that trembled, and tried to make her way around him toward the door.

His mouth, which just a few moments ago had been soft and sensual, was now drawn into a hard, thin line. "So that's it then?" he taunted. "You're not even going to bother trying to explain your behavior, are you?"

Maya drew herself up to her full height, but still she had to look up at him. "Explain *my* behavior?" she repeated through bloodless lips. "Well, I guess I'd say I had too much to drink." Her voice was cold and wounded. "But tell me, what's your excuse Rajiv? Or does the blame lie entirely with me?"

And before he had a chance to answer, she brushed past him, forcing herself not to run but to walk away with her head held high.

CHAPTER 4

Rajiv stared morosely at the road ahead of him, his eyes tired and sore from lack of sleep. It had been a long time since he'd had such a grim and disturbing night, and he guessed that today was not going to be any better. Maya had hardly said a word since they'd left London almost an hour ago. As the powerful Porsche ate up the miles toward Cranthorpe, he was berating himself for being more aware of her than ever after the shameful madness of the night before.

Normally, he found the drive from London to the lush countryside of Wiltshire relaxing and satisfying, but not today. Besides feeling ripped apart with guilt for what had happened, he felt a burning fury toward her for not reacting. She had left with that parting shot the night before, not giving him a chance to defend himself, although how he would have managed that he hadn't quite fathomed yet. Then this morning she had been cool and distant, not a sign of guilt or remorse on that pure and immaculate face. She had her hair tied back today and, although he loved it loose, he had to admit that it gave her an air of innocence pulled back from the classic beauty of her face. Apart from slight shadows beneath her slanted, green eyes, she didn't look as if she'd suffered any ill effects from last night's sexual encounter. She was wearing the same Indian skirt she'd worn the day he'd met her at the station, but with it she wore a tie-dyed tank top in different shades of blue and lilac, and he had to admit that it suited the rather ethereal image of her that was beginning to fascinate him more and more. He was painfully aware of her long slim legs beneath the fine cotton skirt whenever forced to change gears. Not even his deep sense of shame could dull the burning excitement he felt every time he remembered how it had felt to give in to his needs and ravish her the way he had last night. His body still throbbed and his blood thickened at the memory of her warm sensuality as she'd responded to him. God, was she like that with every man who touched her? Was she like that with Sanjay? His hands tightened on the wheel as his emotions veered between lust and rage.

"Will you please slow down?" Her soft accent invaded his thoughts. "You're going much too fast."

He expelled an exasperated sigh and eased his foot off the accelerator. "What's the matter, are you not in a hurry to get there?" he asked caustically, and she gave him a filthy look before turning to stare out the window.

"As a matter of fact, I'm looking very forward to getting there."

Rajiv's jaw clenched as he bit back a spiteful comeback and then wondered if that meant she was looking forward to seeing Jay again. The way she had responded to his lovemaking last night had made Rajiv feel like he was the only man in her universe, but obviously that wasn't the case. Perhaps she'd wanted him to believe that. Perhaps she had decided that he, being the older brother, was a better bet. If his earlier suspicions about her were right, then why should she settle for Jay when she might have a shot at him, the head of Maddox Junta Investments?

He could feel his head beginning to pound. These past

two days were beginning to take their toll. He had known that it wouldn't be pleasant baby-sitting Sanjay's girlfriend, but God, he'd had little idea just how unsettling to his peace of mind it would turn out to be.

℮℮℮

Maya felt the tightly wound tension deep within her ease slightly as they left the village of Steeple Wick behind and followed the narrow road that Rajiv had coldly informed her would take them to Cranthorpe. She wanted desperately to be out of this car and away from him as soon as she possibly could. It had not been a pleasant journey and the atmosphere in the vehicle, irrespective of its opulent comfort, had been fraught with underlying hostilities and recriminations. It was obvious that he blamed her for what had happened the night before. That he saw her as some kind of shameless slut who was ready and willing to jump into bed with the first man that came along. As much as these accusations hurt, they were minor compared to the shame and humiliation that she had already heaped upon herself concerning her behavior the night before. It was so completely out of character for her to behave in such a wanton way. She would love to inform him that his berating of her was quite unnecessary as she was managing it more than adequately herself. But she felt no desire whatsoever to engage him in conversation. Just looking at him caused an unpleasant ache deep in the pit of her stomach. Even with a slightly haggard expression on his haughty face, he still managed to look devastatingly attractive. A helpless languor invaded her limbs every time she recalled how his body had trembled in her arms.

"Here we are."

His low, controlled tones brought Maya out of her gloomy reflections, as the Porsche turned between white-painted gates and followed a gravelled road towards the house.

A smooth green verge sloped away at either side of the row of trees that formed a line along the sweeping drive. Cranthorpe stood huge and majestic before her, and Maya bit back a gasp of surprise at the size and beauty of it. It was built of strong gray brick, the long casement windows flanking an entrance approached by a wide flight of stone steps. Above the stately home, tall chimneys stood welcoming and dignified against the bright blue of the sky.

Maya swallowed back her words of amazement and shock. When Jay had invited her to their country home, she had imagined a small cottage-style house, with a pretty garden, made up of three or four bedrooms, max. This *mansion*, beautiful as it might be, left her feeling anxious and intimidated.

The large double doors opened as the car came to a halt outside the wide entrance and two figures emerged, the first being a beautiful Indian woman who Maya presumed to be Mrs Maddox, and beside her stood the familiar figure of her dear friend Jay. She climbed out of the Porsche without waiting for Rajiv to assist her and smiled gratefully as Jay descended the steps to greet her.

"Maya, it's so good to see you." As he closed his arms around her in an affectionate hug, she felt an unexpected prick of tears and had to swallow hard before saying anything.

"Hello, Jay," she managed at last and, smiling up at him, noticed immediately how thin he looked. He had always been slim, but now he looked positively gaunt, his cheekbones prominent and a tired, hollow look in his eyes that had not been there before. "How are you?" she asked, unable to hide the concern in her voice.

"All the better for seeing you," he said with a heartfelt smile. "Come and meet my mother."

Maya turned to face the slim, elegant woman standing beside Rajiv. "How do you do Mrs Maddox," she murmured politely as the woman shook her hand.

"Welcome to Cranthorpe, and please call me Anna," Jay's mother responded, her sweeping gaze taking in Maya's tie-dyed top and Indian skirt.

Maya couldn't help noticing a similarity in the strong, striking bone-structure between her and her older son. She was tall, almost as tall as Maya, and her dark hair tied back in a classic chignon, which complimented her unlined, classic Indian features. With her slim body clothed in a loose, Indian style, dress and pants suit and a long patterned scarf, she was a picture of sophisticated elegance.

From the corner of her eye, Maya saw Rajiv and Jay embracing each other while Anna Maddox looked on approvingly. It was clear to Maya that their relationship was a close one. Rajiv left Jay and went over to embrace his mother, who told him he looked tired and should stop working so hard. Maya kept as close to Jay as possible, grateful when he draped his arm over her shoulders.

They entered the house through a large sunlit entrance hall with a wide curving staircase hugging one side of the room. The walls panelled in a deep oak, and the floors too, were a light polished wood. Maya had to bite back an exclamation of pure awe at the size and sheer beauty of the place. They moved through to a French-windowed room where the décor was a subtle mixture of green and ivory tones. A pair of damask sofas flanked the Tudor fireplace, and Maya was invited to seat herself on one of the sumptuous settees.

Rajiv hung back at the door. "I told Godfrey I'd see him when I arrived," he stated casually. "I need to discuss a few things with him, but I'll be back by lunch time."

His mother nodded her head and then seated herself on the settee opposite Maya. "So how did you enjoy your stay in London?" she enquired, lifting a perfectly shaped eyebrow.

Jay came to sit beside Maya. "Yes, did you make it to the Tate Modern?" he asked with a reassuring smile, and she nodded, relating her impression of the building and some of the works that she had admired.

"Have you seen it Anna?" Maya asked the older woman, attempting to include her in their conversation.

Anna Maddox shook her head. "I'm afraid modern art is not my thing," she said, her Indian accent music to Maya's ears. "Sharks in tanks, beds surrounded by filth, pornography." She shivered. "No thank you!"

There was an uncomfortable silence, in which the other woman smiled naively, while Jay stared uncomfortably down at the opulent green and gold carpet, and Maya wondered if Anna Maddox knew of her son's passionate interest in modern and existential art. They had both attended art classes in the evenings, which was how they'd met. Maya had an interest in Art Therapy, but Jay had confided in her his love for modern art and, having seen some of his work, she had no doubt that he had the talent for it.

"Ma's love lies with classic Indian art." Jay smiled ruefully, striving to lighten the atmosphere in the room.

The conversation moved on to safer topics while they were served deliciously spiced chai out of fine china cups and those divine Indian sweet cakes she'd tried in London. Maya asked about the history of the house and Anna Maddox informed her that parts of it dated back to the sixteenth century.

Jay remained quiet for most of the conversation and Maya had the feeling his mind was elsewhere, so it was a relief when the older woman finally suggested that he show Maya where she would be sleeping.

The bedroom she'd been given was named the Rose Room, which overlooked the rose-garden below, and in the distance Maya caught sight of large lake shimmering in the sunlight.

"Jay, this is absolutely beautiful!" she exclaimed, gazing out of the window before walking round the spacious room with its dusky pink walls and matching damask silk curtains.

"I'm glad you like it," Jay said, going over to the huge bed, covered in a rose-patterned satin bedspread, and lowering his thin frame onto it. He kicked off his trainers and crossed his legs as his brown hair flopped forward almost covering his warm amber eyes.

There was something hauntingly beautiful about Jay's face. Perhaps it was his deeply sensitive eyes, or his full sensual lips, but whatever it was, it caused people of both sexes to gravitate toward him. Yet Maya had soon realized that he was totally unaware of the affect his looks had on other people.

"You look tired, Maya," he observed, his searching gaze taking in the shadows beneath her eyes and the slight tension in her in her face. "My brother hasn't been giving you a hard time, has he?"

Maya flushed. "Don't be silly, Jay. Your brother's been...very kind." She smiled lamely. "I just didn't sleep very well last night, that's all." She seated herself next to him the sumptuous bed and gave him a solemn look. "So how are you, Jay, really?"

He shrugged his thin shoulders. "Not too good. As you've probably guessed, I feel so isolated here. It's like I'm playing a role, not really being me, just the person people expect me to be." His long slim fingers played with the silken bedspread.

"Have you thought about telling them the truth, your mother and your brother, at least?" she asked gently.

"It's *all* I've been thinking about, besides Kurt, that is," he told her, pushing impatient fingers through his long hair.

"You still haven't heard from him then?"

Jay shook his head. "Not a word, no. We had this huge row the night before I left Edinburgh. He wanted to come down to London with me, to be here when I told my mother, but I chickened out, said I wanted to do it in my own time. He told me I was a coward, that I had no intention of telling her, or anyone else for that matter and then he left. He went home to Switzerland, said he wasn't prepared to live a lie." He turned to face her, his eyes dark and mournful. "And now that I've lost him I feel, what's the point of telling them anyway? What's the point of anything really?" His voice broke and tears filled his eyes as she closed her arms around his heaving shoulders and tried her best to comfort him.

They were still sitting there when a rather loud knock sounded at the door and, before either of them could speak, it swung open. Rajiv stood there, his sardonic gaze taking in the two figures embracing on the bed.

"Sorry to interrupt," he declared, his mouth twisted into a mocking smile. "You forgot your suitcase downstairs."

Maya's face burned as he set her suitcase down just inside the room and straightened up, his eyes flicking over them in a guarded look.

"Well, I guess I'll leave you both to it then," he remarked wryly and strode out, pulling the door firmly shut behind him.

Jay let out a bitter laugh after he'd left. "He probably thinks he's interrupted our reconciliation," he declared. "If only he knew how wrong he was!"

Maya stifled a groan, wishing she could see the humor in the situation, but all she really felt was dull ache in the pit of her stomach.

Jay eventually left her to freshen up, agreeing to meet her downstairs for lunch in half an hour. Maya sank back on the soft mattress, trying not to think about the look of cold contempt on Rajiv's face when he'd walked in on them. God, what must he think of her, she agonized, and now she would have to go downstairs and face him. If only she hadn't kissed him last night, none of this would have mattered. But she had, and it did. She made her way into the ensuite bathroom and stared at herself in the large, ornate mirror. She looked guilty as sin, but she had done nothing wrong. Maya lifted her head and took a determined breath. She would not allow him to make her feel ashamed. The whole situation was ridiculous and she would rise above it. After splashing some cold water on her face, she left the bathroom and went over to the carved Victorian dressing table, seating herself on the padded velvet stool, determined to go downstairs and face Rajiv looking as self-assured and irreproachable as possible.

She felt a little better with some moisturizer and make-up concealing the dark shadows beneath her eyes, and she'd combed her hair into a smooth silky curtain down her back, resisting the urge to change into something more conservative, before making her way downstairs. As she entered, the drawing room, with its French windows standing open to an uninterrupted view of the colorful, landscaped garden beyond, Maya couldn't help feeling that this house was different to the one in London, which had been very gracious but quite formal. Cranthorpe, however, seemed to her to have an entirely peaceful, genial atmosphere about it, thanks to warm colors, beautiful furnishings, and the lush surroundings of the English countryside.

"Do you like it?"

Maya's head jerked at the sound of that all-too-familiar voice. He was standing at the other end of the room, a glass of amber liquid in his hand, and, for a moment, she stared at him nonplussed.

"The house, do you like it?" he repeated, walking towards a small open bar at one end of the room.

"Yes," she answered. "I was just thinking that it has a very welcoming atmosphere about it."

"Very good." He nodded, as if she had passed a test. "Can I get you something to drink?"

"Um, just some mineral water please, if you have it." She walked over to the French windows and stared out at the magnificent view, but even the vibrant flowerbeds and rolling lawns were difficult to appreciate when she was so overly conscious of the man beside her. She couldn't help asking, "Do you know where the others are?"

"They'll be here in a minute, I'm sure." He carried the long frosted glass over and handed it to her. "Why? Is my company not appealing since I interrupted your little reunion upstairs?" he added provokingly.

"You didn't interrupt anything." Her eyes flashed at him. "Jay was feeling upset and I was comforting him, that's all."

"Please." He held up his hand. "You really don't owe me any explanations and, besides, I could do without the details."

Maya gripped the glass with both hands, the desire to slap his cynical face almost overpowering her. The sound of footsteps approaching was a welcome relief.

Anna Maddox paused at the threshold for a moment and then frowned at her son. "Rajiv, isn't it a bit too early in the day for spirits?"

He just shrugged his broad shoulders and drained the glass with a grimace.

She shook her head at his casual defiance and then turned to Maya. "Do you like your room, Maya," she enquired, every inch the gracious hostess.

Maya murmured an appropriate response, all too aware of Rajiv's indolent gaze following her every move.

It was a relief when Jay finally arrived and the four of them went through to another equally bright and attractive room for lunch. Maya found the meal quite a strain. Although the Indian Thali was faultless, she was all too aware of Rajiv at the other end of the table, not saying much at all. But no doubt listening as his mother asked pertinent questions about Maya's life in Scotland and her future plans now that she had completed her studies.

Jay was also rather subdued throughout, even though his mother tried to draw him into the conversation, and Maya guessed that he was finding it difficult to show any real feelings in front of his family. It was a relief when the meal finally ended and Jay offered to show her around the grounds. The weather was still warm and sunny and Maya found the splendor and beauty of her surroundings quite uplifting. The grounds were huge, and Jay told her about the different kinds of wildlife, such as deer, herons, kingfishers, woodpeckers, and ducks that she would get to see here. They walked down to the lake and she lifted her face to the sun with a sigh of pure pleasure.

"It's going to be good having you here," he confided once they'd seated themselves under a tall elm tree.

"Yes," she replied, listening to the excited chirping of the birds and insects around her, and then added tentatively, "I couldn't help noticing how quiet you were during lunch."

He sighed, wrapping his arms round his bended knees. "I know. I feel like I'm expected to perform, to pretend that everything's okay, and I just can't hack it." He stared at her with desperate eyes. "Can you understand what I'm saying, or do I sound as screwed up as I feel?"

Maya shook her head. "You don't sound screwed up at all, just confused, but I can't help wondering, Jay, wouldn't it be easier if you just told them the truth?"

He groaned softly, dropping his head onto his knees. "Oh, Maya, you don't know my mother. She might come across as sweet and naive but underneath it all she's very old fashioned—a traditional Indian woman—and having a son who's a *homosexual* would probably cause *her* to have a nervous breakdown!"

She digested this slowly. "I don't know, Jay. From what I've seen of your mother, she seems like a pretty formidable lady. Do you really think she'd fall apart because you're gay?"

He picked up a leaf and began shredding it meticulously. "Maybe not fall apart, but I can't ever imagine her accepting it." A haunted expression crept into his eyes. "But if her reaction was anything like my father's I think I'd die, and he wasn't even Indian."

Maya stared at him. "You told your father you were gay!"

Jay lips twisted into a grim, humorless smile. "Yeah, I told him the night he died." He took a deep breath and then let out a long sigh. "We were having an argument, which was nothing new. He was always trying to tell Rajiv and me how to live our lives. He was a bully and I think we both despised him. Anyway, he didn't want me studying art, said it was for *wimps*." A bitter laugh ran through him. "He'd been drinking that night, which was nothing new either, but he was a cruel, aggressive drunk and I was terrified of him. Rajiv used to stand up to him but I just couldn't. That night was different though. Something exploded inside me. Maybe 'cause I was finally leaving home, going to university. I wanted to prove I was a man. I don't know. Anyway, I told him. I said, 'I'll never be the son you want, so you might as well give up on me now, because I'm gay. I was born gay and I'll die gay and there's nothing you can do about it!'"

Maya listened in amazement. "What did he do?" she asked finally.

Jay raked his fingers through his hair in a frustrated gesture. "He went ballistic. Thank God, we were alone in the Knightsbridge house. My mother was here and Rajiv was away in India, so there was no one to interrupt us. He hit me, swore at me, called me all sorts of names, and then proceeded to get even drunker. I went up to my room and started packing my bags. I had this notion of moving up to Edinburgh straight away and staying there for good." A tired smile tugged at his mouth. "Who knows? If he hadn't died, maybe that's what would have happened. My life would have been so much simpler."

"So what *did* happen Jay?" she persisted.

"Well, you can guess the rest, really. He decided to visit one of his *lady friends* in his brand new Ferrari, which he ended up wrapping around a pole instead. Luckily, he didn't take anyone else with him. I don't think I could have lived with that." His voice had become almost expressionless now. "He died instantly. And you know something, Maya? For a while I felt glad that I'd killed him!" He pressed his head down onto his bended knees and began to sob quietly.

Maya put her arms around him and leaned her cheek against his slim shoulder. "It wasn't your fault Jay," she soothed. "You mustn't blame yourself."

"Oh yes it was, Maya. There's no getting away from it. If I hadn't told him, he would still alive today."

"You don't know that and he shouldn't have been drunk and driving," she insisted. "As you said, he could have killed innocent people."

He didn't appear to be listening to her. Although he'd lifted his head and the sobs had subsided, there was a dull, detached look in his eyes.

"Have you spoken to anyone else about this?" she asked eventually.

Jay rubbed his eyes in a childlike gesture. "I told Rajiv that we'd had an argument that night, but I didn't go into any details. Just said it was the usual kind of row, which it was really, until I decided to be brave." He picked up another leaf and crushed it in his palm. "Poor Rajiv, I screwed things up for him too. He was also planning to detach himself from our father. Wanted to go away and start his own business in India. But father wouldn't have it, said he had to take over the business here eventually. And of course, when he died that's exactly what Rajiv had to do—take over as head of the family and head of Maddox Junta Investments. He became a workaholic overnight." Jay stared out across the lake.

"What a mess I've managed to make of things, Maya."

CHAPTER 5

S o what do you think of her?"
Rajiv looked up from the spreadsheets in front of him, frowning in irritation as he watched his mother pace restlessly around the book-lined room. It had been like this since she'd first entered the study, disrupting his need for some quiet time in which to try and put his thoughts in order. A task that was proving virtually impossible even without his mother's restless presence to provoke him.

"Think of who?" he asked.

Her mouth tightened in annoyance. "Don't be obtuse, Rajiv," she responded, her voice rising. "Maya Stewart, who else?"

He sighed, leaning back in the soft leather chair. "She seems nice enough, I suppose," he conceded, trying to keep his expression as bland as his words.

"Well I'm not sure I trust her," she stated.

His frowned deepened as a feeling of unease descended at her words. He didn't trust Maya either, but for some obscure reason he didn't want his mother to know this.

"Why do you say that?" he enquired, playing for time.

Her eyes were cold and accusing. "She's got you hooked as well as Jay, hasn't she?"

"What?" Rajiv shot out of the chair in a sudden fluid movement and went round the desk toward her. "What are you talking about, Ma?" he asked, striving for a patronizing tone.

"Do you think I'm stupid?" Her eyes glimmered with anger. "Do you think I can't see how you look at her? I'm not a fool, Rajiv, even if you are!"

He felt a film of sweat break out on his skin as he forced a look of concerned bewilderment onto his face. "Ma, will you please calm down? I think all this stress over Jay is getting to you." He took her cold slim hands in his. "Come and sit down, let me get you a brandy. Your hands are freezing."

She allowed him to lead her to one of the velvet-covered chairs beside the fireplace, but her expression was still hard and uncompromising. He poured them both a stiff brandy from the drinks cabinet.

"Here, drink it," he ordered, pulling up a chair beside her.

"You're not going to change my mind, Rajiv, so don't try your boardroom tactics with me," she declared after taking a fortifying sip. "There's something not right about her. I just can't put my finger on it." Her face filled with tension and Rajiv closed his eyes against her words. "She's hiding something, can't you see that? There's more to her than meets the eye. Jay obviously doesn't see it and now she seems to have you fooled as well!" She swallowed the rest of the drink and set the glass down on the polished desk, her regal face pale and drawn.

"Ma, I think you're overreacting," he said steadily. "Okay, I admit she's a very attractive girl, but she really seems to care about Jay." The words were wrung from him, and he told himself he meant them.

She shook her head despondently. "That might not be enough to save him."

"What do you mean?"

"When I heard she was coming here to see him, I thought perhaps there was a chance of them getting together. Even though she's not Indian, I've prayed to God and made my peace with that. I had always expected both of you to marry Indian women. You know that, but I'm prepared to sacrifice that dream for Sanjay's welfare. You, I know, will marry an Indian girl and that will have to be enough for me. So I was prepared to accept her, as his girlfriend, or whatever." Anxiety marred her classic features. "But seeing them together—something is not right." His mother stared out of the windows behind him, a puzzled frown on her face. "She doesn't appear to love him, at least not in a sexual way. Watching them together. I don't know—it just doesn't fit."

Rajiv tried to quell the thrill he felt at his mother's despairing words, but it soared through him, easing the dull ache that had nagged at him all day. Later, after his mother had left, Rajiv sat staring out of the study windows. If he had felt unsettled before her interruption, it was nothing compared to what he was feeling now. The desire to drink himself into oblivion was a tempting one, but he knew from past experience that that would only make things worse. He had always prized himself on being able to control and guard his emotions. It was imperative in business and something that his father had driven home time, and time again. And now, after a mere two days in her company, this young slip of girl had managed to get under his skin like no one else before.

He needed to get away from her. *Out of sight was out of mind*. Although he had planned to spend several days here supporting his mother, he could now see that that was not a good idea.

Suddenly he noticed Jay and Maya making their way back toward the house, arm in arm, and his expression hardened. There was no doubt that they made a striking couple, both tall, beautiful, and young, he acknowledged grimly. A feeling of jealousy, totally alien to him, stabbed at his guts and strengthened his resolve to leave Cranthorpe as soon as possible.

❦❦❦

The following morning, Maya awoke to the uplifting sound of birdsong outside her room. It was another beautiful summer's day and she climbed out of bed with a positive feeling that she hoped would rub off on Jay when she saw him. In fact, he had seemed a little better after their walk yesterday and, even during dinner, he had chatted with Maya about friends of theirs in Edinburgh and what they were up to. Rajiv had seemed more remote than ever, but Maya had done her utmost to ignore his indolent presence.

Today was a new day, however, and she intended to make the best of it. After a refreshing shower she pulled on a pair of flared hipster jeans and a turquoise ribbed T-shirt She tied her hair back in a ponytail, creamed on some moisturizing sun-block, just in case, and then made her way down stairs.

It was just after nine o'clock when she reached the ground floor and almost bumped into the housekeeper, a friendly Indian lady who had been introduced to her the day before with the rest of staff. An experience Maya had found rather intimidating. Giving orders to servants was something she could never get used to.

The plump, middle-aged woman in a sari smiled at Maya. "Good morning, Miss Maya."

"Good morning, Nana Bibi, isn't it a lovely day," Maya enthused, pleased that the first person she'd encountered seemed to be in good spirits as well.

The housekeeper pointed out the direction of the morning room. "Mr Rajiv already have breakfast and Madam Anna 'as just come." Her Indian accent was strong.

Jay had told Maya that the housekeeper had come to London with his mother, her family having worked for Anna's family in India for generations.

"You like coffee, tea or chai, miss?" the housekeeper asked.

"Coffee please, Nana Bibi."

The housekeeper nodded, saying she'd be back with it "Quick, quick."

Maya smiled to herself, loving the melodic sound of the Indian accent. Then she braced herself, recalling that Jay's mother was in the breakfast room, and hoped she wouldn't ask too many difficult questions about Jay. Hearing raised voices as she approached, Maya slowed down, not meaning to eavesdrop, rather to turn around quietly and get away from whatever it was that was going on. But something stopped her.

"I may be old but I'm not stupid, Rajiv!" Maya heard Anna's voice and stopped in her tracks.

"You're not old and you're not stupid," Rajiv countered in a harsh voice.

"I also know about your weakness for beautiful women."

Maya heard a clatter of cutlery.

"What's that got to do with anything, Ma," Rajiv ground out.

"I saw the way you were looking at her last night again. You can hardly take your eyes off her! She's beautiful and you desire her, but there are thousands of beautiful girls for you. Just leave her alone, please. For your brother's sake!"

Maya heard a groan of frustration from Rajiv, then. "I don't have time for this. I've got work to do, more than you can imagine." There was a short silence. "Ma, please stop your imagination from running wild, *please*. God, is your opinion of me so low that you think I'd try and mess up the one thing that may help Sanjay get better?"

There was a short silence then, "Rajiv, I don't have a low opinion of you. You've been my rock since you were a child. I don't know how I would have survived without you." Her voice broke. "Maybe I am over-reacting, but I just have a bad feeling about this—about her. And I know you're not used to denying yourself. You've been too used to getting your own way, especially with women."

"Ma, that was years ago, a young man sowing his wild oats, or whatever. I'm not the person I was back then. Surely I've proved that to you by now?"

There was a longer silence. Perhaps he was holding her, comforting her. Maya felt sick to her stomach. Her body was trembling and her legs felt like jelly as she stood there her arms wrapped around her midriff.

"Can we drop this subject now? I've got about a hundred emails and phone calls to make," Rajiv said the anger no longer evident in his voice.

His mother may have replied, but Maya was trying to get her legs to move. Nothing could be worse than him finding her eavesdropping at the door. She stumbled along the passage, trying to get her legs to behave normally.

"Maya."

Her only respite was that he spoke softly, so his mother couldn't hear, but she tried to ignore him, walking as fast as she could.

"Maya!" His hand was large and strong, digging into her soft upper arm and she had to bite her lip not to cry out in pain. "Where are you going?"

Maya couldn't look at him. She felt mortified by what she'd heard, so she just stared down at the faded jeans he was wearing, knowing that she couldn't hide from him, or his mother, forever.

"Were you listening at the door?" He was too clever for

his own good and she hated him for it. "What did you hear?"

"Enough!" she choked, trying futilely to release her arm from his iron grip.

"Are you okay?" he asked, concern shadowing his harsh features.

"What did you say to her?" she uttered tremulously, finally finding her voice as her hands covered her pale cheeks.

"I didn't say anything to her, for God's sake!"

"Let me go. I can't bear to look at you," she hissed, trying futilely to free herself.

"Come." His fingers moved down to her wrist like a vice. "We're going to talk about this whether you like it or not."

As he dragged her with him along the corridor, Maya felt too numb with shock to argue. Eventually he stopped along the passageway to open a heavy panelled door, urging her firmly inside. It was a study, Maya realized dazedly and, with the heavy curtains drawn, quite difficult to see much besides a large polished desk and rows of beautiful old books lining the walls. She drew in a trembling breath, too angry and humiliated to care where she was.

"I want to know what you told her," she repeated unevenly, as he shut the door. "God, did you tell her that I tried to seduce you or something?"

"Don't be crazy. I never told her anything." He raked his long fingers impatiently through his hair. "Would you believe she guessed?"

Maya looked up at him, wrapping her arms around her waist. "Guessed what?" she asked in confusion.

"Good question." He grimaced, rubbing the back of his neck tiredly. "She seems to think there's something going on between us."

She continued to stare at him. Her throat tightened

painfully. "And you never said anything to her about—about what happened in London?"

"Of course not. Why the hell would I do that?" He leaned one hand against the dark wooden panelling beside her head. "Do you believe me?" His gaze was serious as he stared at her.

She nodded, looking at the buttons on his white, Indian cotton, shirt, her mind in turmoil. "God, what must she think of me?" she whispered to herself.

He swore softly. "Look, don't take any notice of her. It's me she thinks badly of, not you. She'll get over it, Sanjay seems much better since you arrived and that's all that really matters, okay?" His voice was soft and soothing.

"I don't know what to do." Her hands were still wrapped round her waist and she dropped her head in defeat.

"You don't have to do anything, just concentrate on Jay," he stressed. "Once I'm gone she'll be all right, and as I'm leaving this afternoon—"

"You're leaving?" she exclaimed as she stared into his eyes. She tried to look away but it was impossible and his expression as he stared back at her caused a painful knot in the pit of her stomach.

"I have to get back." His gaze dropped to her mouth. "Business commitments that I can't get out of."

"I—I think I should go back to Scotland," she decided suddenly. "It's not right for me stay here. Your mother obviously doesn't trust me."

"No!" he hissed savagely. "Please, don't even think about leaving. Jay needs you. You can't leave now."

Maya swallowed, her breathing constricted. "I don't know."

"You can't leave now," he repeated in a gravelly tone as he grasped her shoulders.

The warm strength of his hands through her thin T-shirt

left her feeling strangely weak, and when he jerked her toward him, Maya could find no will to resist. He was leaving and she might never see him again. His mouth fastened on hers and her lips parted to accept the heated invasion of his thrusting tongue. She responded instinctively, the idea of resisting him simply not an option. Her hands spread against his chest, the warmth of his flesh palpable through the thin fabric of his shirt. She could feel his heart beating heavily beneath her palm as he slanted his head and deepened the kiss, causing her body to sag weakly against the wooden panelling behind her. Maya's arms moved up to cling around his neck, her slim fingers threading into the thick, silky hair at his nape.

"God, you're driving me crazy," he breathed.

His hands moved down her back, finding and caressing the smooth skin exposed above the waistband of her jeans, and his mouth left hers to trail a path along her cheek to the cavern of her ear. She could hear his harsh breathing as his hands pushed the thin fabric of her T-shirt up and over her breasts.

"Beautiful," he groaned, his hooded eyes moving hungrily over her exposed flesh, her dusky nipples pouting shamelessly at him. "So beautiful."

He rubbed the pads of his thumbs against them and Maya moaned, arching her back instinctively towards him.

"Do you know what you're doing to me?" he demanded, and she could only shake her head in bemusement as he captured her mouth in another drugging kiss.

Once again, her body seemed to have taken on a life of its own, needs she hardly understood overpowering her. She heard herself moan when he cupped one of her breasts and squeezed her aching nipple. She was on fire for him, every nerve in her body desperate for a satisfaction she could hardly fathom. Of their own volition, her arms were pulling him down, to taste the tightened bud, and he needed no second invitation. Maya gasped at the piercing pleasure that darted from her breast to the very heart of her. Heat pooled between her legs and her inner muscles tightened with need.

As he sucked hungrily at her breasts, Maya became aware of the hard length of his arousal through the soft jeans he was wearing. He eased a muscled thigh between her weakened limbs and she shuddered when his hard flesh rubbed against her moist and sensitive core. The wooden panelling was cool against her bare back and she felt a desperate desire to feel his naked body against hers. His hands moved down to cup her bottom, lifting her up and rubbing himself fretfully against her welcoming flesh. She was sure he could feel the moist heat through her jeans but she didn't care. She wanted to feel him inside her, to feel the hot hard length of him filling her and easing this craving that was overpowering her.

"I want you," he groaned, mirroring her thoughts. "I want you now."

In her state of heightened desire, she could only nod helplessly in agreement. His fingers moved to the metal button of her jeans, unfastening it with the ease of experience and pushing the zip slowly down. She trembled with a mixture of panic and anticipation and, as if sensing her sudden uncertainty, Rajiv covered her mouth in a deep searching kiss that blanked her mind of everything except the need to satisfy this desperate craving.

Her hips thrust eagerly against his hand when his fingers began probing the elasticized edge of her panties. Then, through the heavy haze of desire, Maya heard a telephone ringing. It was in the room, a loud incessant noise that simply wouldn't go away.

"The phone," she panted, dragging her mouth away from his.

Rajiv groaned. His hands were trembling as they moved up her body to clasp her shoulders. "Don't move," he breathed against her mouth, his eyes glittering with a mixture of frustration and desire in the dim light. "Just give me a minute to get rid of whoever it is."

Maya felt an unbearable sense of loss when he moved away from her, but as her body rapidly cooled, her brain began to function. Was she out of her mind? This was the second time she had allowed him to overpower her senses, literally to seduce her. And in his study, where anyone could have walked in and seen them! She dragged her T-shirt down over her swollen breasts, the nipples moist and sensitized. She reached for the zip of her jeans, her face flushed with shame at the thought of what she'd been about to let him do. If the phone hadn't rung, she would have allowed him—no encouraged him—to take her, right here, up against the wall of the study like some sex-starved maniac.

Stifling a sob she reached for the doorknob just as he called out her name, but his desperate tone only made her more determined to get away. She wrenched open the door, praying that there was no one was on the other side, and ran from the room, wishing she could run away from herself.

CHAPTER 6

Rajiv drove back to London that same day with a feeling of depression hanging heavily over him. He had not seen Maya after that delirious scene in the study and he told himself it was better that way. He desperately needed to put some distance between himself and her. He could only pray that being away from her disturbing presence would get his emotions back into perspective again. It was difficult for him to conceive the effect she had on him. He was simply not the type of man to be so easily overcome with lust. In fact, on more than one occasion women had accused him of being "a cold fish." He frowned, realizing that he was suddenly seeing those women in a rather unfavorable light, and that wasn't fair. But Maya's unaffected beauty, together with her irresistible sensuality, were impossible to ignore. God, just being around her caused him to break out in a sweat, not to mention how fantastic her body had felt this morning against his. If that damn phone hadn't rung…

Rajiv gripped the steering wheel until his knuckles turned white. It was a *good thing* that the phone had rung, he told himself. His body didn't seem to agree. There was a throbbing ache as his erection swelled against his trousers again, and he was convinced he could still smell her warm feminine fragrance on his skin. Goddammit, she was like a fever in his blood, a fever he could not, for the sake of his brother, succumb to.

୧ଓଓ

For Maya the days after Rajiv left were quiet and tranquil. She felt more herself again without him around. She and Jay spent the days together, going for long walks or swimming in the pool. Sometimes they would drive to the village or some other local beauty spot in the surrounding area.

Anna Maddox also seemed to calm down in the absence of her older son, and her behavior toward Maya was a little warmer. It still shocked Maya to think that the other woman had observed something between herself and Rajiv, if what he had said was the truth. Could he have said things to turn his mother against her? Maya wondered. It was difficult to think clearly about anything that concerned Rajiv. Just picturing him in her mind could leave her in a state of emotional upheaval, and so she tried her best not to think about him at all. It was easier during the day as long as she kept herself busy, but it was more difficult at night when her mind and body became tormented with desires she had never experienced before.

Three days after Rajiv had left an unexpected visitor arrived at Cranthorpe. It had been another sunny day with just a few clouds and a slight breeze in the air as she and Jay made their way back toward the house after driving to Steeple Wick to send a postcard to her mother in South Africa.

"Oh hell," Jay muttered with uncharacteristic vehemence. "I wonder how long she's planning on staying this time."

Maya frowned, following his gaze toward the bright

red Mini Cooper parked in the drive. "Who is it Jay?" she asked with a sense of unease.

"Kirti Patel," Jay responded tersely. "Hoping to become Mrs Kirti Maddox one day soon, if she and my dear mother have anything to do with it."

She stared back at him. "Kirti Maddox? You mean she's hoping to marry you!"

He threw back his head and laughed. "Don't be daft, Maya. It's Rajiv she's after, not me."

Maya felt an unexpected hollowing in her stomach, which she tried to cover with a tight smile. "Oh, what's she like?" The words were no sooner thought than spoken.

"Well, you'll be finding out soon enough," he told her. "She'll be staying the night, I'm sure, so we won't be able to avoid her."

"Oh, come on, Jay. I'm sure she can't be as bad as you're making her out to be." She smiled back at him, trying to ignore the feeling of deflation that was darkening her mood. It should not come as a surprise. After all an attractive, rich and powerful man like Rajiv was hardly likely to be available, especially not to someone like her.

As they entered the house she could hear someone laughing excitedly through the open door of the drawing room, and Maya felt a growing reluctance to interrupt the tête-à-tête. But with a pained smile, Jay clasped her hand and they moved reluctantly forward.

The first thing Maya noticed was the animated expression on Anna's face as she turned to Jay.

"Oh, Jay, darling," she said excitedly. "Isn't it wonderful? Kirti's come to stay for a few days. She took pity on me, all alone now that you have Maya here, and decided to drive over from Surrey to keep me company."

Maya's eyes finally settled on the slim, young Indian woman reclining gracefully on the chaise lounge. She was quite stunning, Maya conceded with a sinking heart. Kirti

Patel was everything that Maya was not: beautiful—as only Indian women could be—dainty and petite, with long sleek ebony hair and elegant, delicate features. The turquoise color of her long skirt matched perfectly with her silk, patterned Indian blouse. Wide, doe-like eyes widened as she came to her feet in a fluid, feminine movement and went to greet Jay, kissing the air close to his cheeks.

"Sanjay darling, how are you?" she asked in a little girl's voice that reminded Maya of an actress from a Bollywood movie. "Your mother's been so worried."

Her accent was perfect polished English with just a touch of Indian melody to it and, although her words sounded perfectly innocent, Maya could see the effect they were having on Jay.

His eyes filled with guilt and his body language mirrored his dejection.

He pushed his hands into the pockets of his jeans and hunched his shoulders. "Yeah, well I keep telling her there's nothing to get wound up about."

"And you must be Maya." Kirti's expression was one of naïveté as she smiled up at Maya. "It was so kind of you to come down and visit dear Sanjay."

Maya shook her hand, trying to quell a feeling of impatience at the girl's tactlessness.

"Anna tells me you're from Scotland," Kirti continued, once they'd seated themselves. "So tell me, are you enjoying the lovely English countryside?"

Maya made some suitable reply, aware of Jay beside her on the long settee. She could sense his discomfort but there was little she could do about it, besides trying to steer the conversation away from him and his depression.

"It's such a pity Rajiv had to go back to London so soon," Kirti was saying. "He really works far too hard, don't you think, Anna?"

Watching the two women, together Maya could see

that Kirti would make a perfect daughter-in-law for Anna Maddox.

"So how long will you be staying, Maya?" Kirti eventually asked, bringing the conversation back round to her.

"Um, about another week I think," Maya replied, aware of the flicker of…something in Anna Maddox's dark eyes.

"Oh, well, we'll have to arrange a little dinner party before you leave, won't we, Anna?" Kirti suggested brightly.

"Oh no," Maya said quickly. "Please don't, that's quite unnecessary. I—um—I'm enjoying the peace and quiet really."

"Actually, Kirti's quite right," Anna asserted. "A dinner party is probably just what we need. It's been too long since we've had one. Don't you agree, Jay?"

Jay gave Maya a resigned smile before answering his mother. "Well, it looks to me like your minds are already made up, and I guess Maya could do with some entertainment before she leaves. It's true, darling," he insisted when she tried to protest. "We haven't done any socializing while you've been here. It's the least we can do."

"Well, that's settled then." Kirti clapped her hands together. "I do hope Rajiv can get away from London. We shall have to telephone him this evening Anna and demand that he be here!"

"How long has your brother known her, Jay?" Maya asked when they'd eventually managed to escape the drawing room.

They were sitting beside the pool after an invigorating swim, which Maya had felt they needed after their encounter with Kirti. The pool itself could be either indoor or outdoor, according to the weather. At present, the screens between the pool-house and the conservatory were rolled back due to the heat of the day. There was something rather extravagant about being able to swim whatever the temperature was.

Maya had always loved swimming and this part of the house was becoming her favorite haunt.

"About 9 months. My mother introduced them," Jay told her as he lay back on one of the cushioned loungers, his face turned toward the sun. "She wants Rajiv to settle down and seems to think Kirti's the perfect candidate, but I'm not sure he agrees with her. Sometimes I think he just goes along with things to keep the peace, and Kirti doesn't make any demands on him so he can put up with her. She's low-maintenance." He frowned for a moment then continued. "He knows that he has to marry soon and Mother has introduced him to dozens of prospective brides in the past two years."

Maya swallowed hard. Rajiv having to marry—his mother introducing him to *prospective brides*? The idea was quiet unpleasant and she couldn't help wanting to know more. "Is she Catholic like your family?" she enquired casually.

Jay laughed. "No, she's Hindu." He shook his head. "But she's made it quite clear that she would be willing to convert if the need arose."

"Why does he have to marry soon?" She tried to project a tone of mild interest, slipping her sunglasses on to cover her eyes.

Fortunately, Jay seemed oblivious to her inner turmoil, his eyes closed, and facing up to the sun. "Many reasons, I guess." He paused, and Maya felt the urge to shake the information out of him. "Firstly, he's thirty one. For an Indian man, that's pushing it, particularly if you want a young Indian bride. Secondly, if he decides to get involved in politics, Indian politics, that is, he'll need to be settled down for people to take him seriously." He sighed. "And lastly, of course, there's my mother. She's desperate for him to get married—big Indian wedding, grandkids, the whole shebang."

Maya tried to process all this information, myriad questions flashing through her mind. "And why does he have to marry an Indian woman?" Was the first one that needed to be answered. "I mean, you're Catholic. Wouldn't that suffice?"

Jay laughed, not a very pleasant laugh. "Rajiv would never marry a woman who wasn't Indian. He hates the fact that he's only half Indian. My father used to call us *half-breeds*. As far back as I can remember, Raj would say he wanted his children to be Indian and proud. Although they will still be one-quarter English. I think he can just about live with that. Besides, if he does decide to get into Indian politics he'll need to be seen as an Indian man with an Indian family."

"I didn't know he was interested in getting into politics," she managed, her brain still trying to absorb all this new information.

"Well, he's very involved in charity work in India and he's very outspoken with his views on the sorry state of the current government. A lot of people and the Indian press are pushing him to get more involved. I think they see him as some kind of savior." Jay shook his head. "Poor Rajiv."

"But what about love?" she had to ask.

"Love! Rajiv?" He threw back his head and laughed. "No way. My brother's far too controlled for that emotion, Maya. I don't think I've ever seen him even mildly infatuated."

He sobered up suddenly. "Mind you, it hasn't been easy for him. Since my father died he's had to take care of everything, including Mother. Before that he was quite wild. Although he got through university with honors, he spent most of his time jet-setting around the world with one woman or another, much to my parents' displeasure. Maybe things would have been different if my father hadn't died, but Raj took over the business almost immediately and managed to prove everyone wrong by becoming an even better businessman than my father was."

Maya bent her head against her raised knees and closed her eyes, remembering Rajiv touching her, kissing her with uncontrolled passion, and she had to conclude that there was a side to him that his brother wasn't aware of. Was she the only woman to see him like that? she wondered. No, it wasn't possible. She was probably one in a long line of woman—not the first and certainly not the last.

She jumped up quickly, unable to remain still with such painful thoughts any longer. "I'm going for another swim. Are you coming?"

Jay shook his head, watching indulgently as she dived gracefully into the water.

Later that night Maya found it impossible to sleep, going over and over the conversation with Jay in her mind. Rajiv was looking for a wife, or rather, his mother was looking for a wife for him! To a British person this might sound absurd, but she felt sure it was nothing unusual in Indian culture. Could Kirti be the one? What had Jay said? She was *low-maintenance*. And beautiful. From what she knew of him, Maya felt Rajiv would want a *low-maintenance* wife, someone who would do his bidding without asking questions.

Would he be unfaithful to her? The thought made Maya feel physically ill. It all sounded so cold-blooded. Would Kirti, or whoever, accept him having discreet affairs while he traveled the world on business? Something told Maya that there were a lot of women out there—Indian and non-Indian—who would accept such an arrangement in order to be married to a man like Rajiv Maddox.

Why the hell was she lying here at one o'clock in the morning thinking about it? The man was nothing to her, really. She had probably been a little distraction to him. Or maybe he had been testing her, trying to find out if she was good enough for his brother. Well, her behavior since she'd met him could only lead to one conclusion. He saw her as a woman, who was supposed to be with one man, but was quite happy for that man's brother to take liberties with her!

The following day, Jay had an appointment with a psychotherapist in Swindon, and Maya offered to accompany him, as he seemed quite nervous about what he called *the ordeal*. It had been obvious to her during dinner the previous evening that she had little in common with both Kirti and Anna, as her and Jay had sat and listened to them chatting away about their involvement in various upcoming fundraising events. Although Maya was intending to begin work with a non-profit organization in the autumn, she was far more interested in the work on the ground rather than in the fundraising part of it. By the end of the meal, she felt quite tired, only politeness preventing her from excusing herself and escaping to the peaceful environs of her room.

Jay was happy to have her along with him on the drive to Swindon. It was the first time he would be meeting the therapist. Maya was hoping it would not be *the ordeal* he was expecting.

"This is probably going to be a total waste of time," he said agitatedly as they approached the outskirts of the town.

"Don't say that Jay," she responded, aware of the tension building up in him with each passing mile. "At least give it a try and see how it goes."

They parked in one of the large shopping malls and Maya went for a walk round the shops after arranging to meet Jay at a chosen café in an hour. It was strange to be around all the hustle and bustle of busy people after the peace and tranquillity of Cranthorpe. Maya realized with surprise that she had not missed this hectic city life at all. Perhaps one day she should think about moving out of her mother's flat in Edinburgh and looking for something in the countryside of Scotland. Not that she could afford it until she'd paid off her student loans, which was going to take quite a few years. And how would her mother feel about living alone? It had been extremely difficult for both of them when her father had been diagnosed with cancer. His death had left her mother at a total loss, but since she'd been in Cape Town with her sister, the children, and grandchildren, she seemed to be in much better spirits, and did not seem in a hurry to return to Scotland. Although Maya missed her, especially just after she'd first left two months ago, she was just relieved to hear her mother sounding so much more upbeat than she had since her father had passed away. They talked on the phone once a week and emailed each other often. In fact, Maya had emailed her last night, having brought her old laptop with her from Edinburgh.

She walked past a small boutique with some eye-catching outfits in the window and, on impulse, went inside. Although she couldn't really afford to buy anything, a dress hanging on the Sale rack immediately caught her eye, and she couldn't resist trying it on. The dress was styled in a way that covered her neck but left her shoulders and arms exposed, and Maya knew it would be the perfect outfit for a dinner party at Cranthorpe. It was black, made from a synthetic knit that ended just above her knees, and clung in all the right places, quite different to her usual style, more sophisticated. But she felt it was just what she needed to boost her confidence. It would help get her through an evening that would undoubtedly have its tensions. Before she could change her mind, Maya pulled out her bankcard and purchased it, telling herself this the kind of dress would never go out of date. And it could always come in handy in the future.

Jay was waiting for her at the café and seemed quite positive about his session with the psychotherapist.

"It was strange," he reflected, sipping his coffee thoughtfully. "I found it easy talking to him and ended up telling him everything: about my sexuality, all about Kurt, my relationship with my mother, everything. Of course, it's all confidential. He assured me of that. Oh, Maya." He clasped her hand suddenly across the table. "It felt so good to be just myself. Like I am with you."

Maya felt like saying, *You don't need to live a lie, just tell them the truth and be done with it.* But she bit her tongue. Since meeting his mother—and brother—she realized just how traditionally Indian they were. While at university, she had come to see Jay as more English than Indian. After all, he was half English. Now that she had spent time with him, in his home with his family, she'd seen a very different side to him. In addition, she was now sure that his mother would have a very hard time accepting her son's sexuality. Jay had told her that some Indian, Hindu, and Catholic families had *disowned* their own children for coming out as gay.

Maybe the therapist could help, she told Jay. Maybe, once he'd settled in with the therapist, they could arrange a family session where Jay may feel more confident in coming out about his sexuality. Jay seemed to consider the idea, but said he'd discuss it with his therapist first and take it from there.

The following morning, Maya made her way down to the morning room for breakfast. The weather outside looked cloudy and decidedly humid and she wondered if there might be thunderstorms later. This was the first gray day since she'd arrived in England over a week ago, so she told herself she had no cause for complaints.

Usually, she ate alone and, although Jay was getting up earlier than before, he was still in bed until around ten o'clock, due to the anti-depressants which he said made him feel drowsy.

So it was a surprise to see Kirti at the table, perfectly made up and looking quite stunning in a lime-green long

collarless shirt and matching embroidered pants, the color
highlighting her striking coloring and long, dark hair.

"Oh good morning, Maya. Isn't it a pity about the
weather?" She pouted delicately. "Anna and I were going to
play tennis with the Langley's but I guess we may have to
cancel now."

Maya smiled sympathetically at her as Nana Bibi arrived to see what she wanted for breakfast. She and the
housekeeper had become quite friendly, and Maya felt a
fleeting sense of impatience toward Kirti for disturbing their
peaceful mornings together, but she suppressed it, telling
herself she had no right to feel this way. One day Kirti
could well become the mistress of Cranthorpe, whereas
Maya was just a passing guest.

After asking for some toast and coffee, Maya made a
concerted effort to be pleasant to the other woman.

"I've managed to convince Rajiv to come for the weekend," Kirti announced, once Maya's breakfast was on the
table. "He'll be arriving tomorrow evening. Isn't that exciting?"

"Hmmm, yes," Maya nodded, biting into her slice of
toast and feeling her stomach contract at Kirti's news.

"So we're planning on having the dinner party on Saturday night. Will that be okay with you?" Kirti enquired,
leaning her elbows on the table.

Maya took a gulp of the strong coffee, needing something to wash down the toast that was now stuck in her
throat. "Fine."

"I hope Jay doesn't mind us arranging this dinner,"
Kirti said, raising her beautifully shaped eyebrows.

Maya was tempted to say, *It's a bit too late to be worrying about that now*, but she bit back the words and shook
her head instead. "I think he's sort of used to the idea now."

"He's been so much better since you've been here, you
know," Kirti confided. "I saw him not long before you ar-

rived and he was terribly depressed, but I noticed the improvement as soon as I saw you with him." She gave Maya
an intimate smile. "The two of you make such a lovely couple and you get on so well together. Why if Rajiv had to
spend so much time with me, he'd probably be bored to
tears."

She gave a little laugh, and Maya was forced to disagree. "I'm sure that's not true, Kirti," she countered, but the
other woman shook her head.

"No, I can see how close you and Jay are," Kirti insisted. "It's obvious that you're madly in love. Rajiv isn't like
his brother, he's not so emotional, you see."

Maya caught her breath, wishing she could disagree
with everything Kirti was saying. What could she say? That
Jay and she were not "in love," or that Rajiv was extremely
emotional from what she had experienced?

She simply could not voice these things, so instead she
just shook her head and tried to move onto a safer topic.
Kirti was not a nasty person, she realized, just very naïve
and, when Maya suggested a swim, she agreed to come
along, although she wouldn't go in the water.

It turned out to be quite a pleasant morning and, in between Maya's swims, the two of them chatted about innocent topics. Kirti was flicking through a magazine, and she
brought Maya up to date on all the celebrity gossip, being
quite an expert on most of the big names. She had even met
a few of them through her charity work.

Maya found some of her stories of out-of-control egos
and vicious tabloids journalists quite fascinating. But all the
while, in the back of her mind was the reminder that tomorrow Rajiv would be back.

Although a part of her was dreading it, she was too
honest to deny that the prospect of seeing him again was an
extremely tantalizing one. With Kirti here, and the mind-
boggling information she'd received from Jay, she knew

that she would need to stay as far away from Rajiv as possible.

He needed to find an Indian wife and settle down, while she needed to get this weekend over with and then make her plans to go back to her life in Edinburgh.

CHAPTER 7

Rajiv could feel a heightening sense of tension as he drove closer to Cranthorpe. He'd left London before the rush hour began and had, therefore, made good time, but he wished he could control this feeling of nail-biting excitement at the thought of seeing Maya again. God, he had hoped that being away from her would help his situation, but it only seemed to have made things worse. In fact, he'd found it difficult to concentrate on anything while he was in London and, on more than one occasion, he had seen the people he worked with giving him strange and worried looks, which was the last thing that he needed. Being the head of an organization as large as Maddox Junta Investments made it vital that people trust and believe in him, and he could not have them doubting his ability to handle things. There had been serious doubts about his ability to manage the company when his father had died. It had taken him a good two years to convince the staff and shareholders that he was up to the job. After all the hard work that had gone into proving himself, the last thing he needed now was people beginning to doubt his abilities again.

Maybe it would be better once she went back to Scotland, he told himself as he slowed down to maneuver around a particularly sharp bend. The thought of never seeing her again left a hollow feeling in the pit of his stomach, but he knew that that would probably be the best outcome.

Unless she decided to continue her relationship with Jay. Rajiv's nerves tightened at the idea of seeing her regularly as his brother's girlfriend—or even his wife! The picture in his head was too disturbing to contemplate. He made a mental effort to push it aside, concentrating on the road ahead with a dogged determination to keep his grasping mind under control.

Then there was also Kirti to contend with. Before meeting Maya, he had half-heartedly been considering the idea of marrying her, but the idea was now becoming more and more unpalatable. Since he'd turned thirty, he'd been seriously contemplating marriage. He was getting too old to continue the bachelor lifestyle he so enjoyed. Besides, he wanted children, and he knew too many men, and women, who'd waited until their forties to have them. That was something he simply didn't want, but the clock was ticking and the pressure was on. Not just from himself, but his mother, who had been searching India as well as England for a suitable Indian bride for him. He'd lost count of the number of Indian women his mother had introduced him to. Most of them had been too young, although Maya was probably the same age as many of them. Indian women in general were quite innocent and naïve until they married. It made him feel quite uncomfortable meeting these youthful, demure girls who seemed almost like teenagers to him. He was thirty-one, for God's sake, and not some pervert who got turned on by girls who were barely out of their teens. He simply couldn't contemplate it.

Maya was a different story altogether. She was mature, confident in her own low-key way, and surely experienced. Though the thought of her with another man, especially his brother, was like a knife twisting in his gut. He had to get over this infatuation. If it wasn't for his brother, he would have had her by now, gotten her out of his system, and been ready to move on to marriage.

It was not yet five o'clock when he pulled up outside the house, and as he killed the engine, Kirti came out to greet him.

"Rajiv darling, you're early. What a nice surprise." She stood at the bottom of the steps with a welcoming smile on her charming face and, just for a moment, he wished that he could feel that gut-wrenching desire for her, rather than for a woman who was way out of his reach.

"Kirti." He brushed her cheek with his lips, trying his best to look pleased to see her.

They climbed the steps together and he forced himself to put an arm round her shoulders and listen to her chat away about what she and his mother had been up to these past days. He could feel his skin prickle in anticipation as they entered the drawing room, but only his mother was there. He forced himself to make polite conversation before asking her where Maya—and Sanjay were.

"Sanjay's taking a nap," his mother informed him. "And I'm not sure where Maya is, probably at the pool. She spends a lot of time there."

He could hear the underlying criticism in his mother's voice, but chose to ignore it. What was wrong with spending time in the pool, for God's sake? He loved to swim, in summer and winter, although he could not recall seeing his mother or Kirti take a dip in the pool. Ever.

He walked to the door, feeling increasingly restless. Now that he was at the house, he felt impatient to see her. "I think I'll go and take a shower." He rubbed the back of his neck. "If you don't mind?"

The two women nodded their perfectly groomed dark heads in unison, and Rajiv made his escape with a heartfelt sigh of relief.

He did go for a shower, but instead of using his en-suite bathroom, he found himself walking toward the solarium. It might be a crazy thing to do, but he wanted to see her now, and if she happened to be enjoying a swim, that was not going to stop him. He opened the sliding doors, which separated the pool area from the conservatory, without making a sound. He moved quietly toward the changing-rooms on his left, catching a tantalizing glimpse of her enjoying a leisurely crawl along the length of the pool. He entered the change-rooms before she could see him and stripped off quickly, stepping under the shower with a sigh of pleasure as the water cooled his heated body. Nana Bibi always made sure a selection of swimsuits and trunks were available for guests and he pulled on a pair of black shorts suppressing the urge to leave them behind and swim with her in the nude. The image of her naked in the water was enough to bring him to full arousal and he cursed to himself as he was forced to climb under the cold shower again before finally exiting the change-room.

♥⁓♥⁓

Maya let out a frightened yelp as she felt someone, or something, dive into the water. She grabbed onto the rim of the pool and watched with a thundering heart as the dark form now under the water made its way swiftly toward her.

"You!" she gasped with a mixture of relief and trepidation when he finally surfaced right beside her, grinning wickedly at her terrified expression.

"Well, who did you expect?" he countered, raking back his dripping hair with long brown fingers.

As she stared into his laughing blue eyes, Maya felt a painful melting feeling in the pit of her stomach. She had missed him, she realized as her throat tightened and breathing became difficult. Something of what she was feeling must have shown in her face, for his gaze darkened, the pupils dilating so that his eyes appeared almost black. He reached out and brushed his thumb against her wet lips in a sensually, intimate gesture, but before she could react to his burning touch he pulled away.

"Race you to the end and back," he challenged, moving away from her. "Come on—or are you scared I'll beat you," he added at her hesitation.

Maya was tempted to refuse but the gleaming challenge in his eyes convinced her. Besides, she was a good swimmer and, although he was bigger and stronger than she, she could still give him a run for his money.

He was an excellent swimmer and, although she beat him—just—she knew that he'd allowed her to. But she enjoyed her moment of glory just the same. They swam for a good half hour and Maya found his playfulness in the water quite invigorating. She and Jay usually swam laps just to exercise their bodies, but this was different. This was pure fun and the fact that she was excited to see him again just added to her pleasure.

Finally, she protested that she was simply too tired to swim anymore and climbed out, on legs that could hardly carry her, to flop down onto one of the cushioned loungers with an exhausted laugh. Squeezing the excess water out of her long hair, she rubbed her body lazily with a fluffy white towel, glancing surreptitiously over at him as he emerged from the pool.

The black, low-waisted shorts moulded to his thighs and his dark brown skin gleamed as droplets of water streamed off his lean muscular body. There was not an ounce of superfluous flesh on his tall athletic frame. She felt the same melting weakness beginning low in her stomach just by looking at the masculine beauty of his body.

"That was just what I needed after the long drive from London," he announced, pushing his wet hair back and helping himself to one of the towels stacked along the side of the pool area.

"When did you get here?" she asked curiously, as he sat down on the side of the striped lounger beside her.

"About an hour ago, I guess," he remarked, rubbing his hair dry with the towel.

He was facing her, his brown feet set squarely on the tiled floor and his knees apart, allowing her a glimpse of lean muscular thighs sprinkled with hair that glinted against his dark bronze skin. He was too close for comfort. Maya looked away, moistening her lips as he dropped the towel and leaned even closer, casually resting his forearms along his thighs.

She sat forward. Under his scrutiny, her black bathing suit seemed suddenly much more revealing than it had before, and she wrapped her arms round her raised knees, all too aware of his intimate gaze.

"Looks like you've caught some sun since you been here," he said "It suits you." His voice was warm and husky, his eyes moving hotly over her body. "Have you missed me?"

Maya's head shot up as she stared at him, wondering if she had heard right. But his darkened, languorous eyes told her that she had heard him correctly. She drew a trembling breath, feeling her breasts swell against the constricting swimsuit and heat pool, like melting honey, between her thighs.

"I don't know what you mean," she lied, her eyes trapped by the desire that flared in his.

"Don't lie to me," he said roughly and reached out to twist a lock of her dampened hair around his finger, tugging at it almost painfully as if to punish her for her deceit.

"So there you are!"

Maya jerked round contritely to see Kirti standing at the glass sliding doors that led to the conservatory. Her high-heels clicked loudly against the tiles as she came toward them, an exasperated smile on her face.

"I've been looking everywhere for you, Rajiv. You should have said you were coming for a swim. I would have joined you."

It seemed that Kirti found nothing unusual about the scene she had just interrupted, and Maya wished she didn't feel so flushed and guilty. After all, she had done nothing wrong. Although it was not difficult to imagine what could have happened if Kirti *hadn't* interrupted them.

"I thought you didn't like swimming," Rajiv responded coolly.

His only concession to his Kirti's arrival had been to let go of Maya's hair, and she felt a sense of unease at his indifferent behavior.

Kirti came to a halt beside them, her smile slightly teasing. "I don't," she agreed. "But I could have kept you company, darling."

"I had Maya to keep me company," he remarked dryly, and Maya stifled a gasp, wanting to slap his lean, handsome face.

He did not seem the least bit bothered by the situation, whereas Maya was squirming with discomfort and shame. As for poor Kirti, she was now at a loss for words.

Sensing the other girl's discomfort, Maya stood up quickly. "Well, I'd better be going." She gave Kirti an encouraging smile and wrapped the towel protectively around her body. "Jay might be looking for me. Um, I guess I'll see you both later then."

Without giving him a second glance, she walked swiftly into the change-rooms, dragging her clothes uncaringly over her damp swimsuit. She then slipped out through the sliding doors like a thief in the night.

Upstairs in her bedroom, Maya fumed at his unfazed behavior and at her own gullibility. God only knew what would have happened if Kirti hadn't arrived, and Maya's blood ran cold at the thought of the other woman discovering them behaving in an inappropriate manner. It was not as if it hadn't happened before, she reminded herself grimly, and only luck had prevented them from being discovered that last time in his study. She bit painfully down on her lower lip. She was too vulnerable where he was concerned. This afternoon proved it once again, and the only solution she could think of was to remove herself from his presence completely.

As she peeled off the damp swimsuit and climbed under the hot spray of the shower, Maya tried to decide when was the soonest that she could leave. Jay would be disappointed of course, but hopefully, his work with the counsellor would help him make the decisions he needed to make. If she told Jay tonight, she could leave sometime next week. That should be okay. She lathered herself with the luxurious soap and tried not to feel despondent. It was not only letting Jay down that upset her, she admitted, it was the knowledge that she would never see Rajiv again that choked her. As stupid as it seemed, meeting him had changed her in some way. What had passed between them was not something she was likely to forget, even if it was just a passing diversion for him.

How could he behave like this with her when he was planning to get married? Even if he wasn't yet sure who his future wife was going to be? Ridiculous, right? Not knowing who you were going to marry, but preparing for it anyway. Perhaps if he had been engaged when she'd first met him, she would not have felt this attraction to him. *Yeah right.* Okay, so nothing could have prevented her from the attraction she felt for him. Or was she just sexually aware of him? Was there a difference? She thought so. Attraction didn't go half-way to describing the level of awareness that she felt around him.

She climbed out of the shower and covered herself in the huge pink bath towel, avoiding the haunting face reflected in the mirror. Was it less than an hour ago that she had felt happy and carefree, laughing and swimming with him as if nothing and nobody else existed? But Kirti existed, and there was no doubt that she would make an excellent wife. Maya pulled the bath towel tighter around her, unable to ignore the painful ache that gripped her. She would have to go downstairs soon and behave as if nothing had happened, and yet her whole frame of mind had now altered.

She forced herself to dress for dinner, wishing she could just crawl under the blankets and forget about everything, if only for a while. But that was impossible, and so she brushed her half-wet hair and tied it in a long plait down her back. Perhaps she should get it cut when she got back to Edinburgh. It seemed like time for a change.

She grabbed the first things that came to her hands from the wardrobe, which happened to be the beaded emerald blouse that she had worn on her first night with him in London. Her lips twisted in a painful smile. How long ago that seemed to her now. With the blouse, she wore a simple, black, silky, wrap-around skirt that fell softly down to her ankles. Realizing that she was late, she added just a touch of gloss to her lips, quite unaware of how young and susceptible her unmade face and simple hairstyle would appear to those around her.

Jay was pouring himself a drink as Anna and Kirti sat chatting together on the settee, while Rajiv was nowhere to be seen, and she tried to tell herself that she was glad.

Jay came to greet her, a look of relief on his face. "Hi, princess." He took her hand. "You look lovely. Come let me get you a drink."

She followed him over to the drinks cabinet, greeting the two women politely as she passed by.

"Did you enjoy your afternoon swim?" Jay asked, and Maya felt the hot color invade her cheeks at his innocent question.

"Mmm, yes, thank you," she said quietly, hoping he didn't notice her discomfort.

"I was just saying I'll need Rajiv to give me some swimming lessons soon." Kirti had obviously heard them and come over to join in. "He says you're a very good swimmer, Maya. I feel quite jealous," she conceded, pulling a face and laughing.

"How would he know?" Jay asked with a frown

"Oh, didn't Maya tell you? Rajiv joined her at the pool just after he arrived. They were swimming for ages, weren't you, Maya?"

She could feel the heat prickling on her skin as they both stared at her. "Well, it wasn't that long really." She took a large sip of the white wine Jay had poured for her and smiled brightly at the other woman. "You look lovely, Kirti. That color really suits you."

It was a relief that she'd chosen the perfect subject to distract Kirti with. Maya pretended to listen with interest to the other woman talking about the Indian designer of the pale-blue dress she had on this evening.

"I'm saving my Versace for tomorrow night," Kirti continued avidly. "Phoebe's bringing her new boyfriend and I'm simply dying to meet him."

Maya nodded absently, hardly taking in a word she was saying, Rajiv had just entered the room and his disturbing presence immediately played havoc with her senses. He looked darkly attractive in a white linen shirt and black trousers. Maya felt her limbs weaken as she met his brooding gaze for a brief moment before she managed to drag her eyes away.

"Sorry I'm late," he announced to no one in particular as he came into the room.

Kirti went to link her arm possessively through his. Even in extra-high heels, she still only reached some point below his chin. Maya found herself watching them with a mixture of fascination and dread. This was the first time, besides earlier at the pool, that she had seen them together as a couple.

"You work too hard, darling," Kirti cooed, running a long painted nail along the soft cloth of his shirt. "Come, let Jay pour you a little drink. You look quite tense, doesn't he, Anna?"

Maya moved quickly toward the French windows, pretending to look out at the blossoming shrubs. It was still quite light outside and, although the day had been a little cloudy, the evening had seen the sky clear. It looked as if they might enjoy another beautiful sunset.

Maya found the evening quite a strain. Kirti monopolized most of the conversation, which was probably a good thing as it meant that her own silence went mainly unnoticed. She was aware of Rajiv's eyes on her from time to time but she managed to studiously avoid meeting his gaze, fearful of the effect those hooded eyes could have on her.

She managed to get away straight after dinner with the excuse of a headache, which was partly true. Having to watch Kirti and him together had not been easy. Observing the other woman as she touched him and flirted with him in a totally proprietary manner had been more difficult than Maya could have imagined. As she pulled off her clothes in the safety of her bedroom and loosened her hair, Maya felt more certain than ever that she had to get away from this place—or rather, this man.

She was just about to climb into bed when a knock at the door made her jump. "Who is it?" she asked, her heart thundering in her ears as she imagined Rajiv, awaiting her on the other side of the door.

"It's me, Jay."

Maya despised herself for the feeling of sinking disappointment at the sound of her friend's voice. Lord, what would she have done if it was Rajiv? Invited him into her room—and her bed?

"Come in, Jay," she said, drawing a steadying breath as she opened the door.

"How's your headache?" he enquired, following her into the room and closing the door behind him.

"Um, a little better I think. Sit down." She patted the mattress beside her, but he moved to the dressing table instead, avoiding her eyes. "What is it, Jay?" she asked, sensing something was not right.

Finally, he turned to face her. "You didn't tell me you'd gone swimming with Rajiv this afternoon, Maya."

His voice was more concerned than accusing, but still she felt her face redden. "I'm sorry. I didn't think it was that important, Jay," she murmured, trying to hide her burning cheeks behind her long, loose hair.

"God, Maya, don't tell me there's something going on between you two!" he exclaimed, moving agitatedly round the room. "When I saw your face this evening—hell it suddenly struck me. You looked so guilty. How long has it been going on?" He stood suddenly still and fixed his fierce gaze on her flushed face.

"Jay, please. Nothing's going on." She stared up at him beseechingly. "Why are you saying these things?"

"Because I saw your face when Kirti said you'd been swimming with him." He began pacing again. "And then I noticed him during dinner. God, he couldn't keep his eyes off you! Kirti must have been blind not to notice." He ran troubled fingers through his long hair. "Maya, you don't know my brother like I do. When we were younger, people always said I was the handsome one, but believe me it was always him who got the girls. Not that I cared a damn, of course." He laughed derisively. "They were crazy about him and he took full advantage of it—love them and leave them, or rather screw them and leave them—that was Rajiv."

Maya listened with a mixture of fascination and horror, not saying a word, and Jay came to sit beside her, taking her cold hand in his.

"The reason I'm telling you all this is 'cause I don't want you to get hurt, and Rajiv is more than capable of hurting you. Do you understand? He's too used to getting—or taking—what he wants where women are concerned. Maybe it's because he could never be free, because all his life, as the oldest son, he knew the family responsibilities would be heaped on him. But whatever it was, it's given him a heartless streak, *especially* where women are concerned.

"He's always had at least one mistress, sometimes two at a time—one here in the UK and usually one in India." Jay paused, clenching his fists in fury. "And as you now know, he's looking for a wife—an Indian wife. I told you. He's always said that when he marries it will be to a traditional Indian woman. Maybe Kirti, but if not, someone of her ilk, if you know what I mean."

Maya dropped her head down between her shoulders. Yes, she knew he wanted little Indian babies, who wouldn't stand out, or be bullied, like him and Jay had been.

"I don't think he's capable of falling in love. I think he just got bored with all the fooling around and decided it was time to settle down. Do you understand what I'm saying, Maya? Because, God knows, I don't want you to end up heartbroken like me!"

CHAPTER 8

I say, Rajiv, you and Kirti will have to come round for a
game of tennis soon."

Rajiv nodded his head absently as he lifted the tumbler
of whisky to his lips and drained the glass, enjoying the way
the alcohol burned all the way down to the knot of tension
that had settled in the pit of his stomach. The room felt
noisy and congested, even though he knew that there were
only ten of them for dinner. Kirti had informed him of the
details more than once in the past twenty-four hours, yet all
the boisterous chatter made the room seem over-crowded
and loud.

There was the local doctor, Craig Somerset, a widower
close to his mother in age, and then there were the Lang-
leys. Erwin Langley, the older man Rajiv was professing to
have a conversation with right now, his wife Susan, and
their daughter Phoebe. Kirti and Phoebe were good friends,
who'd met the first time Kirti had visited Cranthorp. They
certainly had a lot in common, even if Phoebe was as English as they come, Rajiv acknowledged wryly, watching the
two of them gossiping avidly together at the other end of the
room.

Then there was Phoebe's new boyfriend, Timothy Osborne, who had attached himself to Maya like an eager puppy-dog, salivating with excitement at the sight of her.

"Can I get you another drink, Erwin," Rajiv offered, dragging his eyes back to the man beside him.

"And why not?" The older man passed Rajiv his glass. "Same again for me, but make it a single this time, old chap."

Rajiv nodded, moving from the French windows to the drinks cabinet. He tried to avoid looking over at her again, his eyes drawn like a moth to a flame. From the moment, she had walked into the room in that slinky black dress, her bare limbs smooth and tanned, and her vivid hair loosely tied at the top of her head, Rajiv had been overcome with pure unadulterated lust. He poured himself another double whisky and a single for Erwin, quite aware that he was drinking more than he should.

Jay was chatting away to Susan Langley, Rajiv noticed, totally unconcerned that Maya was being hit on by that young idiot Osborne for the past fifteen minutes, at least. Didn't he care? It was a sobering thought and, not for the first time, Rajiv wondered if perhaps his brother and Maya were really just friends. But he shrugged the idea away as wishful thinking. No red-blooded male could just be friends with a woman like her. It was simply impossible.

It was a relief when Nana Bibi announced that dinner was ready and, as they moved through to the dining room, he gained some comfort from the fact that the young toff wasn't sitting beside Maya. His mother occupied one end of the table and he, Rajiv, took his father's place at the other end. On Anna's right, sat the good doctor and, on her left, was Susan Langley. Maya was seated between the doctor and Jay, while Rajiv had to make do with Kirti on his right and Phoebe Langley on his left.

"Rajiv, you naughty boy," Kirti pouted. "You haven't even mentioned my new dress."

"Sorry." His veiled eyes moved over the gold sequined dress and he swallowed a mouthful of the Burgundy wine before saying dryly, "It suits you, Kirti. What there is of it, that is."

Kirti giggled excitedly at his reply, quite unaware of how unfavorably she was being compared to Maya, who turned to smile at Jay and then stopped short as she met Rajiv's heated gaze. Through sheer willpower, he held her eyes, uncaring of who might be observing them. He wanted her to know how he was feeling. She had practically ignored him the whole evening, smiling and conversing with everyone except him, and he resented her for it. Dammit, didn't what had passed between them mean anything to her? His life had become a torment since he'd first laid eyes on her. Didn't she know that? She managed to look away finally, her lovely face flushed with color, and he felt a petty sense of triumph for undermining her cool facade.

"Kirti tells me you're going to teach her how to swim." Phoebe Langley's voice interrupted his thoughts.

Rajiv frowned at her. She was not a particularly pretty girl, but clever make-up and even cleverer plastic surgery had given her a reasonably attractive look. "I am?" he questioned with some irritation.

"Oh please, darling. It'll be such fun." Kirti clasped his arm, gazing appealingly into his eyes. He had to force himself not to pull away from her clinging fingers. "Jay and Maya spend so much time at the pool," she continued. "And it looks so relaxing. I do so want us to do the same."

His jaw clenched at the picture Kirti had painted of Maya and his brother. What else did they do by the pool? he wondered, glaring at the two of them from across the table.

"I don't have the time right now, Kirti," he said, extracting himself from her grasp. "Maybe you should think about hiring a professional." He knew he was being insensitive, maybe even cruel, but he simply could not imagine himself spending time teaching Kirti to swim. In fact, the thought of spending any time alone with her was becoming anathema to him. Why this was, and what he was going to do about it, was not something he was prepared to examine right now.

Kirti was looking sulky and hurt, with Phoebe giving her sympathetic glances that left him feeling guilty and frustrated at the same time. The whole situation with Kirti was beginning to feel like a charade. Looking back, he could see that it was his mother who had thrown them together, and he had allowed the relationship to continue simply out of apathy. He had no real feelings for the girl, and the fact that he had toyed with the idea of marrying her one day seemed ludicrous now. He couldn't get married simply because his mother expected it, and then to choose someone, simply because she was deemed "suitable," seemed totally absurd.

Once again, his eyes were drawn to the woman responsible for all this upheaval. She was talking to Jay, smiling as his brother reached out to caress her smooth naked arm. Rajiv tightened his grip on the delicate wine glass he was holding to prevent himself from leaning over and dragging his brother's hands away from her.

With a deep, steadying breath, he slowly eased his grip on the glass. It wouldn't do to go crushing glasses at civilized dinner parties, he told himself bitterly, and drained the wine instead.

∽∾∽∾

Maya stepped out onto the spacious patio and breathed in the fresh night air with some degree of relief. It was good to get away, even if only for a few minutes, for she knew she would have to go back in and mingle again soon. As she'd expected, the evening had been a strain. Besides the fact that she was not used to dinner parties of this caliber, her awareness of Rajiv, and the feelings he evoked, had left her feeling drained and vulnerable.

After Jay's outburst last night Maya had told him of her plan to leave within the next few days and, although he had been disappointed, even angry, eventually he'd agreed that she needed to do what she felt was best.

"All alone?" That deep velvety voice caused her heart to thump heavily in her chest.

Maya felt heat prickling on her skin as his gaze moved from her face to her bare shoulders and down the length of her legs. "I needed some fresh air," she said with more coolness than she felt. "That's all."

"That dress suits you," he said softly, his blue eyes electric as they settled back on her face. "It's no wonder he's been drooling over you like a puppy-dog."

"I don't know who or what you're talking about."

"Your latest conquest, who else?" He moved closer and she took a step back, but the balustrade effectively blocked her in. "Did he tell you his father's an Earl? Could be quite a good catch, don't you think?"

She could smell the alcohol on his breath as he regarded her through hooded eyes, and the realization that he must have drunk too much made her feel more confident.

"Why, Rajiv, surely you're not jealous," she challenged, leaning back against the balustrade and pasting on a fake smile.

"Maybe I am," he acknowledged tightly. "Or maybe I don't like seeing my brother made a fool of."

Maya threw back her head and laughed. "Jay wouldn't mind in the least," she managed eventually and watched his eyes darken with anger.

"I see." He reached out and trailed a finger slowly down her bare arm. "I suppose this has something to do with the so-called 'open relationship' you and my brother have." He lifted a mocking eyebrow. "Is that right?"

She forced herself calmly to return his gaze, holding back a shiver at the casual touch of his finger. "What about you and Kirti?" she returned, deliberately evading his question. "Is that an open relationship too, or are you planning on being faithful till death do you part?"

His hand closed round her wrist in a vice-like grip. "Stop playing stupid games, Maya." She could feel the heat of his body as he moved closer, and she glanced anxiously toward the room behind him, but nobody else seemed to have noticed their heated exchange. "Or are you deliberately trying to torment me?"

"*Me* torment *you*?" Her voice rose, and then she gasped as he pressed himself against her, his powerful thighs leaning into her. "Raj, are you crazy? God, anyone could see you!"

She could feel the bold thrust of his erection through the lightweight trousers of his suit and she despised herself for the spread of languid desire that invaded her body, allowing him to slant into the melting heat between her legs.

"Touch me," he demanded, as he took her hand in his and drew it down his body, pressing her palm against the heated bulge that strained against his zipper.

Maya drew a trembling breath, her whole body suffused in heat. She could feel the pulsating throb of his erection as her hand began to explore his body of its own accord.

Rajiv shuddered uncontrollably. "God, that feels good," he groaned, his breath hot against her neck. "I want you—I want you now. Let me come to you room later, let me please you. You know you want it, too."

Maya listened to his words with a mixture of pleasure and pain. How many women had he whispered those words to before? she wondered. If only Jay's accusations were not so fresh in her memory, if only Kirti wasn't there in the very next room.

Even as her body cried out for fulfilment, she knew she could not allow it. Dragging herself away from him was the most difficult thing she had ever done. It tore her apart. She almost ran back into the warmth of his arms as her body cried out for his.

"No, Rajiv," she breathed raggedly, her chest rising and falling as she fought for control. "I won't allow you to use me."

He was breathing hard, a pulse beating at his jaw line. "Don't talk rubbish," he grated, buttoning up his jacket with trembling fingers. "You want me as much as I want you. Nobody's using anyone."

"And what about Kirti? Don't you care about her feelings?" she challenged..

His mouth twisted sardonically. "I could ask you the same about Jay," he countered swiftly.

"That's different."

"How is it different? Tell me please. I'd love to know."

"So there you are, princess!" It was Jay, concern evident in his eyes, and she smiled reassuringly back at him. "Are you going to join me for a coffee liqueur?"

Maya nodded, walking shakily toward him. "I'd love to. Thank you, Jay," she replied, taking his hand.

Jay turned to his brother. "Oh, Rajiv, I think Kirti's been looking for you," he remarked with a cold look and then guided Maya swiftly back into the room.

ℰⱭℰⱭ

Rajiv finished off his second cup of coffee and checked his watch once again. It was nine-fifteen in the morning and he was paying for his over-indulgence the night before. It wouldn't have been so bad if he'd been able to sleep off the effects of the alcohol. But by the time he'd made it to bed, having fought off Kirti's clumsy overtures, he'd felt wide awake. Then he spent a restless night, tossing and turning, tormented with thoughts of Maya and how exquisite her soft, pliant body had felt against his.

Nana Bibi had informed him with a knowing twinkle in her eye that Maya usually came down around nine o'clock for breakfast, and so here he was, hanging around like some eager adolescent with a hard on, while she was probably enjoying a Sunday morning lie in. He stood up and went to stare with brooding intensity out the long windows. The day was overcast and slightly cool, not that he cared one way or the other. He shoved his hands into the back pockets of his jeans, his mouth tightening into a thin line. Gone were the carefree days when all he had to worry about was the weather and the prospect of rain spoiling his plans to spend the day outdoors: riding his motorbike, playing tennis, swimming in the pool or in the lake.

It seemed the man he was before meeting Maya had lived a rather shallow existence, incapable of extreme highs and lows. But now that's all his life seemed to be about: the thrill of being around her and, especially, touching her and the gut wrenching pain of seeing her happily involved with his brother.

"Oh. Good morning."

It was her.

His jerked round, his whole body tightening with excitement. "Hi." He tried to sound casual, as if it was only by chance that he'd encountered her here, while his eyes moved hungrily down her body.

She was wearing a lilac colored cardigan and, although buttoned almost to the top, he could have sworn that she wore nothing underneath it. Made from soft, fluffy wool, it hugged lovingly at her pointed breasts and he quickly veiled his eyes, concealing the naked desire that he knew would be visible in them.

Her hair was hanging long and loose down her back,

except for two slim plaits at the front, framing the soft sensual beauty of her face.

"Good morning, Miss Maya."

Nana Bibi followed her into the room carrying a tray, and he watched with interest the easy familiarity evident between them, knowing his mother would not approve.

The housekeeper gave him a covert smile. "I've made up a large pot of coffee for the two of you."

"Thank you Nana Bibi," he responded, turning away from the window. "Did you sleep well?" It was a loaded question. He asked it to unsettle her—and to punish her for the discomfort he had endured throughout the night.

"Very well, thank you," she answered coolly, helping herself to a slice of toast. "How about you?"

"Fine." He shrugged dismissively. "I noticed you disappeared quite early last night. Was the party not to your liking?"

Her mouth tightened slightly, but her expression remained composed. "The party was fine. I'm just not used to late nights, that's all."

Rajiv watched her with brooding eyes. She was not a fussy eater. He had realized that from their first meal together at the house in Knightsbridge, and there was a certain pleasure in watching her enjoy her food. He wondered if she enjoyed sex in the same way, if she abandoned herself to it without any inhibitions, savoring each sensation, unafraid to try anything new. Damn, he swore silently to himself. Why did it always come down to sex with her?

"I'm driving over to the village this morning," he said with an indifference he was far from feeling. "Would you like to come with me?"

Her eyes widened and then narrowed into a frown. "I don't think so." She paused for a moment. "Is Kirti going?" she asked, and he bit back a harsh retort at the stupidity of her question.

"No. Kirti's probably still in bed. I don't think she'll be up for hours." She was going to refuse. He could tell by the way she carefully moistened her upper lip, like she always did when feeling ill at ease. He moved toward the table, gripping the back of one of the chairs. "For God's sake, Maya, it's just a drive to the village," he ground out, losing patience. "I promise to behave myself, okay. Is that what you want to hear?"

He could see the uncertainty in those bright emerald eyes, but his gaze didn't waver and eventually she agreed with a reluctant nod of her head.

"All right. I'll come, but just for a short while. We'll have to be back before Jay wakes up."

"Fine." He nodded in agreement, straightening up from the table, carefully masking the satisfaction he was feeling at the prospect of a morning alone with her. "Shall we meet in the hall in, say, half an hour?"

Rajiv left the room quickly, before she could change her mind, trying to subdue the ridiculous sense of excitement that coursed through his body.

Thirty-five minutes later they drove away from Cranthorpe and Rajiv expelled a quiet sigh of relief. They had managed to get away without encountering anyone besides Nana Bibi, who was sharp enough to relay only what was necessary to whoever might notice their absence. He felt a sense of carefree insouciance as he drove along the narrow country road with Maya sitting quietly at his side. Just for now, he would allow himself to enjoy the moment and forget who she was, who he was, and the impossibility of their situation.

Steeple Wick was a small market town and, with it being a Sunday morning, there were small groups of people coming out of the old church, which was situated close to the main square. He parked the car and they walked through the square where a weekly crafts and antiques market was being held. He often drove to the village on a Sunday morning, always on his own, and enjoyed browsing through the market, sometimes purchasing the odd tool or old country bric-a-brac that caught his eye.

"This is lovely," Maya enthused. "What a perfect way to spend a Sunday morning."

Rajiv smiled, pleased with her reaction. She was so different to the women he usually associated with who wouldn't be seen dead in a second-hand market. He watched her chatting away to one of the stallholders with that unaffected charm of hers that had the old man eating out of her hand in no time. Rajiv allowed himself the pleasure of observing her as she moved along the rows of stalls. She was wearing a floral skirt that ended just below her knees, and his lazy gaze roamed freely along the supple lines of her long legs up to the rounded curve of her buttocks. It was incredible, the effect that she had on him. Her clothes were not particularly provocative and yet, just looking at her, caused him to become aroused. He could not remember, even as a teenager, any girl exciting him the way she did.

Eventually he managed to drag her away, but not before she'd purchased a1930s cake stand for his mother and a silver-plated picture frame for Nana Bibi. The sky was beginning to darken and he suggested they pop into the local pub before making their way home.

The Grafton, as it was called, was filled with people enjoying a pre-lunch drink and Rajiv waved to a few familiar faces but didn't stop to chat. He was not prepared to share Maya with anyone else, not when his time alone with her was so precious, leading her determinedly toward a quieter part of the room.

"Coffee or something stronger?" he asked, after seating her at a tiny table for two.

She looked toward the bar, biting into her bottom lip. "Um, what are you having?"

"Just a half lager, I think," he said, lifting his brows. "Would you like to join me?"

She agreed and he fought his way through to the front of the bar, impatient to get back to her, becoming aware of a group of young men standing at the bar, their keen eyes focusing in on her.

"Cheers." He raised his glass to her on his return and drank thirstily, enjoying the bitter taste of the chilled lager while trying not to stare at her licking the foam off her lips.

"So how do think Jay's meeting with the counsellor went?" he asked eventually. It was something he'd been meaning to talk to her about since his return to Cranthorpe.

She set her glass down, her long lashes veiling her eyes. "He seemed pleased with the session, I think," she mused, finally meeting his gaze. "He wasn't at all keen to begin with, but afterward—well, he was quite excited." She paused and he waited silently, sure, that she was being careful choosing her words. "I think the therapy could be really helpful, giving him time to explore what he's feeling, what he wants for the future. Did he say anything to your mother or you about it?"

He shook his head. "Not much. That's why I thought I'd get your opinion."

Her expression became guarded and Rajiv felt that sense of suspicion he'd had about her in London. What was she trying to hide?

"He seems better though, don't you think?"

He dragged his mind back to what she was saying. "Yes, much better. And it's all thanks to you, Maya."

She tried to disagree but he could tell she was pleased with his response. "I think it'll be good for him to open up a bit more."

He frowned. "You mean with the counsellor?"

"With everyone—and-and the counsellor," she added quickly.

Rajiv watched her. She was not saying what she meant. "What does he need to open up about, Maya?"

A faint tinge of color flushed her cheeks, but she managed to meet his gaze. "I just mean that it's probably good for him to talk about…things," she finished lamely, and he bit back a sound of frustration.

"Talk to who? Me, my mother? Who?"

"B—both of you, I suppose." She looped one of the plaits behind her ear in a nervous gesture. "Please, Rajiv, don't let's argue. It's been such a lovely morning let's not spoil it."

He blew out a frustrated breath, suppressing the urge to reach over and shake her. "You're right. Forget it." He drained the lager and reached into the pocket of his jacket, pulling out a slim velvet box and laying it on the table in front of her. She leaned backward almost as if afraid to touch it and he laughed at her expression. "It's not going to bite you. Go on. Open it."

Finally, she reached out tentatively and opened it. "But when—how did you know?" She stared at the silver and amethyst chocker in amazement.

"I saw you admiring it and went back to the stall when you weren't looking," he explained, enjoying the look of pleasure and surprise on her expressive face. "Come on then, try it on. Let's see if it fits you."

He lifted it out of the box. It was quite old, probably 1920s, and delicate, the purple stones sparkling, almost the same color as the cardigan she was wearing. He passed it over to her.

"I don't know." She hesitated. "Rajiv, you shouldn't have."

"Why?"

"It was much too expensive."

He threw back his head and laughed. "Expensive! Oh, Maya, sometimes you seem so naïve, so full of contradictions."

For a moment, she seemed unsure how to react, but as he continued grinning at her, she gave in and smiled back at him. A real smile, the kind of smile he felt right through to his groin. The atmosphere became charged and intimate, until finally she dropped her gaze looking down at the chocker, her long, slim fingers caressing the glowing stones.

"Do you want to try it on? The stall-holder says he can adjust it if it doesn't fit." She hesitated, as if still uncertain about accepting it. Could it be an act? All the women he gave gifts to would turn their noses up at silver. It had to be gold or platinum for them. As for semi-precious stones, they simply didn't feature in a woman's jewellery collection. "Need any help?" He forced himself to ignore the growing irritation he felt at her uncertainty about accepting the gift.

Finally, she lifted the chocker to her neck and, after a moment, found the clasp at her nape and fastened it.

"It fits you perfectly," he said with pleasure, admiring the way the sparkling stones complimented her untimely beauty. "All you need now is a medieval gown and you'll make the perfect princess."

She laughed at his flowery compliment, fingering the ornate silverwork with obvious pleasure. "Thank you, it's beautiful," she said softly, her emerald eyes warm and glowing in the dim light.

He reached out to tug gently at one of her plaits, resisting the urge to pull her mouth to his. He wished time could stand still, that he could spend the rest of the day with her, listening to her beautiful voice with that soft accent that sent prickles down his spine. Getting to know her, what it was that made her so special. She was still such an enigma to him. But time was running out and if they didn't leave soon, their absence would be noticed. He was not in the mood to have to explain himself to his mother, or Kirti, or especially Sanjay.

It was raining quite heavily as they left the pub and, although he offered to bring the car over, she insisted on running with him through the summer downpour. They reached the car, laughing and out of breath. Throwing his jacket into the back, Rajiv tried to quell the looming sense of emptiness at the thought of returning to Cranthorpe where they'd be surrounded by people, where he'd have to hand her back to Sanjay.

He loved his brother, but seeing them together was making him feel mean and resentful—and guilty, guilty for wanting the one thing that was bringing Sanjay out of his depression.

She laughed, running her fingers through her damp hair. "Well, that was quite refreshing."

He dragged his eyes away from her, to start the engine. In the quiet intimacy of the car, the desire to touch her was beginning to overwhelm him.

His body felt over-heated and he gripped the steering wheel with unnecessary force.

"Gosh, is that the time already?" She stared at the clock on the dashboard, her face becoming serious. "Jay will be wondering where I am."

"He can manage for a few hours without you, can't he?" His voice sounded harsh, and he thrust the car impatiently into gear, moving off through the rain with unnecessary speed. There was a long uneasy silence and he cursed himself for spoiling the warm, effortless atmosphere that had been growing between them.

"Look, I'm sorry, Maya. I shouldn't have said that." Forced to keep an eye on the wet road ahead, he couldn't see her expression. "It's just that...I don't know." He dragged his fingers through his damp hair, trying to find the right words. "Sometimes you bring out the worst in me."

"Well, it won't be for long." Her voice was almost inaudible through the pouring rain.

He slowed the vehicle down and glanced at her cautiously. "What's that supposed to mean?"

"It means that pretty soon I'll be out of your hair," she said tightly, staring straight ahead.

"When?" he asked bluntly, a sinking feeling beginning low in his stomach.

Her eyes slid over him and then away. "Tuesday,"

"*What*?" He braked suddenly, causing the car to skid dangerously on the wet road. She gasped, grabbing tightly onto her seatbelt. He pulled onto a grassy verge at the side of the road. "The day after tomorrow?"

He killed the engine, undid his seatbelt, and turned to stare at her.

She was looking straight ahead and he saw her throat clench as she swallowed. "Yes. I've booked the train from London on Tuesday evening."

"And when the hell were you planning on telling me?" he demanded, his eyes dark and accusing as he watched her face flush with guilt. "You weren't going to tell me, were you?" He squeezed his eyes shut, trying to control the burning anger rising up inside of him.

"That's not true. I would have told you at—at some point."

He stared at her in disbelief, angry not only with her, but with himself for feeling so desperate at the idea of her leaving. Wasn't that what he wanted? What he'd decided would be best? His lean mouth twisted into a tight, painful smile. Well, now he was getting what he wanted—and probably what he deserved.

Something of what he was feeling must have shown on his face, for she reached out and touched his leg. "It's for the best, Rajiv," she murmured.

But he wasn't listening. The heat of her hand just

above his knee was a tantalizing torment, sending tiny shockwaves up his leg toward his crotch and flooding him with desire. The perfume she wore, together with her soft womanly scent, invaded his nostrils, and he leaned toward her, covering her hand with his.

Her eyes widened. "What are you doing?"

Bending his head, he breathed in the subtle jasmine fragrance of her silky hair. "What does it feel like?" he countered huskily.

"Rajiv, you promised—"

He closed his other hand round the nape of her neck. "To behave myself. I know, but that was before you told me you were leaving."

And before she had a chance to reply, he'd unclipped her seatbelt and pulled her toward him, covering her mouth with his, trying to force her lips, to open to accept the heated invasion of his tongue. She tried not to respond—he had to give her that—keeping her lips together and pushing against his chest, but finally she relented. Her mouth softened, allowing the hot, wet invasion of his tongue to slide between her lips. He pressed her back against the seat, plundering her mouth with deep urgent kisses that she returned with delicious sweetness, her tongue entwining with his. His blood thickened and pulsed with an urgency that was getting stronger by the second.

"God!" He dragged air into his starving lungs and heard her moan softly in commiseration.

Her hands were clinging to him now, creeping inside the collar of his shirt, around the back of his neck, desire spiking down his spine. His hand dipped to the soft wool of her cardigan, tracing the shape of her breast, feeling her arch instinctively against him. He found the hard flesh of her nipple, circling it with his finger, his mouth longing to taste her. With hands that shook, he forced himself to slowly unbutton the cardigan, controlling the urge to tear the clothes off her, and expose her naked breasts to his hungry eyes.

"I knew you had nothing on underneath," he breathed unevenly, running soft, wet kisses down from her neck over the choker until the tip of his tongue found and captured her nipple in his mouth. He sucked hard, rubbing his tongue against her erect nipple. Her fingernails dug into him, gasping with each pull of his mouth.

She was squirming in the car seat, fingers raking through his hair, pulling him furtively against her pointed breast, pleasing him infinitely to know that she was as close to losing control as he was. The fact that they were in a car on a public road hardly registered in his languorous mind, except in the instance that it prevented him from pressing his aching erection against her pliant flesh. He wanted to lose himself inside her, to feel her tight muscles closing around him. God, how he wanted her!

His hand slid down over her flat stomach to caress the smooth skin at the edge of her skirt. He heard her moan out his name before dragging his mouth back to hers. She must have sensed what he was about to do, for there was a kind of desperation in her kiss. He used his lips and his tongue to ease the tension from her, nibbling softly at her lower lip and sucking gently at her tongue until she was lost, once again, in the sensations of her body.

All the while, his hand moved insistently beneath the hem of her skirt, a satisfied sigh escaping him as he discovered the warm bare flesh of her thigh. Her knees parted willingly and he caressed the inside of her soft silky skin, forcing himself to take it slowly, though every nerve in his body was screaming for fulfilment. Her heady, warm scent was driving him mad. He pushed his hand higher allowing his thumb to brush against her panties, groaning with pleasure at the hot moistness that had seeped through the thin fabric.

"Oh, baby, you feel like heaven." He was hardly aware

that he had spoken out loud, his fingers becoming bolder, moving in to explore the very core of her.

She jumped, her bottom lifting off the seat and then, just as suddenly, she closed her legs, trapping his hand tightly in between.

"No." She stared dazedly around her, her copper hair deliciously tousled and her cardigan pushed aside to expose those beautiful, pouting breasts. "This is crazy!" She pushed his trapped hand roughly aside, forcing her skirt over her knees and buttoning up her cardigan with shaking fingers.

"Take it easy." Breathing like he'd just run a marathon, Rajiv dragged himself back from the edge of insanity. "Nothing happened, okay?" He reached out to touch her glorious tumbled hair, desire still raging through him, but she drew away with a look of panic in her wide eyes.

"Please, don't touch me!"

Her voice broke, and Rajiv felt frustration spiking through him. "Aren't you over-reacting just a little?" he grated, still trying to catch his breath. "After all, you were practically begging for it a few seconds ago."

Her face paled visibly and immediately he regretted his cutting words. But he told himself he was justified in saying them. For God's sake, she had been with him each step of the way until she'd suddenly come to her senses. He rubbed the aching muscles at the back of his neck, trying to ignore the more insistent throb of his erection, his body still clamouring for fulfilment.

The drive back to Cranthorpe was completed in stony silence and, although he knew he had no right, Rajiv still felt cheated and let down by her. Not only for rejecting him so offensively, but for her plans to leave without telling him. Her departure should come as a blessed relief but, instead, it was tearing him apart.

CHAPTER 9

Rajiv went back to London later that same day and Maya tried to tell herself it was for the best. The realization that she would not be seeing him again was taking its toll. All she wanted now was to go home to Edinburgh and try her best to forget about him and the emotional rollercoaster she'd been on since meeting him. Their return journey from Steeple Wick to Cranthorpe had left her feeling drained and exhausted. Once back in the safety of her bedroom, she had climbed into a hot bath and allowed the tears to flow, berating herself for allowing him to get under her skin. After what Jay had told her, she should have known better than to spend the morning alone with him. But when he'd asked her—no pleaded with her—to accompany him, she'd given into the crazy impulse and agreed. She had *wanted* to go with him. There was no denying it. And to begin with, the outing had gone well, not just well, it had been quite special.

She had enjoyed every moment of their time together, until she'd told him of her plans to leave. His reaction had surprised her. She could have sworn that she'd seen real desperation in his eyes. That was why she'd reached out and touched him, just to comfort him really, but what had resulted had had little to do with comfort. Once again, he had managed to seduce her almost to the point of no return. God, just thinking about it left her weak and shaky, a tiny pulse throbbing insistently between her legs. Thank God, she had come to her senses. *And what if she hadn't?* Would he have made love to her there in the car on the side of the road?

Maya tried to feel outraged at the thought, but all she really felt was a sense of loss and a very physical need that cut right through her. Her body felt languid, yet restless, a heaviness invading her limbs and making it difficult to do anything, while struggling to behave normally under Jay's eagle eye.

A knock on the door heralded her friend, a trace of concern shadowing in his perceptive gaze. "How's the packing going?" he asked, sitting on the edge of the bed beside her open suitcase.

"I think I'm getting there," she answered, carefully folding the little black dress and resisting the impulse to press it to her face.

"Are you feeling okay, Maya?" Jay asked, and she forced herself to return his gaze.

"Yes, of course. Why do you ask?"

Fortunately, he had not learned of her outing with Rajiv the day before. In fact, she did not think anyone, besides Nana Bibi, knew that they'd gone out together. And she hoped that Jay hadn't somehow found out about it now.

He sighed, his shoulders slumping forward and his long hair almost covering his face. "I dunno. You just seem sort of quiet lately. You're not upset because of what I said about Rajiv, are you?"

Maya was genuinely surprised. "Of course not. You were only being honest and concerned for me. Weren't you?"

He nodded. "Yeah, but maybe you didn't want to hear

it. Sometimes it's easier not knowing the truth, isn't it?" He looked up at her, and Maya knew he was not only talking about her situation.

She sat down on the bed beside him. "Jay, in the long run, it's always better to know the truth. I personally would never want to live in a state of denial. Never," she ended emphatically and he put his arms around her, squeezing her tightly.

"I'm going to miss you." His voice was muffled against her hair.

"Me too," she choked, holding on tightly to his thin frame.

ფფ

The following morning, the day of her departure, Maya felt in slightly better spirits. Jay and she had been to a small hotel nearby for a goodbye dinner the night before. It had been nice to spend the evening out alone together. Kirti had left earlier that same day, seeming genuinely sad to say goodbye to Maya, who had come to like her despite the differences in their personalities and lifestyles. Although they had invited Anna to join them for dinner, it had been a relief when she'd declined.

Now Maya's suitcase was packed and she had only to change into the flared jeans and turquoise T-shirt that she'd left hanging in the huge wardrobe. She climbed out of the shower and towelled herself dry with a feeling of nostalgia. This was her last shower here and she realized that she had truly enjoyed staying in this house. Besides its obvious luxury and comfort, there was a therapeutic quality about Cranthorpe that she would definitely miss. She ran her fingers affectionately along the polished wood of the dressing table before reaching for the terry-cloth bathrobe at the foot of the bed.

A knock at the door disturbed her melancholic thoughts.

"Come in," she called, presuming it was Jay and turned to face him with a welcoming smile.

"Hi."

It was not Jay, but Rajiv, who entered the room, closing the door softly behind him. Maya's jaw sagged, and she wondered if her desperate mind had conjured up this tall, enigmatic figure leaning indolently against the door. In a plain black T-shirt and faded Levis his masculinity hit her like a physical blow. The fact that she had not expected to see him again made his presence even more electrifying to her soaring senses.

"What are you doing here?" It came out in a whisper.

"I'm driving you back to London," he announced, his eyes flickering down to the gaping cleavage of her robe. "You didn't think I'd let you go without saying goodbye, did you?"

Maya pulled the lapels of her robe together. "But there's no need. I've already booked a seat on the coach back to London."

He gave an unconcerned shrug, his gaze warm and lazy on her flushed face. "Too bad, I've driven all the way over here and I'm driving you back."

She continued to stare at him, his casual attitude leaving her speechless. His hair was black in the morning light, his dark skin shining like polished bronze, and his eyes gleaming blue like the sky outside. A warm glow began to invade her body and her naked breasts beneath the robe swelled and hardened, sending quivering messages down to the ache between her legs.

"I didn't expect to see you again," she said huskily, and his eyes darkened in that all too familiar way.

"Does that mean you're pleased that I came?" he asked, moving closer.

She stared into his heavy-lidded eyes, mesmerized by the message in them. "I don't know," she murmured truthfully and the room suddenly filled with a sizzling tension.

"Are you wearing anything underneath that?" he demanded thickly, his eyes moving hungrily over her body, almost burning her with their intensity. Then abruptly he shook his head. "No, don't tell me, I promised myself— hell, I'd better get out of here now." Moving determinedly away, he grabbed the doorknob, pulling the door open and—

"Rajiv." It was Jay's voice, filled with surprise—and something else. "What are you doing here?"

Rajiv pushed the door completely open so that Maya was visible behind him. "I've come to take Maya back to London," he stated coolly.

"That wasn't necessary." Jay's mouth tightened. "She's booked the coach back and then a taxi will take her to the station. It's all arranged."

"Well, I can drive her directly to the station." Rajiv leaned one shoulder against the doorjamb and regarded his brother dispassionately. "And I'm sure she'll find the drive a lot quicker and more comfortable." He turned his challenging gaze on her. "What do you say, Maya?"

Maya stared from one brother to the other feeling torn in half. "I really don't mind either way," she mumbled awkwardly, holding the lapels of her robe together like a lifeline.

Jay was obviously not happy with the situation, but there was little he could do or say. Rajiv was here now and it would be ridiculous to expect Maya to take the coach when he was driving back. A situation Rajiv was quite aware of.

He straightened up with a wry smile. "Well that's settled, then," he said. "What time would you like to leave?"

They left her alone after agreeing on a time, and Maya

fell onto her bed, expelling a shaky sigh of relief. Jay had looked on the verge of losing his temper, so she'd ended the exchange as quickly as possible, unable to quell the underlying excitement that coursed through her at the prospect of driving back to London with him. It was ridiculous to feel like this, she told herself, but to no avail. In these past few days, or weeks, her body seemed to have taken on a life of its own, and no matter how she might try to govern it with a cool, level head, it was not taking any notice of her.

Saying goodbye to Jay was not easy—for either of them.

"You know you're welcome to come up and stay with me in Edinburgh anytime and for as long as you like," she told him, her eyes serious as they stared into his. "There's more than enough room. With my mother in South Africa, it's just me and Josie," she said, mentioning her friend who Jay knew quite well.

They were at the bottom of the staircase. Rajiv and his mother waited discreetly outside.

"I know and thank you, Maya, but I can't keep running away." There was a resigned look in his eyes and it worried her. "Ma's trying to convince me to go to India with her, but I'll probably stay here and continue with the therapy."

"I think you're right to continue with the therapy," Maya agreed. "But do you think it's a good idea for you to be here on your own?"

"Better than being with her, searching the upper classes of Indian society for a suitable wife for Rajiv." He rolled his eyes. "I think she's finally realized that it's not gonna work with Kirti, so the search begins again."

Maya's stomach hollowed, but she managed to keep a smile pasted on. Whether it was Kirti or some other perfectly beautiful Indian woman, did not make any difference. Not to her at least.

She grimaced and squeezed his slim, delicate hands.

"I'll phone you when I get back, and I want you to think about coming up to stay with me and Josie. Please Jay? It'll be fun, just like the old days."

He gave her a reassuring smile and then put his arms around her. "Okay. I'll think about it. And Maya…"

She pulled away slightly. "Yes?"

"Don't let him convince you to stay with him in London."

"Of course not!"

"Don't look so surprised." His expression was serious. "I'm sure that's what he wants."

She bit into her bottom lip. "No, it can't be. He's just being helpful."

"Don't be naïve, Maya. It doesn't suit you. Now off you go. We don't want you missing your train. Then you'd *have* to spend the night in London."

They left the house together, arm in arm. Rajiv and his mother were standing by the Porsche and Maya went over to thank the older woman for her hospitality.

"Well, your presence has definitely perked Jay up," Anna conceded with a smile. "So I think it's we who have to thank you for coming."

"Not at all. Spending time here in your beautiful home, and with Jay, has been a real pleasure for me," she insisted and meant it. Much to Maya's surprise, the older woman reached out and hugged her. Maya hugged back, having to hold back tears once again.

She gave Jay one last tearful embrace before climbing in beside Rajiv and turning back to wave as he pulled smoothly away.

She felt quite emotional watching the courtly house disappear from view. Somehow the place had wormed its way into her heart and she knew she would miss it.

They came to the end of the property and he gave her an enquiring glance before turning onto the public road.

"You okay?"

"Yes, I'm fine," she murmured, pretending to look around her with interest. "How long will it take us to get to London, do you think?"

"If we're lucky about two and a half hours." He maneuvred the powerful vehicle with ease and, although he drove quite fast, Maya felt confident with him. "What time does your train leave Kings Cross?"

"Six-fifteen. We will make it won't we?" she asked, Jay's warning echoing in her ears.

He smiled knowingly. "It's not even two o'clock, Maya. Don't worry. I'll get you there on time."

It turned out to be a pleasant drive. Rajiv knew a lot about the area and its history. He kept her entertained with stories of Stonehenge and his memories as a young boy of the place filled with hippies and travelers during the festivals at Summer Solstice.

"My father detested them," he told her. "But I envied them, especially the kids. They looked so free, not a care in the world."

Maya nodded sympathetically. Those children may have had very little materially, compared to him and Jay, but they probably had a lot more in other ways than the heirs of Maddox Junta Investments.

"I suppose Jay told you all about our dear father," he said, cutting into her thoughts.

"He told me a little about him," Maya said carefully and he gave a bitter laugh.

"None of it very pleasant, I'm sure.

"No it wasn't," she answered truthfully.

Later they stopped for a coffee break along the motorway and Rajiv asked her about Jay.

"How do you think he'll cope without you there," he enquired, one arm hooked over the back of the chair while his compelling blue eyes studied her with disturbing intensity.

"It's difficult to say, really. He told me your mother wants him to go to India with her," she said—recalling Jay's words about Anna hunting for a wife for the man sitting opposite her—trying to gauge his reaction to her comment.

"Yeah, she told me." He took a sip of his coffee, avoiding her gaze. "Do you think he'll go?"

"He didn't seem very keen," she murmured.

Was he deliberately avoiding looking at her? She would have loved to ask him how he felt about his mother picking out prospective brides for him, but knew it would be totally inappropriate. Besides, she didn't want to spoil the last few hours they had together—and maybe she just didn't want to know about his marital plans for the future. In addition, there was still Kirti, who would probably make the perfect Indian wife.

"Can't say I blame him. Those fossilized old friends of hers in India are enough to put anyone into a state of depression."

Maya giggled at the picture he'd painted and his eyes darkened. "I love it when you laugh—not that you do very often around me."

Maya felt her cheeks warm, while his eyes focused on her mouth.

"I told him he's more than welcome to come to Edinburgh and stay with me anytime," she said, striving to move onto a safer subject, but his mouth tightened at her words.

"And what did he say to that?" he asked, his long lashes veiling his gaze.

"He said that he can't keep running away," she told him, lifting her cup to her lips.

"Running away from what?" He stared up at her with questioning eyes, but she shrugged her slim shoulders unable to answer his question. "Do you think his depression has something to do with my father's death?" he asked with a frown.

"What makes you say that?" she asked, stalling.

Rajiv raked inpatient fingers through his hair. "I don't know. He told me they'd had an argument just before the accident, and Jay has this foolish notion that it was his fault. I said it was crazy. Our father had been drinking when he crashed. He was always drinking and driving, an accident waiting to happen." He drained the last of his coffee and grimaced. "Did he tell you about that?"

Maya stared down into her cup. "Yes".

"So it's still bugging him." It was a statement.

She nodded, wishing she could tell him the whole story as his eyes questioned her.

"Do you know what it was that they'd argued about?" he asked. "He never did say."

She moistened dry lips with the tip of her tongue, sorely tempted to tell him everything.

"You know, don't you?" he stated grimly, but still she didn't reply. "Why all this subterfuge? He's my brother, goddammit!"

Maya would have given anything to tell him the truth right there and then, and her heart went out to him as he searched her face for clues that she couldn't give him.

"You need to talk to Jay about these things, Rajiv, not me."

His eyes narrowed. "In case you haven't noticed, my brother's opinion of me seems to have taken a dive since you came on the scene."

Maya squirmed at his words. "I'm sorry. Maybe things will improve now that I'm leaving."

"It's not your fault," he said softly. "Are you going to come back?"

She frowned. "Come back?"

"Here to England—to Jay?"

"Oh, no." She paused. "Well, at least not in the near future anyway."

After a long strained silence, he pushed back his chair. "Shall we go then?"

Maya couldn't tell if he was pleased with her answer or not.

Once back on the motorway, the atmosphere eased and Maya got the impression that he was making a concerted effort to keep things light and amicable. He put some music on, an oldies radio station, which left her feeling sad and melancholy. All too soon, they were entering the outskirts of London and Rajiv had to slow down as the traffic became heavier. Maya allowed herself to relax and enjoy the precious moments left, glancing surreptitiously at his profile while he concentrated on the busy road ahead, imprinting his chiselled features on her memory. The sensual shape of his mouth; his thick, straight lashes; and the way his hair fell forward over his brow, its darkness catching the light whenever he moved. It wasn't fair, she thought, closing her eyes against the sudden ache in her chest. If only they'd never met, if only she could go back to being the cool controlled woman that she'd been before he had come along and turned her world upside down.

It took ages to get into central London, but she didn't mind, cherishing each minute they had together and dreading the thought of saying goodbye. Although they didn't talk much, there was a deeply intimate mood in the car and a longing every time their eyes met, making it difficult to look away. The radio began playing a slow, sexy Eric Clapton tune, and Maya felt her whole body suffused in a sensual heat. She closed her eyes, allowing the haunting guitar to drug her senses with its melody.

"We're here," Rajiv said softly and she opened her eyes with a sinking feeling.

He reversed into a parking space while she looked

around, vaguely recognizing the area from when she'd first arrived. So this was it. She took a deep breath and turned to face him.

He dug some change out of the front pocket of his jeans. "I'll just feed the meter and then we'll go. You've still got loads of time."

"There's no need." She reached out to stop him as he opened the door, her fingers clinging to the soft cotton of his T-shirt. "I mean, you don't have to come with me," she finished tremulously, her hand dropping back onto the seat.

"Maya, there's no way I'm leaving you hanging around Kings Cross station on your own," he said, climbing out of the car.

A minute later, they entered the station and she had to admit to feeling a lot more confident with the tall steely male at her side, her suitcase looking light and flimsy in his capable hands.

They were an hour early, but he insisted on finding out which platform her train left from straight away, so they made their way over to the Information Desk.

The young blonde woman gave Rajiv an apologetic smile after checking Maya's ticket. "I'm afraid this train has been delayed. There's a problem with the line and all trains to Edinburgh have had to be postponed. Would you like some information on overnight accommodation?"

"That's not necessary," he responded quickly. "We have accommodations. Can you give us a phone number to call for information on when the trains will be running again?"

The woman was more than happy to assist him, but Maya hardly noticed, her mind trying to grasp the implications of this change of plans. She was going to have to spend the night in London! The world seemed to shrink around her as she looked up into Rajiv's glittering eyes, the air throbbing between them.

"Shall we go then?" he murmured and, as his gaze held hers, Maya knew there was no turning back.

They were going to spend the night together and nothing could change that now.

CHAPTER 10

Not a word was spoken between them as they drove through the busy London streets. Maya was in a daze, unable to think clearly as she stared out of the car window. She had allowed him to take control of everything, from dealing with the woman at the Information Desk to getting all the necessary information and propelling her gently back to the car. Her body trembled with a mixture of fear and anticipation at the thought of where *exactly* she would be spending the night. Was she a fool to want this? Was he just using her? And did it really matter?

Tomorrow she would be on that train back to Edinburgh, but at least she'd have her memories to take with her. A night together with Rajiv was something that she would cherish for the rest of her life, so why not grab the opportunity now that it had presented itself? For him it might only be a casual one nightstand, but that was his concern. For her it would be something to treasure.

Maya slowly realized they seemed to be driving a different route from the one they'd taken on that first day she'd arrived in London, and when he drove the car into the underground parking area of a tall building, Maya's head jerked around to stare questioningly at him.

"Where are we, Rajiv?"

"My apartment," he murmured and then added with a look of uncertainty, "If you don't like it, I'll take you to the house in Knightsbridge, okay?"

Maya kept silent, not sure what to say.

He maneuvered the Porsche into a designated parking space and turned off the engine. It was dark and quiet underground and she looked around her, still puzzled.

"I didn't know you had an apartment," she said with a frown. "I thought you lived at the house in Knightsbridge."

"I need my privacy, Maya, just like anyone." He turned in his seat to face her. "Now and again I stay there overnight but this is my London home."

"So you only stayed there because of me?"

He smiled wryly. "Well, I couldn't very well have brought you here, as much as I would have liked to."

Maya stared at him for a long moment as uncertainty clouded her mind. "But you've brought me here now," she challenged softly.

His expression became serious. "Yes, do you mind?"

She paused for a moment then shook her head. "No, I don't think so."

"Good, shall we go up then?"

They took the lift up to the penthouse floor and entered the apartment. It surprised Maya how large it was—large, white, and minimalistic—high ceilings, parquet flooring, pure luxury. She walked over to the long windows, which took up one side of the room, catching her breath at the view. The sun hung low over the city. She could see the Thames right below them, curving up and away, toward what looked like Albert Bridge in the distance. For a few moments. she lost herself in the fairy tale scene below her, forgetting the reason why she was here. But a movement behind brought her swiftly back to the present. She turned, hardly noticing the understated opulence of the enormous

room, her eyes clashing with the man standing tautly opposite her. His expression was tense, a muscle jerking along
his jaw line, and Maya found it strange how completely
calm she felt. It was as if all this was meant to be. From the
moment they had first met at the train station, everything
had been moving—just like the Thames below them—
toward this moment and nothing could change that. And so
here she was, ready to accept her fate.

"Would you like a drink, or something?"

He motioned toward a drinks cabined and she shook
her head. That was not why she'd come.

Rajiv stared at her, his face tight with suppressed tension. "Nor would I," he muttered, slowly coming toward
her.

Her green eyes watched curiously, as he stopped in
front of her, their bodies almost touching. Reaching out he
cupped her face in his hands, caressing her cheekbones
slowly with his thumbs.

His eyes veiled as she stared up at him, only his labored breathing betrayed what he was really feeling. When
his thumb moved downward to trace the outline of her lips,
Maya began to feel the heat from his fingertips, transferring
through to her their message of need. Her lips parted automatically and he rubbed gently at the smooth moistness inside with the pad of this thumb. She bit down on it gently,
her eyes never leaving his, which were almost black in the
soft lighting. He seemed content to watch her through hooded eyes, one hand resting at her jawline, the other moving
slowly down from her throat to her breast. It was her turn to
breathe heavily now. His hand cupped and squeezed her
breast, causing her nipple to tighten with pleasure.

"Are you wearing a bra?" he asked huskily, and Maya
nodded unable to find her voice. "Well, not for long."

He let out a trembling sigh and pulled her into his arms.
His tongue teased at her parted lips, softly nibbling at her

sensitive bottom lip, while his fingers reached under her T-shirt to caress the warm flesh at her midriff. Maya's arms snaked up around his neck, her hands threading through the strong silkiness of his hair, where it overlapped his collar. Her eyes closed, shutting out everything but the touch and smell of him. She moaned softly when he cupped her aching breast through the smooth satin of her bra, brushing lightly at the budding peak and sending ripples of desire through her body to pulse hotly between her legs. She began to move restlessly against him, wanting more than he was giving her.

"Rajiv, please," she breathed softly against his mouth.

"Are you sure about this?" he asked tightly. "Because once we start there's no going back."

"I'm sure," she responded, her fingers twisting into his thick hair.

And finally, he unleashed the passion he'd held in check. His hands slid down the curve of her spine to her hips and he pulled her against the solid, masculine strength of his body. His heat inflamed her senses and the urgency of his caress left her in no doubt of his needs. He kissed her many times, his mouth plundering and bruising, as if he couldn't get enough of her, and she responded wantonly, her body soft and pliant in his arms.

"I can't believe you're here with me," he choked. "It's surreal."

But for Maya it was all too real. The feel of his strong hands cupping her buttocks and pulling her up against the hard swell of his erection was wonderfully real. He ran a tantalizing finger along the cleft of her bottom causing a ball of heat to uncurl itself and spread through her thighs, her legs almost buckling beneath her. Rajiv must have sensed her state of helplessness, for he scooped her up into his arms and carried her across the room. Maya did not bother to look where he was taking her. Her body and mind were focused only on him and the desperate sensations he aroused in her. Snaking her fingers around his neck, she pulled his mouth down to hers once again.

"If you carry on like this, we won't make it to the bedroom," he breathed unevenly and turned to kick open a door to their right.

The curtains were drawn and, through the dimness, Maya's impression was one of space and luxury as Rajiv laid her down on the huge bed. The Indian-cotton bedcover felt wonderfully smooth and cool against her palms. She lifted herself up onto her elbows as he snapped the side lamp on, casting a soft golden glow around them.

"I want to see you," he bit out, pulling off his T-shirt with unconcealed impatience. "Every inch of you."

He dropped his T-shirt onto the floor, his hard, muscular torso catching the light. Maya stared, drinking him in. His skin was a glossy, golden brown, his body that of an athlete—all lean, sculpted muscle, almost hairless except for the trail that led down from his belly-button to disappear below his jeans. He came down on the bed beside her, pulling her T-shirt up and over her head in one smooth move, before kneeling back to gaze at her with smouldering eyes. Maya watched him watching her, his pupils glittering blue in the warm light. Her body felt hot and tight and she brought her hands up to her breasts, fingering the sensitive nipples through her bra until he suddenly gripped her wrists.

"God, Maya, you drive me crazy!" he breathed harshly, dragging her hands away and pushing her down with his weight into the covers.

He ground his mouth against hers, his hands gripping her wrists, holding her arms high above her head. Slowly, still binding her wrists with one hand, he ran his fingers down her arm to cup her breasts, one at a time through the bra. Squeezing until the dusky nipples strained, he lowered his head and sucked wetly through the sheer satin. Maya felt the blood thicken like lava in her veins, her body arching off the bed with a chocked sob. He was lying between her legs, but they both had their jeans on, and the thick cotton barrier was much too much for her. She shifted her hips impatiently. Finally he let go of her wrists and reached behind to unclip her bra. It was wonderful to feel her breasts swell freely out of their constriction. Rajiv seemed to enjoy it just as much, his tongue circling and sucking at her nipples greedily. Maya's body jerked as sensual pleasure assaulted her, her fingers luxuriating in the feel of hard muscle covered by satin smooth skin, scratching her nails instinctively along his back, while he bit softly at her nipples until she cried out in sweet agony.

His hand finally reached the zipper of her jeans and, with slow deliberation, he pushed it down, tracing the elastic of her panties with unsteady fingers. She lifted her bottom eagerly, allowing him to peel the jeans off her. The heat between her thighs was becoming unbearable and she let out a mindless sob as he cupped her crotch with the palm of his hand. She could feel the warmth of his palm through her dampened panties. Her legs fell helplessly apart as he traced his finger down along the soft fabric, tormenting her with his restraint.

"You're wet," he breathed. "Hot and wet."

Maya felt her face flush, but her desire was more powerful than the embarrassment, which ebbed away at the obvious pleasure in his eyes. "Raj, please."

"Do I need to use a condom?"

She blushed again. "Um, I don't know." Moistening her swollen lips. "I'm on the pill—"

Rajiv released a heartfelt sigh, leaning his forehead against hers. "Do you trust me?"

She didn't hesitate. "Yes, of course."

Her shaky inexperienced hands moved to the button on his jeans. She could wait no longer, and Rajiv shuddered as her fingers brushed against his aching erection through the soft fabric. With jerking movements, she managed finally to undo the button. As she unzipped his fly, it suddenly occurred to her just what she was doing. To him she must seem like an experienced woman of the world, but in actual fact, she had never undressed a man before. She had never even wanted to. Not until now.

"Maya."

His groan of frustration brought her back to reality, and she realized that he was waiting for her to dispense with his underwear. She pushed the boxer shorts down over the taut muscles of his hips and then bit back a gasp as his engorged shaft spilled out into her hand. He shuddered as she ran her curious fingers along the pulsing length, alarmed by the size of him.

She drew in a trembling breath, her body suddenly taut with apprehension. He was too big. There was no way her body could accommodate him.

"Maya?" He sensed her hesitation. "What is it, baby?" His voice broke as the tension between them grew.

"God, Raj. I—I don't know if I can—" Her eyes fixed on the almost aggressive image of his erection.

His eyes followed her gaze and he drew in a trembling breath. "Shh, it's okay." His tone was soothing. "I would never hurt you. I promise."

Somehow she knew that might be true if she wasn't a virgin, and she was tempted to tell him the truth, but a part of her was hoping that he wouldn't realize how pathetically innocent she was.

Her hand continued to explore the smooth length of his bold shaft, fascinated by the hard, throbbing heat of him.

"Don't—" He pushed her hand roughly away before she could explore the moist tip with her thumb and she looked up at him with a puzzled frown. "Not now, Maya. Please."

There were beads of sweat glistening on his forehead. She brought her hand up lovingly to wipe them away with a dawning realization of the control he was holding himself under.

"Make love to me, Raj. Now," she whispered, his blatant desire making her feel bold.

Rajiv needed no second invitation, his fingers tugging the flimsy panties down over her ankles. "I knew you were a natural redhead," he breathed huskily.

His eyes were fixed at the juncture of her thighs and she almost covered herself with her hands, but stopped as he eased his hand between her legs and allowed his thumb to probe at the moist heart of her. An explosion of pleasure overtook everything else. Her legs splayed apart and her spine arched in exquisite agony at the ministrations of his expert fingers.

He knelt between her legs, his face flushed and taut with desire. "This was what I wanted from the moment I saw you," he said raggedly and then lowered his body onto hers.

Maya sighed with pleasure as his hard body pressed down onto hers. She could feel the swollen ridge of his erection rubbing intimately against her. Pushing up against it, she reveled in the quivering sensations that washed over her. But then he pulled back, and she cried out in despair.

"I'm sorry Maya, but I can't wait. Not another second."

Suddenly Maya felt that hard, swollen head seeking and pushing into her. A moment of pure panic attacked her, and her body froze.

"Relax," he chocked, beads of sweat rolling from his face down onto her breast. "For God's sake, Maya, *relax.*"

He reached down between them and ran his finger along the throbbing sexual bud at the top of her sex and immediately the pain dissolved into that weak dragging pleasure again. He drew back from her, placing his fingers at her tight entrance, easing two of them inside of her. It felt wonderful. With his thumb circling her clitoris and his fingers moving inside of her, drawing the hot moisture out, she could only moan softly, circling her hips with restless impatience. Finally, he removed his fingers, staring at her with glazed eyes, sucking them into his mouth one at a time.

Maya was drowning in the hot desire of his gaze, overcome with need she could barely understand.

"You taste like heaven," he breathed.

Gripping his shaft in his fist, he guided his engorged penis to her tight entrance, pushing himself into her. A loud yelp of pain escaped her, her inner muscles tightening instinctively against the invasion of the thick head of his erection.

"What the—" Rajiv stared down into her eyes, now filled with tears of pain. "God, Maya, why?"

The pain eased somewhat as she took some much needed oxygen into her lungs. She needed to do this, wanted to do this with him and no one else, so when he tried to withdraw from her she locked her long legs around him and dug her nails into the bunched muscles of his back.

"Don't stop," she choked. "Don't you dare stop now!"

Hanging over her, breathing heavily, Rajiv hesitated for a second and then with a groan of resignation thrust against the tight barrier of her hymen. Maya cried out at the sharp, burning pain that pierced her body. Tears of hurt and frustration filled her eyes. He was deep inside her now, not moving except for the trembling of his body.

"God, Maya," he said in a strangled voice. "I don't want to hurt you, but if you want this—"

"Don't stop." Tears were leaking down the sides her face. "Just get it over with."

He withdrew slowly, but then pushed in again, even deeper this time, with a groan of pleasure or...something. She wasn't sure.

The sharp pain had now turned into a deep, burning ache, causing her body to tense up as he eased back out again.

"Breathe, Maya," he groaned. "For God's sake, breathe!"

And she forced herself to draw a trembling breath.

Slowly, he set an agonizing pace: advance and retreat, advance and retreat. Maya swallowed a sob, biting down hard on her lower lip. She wanted to scream at him to stop, but she suffered in silence instead, until suddenly his whole sweat-slicked body stiffened. Arms braced on either side of her, he arched his back and drove into her one last time with a strangled moan.

His breathing was ragged but thankfully, he didn't collapse onto her, although his arms, in fact his whole body, was trembling and drenched in sweat. Maya closed her eyes, unable to look at him. Slowly he eased himself out of her, and she gave a desperate moan of relief. Leaning back on his knees, he hovered between her spread thighs and she covered her eyes with her arm. She was desperate to close her legs. She felt exposed and angry, with herself as well as him, the unpleasant stickiness between her limbs only adding to her regret.

"Maya—I'm sorry." He swallowed, trying to catch his breath.

"Could you please move," she said in a tight voice, her arm still covering her eyes.

"Of course."

She felt him move and closed her legs tight, a trembling sob escaping from deep in her throat.

ભૂભૂ

Rajiv climbed off the bed and made his way to the ensuite bathroom, his mind in turmoil. *A virgin!* How the hell was that possible? He grabbed a small, white hand towel and soaked it under warm water, staring at himself in the mirror. Why the hell hadn't she told him?

He would never have touched her if he'd known.

He swore crudely at the face in the mirror. She had never given him any indication that she was untouched. He closed his eyes, unable to bear the face staring back at him. And what about Sanjay? Did this mean they weren't lovers? Of course, they weren't lovers! How could they be? Too many questions were clamouring in his head, making it impossible for him to function. Right now, he had to see to her needs, try and ease her pain, even though she probably hated his guts. After this fiasco, she wasn't going to let him touch her again. Rajiv quashed the thought. It was too depressing to contemplate. He caught a glimpse of his lower body in the mirror and he felt sick with guilt at the sight of Maya's blood smeared with his semen. He washed it off quickly at the basin, wishing he could jump under the shower and try to wash away some of the guilt and remorse he felt, but there was no time. He needed to see to Maya first.

Squeezing the excess water from the towel, he took a steadying breath and made his way back into the bedroom. Thankfully the light was dim, just the one lamp beside the bed casting a soft glow over the room. She was lying on her side, facing away from him, curled up like a wounded animal. He felt his stomach knot. Accepting that he had done this to her, he made his way round to her side of the bed and sat down.

Her eyes closed and he gently brushed her hair away from the side of her face. "Maya, baby."

She didn't respond, so he folded the damp towel into a small square and laid it gently against her skin.

"Maya, let me wipe your face."

For a long moment, she didn't respond, and then slowly she turned to him, avoiding eye contact. He wanted to say something: apologize, beg, plead, but his brain told him to keep silent. He opened the towel and gently wiped her face. She was looking straight ahead of her, but he just continued smoothing the cloth from her forehead to her chin, wiping away the remnants of her tears, keeping his mind blank of everything except easing her discomfort. She closed her eyes and he laid the towel across them, gently stroking her damp hair. Her eyes stayed closed when he drew the cloth downward, smoothing it along her neck and shoulder, then slowly, carefully eased her onto her back and began wiping her chest, above her breasts. As he moved downward, she tried to resist, covering her breasts with her arms.

"Please, baby, let me do this." His voice was hoarse. "I don't know what else to do."

She must have heard the desperation in his voice, for she relented, moving her arms stiffly to her sides and straightening her legs, but keeping them tightly held together.

He wiped around her breasts and then slowly circled the cloth over each beautiful mound. When he stood up, her eyes opened, huge and vulnerable in the dim light.

"I'm just going to rinse out the towel," he told her. "I'll be back in a minute."

She closed her eyes and let out a long sigh.

He was back in less than a minute. She was lying in the same position, her body held tightly together. Rajiv sat down again and continued his ministrations. Wiping her midriff and then moving slowly down to her soft, flat stomach. She tightened her legs when he reached the top of her pubes. God! The color of her pubic hair was beautiful. A few shades darker than her head, it was a deep copper, the texture fine and silky, beginning low down her mound and barely covering the soft, pouting folds of her vulva. He felt the heat rush to his groin and clamped down on it with an iron fist. He'd never seen anything so erotic, so tempting in his life.

He ran the cloth along her hip and down one long, supple leg, then began at the bottom of her other leg and, in slow circular movements, wiped up to her thigh and finally ended at her right hip. Her body was more relaxed now, her eyes still closed, but her breathing was calm and deep. He stood up once more to go and rinse a fresh towel.

When he came back her eyes were half open, sleepy looking and, without hesitating, he laid the warm, damp towel at the apex of her thighs. Her eyes widened, but she didn't move.

"Maya, let me do this, baby. You'll feel much better." That vulnerable look was back in her eyes, and he shook his head in self-deprecation.

She closed her eyes, and he felt, rather than saw, her relax. He folded the towel and wiped slowly downward. Her legs parted ever so slightly. There were smudges of her blood mixed with his semen smeared between her thighs and a wave of shame washed over him. He bit back a groan and continued cleaning the insides of her legs. Finally, he folded the towel lengthways and covered her sex with it. She let out another long sigh, which he hoped was one of relief, and bent her knees in a way that allowed her thighs to spread a little more.

It was killing him not to touch her, but he dreaded her rejection. He stood up and, realizing he was naked, made his way into the walk-in closet and pulled on a fresh pair of boxers. Moving to the other side of the bed, he lay down beside her, careful not to touch her. Bending his arm, he rested his head in his palm so that he could look at her. She gazed warily at him out of the corners of her eyes and lifted her hand to press it gingerly against the towel between her legs.

"Are you very sore?" he asked softly.

"No."

It was the first word she'd spoken since she'd asked him to get off of her and relief washed over him. He wanted to ask her a thousand questions, the first one being: *Why didn't you tell me?* But he refrained from doing so. Now was not the time so, very slowly he lifted his hand and ran his finger very lightly down her arm, waiting for her to flinch. She didn't.

"Would you like something to drink?" he asked. Anything to bring some normality to the situation. "Water, juice, anything?"

She moistened her lips. "Water would be good, please."

Rajiv jumped up, eager for something to do for her. "One water coming up."

While he was pouring water for both of them, he remembered the Calendula cream his mother used to use, for cuts and bruises, on him and Sanjay when they were kids. He rifled through the kitchen cupboard and found a jar of it. Returning to the bedroom, he placed the jar on the bedside table and waited for Maya to sit up before handing her the water.

"I've got some cream here that will help ease the soreness," he murmured, trying to keep his voice steady.

⚬⚬⚬

Maya gulped down the water, staring at the jar of cream. Anything to avoid the eye contact, which left her embarrassed yet breathless at the same time. "What is it?"

"It's Calendula cream, from India." He smiled. "My mother used it on Sanjay and I when were kids. It's great for cuts, scrapes, bruises—anything really." He took her glass and placed it on the bedside table. "Lie down and relax."

Maya hesitated and then wriggled down so she was lying flat on the bed, feeling shame and regret. She still felt
sore where he'd entered her and there was a burning ache
deep inside her body. The sex had been far from pleasant. In
fact, it had been a lot more painful than she'd expected, and
she wasn't keen to try it—ever again.

"Relax, Maya, this is going to make you feel a lot better. I promise."

She took a deep breath and let it out slowly. He bent
over and kissed her chastely on the lips. Then he opened the
jar, digging his finger inside and bringing it out with a liber-
al amount of cream.

"Open your legs for me, baby," he said softly.

She stiffened as he slowly withdrew the towel from between her legs and dropped it by the side of the bed. Pulling
her leg toward him before she could protest, he swiped his
creamed finger along the seam of her sex. Rubbing gently,
he paid particular attention to her sore, swollen entrance.

Maya's eyes closed as sensation engulfed her body.
Beginning between her legs, swirls of pleasure resonated
through her body, shocking her with its intensity, causing
her bottom to lift off the mattress. His finger moved up
again, rubbing, circling her clitoris, and a moan escaped her
lips. After all the pain and unpleasantness of the sexual act,
she hadn't ever expected this lush, wanton sensation to suddenly consume her.

"You like this." It was a statement, and Maya dragged
some oxygen into her lungs, unable to answer him, as his
finger continued to weave a web of carnal pleasure around
her.

The cream felt slippery and moist between her legs.
She tried to grab back some control, but he was relentless,
moving expertly from her throbbing nub of pleasure down,
rimming his finger around her sensitive entrance. Slow then
quicker, soft and then firm. Up, down and then around—

again, and again. Her breath was coming in short gasps and, when he bent over to nuzzle her hair, she heard his breathing, harsh and uneven, warm against her ear. She turned her head, searching for his mouth, and he responded, drawing her into in a deep, drugging kiss. Maya had lost all sense of reason. Her fingernails dug into his hair as his desperate, probing mouth, together with his fingers, went on, and on. Suddenly he pushed a finger inside her and her body stiffened. All the nerve endings inside of her protested at his invasion, yet tightened in sweet, pleasurable pain. His finger twisted around inside her, his thumb teasing her nub of pleasure, rubbing and then pressing down firmly, again, and again. Maya dragged her mouth away from his to gasp and then let out a long, trembling moan as her body convulsed into a tightly wound knot that exploded, sending shockwaves throughout her writhing body.

Rajiv covered her mouth in another long soulful kiss, easing his finger slowly out of her and cupping her hot mound with his hand.

She was trembling, the aftershocks of sensation, mixed with the sensitized flare of her nerve endings, sending ripples of pleasure from her thighs to every part of her body. Raj was pressing light kisses to her moist face, her eyes, her cheekbones, softly nibbling at her earlobes, until her breathing finally slowed down.

"I'm sorry, baby." His breathing was still uneven and she could feel the heat of his erection, through the thin cotton of his boxers, hard against her hip. "I didn't mean to get carried away."

He didn't ask if she was okay and Maya was glad, because she wouldn't have been able to answer him. The feelings had been…overwhelming…and just a little scary.

CHAPTER 11

Rajiv was laying on his side, facing her. She squeezed her trembling legs together, forcing him to move his hand away and rest it on her stomach. But he wasn't finished with her yet. "Maya, why didn't you tell me?" There was a hint of accusation in his voice.

"Was it that bad?" *No, worse!*

His eyes darkened in anger. "Yes it was—for you," he ground out. "And if I'd known it would have been a lot less painful."

She squirmed. "Do we have to talk about this now?"

"Yes, we do." He lifted his hand from her flat belly and raked his hair away from his face. "I would never have seduced you if I'd known."

"You didn't *seduce* me!"

He lifted himself up and looked down at her, his blue eyes bemused and questioning. "I'm asking you again. Why didn't you tell me?"

She wanted to look away from that almost-hurt expression. She felt trapped, cornered—awkward. "I—I guess I was embarrassed."

"Embarrassed!" He swore softly to himself. "Why the hell would you feel embarrassed?"

She tried to cover her eyes with her arm, but he stopped her. "I was hoping you wouldn't notice."

"Were you ashamed of being a virgin?" His voice was soft, but deadly serious.

Maya drew in a deep breath. *He just wasn't going to let this go.* "Yes…maybe. After all I am over twenty-one," she finished lamely.

He moved abruptly, sitting up and crossing his legs, dragging both hands through his hair in frustration. "I would never have touched you if I'd known."

A wave of dejection washed over her, she didn't want to believe him. "Are you sure?"

"Yes, I'm sure." It was a statement.

Maya felt utterly deflated. She searched his face, but his expression was hard and detached.

"I would never have taken your virginity," he continued in a level voice. "Not when I can't even offer you marriage."

A nervous giggle bubbled out of her. "*Marriage!*"

"You find this amusing?" His expression was really angry now. "I don't know what it's like in your culture, but where I come from taking a woman's virginity is a very serious matter."

"I'm sorry, Rajiv, but I don't want to get married." She hesitated and then forced herself to continue. "I don't even know if I believe in marriage."

He looked genuinely shocked, then his eyes narrowed, as if he was coming to a conclusion, a conclusion that turned his face as hard as granite in the low light. Only his eyes were alive, alive and blazing with accusation. "So what? This was just an experiment for you?" In less than a second, he was straddling her, gripping her hands above her head, hanging over her like a wild animal.

"Raj! Please, you're hurting me."

He ignored her pleas, nudging one knee between her

legs. When she tried to struggle, he simply lifted his weight and lowered himself down onto her. "So when did you decide that I should be the one to *assist* you in getting rid of your virginity!"

His face was almost touching hers, as his words sliced through her like a knife. Why was he so angry? Just because she had been a virgin? He was breathing hard and so was she. She struggled to push him off her, while his hands bruised her wrists in their iron grip. When she felt his erection pressing against her thigh, a prickle of fear ran down her spine. He was so big and, if he lost control, he would hurt her again. The thought of his thrusting that huge…thing into her raw and aching body again was too much.

"Please don't hurt me again," she sobbed, and suddenly he stilled, only his ragged breathing betraying the stress he was feeling.

"God, Maya, what are you *doing* to me?"

He released her wrists and brought his hands down to cup her face. "You make me hate myself."

And then his mouth was on hers, hard and demanding, slanting his head for a better, deeper fit. Hot, possessive kisses that left her weak and clinging to him. God, the man knew how to make love with his mouth! She slid her tongue against his, allowing him to suck gently at it. Heat was unfolding between her legs and she knew he felt the same when he ground himself against her.

She wanted him, craved him, but she was still sore, and the huge bulge of his shaft pressing against her was a stark reminder of the pain she just did not want to endure again. Was she prepared to go through it for him? She wasn't sure. All she knew was that she didn't want to stop and she didn't want *him* to stop. So when his mouth moved down from her throat to finally suckle at her aching breast, she gave herself up to the craving sensations that seemed to have a hotline from her breasts to the sweet, tight pleasure that was beginning to throb between her legs. His pace became less urgent, sucking and gently biting each breast, taking his sweet time and Maya writhed beneath him, digging her hands into his thick hair, arching her body—wanting more.

Rajiv gripped her hips, holding her still while he moved his mouth slowly down her midriff towards her stomach. She dug her nails into his shoulders and wrapped her legs around his, rubbing the insteps of her feet invitingly along his legs, egging him on even though she knew it was stupid and reckless. She wanted, needed…she wasn't even sure what, but her body felt like it was being wound up tighter and tighter. His mouth was at her belly button now, his tongue maddeningly slow as it circled and licked at it before traveling downward. His hands gently eased her thighs apart, and then his hot mouth was there, on her exposed, swollen flesh. Her body jerked, a surge of lush pleasure claiming her and emptying her mind of everything but his tongue, mouth, lips, even his teeth.

She was going to pass out. It was too much, and she struggled, pushing at his shoulders, yet thrusting her hips against him at the same time, her senses in turmoil. His tongue swirled and licked at her aching bud. She dragged air into her lungs, sure her body could take no more of this sexual onslaught. A pleading sob escaped her, but he took no notice. Using both hands, he lifted her bottom off the bed for better access and continued to plunder her aching, feminine core. She was being wound, tighter and tighter, until she was begging—what for, she wasn't sure. Her cries were high and piercing, but he was merciless, his mouth and tongue sliding and circling against her squirming flesh.

Suddenly, he pushed his finger deep inside her and Maya exploded, her sensitive nerve endings clamping tightly around that intrusive finger as waves of unbearable pleasure burst through her, sucking her down into a whirlpool of drowning sensation. Her breath was coming out in sobs as he removed his finger, ever so slowly, his mouth still pressing hard against her vulva.

Finally, she felt herself slowly relax, soft throbs of pleasure continuing to wash over her trembling body. Rajiv lifted his head and moved over her, covering her mouth with his. She was barely conscious, her body boneless across the bed. She could taste herself in his long, languorous kiss, her tongue entwining with his, the only part of her body that would do her bidding. Her eyelids felt heavy and a warm lethargy was enveloping her. She allowed herself to drift as his lips spread feather light kisses over her face.

ⅇ⌁ⅇ⌁

Rajiv stood by the long sliding glass doors, feeling the warm breeze against his heated skin. It was a hot night and he'd opened the door that led to the balcony, staring with unseeing eyes at the flickering lights below. Maya had fallen asleep immediately after her orgasm, leaving him hard and aching. Desire raged through him, ruthlessly demanding release. He'd taken a cold shower to cool his heated flesh, but that hadn't worked, so he'd done what he had to do— Swearing explicitly through tightly ground teeth, he'd closed his fist round his swollen shaft and within seconds hot jets of semen had swirled down the shower drain, together with the icy water. He'd found relief, no pleasure that he could recall, but at least his mind could function now.

He had no intention of making love to her again. Maybe he was fooling himself, but perhaps he had not completely broken her virginity. Technically, she might still be a virgin. He'd climaxed within seconds of entering that excruciating tight channel of hers. Rajiv's senses quickened at the memory, but he suppressed it. At least he'd managed to make her come, given her a taste of how good it could be. God, how he'd love to be the one to introduce her to the pleasures that he knew her body was capable of. He'd never expected her to climax so easily, especially after the pain he'd put her through. But she was so responsive! Her body was like a musical instrument beneath his hands, and she couldn't control it, no matter how hard she tried. Would she be like that with another man? With Sanjay? The idea was like a knife twisting deep in his gut—her body aroused and writhing beneath another man, just as it had writhed beneath him. He raked his fingers through his hair, trembling with rage. He had to let her go. It was the only way to redeem himself and, besides, he was sure she would not want a re-peat performance of the disastrous excuse for love-making he'd put her through. *But I could show her how good it could be.* He sucked air through his teeth. *No*! He would not be able to live with himself. Besides, the more she liked it, the more chance she'd be wanting it *from another man.* The knife twisted in his gut again.

A movement from the bed sent his head jerking toward her sleeping form. His breath caught in his throat. She'd moved onto her stomach, her right leg bent high on the mat-tress, the left one lying straight and long, free from the co-vers shoved down to the bottom of the bed, her body com-pletely exposed to him. His greedy eyes moved down, over the bare curves of her high, pale buttocks to the silky folds of her pear shaped feminine cleft, warm and moist in the soft light.

Rajiv felt his whole body tremble and break out in sweat. He sucked air into his desperate lungs. She was in a deep sleep, exhausted probably from the physical and emo-tional rollercoaster he'd put her through. But he was wide awake, his erection throbbing painfully, unable to drag his gaze from that inviting feminine flesh, unconsciously ex-posed to his hungry eyes.

Lust surged through his body in waves. His heart was pounding, but he had to take control of it. He'd promised himself. *But I could lie with her, maybe even touch her while she sleeps.* He would never get another chance. Soon it would be daylight and then he'd never see her again.

Before his conscience forced him to change his mind, he climbed slowly onto the bed beside her. He still had his boxers on. *And you'll keep them on,* he told himself grimly. He tried to control his breathing, but his lungs were starving for more oxygen. Each breath deep and ragged, he squeezed his eyes shut, trying to erase the image that had brought him to the brink of losing control. His lungs eased just a little, but his body was still covered in a film of sweat and there was nothing he could do about it. He had to touch her, *just touch her.* He ran a trembling finger along her spine. Her skin was like satin.

His hand itched to cup her silky rounded backside. God! He wanted to caress and squeeze those pale, inviting globes. He stifled a groan and moved his hand sideways to skim along the curve of her thigh to her waist, to the side of her breast, pressed against the mattress. He moved in a little closer, the front of his body brushing against her side. Her head was facing away from him and he pressed his face into her tumbled, silky hair, breathing deeply. He smelled jasmine and that unique scent that was all hers. His hand resting on her lower back, he clenched the muscles of his buttocks, so that his shaft pressed softly against her hip, and ground his teeth to suppress the agonizing groan that rumbled in his chest.

She sighed softly and adjusted her position, turning onto her side, pressing her bottom fully against him. Rajiv lie dead still, waiting for her to awaken, but her breathing was soft and deep. Slowly he allowed himself to relax against her, almost sobbing his pleasure, as her body leaned back into his. He caressed the indentation of her waist then allowed his hand to splay against her flat stomach.

She breathed another deep sigh and wriggled herself

against him. It was too much. He needed to get away before he lost control. *You're not going anywhere,* his body told him. *You're just holding her.* His brain was in agreement, so he allowed his trembling hand to caress her stomach, her hip, her thigh, and back up again. Soft, searching caresses, memorizing the long, curving shape of her sensual, made for love body. Knowing he would never forget this night as long as he lived.

Rajiv's hand was at her midriff, caressing the underside of her breast when she mumbled something and pressed her backside into his groin again. He groaned.

"Raj?" she breathed sleepily.

He moved his hand to her hip. "Shh. I'm just gonna lie here. Go back to sleep." He sounded breathless.

"Wasn't sleeping," she mumbled. "Just dozing."

"I just want to hold you," he breathed, caressing her hip lightly.

"Mmm." She wriggled her buttocks again and he caught his breath.

"I won't do anything, baby," he said softly, knowing she must be feeling the hard bulge through his boxers pressing into her. "Just hold you while you sleep."

"Why?" She sounded more awake now and Rajiv cursed himself.

"Why what, baby?"

She arched her back and circled her hips against him. "Why won't you do anything?"

"Maya, please!" The words were torn from him.

She turned onto her back, covering his hand on her belly, and stared at him with heavy, sensual eyes. "Don't you want to make love to me?"

"Yes. No!" Lust was clouding his brain as he tried to make sense of what she was saying.

"No?" She lifted her hand to caress his sweat dampened face. "Why not?"

Rajiv closed his eyes, revelling in the sweet touch of her fingers on his skin. God, how would it feel to have those fingers closing around his throbbing shaft? His erection jerked, but he didn't lose control.

"Maya." He tried to keep his voice steady. "What I did was wrong. You may still be a virgin—technically. I can't make love to you again, knowing how innocent you are."

She closed her eyes and sighed then opened them. "Oh Raj." He loved the way she shortened his name. "You're so…"

"So what?" *I'm not gonna like this.*

She almost smiled. "So Indian."

"That sounds like an insult."

"No. Not at all. It's quite sweet, really." She arched her naked body against him, his erection pressing against her firm, flat stomach now. "It means I want you to make love to me—properly this time."

Blood rushed from his head to his groin, emptying his brain. He struggled to recall why he should not make love to her, but her fingers were in his hair now, pulling his mouth down to hers. It was impossible to resist. *She* was impossible to resist. Her soft, swollen mouth sucked at his bottom lip, nibbling with her teeth, teasing him! Already she was learning the power of her feminine sensuality, her capacity for giving and receiving pleasure. Once again, anger raged with lust inside him. She could be everything a man wanted in a woman. And one day she would be. Without a doubt she would be. *But it won't be me.*

Rajiv felt his control snap. He sank his fingers into her hair, twisting and pulling her head back into position for his punishing kiss.

꘎꘎꘎

Maya felt a shiver of trepidation at his demanding, possessive mouth, bruising her lips. But she'd asked for this, especially when he'd tried to deny her what she so desperately wanted—*him*. His lips softened, his tongue circling her mouth, before darting in and out, giving her a taste of what was to come. Pressing down onto her, heavy and hard, he eased her legs apart, cradling himself between her thighs. He still had his boxer shorts on and she could feel his erection rubbing against her moist core through the thin cotton. That scary, sweet sensation began building up inside her, and she moaned his name.

Maya could tell he was under tremendous strain, his body slick with sweat, his heart pounding against her breast. Yet he moved slowly, deliberately, savouring each kiss, each caress. His hand stroked then squeezed her breast, pushing the nipple upward, covering it with his mouth and sucking hard. She jerked into him and began to shake. Once again, the pleasure darted straight to her core, her body arching at the melting heat between her legs. He was at her other breast now, suckling greedily. Maya's breath was coming in short gasps, her body writhing beneath him as her insides twisted tighter and tighter until she felt she might combust.

He ran his hand lightly down over her stomach to the apex of her thighs, stroking and searching between the slick folds of flesh. She was wet, but her embarrassment dissipated at his groan of delight. His expert fingers slid along her moistened cleft and then found her swollen nubbin. Maya let out a long moan, circling her hips, mirroring his movements. She caressed his taut, muscled back, damp with sweat, until she reached the elastic of his shorts and slid her hands inside, digging her nails into his smooth, firm buttocks. Rajiv expelled a strangled groan, making her feel bolder. She hooked her thumbs into the elastic edge, pushing them over and downward.

He lifted his hips. "Help me here, baby," he choked,

and she gripped the front of the boxers, sliding them down over his swollen shaft. Immediately he sank back between her parted legs, gritting his teeth when his heavy groin rested against her wet, welcoming flesh.

Maya slid her hips back and forth, pleasure exploding as his bold, smooth shaft slid against her drenched heat. She too was trembling now, but not just with pleasure. She'd forgotten how big he was and trepidation was edging into her desire. He pulled back slightly, positioning the swollen head of his member at her entrance.

"Open your eyes," he groaned, his arms braced on either side of her, and then slowly pushed himself inside her. "Look at me, baby."

Maya drowned in those dark, glittering eyes, sucking in gasps of air. It was not as painful as before and she tried to relax her muscles, but as he thrust, again she heard herself cry out at the sense of invasion, nerve endings protested in pain as he stretched her raw, sensitized entrance, her inner muscles tightening to prevent his alien invasion.

"Relax, baby," he gasped, his face dripping with sweat. "Sweet Jesus, relax!"

He thrust against her protesting muscles, then recoiled and thrust even deeper, until completely buried inside her. Different sensations began to build. He kept still for a moment, allowing her body to stretch and then tighten around his pulsing shaft. Maya moaned and circled her hips slowly, experimentally. Waves of hot sweetness built inside her, threatening to overpower her. He retreated and then thrust deeply into her again, slowly at first then picking up speed. It was too much. She feared was going to explode. She pushed against his shoulders, trying to get away, but he held her down, thrusting in and then out as she threw her head back and sobbed.

"Don't fight it, baby," he soothed. "Wrap your legs around me."

But she couldn't. It was impossible to do anything except try to fight the tidal wave that was threatening to drown her. Rajiv gripped her squirming buttocks and lifted her up against him. She cried out as he buried himself even deeper, grinding into her, while his pelvis rocked and rubbed against her clitoris.

She gave a shuddering moan as the powerful heat of him filled and consumed her, causing her to cry out in pleasurable pain. Time stood still, the world shrinking around them. Finally he moved, rolling his hips, sending sensations rocketing through her, then thrusting again, and again, each time stronger and harder until she felt she would burst from her skin and die.

The orgasm that rocketed through her was like a kind of death, each shuddering spasm of pleasure exploding and expanding through her. Then the flooding liquid heat as Rajiv joined her, throwing back his head and releasing a strangled groan, his whole body arched, and convulsed in a powerful climax before he slumped weakly into her waiting arms.

Maya was mindless, awash with lush sensation. She had survived, not only survived, but she could still feel little explosions of sweet, painful pleasure darting through her. She felt tears leaking from her eyes as a small sob interrupted her ragged breathing. Never in her wildest dreams had she imagined something so powerful, binding them together in a cocoon of intense intimacy.

He was kissing her now, tasting her tears. "Maya, why are you crying?" his voice hoarse, gasping for breath. "Did I hurt you?"

She tried to shake her head but she was too weak to move. "No. It was just too much," she whispered. "I don't know how I survived."

He buried his face in her hair. "I know," he murmured, his breath warm against cheek.

CHAPTER 12

Maya climbed silently from the bed, listening carefully for any change in Rajiv's deep slumberous breathing. An Indian cotton shirt was lying on the carved, wooden chest at the bottom of the bed. She reached for it, shrugging the soft fabric onto her slim shoulders. It hung down to mid-thigh on her. She buttoned it up, breathing in the clean, soapy smell underlined by his unique, masculine scent, enjoying the sensation of his clothing against her naked skin. The door was slightly ajar and she tiptoed toward it with a quick glance back at his sleeping form before leaving the room. He looked quite beautiful stretched out across the bed, the dark golden skin of his naked back contrasting with his sable tousled hair.

Memories of the night before caused her skin to prickle, heat flooding through her veins. After that earth shattering orgasm, they had lay entangled together, kissing for what seemed like hours, caressing and familiarising themselves with each other's bodies. She'd loved the freedom of being able to touch and stroke his hard, muscled body, covered by his satin smooth skin. She savored the power she had to give him pleasure, driving him to the edge. Fascinated by the bold thrust of his arousal, she had found the courage to touch and stroke him, allowing him to show her just what he needed from her. Her wantonness had surprised herself as well as him. She'd wanted to take him in her mouth, but he'd stopped her. His old fashioned values getting in the way, as he told her she was too new to this, moving too fast. She was too sore and tender for them to have sex again, but he'd pleased her with his hands, his mouth, his body, making her climax over and over again. He seemed fascinated by the fine, dark red hair covering her femininity, feasting on it until her body felt like a vessel of ecstasy, not able to think, or come down to earth, before he found some other way of drowning her in new sensations, leaving her mindless and overdosed on pleasure.

She managed to give him some relief as well. He was insatiable, permanently aroused. Although he wouldn't allow her to go down on him, she used her hands and her body to take him over the edge, even though he kept telling her she didn't need to, that tonight was all about her. But she wanted to give him pleasure, loved seeing him lose control, groaning and burying his face in her hair as she stroked and caressed him until he was weak, trembling and groaning in her arms, spilling his seed over her lower stomach and thighs .

There were slivers of light peeking through the curtains, so she knew it must be early morning, very early, as the sun rose around five o'clock at this time of year. It was quite easy to find the living room, even if she hadn't really noticed where he was taking her the night before. The apartment was big, probably three or four bedrooms, she guessed as she stepped into the brightness of the living room with its white walls and long, pale sofas, set around a large, wooden coffee table. Modern artwork and sculptures added to the sleek lines and created beautiful focal points that immediately caught her artistic eye. The open-plan kitchen was to her right, separated by a long marble-topped counter with four stools, and at the far end of the room was a dining table with seating for about ten people. He obviously entertained here as well. She forced her mind back to more pressing matters.

Where was her bag?

Her eyes swept the room, finally settling on her bag lying on one of the cream couches. She needed to check her messages and then call the train station. There was one text from Jay, wishing her a safe trip and asking her to text him when she arrived. She hated lying, but hit the reply button and sent him a message saying she'd arrived safely and would text him later in the day. She saw a cordless landline on a side-table and decided Rajiv wouldn't mind if she used it to find out about her train. Dialling Directory Enquiries, she obtained the number for Information at Kings Cross Station then called them and asked when the train to Edinburgh would be leaving.

"The train from London to Edinburgh's Waverly Station will now be leaving Kings Cross at 10 am this morning," a female voice informed her, and Maya thanked her before quietly hanging up the phone.

She glanced up at a sleek, silver clock on the wall. Ten minutes past five, almost five hours before the train left.

"Planning on running out on me?"

Maya almost jumped out of her skin at the sound of that cool voice behind her and, with an inward groan, turned her trembling limbs round to face him. He was standing at the doorway, naked, his expression unreadable.

"No, of course not," she managed to say, running her sweaty palms along the sides of the cotton shirt. "I was just checking to see when the train leaves."

He crossed his arms, leaning one shoulder against the doorjamb, and Maya had to force herself not to look below his waist. It was ridiculous, really, after what they had shared the night before, but she felt embarrassed and awkward, while he was obviously quite at ease with his nakedness.

"So what time does it leave?"

"Ten o'clock this morning."

His eyes dropped to her legs as she shifted from one bare foot to another.

After all the heat and passion of last night, the atmosphere suddenly filled with tension. His hooded gaze traveled upward to meet her eyes.

"We need to talk,"

"Please, Rajiv, do we have to have a post-mortem.?"

"You're a puzzle, Maya, and I don't particularly like puzzles. I like to know what I'm dealing with."

"*Dealing with*?" She froze. "Is that how you see me? Something you have to deal with?"

He straightened up, leaning one hand against the doorjamb and rubbing the back of his neck. "There's something I have to know."

Maya crossed her arms in a defensive stance. It looked like he was determined to have a post-mortem. "What?"

"Were you saving yourself—for Sanjay?"

It took Maya a moment to grasp his question. Then she wanted to laugh, but knew that would infuriate him. She didn't want him angry.

They only had a few hours left and she wanted him caring and passionate, sweet and gentle. The way he had been last night.

"No, Rajiv, I was not saving myself for *anyone.* Why would you think I was saving myself for Sanjay?"

"You told me you were on the pill."

"So?"

"Are you on the pill?"

"Yes, of course I am. Why would I lie?"

"There are women who lie about things like that."

Once again, it took Maya a moment to get his meaning.

"You think I was trying to *trick* you? Trap you into getting me pregnant!" Her chest rose and fell in fury.

"Actually, no, that wasn't my assumption," he answered softly and Maya took a few slow breaths to calm herself.

"Well then, please do tell. What was your assumption?"

"That you and Sanjay were planning on marriage, or at least taking your relationship to the next level."

Maya was lost for words.

There was a long silence. He was waiting for an answer, but Maya refused to dignify his *assumption* with an answer. He was getting angry at her silence. His eyes bored into hers, but still she said nothing.

"Otherwise why were you on the pill?"

Maya moistened her lips. "I have painful, irregular periods, the pill really helps."

He looked away and it gave her childish pleasure to see a flush on his perfect cheekbones. "I never thought of that."

"Yes, well, we women don't have it as easy as men." Now she sounded petty.

His eyes were searching hers again. "It's strange that you've never been with a man before."

Maya felt like slapping him. He just wasn't going to let it go. Like a dog with a bone.

"Well, I'm sorry you find it strange, but that's the way it is." She wasn't going to go into detail about her past experiences, or non-experiences, with men and especially the fact that he was the first man she'd met that she'd wanted to have sex with. His ego was probably inflated enough as it was.

"Why me, Maya?"

He seemed really mystified, confused, and perhaps if his mother wasn't out there looking for a suitable Indian wife for him, if he wasn't planning on getting married, she might have been more forthcoming about her innocence and her irresistible attraction toward him, but what was the point?

"Raj, what happened last night, happened." Her voice softened as she tried to reason with him. "It was special—for me, anyway, but it's over now. I have to go back to Edinburgh and you—you have your future plans to get on with." She drew a breath. "Can't we just leave it at that and at least part as friends?"

"Friends!" Her words were meant to sooth the situation, but they seemed to infuriate him even more. "After last night you want to be my *friend*?"

"Rajiv." She was getting angry again and she really didn't want that. "We'll probably never see each other again. What happened last night was wonderful. I'll never forget it—or you, but it's over and, if you don't want to part as friends, let's at least leave it amicable."

"God, you're a cool one, aren't you?"

It seemed that no matter what she said it was the wrong thing. Better that she didn't say anything at all.

"Who would have known you were a virgin just a few hours ago." His eyes traveled down her body in an almost insulting manner and he shook his head. "So fucking blasé."

Maya was speechless, not only by the insolence of his words, but she had never before heard him swear. And he was swearing at her!

"So what do you suggest?" Her heart- rate had sped up with her breathing. As much as she tried to control herself, she was now furious with the way he was treating her, especially after all the caring tenderness he'd shown her last night. "Would you like me to stay on and become another one of your many mistresses? While your mother runs around India searching for a sweet, suitable *bride* for you?"

Rajiv's moved in a blur of speed. Before she knew what was happening, he had pinned her to the wall behind, his hands holding her wrists high above her head in a bruising grip.

"What do you know about my *mistresses*?" His voice was soft but his breathing betrayed the fury he was feeling. "Tell me, goddammit!"

"What difference does it make?" she gulped, shocked by how quickly things had turned vicious. "It's the truth isn't it?"

"For your information, Maya," he breathed against her cheek and leaned the hard length of his body into hers. "I haven't *touched* another woman since the day I picked you up from that damn train station."

Maya could feel heat burning through the thin cotton fabric. As she struggled futilely to twist away from him, the stirring bulge of his arousal became evident through the gaping slit of the shirt.

"Damn you," he swore as his body betrayed him, growing, and lengthening against her soft skin, and Maya felt that all too familiar weakness seeping through her thighs.

But she fought against it. "Let me go, Rajiv." Her voice sounded husky and breathless, and his gaze dropped to her mouth.

His body was heavy, pressing her back against the wall, leaning into every inch of her. The shirt was pulled up high above her thighs by her arms, which he continued to hold painfully tight above her head. In the sudden silence, he ground his swelling arousal into her, just above her pubic bone.

"I can't," he said, suddenly out of breath. "I wish I could, but I can't help myself."

His tongue began teasing her ear and she felt her body break out in a wave of heat, every nerve suddenly on high alert, like a drug addict ready for the next fix. He continued to rotate his hips, moving down to the naked juncture between her thighs and finding her moist cleft with his shaft.

Maya legs wobbled, heat pooling between her thighs and, acknowledging that he had won, Rajiv loosened her wrists and ran his hands down her body to the hem of the shirt.

"See, you're not quite ready to leave me just yet, are you, baby?" he whispered against her hair, and much as she wanted to feel outraged by his arrogance, her body simply didn't seem to care.

His erection working insistently against the wet heat at the juncture of her thighs was sucking her under, to that place where thought was impossible, and the craving needs of her body overtook everything else.

When his hands gripped her buttocks and pressed her up against him, she knew there was no hope left for her.

"God, you feel good," he muttered hoarsely, his teeth biting into her neck, guiding her hand down between them. "So good."

His manhood was hot and heavy in her palm, slick with the juices of her desire, and he shuddered as her fingers closed around his throbbing flesh. Squeezing and stroking from the base to the tip, just the way he'd shown her during the hours of mindless passion they'd shared throughout the night.

"Sweet Jesus, Maya," he hissed through gritted teeth. Thrusting his hips against her stroking hand. "What are you doing to me?"

She lifted heavy lids to look into his glazed eyes, wondering if he expected her to answer him. Instead he covered her mouth with his, closing his hand around her throat, holding her still while he slanted his head and deepened the sensual onslaught of her mouth, continuing to thrust his hips against her enveloping hand.

Maya's back arched away from the wall, guiding the swollen head of his sex to rub against her slick vulva with each thrust of his hips.

"God, Raj." Pure, aching lust was drenching her body from the inside out, driving her to the edge of an orgasm.

"No, I want you to come when I'm inside you," he choked, tearing her tormenting hand away and running the underside of his shaft flush against her inviting flesh, almost pushing her over the edge.

Suddenly he moved away and she cried out in frustration, but he cupped her bottom and lifted her off the floor, forcing her to spread her thighs and wrap her legs around his waist.

"For pity's sake, Maya." He shoved her hand back to his swollen erection. "Do it. Now!"

She guided him to her tender core, shocked at how much she had learned in so little time, and then thought became impossible as he thrust aggressively into her, groaning as her sensitized inner muscles tightened around him. His fingers dug almost painfully into the soft flesh of her bottom as he plunged deeper and harder, her sobbing moans driving him wild.

She felt herself sucked into that whirlpool of sensation, deeper and deeper, until the explosion gripped her and pulled her under, her body convulsing and spasming around his exploding penis, hot jets of liquid spurting deep inside her. His hips kept thrusting into her. Even though he'd climaxed, he seemed unable to stop, his semen seeping out moist and slick against her thighs.

Maya must have actually lost conscious for a short while.

She was hardly aware of him carrying her back to the bedroom, laying her gently on the bed and covering her up. She snuggled into the luxurious softness of the linen, enjoying the warm musky smell that their lovemaking had left behind.

Sunlight streaming through the long windows and onto the bed drew Maya out of a deep and dreamless sleep. Rajiv stood beside the pale brown curtains he had just opened, his face set in an expressionless mask.

"It's eight-thirty and I presume you don't want to miss your train," he said, avoiding her eyes. "The bathroom's through that door, as you know. I'll make some coffee."

She watched him walk toward the door, a tight pain twisting deep inside her. He was half-dressed, a pristine white shirt hanging open to expose his muscled brown chest with that line of sleek dark hair narrowing down into the low waistband of his smart gray trousers. In the past twelve hours, she had come to know his body intimately, as he had come to know hers, and, for Maya, this was something completely new—and wonderful—yet here they were, behaving like strangers.

She shivered slightly. His eyes had been like pale chips of ice this morning and there was nothing she could do about it.

He was going to marry another woman, and she was going back to Scotland to try and pick up the pieces of her life. Ships that pass in the night. But it had been a night that she would never forget, and she did not regret it, not one bit.

She looked around her, seeing his bedroom properly for the first time. The curtains and bedcovers were colored in different shades of beige and light brown, while the walls were painted white, like the main room. A door to the left of the bathroom stood ajar and Maya realized it was a walk-in closet. She stood up, pulling on the terry-cloth robe that he'd laid out at the bottom of the bed, and went over to the long windows. As she'd expected, the view was as gorgeous here as it was in the living room, the morning sun reflecting brightly onto the gently flowing river.

Her suitcase was placed on a large, carved-wooden chest at the bottom of the bed. She went to open it, taking out her toiletry bag and fresh underwear.

The white-marble-tiled bathroom looked large and ra-

ther masculine in its simplicity, with its range of expensive
aftershaves and soaps for men. Besides the huge shower,
there was also a large, oval sunken bath. Maya savored every minute of it, touching and smelling all his toiletries and
imagining what it would be like to have *him* here in the
shower with her. The idea was a tantalizing one, especially
as her body was still sore and sensitive from the night before—and this morning's—frenzied coupling. The muscles
of her upper legs were aching and there were slight bruises
on her thighs and bottom, probably from when he had lifted
her up off the floor, driving himself into her with madden-
ing passion.

Maya felt a surge of heat invade her, leaving her weak
and breathless with longing. She squeezed some shower gel
into a large luxurious sponge and gently soaped between her
legs. She was sore and swollen down there—and no wonder! She'd had more sex in one night than she'd had before
in her entire life.

Making her way back into the bedroom, she felt a mixture of relief and disappointment that he was not there.
What was she hoping for, some kind of reconciliation? *Well
it's not going to happen,* she told herself sternly, impatiently
untying her hair from its topknot as her eyes scanned the
room. The clothes she had worn the night before were folded neatly on an armchair in the corner. He must have done it
this morning while she was sleeping. Had he stayed awake
after they'd had sex in the living room? she pondered, feeling slightly disturbed at the thought of him pottering around
the bedroom while she lay in his bed, naked and dead to the
world.

Maya packed the clothes back into the suitcase and
pulled out the first things that came to her hands, surprised
to see that it was the same lilac top and flowing Indian skirt
that she'd worn on her arrival in London. Fate still seemed
to be playing games with her. She ran a brush through her

hair and left it to hang loose, not bothering with any make-up, just some moisturizer, before going through to the living room with a heavily beating heart.

He was standing at the window, a mug of coffee in his hand, staring out at the view, an inscrutable expression on his face.

"Help yourself to coffee." He motioned to the coffee pot and matching crockery on the large, wooden coffee ta-ble. "I've asked Bijal to pick you up at around nine fifteen, if that's okay with you?"

Maya nodded. So he wasn't coming with her. She told herself it was better this way, that saying goodbye at the station would have been awkward and uncomfortable, while saying it here was much more civilized. Seating herself on one of the soft leather sofas, she poured some coffee into a long white mug. He was still standing at the window and it was a relief to see that his shirt was now buttoned almost to the top, but he hadn't bothered with the cuffs or tucked it in. There was a kind of casual intimacy about him walking around like that.

It squeezed at her heart. How she would love to go over and put her arms around him, to slide her hands beneath his shirt, and caress the hard muscles of his stomach. Her soft dreamy eyes clashed with his darkened gaze and, for a sec-ond, time stood still.

Then he moved, setting down the coffee mug and rak-ing his fingers through his hair.

"It's too late to apologize for what happened," he mut-tered, pushing his hands into the pockets of his trousers. "What's done is done."

Maya moistened her dry lips. "I wasn't expecting an apology," she stated evenly.

"No, I guess you weren't," he countered grimly.

She frowned, not sure she liked the tone of his voice, but then continued anyway. "I was as much to blame as you were and, as we won't be seeing each other again, I think it's best if we just forget it," she finished quietly, quite proud of how calm she sounded.

His mouth tightened into a derisive line. "God, you really are Miss Cool, aren't you?" he muttered, and Maya felt like shouting out that the last thing she felt right now was cool. "And what makes you so sure that we won't be seeing each other again? Aren't you and Jay planning on keeping in contact?"

She hesitated, feeling mean and deceitful. "Yes, of course, we'll be staying in contact, but I'm not planning on coming back to London."

"So will he be going up to see you then?" he persisted.

"That's up to Jay," she replied, looking straight at him. "He knows he's always welcome to come up and stay as long as he likes."

What was the point of trying to convince him there was nothing between his brother and her? What would he want then? To see her on the side while his mother ran around India looking for a wife for him? No, it was best for her to slip quietly away and try to forget him.

Maya set her mug down on the coffee table. "If you're so interested in his future plans, perhaps you should ask him yourself," she suggested, unable to conceal the irritability in her voice.

With the speed of a feline, he was hanging over her, leaning his arms on the sofa above her head. "And what would you like me to say to him?" His face was almost touching hers, tight with rage as he glared down at her. "'Excuse me, dear brother, but I've got the hots for your girlfriend, so would you mind stepping aside while I screw her senseless and I'll let you know when I'm done?' How does that sound to you then?"

Maya felt her face drain at his cruel words, but before she could retaliate, the doorbell pealed loudly and Rajiv's hands fell abruptly away. He moved toward the door, thrusting his shirt impatiently into his trousers.

It was Bijal, come to collect her. As she answered his polite greeting, Maya wondered what he must think of her being here in Rajiv's apartment rather than at the house. Rajiv disappeared to collect her suitcase in the bedroom. She walked awkwardly to the windows, trying not to look as guilty as she felt.

Rajiv eventually reappeared with her suitcase, seeming quite unconcerned with the situation, and she felt a deep resentment toward him for being so thoughtless. He handed the chauffer her suitcase. "If you'll just take this down, thank you Bijal. We'll be along in a minute."

"What did you tell him?" Maya hissed as soon as the older man had left.

Rajiv raised his eyebrows. "Tell him? Nothing. Why?"

She glared at him in frustration. "What must he think of me being here in your apartment?"

He shrugged indifferently. "It's none of his business. I pay him to drive, not think."

Maya collected her bag from the sofa, her hands shaking. "Well, thank you for your hospitality," she said stiffly, walking toward the door.

"Wait. I'll take you down."

He buttoned the cuffs of his shirt. She turned away, unable to bear the pain of watching him, knowing that she would never see him again.

"Are you sure you have everything?" he asked, opening the door

Maya nodded, her throat tight with emotion. The atmosphere between them was tense and awkward as they entered the plush mirrored lift. She heard him draw a deep, steadying breath as she turned impatiently to face the doors.

"You can't wait to get away from me, can you?" he said grimly, his breath warm at the back of her neck, and

Maya trembled when his hand curved round her waist, his thumb brushing the underside of her breast. "Why is that? I wonder. I thought we were quite good together."

His lips moved against her hair and the temptation to lean back against him was overpowering. Long fingers splayed across her flat stomach, the heat of his palm burning through her thin cotton skirt as he pressed her back against the hard length of him.

God, why did he have this power over her?

His hand moved down to the heated juncture between her thighs, but before she could melt weakly into him, the lift came to a smooth halt at the basement, allowing her the strength to pull away.

A wave of shame flushed her cheeks at the ease with which he could seduce her senses.

They stood facing each other beside the vehicle, Bijal sitting expressionless in the driver's seat, as Maya swallowed, trying to find her voice.

She held out her hand in a polite gesture. "Thank you for—for everything," she said tightly.

A pulse throbbed at the taut line of his jaw and he stared at her outstretched hand for a long moment. "So that's it then?" he stated curtly, finally clasping her cold hand in his.

"Yes. Well, take care of yourself." She pulled her hand away, conscious of Bijal waiting patiently for them to finish.

"Goodbye, Maya."

He held the door open and she climbed in, pulling the folds of her skirt around her.

As the car sped, away Maya stared fixedly in front of her, battling against the overwhelming temptation to turn round and look back at him just one last time.

ℰﬤℰﬤ

Rajiv watched her drive away, feeling a ridiculous urge to run after her and beg her to stay, even just for one more night. He stood there long after the car had disappeared, wishing that he could hate her for the feelings she evoked in him. His life seemed suddenly dull and empty now that she was gone. He realized that he had never before felt as alive as he had from that fateful day when he'd collected her from the station. And making love to her last night had left him feeling desperate. Usually, he'd be quite impatient for the woman to leave after sex, but with Maya all he'd wanted was for her to stay—to get to know her, mentally as well as physically, and that's why he'd been so furious when she had sneaked out to phone the station. Was she so anxious to get away from him? God, he'd thought they were good together—more than good—more than he'd ever imagined, and he'd imagined a lot.

He'd felt gutted when he heard her on the phone and, for one crazy moment, he'd imagined it was Jay she was calling, that she was going to end their relationship, but what would be the point of that? As he'd already told her, it wasn't as if he could offer her marriage—or even a *Let's see where this goes* relationship. If he was really honest with himself, the reason he'd lost it earlier in the lounge was because sub-consciously, he *had* been thinking about making her his mistress, making her *his*. To do with as he pleased. God, just the thought of it made him hard. He hadn't wanted to let her go, even after he'd discovered she was a virgin. So innocent, yet so responsive. He wondered what she'd think if she knew what a sicko he really was, what he would really like to do to her. What he did with all the *mistresses* he'd had here in London. Not the ones in India, of course. That was not their style, or his for that matter. With a sick feeling, he realised that he was just used to getting what he wanted, had been for most of his life and especially since his father's death. He took it for granted,

especially when it came to women, and he wanted Maya.
More than anything he'd ever wanted—anything or anyone.
And he couldn't have her.

Sexually they'd just scratched the surface. He broke
out in a sweat as he imagined exploring the realms of sinful
pleasures her sensual body was capable of. With her being
so responsive, there was no telling how far he could take
her—if she was his. *But she isn't yours and she never will
be.*

That age old, familiar guilt sliced through him. He was
a sick, perverted man. How could he even think of Maya—
an innocent—in that manner? It was bad enough that he indulged his needs with sexually experienced women who
enjoyed it. Now he was stooping even lower, wanting to
introduce Maya to his debauched lifestyle.

His plan was to marry to an Indian woman, confess his
sins to a priest, and become a family man, leaving his sinful
life behind him forever. But that was before he'd met Maya.

He exited the lift and entered the apartment. Tempted
to pour himself a stiff drink, he went for the coffee instead.
He'd have to wait, at least until the afternoon, before he
could allow himself alcohol.

Who had told her about his private life? he wondered
grimly. Sanjay? How the *hell* did Sanjay know? And worst
of all, just how much did Sanjay know about his very private sex-life? Surely nothing. God knew he'd always been
discreet to the extreme. Clara would sometimes make fun of
his paranoia regarding his privacy, and she'd get punished
for it as well, not that she'd minded, of course. Anyway,
Clara and all the ones that had come before, as well as
Anushka, in India, were history now. The truth was that he
hadn't been with another woman since he'd laid eyes on
Maya. The thought of even touching another woman was
almost repulsive to him, yet touching her, making love to
her, had shifted the ground he walked on.

But this morning had been a disaster! He threw himself onto one of the sofas, recalling his unreasonable behaviour toward her. His anger at having her and then having to let her go had driven him to the edge. Yet his rage had not been able to prevent him from taking her once again in a wild and frenzied manner that was completely alien to him, who'd always prided himself on being in control. That had always been one of the highlights of his sexual perversions, being in control. Yet, it seemed that he had no restraint where she was concerned. And his needs completely overtook him in a way that was altogether too disturbing. Then there had been that tenderness as well, another dimension of himself that was completely new and even more disturbing. Caring and tenderness were just not his *thing* and had certainly never turned him on before, not until last night, that is. When he'd carried her supine body back to the bedroom and laid her on the bed, he had sat there for ages just watching her sleep. She had looked so beautiful, lying there with her glorious hair spread out across the pillow, her face as pure and innocent as a child's, and all the anger had disappeared, leaving just a gaping hole of emptiness that was still with him now. Nothing could assuage this feeling, except having her back with him, and that was not going to happen. He made his way into the bedroom, gazing at the tousled bed with anguished eyes, instinctively he grabbed the white terry-cloth robe she had worn and, with a tormented groan, pressed it to his face.

CHAPTER 13

Maya walked briskly along the wide sidewalks of Princes Street, relieved to see that the throngs of shoppers were becoming steadily less with each passing day. It had been two weeks since she'd arrived back in Edinburgh and the Festival had just been winding to an end. Although it was over now, there were still quite a few tourists about, and the locals had just about had enough. She turned into Hanover Street, impatient to get home and out of the steady drizzle. It had been a long but interesting day and she was looking forward to starting work at the Bradfield Center at the beginning of October. She would be working with young people, teenagers mostly, with all sorts of emotional problems from anorexia to family problems to drug addiction. And she was feeling quite enthusiastic about being able to use her skills to help others.

Finally, she reached the three-story, old building in which her flat—or rather her mother's flat—was located, climbing the curved staircase to reach the door at the very top.

The flat was large, taking up the whole of the top floor: three double bedrooms and a spacious living room connected to the open-plan kitchen. She was happy here. It was far from luxurious—half the size of Rajiv's apartment—but it was comfortable and homely, and she loved the views of the bay in the distance.

"Hi." Josie, her friend, who rented the third bedroom, was in the kitchen frying onions. "So how'd it go at Bradfield's?"

"Really good." Maya shrugged off her damp, brown suede jacket and threw it onto the sofa. "Stuart McClaughlan showed me around and introduced me to the staff, who work on a Saturday. *And* I have my own office!"

Josie grinned, shaking her silky, black, bobbed hair. "Wow." Her big blue eyes shone. "I'm impressed and glad to see you excited about something for a change."

Maya smiled, dropping down onto the sofa beside her jacket, ready to change the subject. "So what are you cooking?" she asked, leaning her head back and propping her boots on the oval coffee table. "Those onions smell yummy."

"Jay's baked beans, Indian-style," Josie said, stirring the onions with a wooden spoon. "Remember when he first made it for us and we were like—*curried baked beans*? *Yuk*! Then we ended up scoffing the lot."

Maya smiled, but there was a hint of concern in her eyes, thinking about Jay and the fact that communication with him had been minimal since her return to Edinburgh. "Oh yes, I remember, the good old days."

"Has he replied to your last email?" Josie asked.

"Yes, but it was very short and didn't really say much." Maya sighed. "Since he moved back to London, his emails have been shorter and sparser, plus his damn phone is always switched off or going straight to voicemail." She paused, frowning. "I think I'll give him a call tomorrow on the landline. He's staying at the London house now."

She'd been putting off calling the home phone with the silly notion that Rajiv might answer it, but that was highly unlikely. He hardly lived there and, even so, it was usually Mrs Travis who answered the calls.

It might be a good thing to talk to Mrs Travis, find out from her how Jay was doing.

"You've got that look on your face again."

Maya stared up at her friend. "What look?"

"That sad troubled look you've been carrying around ever since you got back from London."

"Oh, Josie, don't start on me again!"

"I can't help it, Maya. You're my friend, my best friend! And you've been wasting away these past two weeks. Look how much weight you've lost and, God knows, you were slim enough to begin with!"

"I'm just worried about Jay, that's all." Which was partly true, at least.

"Yeah." Josie wasn't convinced. "And I don't suppose it's got anything to do with that mega-bucks brother of his, who sent you the anklets."

Maya dragged her hands through her rain-dampened hair. "The anklets were a thank you gift for me helping Jay through a difficult time. You read the note yourself!"

"Come on, Maya, I wasn't born yesterday." Josie crossed her arms, leaning against the kitchen counter, ready to do battle. "When are you going to tell me what really happened?"

"I already told you, there was this…attraction, but he's looking to settle down with an Indian wife. It may be Kirti, the girlfriend I told you about." Josie nodded, watching her intently. "Or perhaps some other suitable Indian girl."

Josie nodded again. She'd already heard most of this. "Okay, but you haven't told me how far this attraction went. Did he talk to you about his feelings, the fact that he's planning on getting married, yet he wants you? He's obviously still into you, otherwise, he wouldn't have sent you a pair of platinum anklets."

"They're not platinum, Josie, they're silver."

"They're platinum, Maya. Now are you going to tell me what the hell's going on, 'cause the guy sounds like bad news to me!"

"He's not *bad news*." Why was she defending him? "And he was honest and upfront with me." She couldn't help smiling at the memory. "He told me he could never offer me marriage."

Josie's eyes widened. "God, when did he say that?"

Maya hesitated. "The night before I came back to London. I told you the train was delayed." Josie waited, saying nothing and eventually Maya continued. "We ended up going to his apartment."

"His *apartment*? I thought he lived in that mansion in Knightsbridge."

"Yes, well he has his own apartment, as well, by Chelsea Harbour."

Josie shook her head. "God, how the other half live." She paused. "So, did you do it?"

Maya nodded, unable to look her friend in the eye.

"You did it!" Josie turned off the braising onions and scrambled onto the sofa opposite Maya. "You finally did it! So how was it?" Her eyes glued to Maya, a mixture of excitement and concern on her gamine face.

Maya dragged her boots off and crossed her legs, trying to find the words. "It was…well, it was bloody painful, if you'll pardon the pun."

"Oh, Maya, I'm sorry. I know. Not like they make it sound in those stupid novels we read."

Maya nodded. "Yes, but afterward, he was really sweet and caring and then, eventually when we did it again—God, Josie, it was wonderful." She swallowed hard, determined not to shed any tears over him.

"Oh, Maya, baby." Josie jumped off the sofa and came to sit beside her, stroking her hair and making soothing sounds. "Was he shocked when he found out you were a virgin?"

Maya nodded, suppressing the tears and trying to find her voice. "He was totally shocked, angry even," she managed eventually. "That was when he told me he could never offer to marry me," she ended with a tight laugh.

"God, he sounds so complex, all modern man of the world and yet so old-fashioned at the same time."

"Oh, he's complex all right, and don't forget he still believes there's something between Jay and me, so he kept going on about betraying his brother."

"Maya, why didn't you just tell him?"

"I was tempted, believe me, but besides it being Jay's secret to disclose, I realized it's better this way."

Josie frowned. "Better, why?"

"Because there's no point, that's why. He's still going to marry an Indian woman, not that I'm interested in marriage and I told him so. There's no future for the two of us. Even if he wasn't getting married, I live in Edinburgh, he lives in London and travels constantly. We're worlds apart. His life is so completely different from mine." She paused. "And last but not least, can you imagine what it would do to his poor mother? One son's gay and the other's having an affair some weirdo Scots girl!"

They both giggled at her description of herself and the atmosphere eased.

"Okay." Josie stood up. "I'm going to carrying on cooking us a lovely dinner and you are going to eat! We need to fatten you up, girlfriend. So we shall continue this conversation over dinner. I still want to know all the details." She winked suggestively and made her way toward the cooker as Maya stood up and grabbed her boots

"Maya." Her friend's voice was suddenly serious.

"Yes, Josie?"

"He still wants you. You know that don't you?"

Maya stared at her, recalling the morning after and the manner in which they'd parted. "No way! It's over, believe me."

"Those anklets say it all. He still wants you.

"Josie, I told you they were a thank you gift!"

"Not platinum anklets. There's something very personal about a gift like that, almost sensual. Marriage or no marriage, he still wants you."

Maya went to take her shower, feeling better than she had since leaving London. It was good to get things off her chest. Trying to pretend all was well had not been the right approach to take and, as Josie had said, she wasn't born yesterday. Besides that, Maya was really looking forward to starting work. Her visit to the Bradfield Center had left her feeling excited for the first time since arriving back home.

The only thing still niggling at her was that she'd heard so little from Jay. Maybe it was better this way, make a clean break from the whole family. But a part of her was still concerned about him. It was strange for him not to have answered his phone and those short emails were not really telling her anything about his state of mind. She would have to call the London house tomorrow.

හ⁄ඉ⁄හ

The sound of the phone ringing brought Maya suddenly awake and she gazed sleepily at the bedside clock. A quarter to seven on a Saturday morning. She and Josie had stayed up late last night, drinking wine and talking about Jay and Rajiv, of course. Josie had wanted to know all the details and Maya, being a little tipsy, had given them to her, telling her of their time together and the complexities of his traditional Indian values.

Her cell phone was switched off and her mother usually texted before calling the land-line, so it could be her. She padded over to the living room as the ringing continued, a slight feeling of anxiety rearing its head inside of her, but she shook it away. It had to be her mother calling from Cape Town to see how her visit to the Bradfield Center had gone yesterday.

"Hello." She gripped the receiver tightly in her hand and felt her legs turn to mush at the familiar voice on the other end.

"Hello, Maya, it's Rajiv here."

Although her heart soared at the sound of his velvety voice, something in his tone was not quite right. "Rajiv, h— how are you?" She tried to sound pleasantly surprised, but failed miserably.

"I'm okay, I guess." She squeezed her eyes shut as he spoke, allowing her senses to drown in the low, faintly husky tone of his voice. "It's Jay that I'm calling about actually."

Her eyes flew open. "Jay? Why? Is he all right?"

He hesitated. "Yes he's all right. Now." A pause. "Maya, Jay tried to kill himself last night."

She sank to her knees on the hard wooden floorboards as her vision clouded over and her mind began racing. *I should have phoned him. I shouldn't have left it so long!*

"Maya, are you okay?" Rajiv's voice sounded tense and uneasy through the phone line. "He's all right. Do you hear me? He's going to be all right."

She nodded, weak and shaky with relief. "I hear you. Oh, Rajiv, I should have called him. I was planning on calling today, but I shouldn't have waited so long."

A sob rose in her throat, making it impossible for her to continue.

"So when was it that you spoke to him last?" he asked tautly.

"Um, just before he left for London, I think," she replied, forcing her mind to function.

"And you didn't tell him about us, did you?"

Maya caught her breath. "Of course not!"

"Thank God." She heard the tension leave his voice. "Thank you, God. I thought maybe—maybe he'd found out, and that was why he'd taken the overdose."

Josie walked into the room, her expression sleepy but concerned. Maya shook her head.

"Rajiv, listen to me. Jay's mental state has got nothing to do with you and me," she said earnestly. "You have to believe me. I wish I could say more, but please believe me when I say it's not because of you."

She heard him draw a shaky breath. "God, I hope you're right," he muttered, and she would have given anything to have put her arms around him right there and then. "Last night was pure hell. I was so sure—never mind. That's not why I'm ringing. He wants to see you, Maya. You were the first person he asked for when he regained consciousness."

ॐ

Maya stared down at the River Thames below her as the plane circled Heathrow Airport. Would this river always remind her of Rajiv? she wondered with an aching heart. It seemed unreal that she was back here again, but Jay's suicide attempt was all too real, and Rajiv had booked her on the first available flight to London. She tried to ignore the curious gazes from the executive businessmen who had boarded the plane with her. But in a long denim skirt and her lilac, lamb's-wool cardigan, she felt she stuck out like a sore thumb.

Her eyes scanned the people waiting at Arrivals and she tried to remember who Rajiv had said would be meeting her here. Probably Bijal, she surmised, and then she felt her world suddenly tilt on its axis as her gaze clashed with a

pair of blue eyes fringed with thick black lashes. He was
leaning against one of the airport pillars, and she watched
hungrily as he straightened up and came toward her. His
white shirt was creased, open at the throat, and his black
hair was tousled. A stubble of growth darkened his mouth
and jaw-line, but he was still the most attractive male she
had ever seen. It took all Maya's willpower to restrain herself from falling into his arms.

"Hi," he said softly, taking the bulky embroidered bag
from her and slinging it over his shoulder. His eyes had not
left her face, and she felt a trembling relief when he took
her hand and led her out of the airport. "Come. Bijal's waiting to take us to the hospital."

She nodded dumbly, gaining strength from the warmth
of his hand. Once seated in the back of the Mercedes, driving along the wet London roads, Maya began to feel a little
more herself. The glass partition between them and Bijal
closed and she felt able to speak openly.

Intense blue eyes bored into hers, before dropping to
roam intimately down her body. "You look different." He
frowned. "Have you lost weight?"

"Maybe, just a little. I've been really busy," she lied.
"But Josie, my flatmate's, determined to fatten me up."

"Josie? Is that a male or a female flatmate?"

"Female, of course," she answered. "She's like my best
friend. We've known each other since school. She's also
very worried about Jay. I'll have to call her as soon as I've
seen him."

He continued to gaze at her, the dark stubble and shadows beneath his eyes, somehow adding to his undeniable
attraction.

"So how is he since we spoke on the phone?" she
asked, hoping he wasn't going to bring up her weight loss
again. "Has there been any change?"

Rajiv nodded, looking gaunt and tired. "The doctors are

pleased with his progress, although they keep stressing how lucky he was." He leaned his head back against the soft leather seat and turned to gaze at her with heavy lidded eyes. "And they're absolutely right. If Mrs Travis hadn't found him—God knows." He closed his eyes at the thought.

"What time did it happen?" she asked, longing to reach out and stroke his lean, tired features.

"Around nine o'clock last night," he told her. "Mrs Travis was hanging about a little later than usual, thank the Lord. Jay had gone upstairs about an hour before, when the phone rang." He raked long fingers through his tousled hair. "Thank God for that phone call! It was a friend of his from Switzerland, I think, so Mrs Travis went up to call him. He wasn't in his room. She found him in my mother's room. He'd discovered some sleeping tablets in her cupboard, poured himself a glass of water, lay down on her bed, and taken the whole bottle."

Maya felt sick at the picture he painted. She reached out and clasped his hand, the urge to touch him too strong to resist. "Have you told your mother yet?"

"No." He looked down at her hand before lifting it to his mouth. "She's still in India and Jay begged me not to tell her, so we'll wait and see." He pressed his lips against her palm, and Maya felt her body melt. "I swore to myself that I wouldn't touch you," he murmured as her fingers traced the sensual shape of his lips and, with an unsteady groan, he cupped the back of her head and brought her mouth unwaveringly to his.

Maya drowned in the raw urgency of his kiss, her hands sinking into his hair as the top half of her body pressed urgently into him. His mouth was ravaging hers, his fingers holding her head fast as his tongue forced a response from her.

The taste and smell of him was overpowering her senses, molten lava surging through her veins. Time stood still.

She forgot where she was, why she was there, and all that mattered was that he continue holding her and making love to her mouth.

"God, I've missed you," he breathed against her lips. "My life has been pure hell without you!"

He spread out her long hair, twisting and tangling it against his face before bringing her mouth back to his once again.

She caressed his neck, the strong column of his throat, her tight nipples rubbing erotically against his chest. It was heaven to be in his arms again and, of their own accord, her fingers moved down over his flat stomach to find and cup the thrusting heat of his manhood, pressing tautly against the cloth of his trousers. Suddenly, he stiffened and expelled a shuddering groan, dragging her hand roughly away.

"No Maya. No!" He breathed raggedly, his fingers still gripping her wrist. "Listen to me. I promised myself that I'd keep away from you, and God help me, that's the way it's got to be."

She pulled away from him feeling mortified and hurt. "Why?" It came out in a whisper.

He shut his eyes against her alluring beauty and swore with frustration. "Because of Jay, Maya. Why do you think?"

As if on cue, Bijal brought the car to a halt outside a tall building, a private clinic—manicured lawns and neatly trimmed hedges enjoying the steady drizzle of the damp and dreary day.

The walk through the hospital accomplished in silence. There was nothing to say, she felt, and besides, she needed to prepare herself for Jay.

After all, he was the reason she was here, and it seemed she needed reminding of that.

"I'll wait for you in the lounge over there," Rajiv said, pointing to a brightly lit room at the end of the passage.

"Here's the nurse now. She'll show you to Jay's room. Take as long as you like. I don't mind waiting."

The expression on his face was inscrutable, and Maya had no choice but to leave him and follow the nurse.

Jay looked pale and weak, lying there on the hospital bed, but he offered her a wan smile as she entered the small comfortable room. Pictures on the wall gave it a homely feel while the window looked out onto the gardens below.

"Maya. Oh, Maya." He held out his hand. "You got here fast. My brother's doing I presume."

She bent over the side of the bed and hugged him. "Jay, you gave us such a fright." Her voice was choked with emotion and her eyes filled with tears.

"I'm sorry, so sorry."

They held each other for a long time, words unnecessary between them.

Finally, Maya lifted her head. "Do you want to talk about it?"

He took a deep breath and wiped his eyes on the plush linen sheet. "I don't know where to start."

"Wherever you like," she suggested gently.

"Well, I thought that being back in London would somehow perk me up a bit, but it didn't." He squeezed her hand as she sat patiently on the bed beside him. "You see that house holds some bad memories for me. That's where my father and I argued before he had the accident, and I feel his presence in so many places."

"Oh Jay," she responded tenderly. "Why didn't you leave? Why didn't you come up to Edinburgh."

He shrugged his shoulders. "It's a strange thing, depression. You seem to lose all your energy. I felt so drained, I ended up just moping around." He stared off into space, dark smudges visible beneath his eyes. "Rajiv came round for dinner sometimes, but to tell you the truth, he seemed quite down in the dumps as well, even though he tried to hide it. He's broken up with Kirti, you know," he told her with a shrug of indifference.

Maya shook her head, not allowing herself to feel pleased about that.

"Anyway, last night I went into my mother's room, looking for some old photos of my father, and Rajiv and I when we were kids. Maybe I shouldn't have done that 'cause looking at them made me feel even worse, and then, in the drawer right next to the photo album was this bottle of sleeping tablets. It felt like they were meant to be there. Meant for me!" He covered his face with his hands and Maya reached over to stroke his hair. "Next thing I remembered was waking up here, feeling like absolute hell." His voice was muffled as he fell back against the pillow, pressing his palms to his eyes.

"Did you know that Kurt phoned you last night?" she asked, suddenly remembering what Rajiv had said on the drive over here.

Jay jerked up again, staring at her. "No. Are you sure it was him? Who told you?"

A smile touched her lips. "Rajiv told me on the way over here. In fact, that phone call probably saved your life. That's why Mrs Travis came to find you."

"Do you know if she spoke to him afterward?"

Maya frowned. "No, I don't. He might be worried about you Jay. Why don't you contact Mrs Travis and ask her what happened?"

He nodded eagerly, reaching for the phone beside the bed. As she observed him talking to the housekeeper, a glimmer of hope flared within her. He looked more animated than she had seen him in a long time, asking detailed questions and listening with avid interest to what Mrs Travis had to say.

"You were right, Maya, it was Kurt," he said excitedly once he'd put down the phone. "After she found me unconscious, poor Mrs Travis was in a terrible state. She ran downstairs to call Rajiv, grabbed the phone and asked Kurt to hang up so that she could call an ambulance. He wanted to know what had happened. She just told him there was an emergency and to call back later, which he hasn't done." He paused, frowning hard. "What should I do now?"

"You phone him, of course. He must be worried. Do you have his number?"

Jay nodded. "Of course. I know his number better than my own. I've been tempted to phone him so many times."

"Well, now's your chance," she encouraged, praying that Kurt's response would be a positive one. If Jay could sort things out with Kurt this whole situation might finally be resolved.

He dialled the number with trembling fingers and waited taking her hand and squeezing it tightly. "There's no reply," he said finally. "It went straight to voicemail. Damn, damn, damn it."

He fell back against the pillows, looking suddenly exhausted, his face shiny with sweat and his breathing labored.

Maya poured him some water, unsure of what to do next, when the nurse entered and, seeing how pale and tired he looked, told Maya that she would have to say her goodbyes and leave.

Maya wiped the moisture from his brow. "Jay, before I go. Your brother's very worried about you. Have you thought about telling him?"

His gaze was unwavering. "Yes, I'm going to tell him—soon. Just let me get hold of Kurt. I need to speak to him and I promise I'll tell Rajiv."

She breathed a tremulous sigh. It might be convenient having Rajiv thinking there was something between her and Jay, but the whole deception was beginning to wear on her.

ल्ल्ल्ल

Rajiv gazed out at the wet weather with unseeing eyes. He'd spent a lot of time in this waiting room and in the hospital chapel. Most of that time had been a torment, not knowing if his brother was going to live or not. He'd prayed, really prayed, like never before: Hail Mary's, Our Father's, Glory Be's, the lot.

Thank God, it was over.

Or was it?

He still did not know why it was that Jay had attempted suicide, although he was becoming convinced that his affair with Maya might not be the reason. *If you could call it an affair.* It may have been only one night of mindless passion but it had affected him more than anything in his life. He was obsessed with her, infatuated. And these past weeks since she'd left England had been pure hell. Much as he had tried to carry on with his life as before, it had been almost impossible to do so. He had ended up drinking far too much, not eating for days on end, and he knew that he'd been hell to work with too.

Seeing her again today had been an exquisite kind of torture. He had sworn on his brother's life that he would not touch her, that if his brother survived, Rajiv would do everything in his power to bring the two of them together again. Though he had sworn to keep his distance, it hadn't taken him long to succumb to his desires. Dear God, only a few minutes with her in the car and he'd been all over her. *But she had started it,* he tried to justify to himself. Was God deliberately tormenting him?

He had to keep his distance. What kind of a man made a promise to God, with his brother's life at stake, and broke it within minutes? He rubbed the aching muscles at the back of his neck and wondered, not for the first time, if there was a reconciliation going on in the room down the passage.

The thought clawed at his insides with sadistic zeal. What if they decided to marry? Could he bear to live with Maya as his sister-in-law? And yet if that was what it took to save his brother, then wouldn't it be worth the pain? His hands were shaking slightly, and a film of sweat had broken out on his skin. God, he'd sell his soul for a glass and a bottle of whisky right now. A movement caught his eye and he turned to see her walking toward him, her flawless features serene under the stark fluorescent lights. And as always, he felt the sharp kick of desire at the sight of her.

He thrust his hands into his trouser pockets where they wouldn't be tempted to touch her. "Everything okay?" he asked, searching her delicate face for clues.

"Yes, fine." She lifted her head to look at him, her lips tilted upward and he wondered what the hell she looked so pleased about. "He needs to rest. The nurse says we can come back this evening."

Bijal was waiting for them downstairs in the parking lot, concern evident on his face. Rajiv reassured him that all was well. The chauffer had known Jay since childhood and the shock of his attempted suicide had hit all of them hard.

"Can you take us to Knightsbridge, please Bijal?" Rajiv said. He needed to put some space between them, to take control of his emotions. He would drop her at the house and then go back to his apartment for a much-needed drink. Leaning against the car door, he tried to still his leaping senses as the familiar smell of her invaded his nostrils.

"Do we have to go to Knightsbridge?" she asked softly, her cat eyes giving out signals that he could not resist. "Take me to your apartment, Rajiv. Please."

A wave of heat invaded his body as he stared back at her. Did she realize what she was asking?

"Maya, I don't think that's such a good idea," he said through clenched teeth, aware that Bijal could hear most of their conversation with the partition now open.

His gaze was drawn to her mouth as her tongue gently probed her upper lip, and his body responded automatically. He'd promised himself, and God, that he would keep away from her. If he took her back to his place, there was no way in hell he could keep his hands off her, and it didn't look like that was what she wanted, anyway. What the hell kind of game was she playing?

"We need to talk, Rajiv." Her voice had a husky intimate sound to it, and her chest rose and fell as her breathing quickened. His eyes focused on her breasts and he realized with a stab of lust that he could see her nipples clearly outlined through the soft lamb's wool.

Talking was the last thing on his mind right now. "Leave Knightsbridge, Bijal." His voice sounded hoarse. "Can you take us to my apartment please?"

It didn't take them long to reach the tall apartment block close to Chelsea Harbour, and he waved the chauffer away with a feeling of relief. He trusted the man to be discreet. Bijal was too loyal for anything else, but *hell,* what must it look like leaving Jay at the hospital and going straight to his apartment with her?

Rajiv bit back a wave of self-disgust. It was not his fault. He had tried to be strong and take her to the house. God was playing games with him, pushing him and his empty oaths to the edge. She was the one who insisted on coming here, tempting him with her inviting body and intimate looks. And here he was playing right into her hands.

"Let's go," he said abruptly, throwing her bag over his shoulder and climbing the steps that led to the foyer of the building, uncaring that she had to run to keep up with him.

They said nothing going up in the lift and, even though he avoided looking at her, he was still torturously aware of her. The fact that they would soon be alone in his apartment was filling him with a mixture of dread and desire.

The apartment was bright, irrespective of the dull damp

weather. The huge windows took advantage of every scrap of light as the building was taller than most of the others around.

He dropped her bag onto one of the sofas and walked straight over to the liquor cabinet. "Would you like a drink, because I could certainly use one?" he said tightly.

She was standing in the middle of the room, her hands linked together and he realized that she didn't seem as sure of herself now as she had been before in the car.

"Um, yes why not?"

He watched her tongue sneak out to moisten her upper lip. She was nervous all right.

"I'll have whatever it is you're having."

He raised his eyebrows. "Whisky, you sure?"

She nodded and he turned to pour himself a large—and her a single—measure of whiskey, sure that she was having the drink to steady her nerves. *Well, join the club, sweetheart*, he thought with a cynical twist of his lips. He handed her the crystal tumbler and then moved back, keeping a safe distance between them before savoring a mouthful of the burning liquid. Her presence here was stretching his nerves to breaking point, particularly after what he'd gone through in the past twelve hours.

He turned to face her. "Okay, now do you mind telling me what the hell game it is you're playing, Maya?"

She gagged on the neat whisky, her eyes wide and innocent. "I'm not playing any games, Rajiv. How can you say that?"

He knocked back the remainder of his drink, enjoying the way it settled and eased the knot in the pit of his stomach. Depositing the tumbler back onto the tray, he turned his suspicious gaze on her.

She pushed her hair back with nervous fingers and he noticed how the movement lifted her breasts and separated the cardigan from her denim skirt, offering him an enticing glimpse of bare, pale skin. Damn, the whisky was weakening his resolve, causing a twist of lust to curl deep inside him.

"I'm saying it because I value my brother's life and I think it would destroy him to know there was something between us." It was a warning to him, as well as her.

His pulse quickened as she came toward him.

"You're wrong Rajiv, Jay doesn't want me—not in that way."

His lean mouth curved sardonically. "I wish I could believe that."

"You have to believe it. It's the truth," she stopped just inches away from him, those emerald eyes warm and inviting. "I can't explain but, hopefully, soon you'll come to understand everything."

Her nearness was playing havoc with his senses. When she reached out and put her glass down beside his, he felt the firm swell of her breast against his arm. "You're talking in riddles, Maya," he ground out, as the blood rushed through his veins.

The fresh jasmine smell of her hair was teasing his nostrils, evoking memories all too vivid, and he longed to press his face into the sensual silkiness of it, forgetting everything but the desperate need to lose himself inside her again. To feel that frenzied release just one more time.

Her hand reached out to cup his tautened jaw and he flinched, gripping her wrist and yanking her up against him as his control finally snapped, giving way to the flood of overwhelming desire.

"Wait, Rajiv." She was in his arms now, soft and pliant, but her mouth evaded his.

"For God's sake, Maya." He sank his fingers into her hair, twisting it painfully in his grasp. "Stop playing with me!"

"I need you to know—" Her mouth was lush and tormenting, but she wouldn't let him have it. "Why it is I'm doing this."

Rajiv frowned, his brain having difficulty functioning. Her breasts swelled against his chest, the nipples boring holes through his shirt, and he reached down to cup her pert bottom and press it against the aching ridge of his erection. "Why?" He almost groaned out loud at the pure pleasure of it. If he didn't get inside her soon, he was going to go crazy.

"Seeing Jay—it just made me realize how fragile, how precious life is."

He swore savagely, his mouth hungry for her. "And what's that got to do with this, with us."

"I want to be with you, even though I know there's no future in it."

His teeth grazed her exposed shoulder. "I don't want to talk about the future. I don't want to think about it. All I want is you," he growled deep in his throat, twisting her hair tight in his fist, his mouth finally capturing hers in a forceful, plundering kiss.

He was fully aroused. The swollen ridge of his erection pressed against her soft belly and she moaned softly, lifting herself onto her toes so that he was now cradled in the yielding folds between her legs. Her mouth was driving him wild. Her swollen lips suckling his tongue made him break out in a film of sweat.

He lifted her up by her bottom and carried her to the sofa, knowing that he simply couldn't make it to the bedroom this time. Lowering her onto the soft leather couch, he knelt between her thighs.

Her skirt was almost at her waist, some of the studs having popped open, allowing him a tantalizing view of long bare legs and virginal white panties. With shaking fingers, he pulled open the rest of the studs, suppressing the urge to rip off her panties and thrust himself into her.

"God, Maya, do you know what you do to me?" he

breathed as the skirt fell apart, exposing her slender hips to his gaze.

She stared up at him through half closed eyes. "I know what you do to me," she whispered huskily, her legs splayed helplessly apart.

He reached down to undo the buttons of her cardigan, exposing her swollen breasts with their dusky nipples to his hungry eyes.

With a tormented groan, Rajiv lowered himself into her waiting arms. It was pure heaven to feel her soft, yielding body with him kneeling in adoration before her. The potent heat between her legs seeped through the barrier of his trousers to the turgid swell of his loins. Her fingers were in his hair, her nails scraping against his scalp, as he pulled his mouth from hers to drag some air into his lungs. His body was ready to explode, yet he was still fully clothed. As if reading his mind, Maya's fingers slid down to unbutton his shirt.

Her pert breasts felt wonderful against his bare chest, her nipples tight and inviting. He needed to taste them, to feel them surge against his tongue. He heard her gasp with pleasure as he pushed them together, with his hands and them suckled greedily on each of them in turn.

She began to move restlessly, grinding her hips against his throbbing flesh and driving him wild with her impatience. He swore savagely. Didn't she realize his entire body was ready to shatter? The ache between his thighs was unbearable. He reached down to unfasten his trousers with fingers that shook, expelling a groan of relief as his straining flesh spilled free and he shoved his pants down to his knees. God knew, he wanted to be completely naked with her, but his needs were too urgent to allow time for anything else.

A shudder of pure lust tore through him as her cool slender fingers closed around his rock hard erection.

"Don't. For pity's sake, Maya, don't do that." His voice broke as he pushed her hand away from his engorged flesh.

With a superhuman effort, he hooked his fingers into her panties and pulled them down, over her ankle boots. His breathing was hard and urgent as he stared down at her beautiful nakedness, that inviting mound barely covered by soft coppery hair. Running his hands up the inside of her legs to the soft damp opening between her thighs, he spread those pouting lips, sliding his fingers into her drenched cleft. Her body jerked when he found that swollen nub and circled it insistently, watching her body tauten and unfold through a haze of lust.

He eased one finger deep inside her, releasing a gush of moisture. When her slick inner muscles eagerly clasped at that firm intrusion, Rajiv's control totally gave way. Lowering himself onto her, he sucked in his breath at the sensation of her smooth hot silk against his swollen shaft. Then with unerring accuracy, he thrust himself into her eager waiting flesh.

He threw back his head and groaned as her muscles tightened around him, grunting with each short powerful thrust of his hips, straining to hold onto the exquisite pleasure of it, to hold back the tidal wave of sensation building up inside him. But as Maya sobbed softly, digging her nails into his backside, he felt her orgasm shudder around him, and his own climax exploded, wave after wave sweeping him away in sweet, hot delight as he emptied himself into her inviting womb.

CHAPTER 14

Maya stretched her slim aching body, feeling rather like a sleek and satisfied cat. She turned her face to gaze at the dark, tousled head sleeping beside her and smiled softly. It was no wonder that he was fast asleep. The man had to be utterly exhausted. He had spent the night before pacing the hospital floor, waiting to see if his brother would survive, and then he had brought her back here and made mad and passionate love to her for hours on end.

After their first frenzied coupling in the living room, he had carried her into the shower and made love to her all over again, but this time he'd been exquisitely sweet and indulgent, and she shivered with delight at the memory of it.

She had licked and tasted every inch of his body, moving downward to kneel in front of him. He had tried to stop her, of course, but this time she'd been determined. Life was too short. Jay had made her realize that. She was determined to make the most of every minute she had together with this man who was the only one in her universe that could make her feel so mindlessly wild and passionate.

So she had knelt before him, stroking away his protests and finally taken him in her mouth. Rajiv seemed crazed by the sight and sensation of her lips driving him to the edge and back. She had loved the feel of rock-hard flesh covered by such fine skin and taken him deep into her mouth. Hearing him gasp and groan had only egged her on. Leaning his arm heavily against the shower wall, while the other cupped her head, he gently thrust himself into her warm, welcoming mouth. His head hung weakly from his taut shoulders as he gazed down in agony at her innocent, experimental ministrations.

Finally, he could take no more and dragged her up, locking her legs around him, pounding mercilessly into her, bringing them both to a shattering orgasm that seemed to go on, and on, and on.

They had eventually ended up here in the bed and, by that time, she'd felt the need of a soft mattress beneath her. Delighting in the awareness of just how much power she seemed to hold over him, she ran her fingers over her protesting thigh muscles, enjoying every ache and pain. It was wonderful to watch his eyes darken and his breathing quicken with just the right touch or look from her. And she would love to spend many hours discovering just how far this uncontrollable passion could take them.

She frowned. He had to know that this was just a passing interlude. Didn't he? Even though, after making love on the bed, Rajiv had taken her into the kitchen and made them both a sandwich, the conversation had centred mainly round her and her upcoming job at the Bradfield Center. He seemed interested in the issues facing the youth and her role within the Center. From his pertinent questions, it was obvious that he knew a lot about non-profit and non-governmental organizations. Maya recalled Jay telling her that Rajiv was involved with many charities in India, that he was a well-known and respected figure over there. Of course, that was just another reason why he needed an Indian wife at his side, she surmised glumly. Anyway, it was pleasant to talk about things unrelated to their current situation, things that didn't lead to arguments or tensions. Conversations which did not leave her feeling depressed and uncomfortable with herself and her role in this complex and completely unique family of his.

Once they'd finished eating, he had insisted on taking her back to the bedroom and, getting out an impressive-looking hair dryer, proceeded to dry her dampened hair. Lovingly brushing it, he held it up to his face in a way that caused a melting desire deep in her body. Her heady newfound powers had incited her to press him back onto the bed and climb on top of him, teasing and tormenting him—until, with one smooth move, he'd flipped her onto her back and taken control, his powerful body seducing hers into sweet surrender.

But nothing had been said, that nagging little voice at the back of her mind echoed insistently. They had not spoken about Jay at all, and she felt that if they had, she probably would have blurted out the truth. For, after what had passed between them, Maya knew that she could no longer deny Rajiv anything. The only way to prevent this from continuing was by staying away from him. As soon as Jay was well again and, hopefully back with Kurt, she was going back home to get on with her life and this *affair* would end. It was devastating even to contemplate, but she refused to be cowed by it. It would be hell not seeing him again, but she was not prepared to be his mistress or…whatever…on the side.

She reached over his sleeping form, careful not to disturb him, and peered at the time on his slim platinum watch lying on the bedside table. It was almost five p.m., and Maya couldn't help wondering how Jay was doing. Had he managed to get hold of Kurt? It would be wonderful if they decided to reconcile, and it would surely do Jay good to have the constant support of the person that he loved. She sighed to herself. Would his mother ever be able to accept it? Pressing her lips to the smooth brown skin of Rajiv's shoulder, Maya closed her eyes and, ignoring all the doubts that were niggling at her brain, savored the pleasure of just feeling his body against hers.

The insistent ringing of the phone coming from the living room awakened her and Rajiv, who lifted his sleepy head.

"God, Maya, have I been out for long?"

He raked his tousled hair back with a lazy hand, and Maya felt a stab of lust. God, she was as insatiable as he was.

"About an hour," she murmured as his hand moved possessively from her thigh to the curve of her breast. "But you needed the rest."

"Hmm, I guess did," he agreed, pressing his lips against the delicate curve of her jaw. "You make me feel like I'm sixteen again."

The phone, which had stopped ringing, began again and he raised his head, a worrying look clouding his eyes.

"Do you think it could be the hospital?" he questioned, drawing away from her mentally as well as physically.

"It could be. We're supposed to visit this evening," she said, trying to keep the tremble from her voice. The whole atmosphere had suddenly cooled.

"God!" he exclaimed, climbing swiftly out of the bed. "What if he's found out that you're here?"

Even in the dim light Maya could see his face had paled at the thought, and she bit back the words: *It doesn't matter*, because actually it did matter. Jay would be devastated to know that she was sleeping with his brother, and she didn't want to upset him in the state he was in just now. Rajiv strode out of the room and a few seconds later the phone stopped ringing.

Throwing back the covers with a growing sense of despondency, Maya wished that she could put some clothes on, but her bag was in the living room and the skirt and cardigan she'd been wearing were probably still strewn across the living room floor. The white bathrobe she'd worn earlier was lying at the bottom of the bed. With a shiver running through her, she quickly pulled it on and stood uncertainly in the middle of the room. She would wait until he finished on the phone before going to collect her clothes. Walking across to the window, she pulled the curtains open just enough to gaze out at the dull sky.

It had stopped raining, but there was an atmosphere of damp grayness about. Even the river looked quite murky and dismal. Rather like her mood, she recognized, feeling suddenly close to tears. Damn it, she was so tired of this whole charade, this deceit! And this was not just about Jay anymore. It concerned Rajiv who was being put through hell for his supposed sins.

Earlier, in the shower, she couldn't help noticing that he had also lost weight. His hipbones were more prominent, his stomach, almost concave. This situation was dire and could not continue. Once he knew the truth, they could both get on with their lives, but she could not continue to see him. The thought twisted through her like a knife, and she squeezed her eyes shut against the pain. She needed to be strong, to be ready for whatever blows fate held in store for her.

Rajiv re-entered the bedroom, naked and looking more upbeat. "It was Jay," he said. "Thank God, he didn't know you were here."

She stared at him with a mixture of sympathy and anger. How would he feel once he knew there was only friendship between her and Jay? Would he be happy and relieved, eager to continue seeing her on the side, his dirty little secret? Was she strong enough to deny him?

"Maya, are you all right?" He moved toward her.

"Have you heard a word I've said?" His expression hardened as she stepped away from him.

"I'm sorry. What were you saying? How is he?" she murmured, holding the lapels of the robe tightly together.

Rajiv shook his head and sighed. "He sounded good, almost excited really," he remarked, rubbing absently at the hard muscles of his chest. "He wants to see me—and you. He asked me to pick you up on my way to the hospital."

"Well, that's a relief then, isn't it?" she pronounced tightly, and his eyes searched her face.

"You're angry with me, aren't you?" he murmured, and she turned away from his caressing eyes.

"I need to put on some clothes," she stated, walking toward the door.

"For God's sake, Maya, I'm concerned for the well-being of my brother," he appealed. "Do you despise me for that? I'm afraid of how he'll react if he finds out about us. He's very vulnerable at the moment, and you know that."

She turned to face him. "And what if he didn't mind?" she questioned deliberately. "Would that please you?"

He stared at her blankly. "If he didn't mind?" She nodded, watching him carefully. "I'd be extremely happy and relieved, of course," he continued with a frown.

Maya's expression was sceptical now. "Really?" Her lips twisted wryly. "I thought perhaps I might just be a case of the forbidden fruit tasting that much sweeter."

His face became a cold mask as the implications of her words dawned on him, and Maya shivered with sudden regret. Why had she said that? He had done nothing to warrant such an accusation, and her heart shrank at the hurt and anger in his eyes.

"You think I would deliberately set out to seduce my brother's girlfriend just for the hell of it?" he ground out. "That's basically what you're saying, isn't it, Maya?"

There was censure in his steely blue eyes, and she

wanted to run and beg his forgiveness, but felt rooted to the spot.

"Well, it seems your opinion of me has reached an all-time low—and I probably deserve it. God knows, my behavior hasn't been particularly honorable of late. Just don't forget who instigated us spending time alone here today." He moved toward the walk-in closet, his face tight with self-deprecation. "I suggest you get dressed now. Jay sounded impatient to see us, so the sooner we get out of here the better."

Maya went to get her bag from the main room. "Just give me a few minutes to get dressed," she said on her return, avoiding his gaze and sighing with relief when he finally left the room. She had to concentrate on Jay now, her reason for being here.

She had thrown a change of clothing and underwear into her bag in Edinburgh, being in a state of shock at the time. Now she pulled out the skinny jeans and white, long sleeved T-shirt she'd brought with her. Her suede jacket was in the lounge. She'd need that as well with the weather being so cool and dismal. Making her way into the en-suite bathroom, she pushed the erotic memories of the shower they'd shared earlier out of her mind, ignoring the water puddles and damp towels strewn across the floor.

Maya grabbed the brush he'd used to dry her hair, trying to tame its dishevelled, tousled state. Everything around her reminded her of their love-making, and it took all her self-control to focus on the job at hand. There was no time to shower, so she washed herself at the basin, filled with regret for spoiling the mood between them. Making her way into the bedroom again, she pulled on her ankle boots and, glancing in the long mirror, decided she looked reasonably presentable, except for her flushed cheeks and lips—and the dazed expression in her eyes. Surely, no one would know by looking at her that she had just spent the past few hours having wild and wanton sex with a man who was way out of her reach.

Taking a deep, steadying breath, she made her way to the main room just as the intercom buzzed.

"That must be Bijal." Rajiv said, his eyes roaming over her, lingering on her swollen mouth.

"Bijal." He lifted the receiver to his ear as Maya shrugged her suede jacket on, waiting. "Sorry Jackson, what is it?" he said tersely.

She knew Jackson to be the concierge who manned the opulent lobby downstairs. Although she had never been properly introduced, she had heard Rajiv greet him by name.

"Okay, send her up." He slammed the receiver back onto the wall unit with unnecessary force. "Shit!"

She gaped at him, still not accustomed to hearing him swear. "What?"

His gaze touched hers and slid away. "I completely forgot. Clara a—friend—was coming round today." Raking his fingers through his hair, he finally looked at her with that flat, cool look she was becoming familiar with. "She needs some advice—business advice—stocks, shares, that type of thing."

Maya shoved her hands into her jacket pockets, not saying anything.

"She inherited some property and funds when her father passed away," he continued, though she wasn't really interested. "Now she needs some advice, doesn't really understand investments, managing finances, that sort of thing."

He was giving her far too much information, and Maya's stomach hollowed. She didn't want to meet this Clara. And she didn't want to hear about him giving her *business* advice. The doorbell pealed and Maya took a step backwards feeling trapped, not wanting anyone to know she was here in his apartment, especially not one of his women, for she was sure that's who this was.

Rajiv opened the door to a petite, striking, blonde woman with a warm smile on her face.

"Rajiv, how are you, darling?" She clasped his shoulders and kissed both his cheeks. "You look tired, baby," she said, still holding onto him.

Maya watched their interchange with an unpleasant, avid curiosity. The woman, Clara, looked to be in her late twenties, but it was difficult to say. With her sleekly styled hair and perfectly made up face, there was an air of sophistication about her that gave the impression of someone older. Wearing a short, black skirt, fitted white shirt, and a long, black trench coat, she looked like she'd just stepped out of a fashion magazine.

"Clara." Rajiv took a step back, forcing her to drop her hands. "This is Maya." He held out his arm and it forced Maya to move toward them with as much composure as she could muster.

Clara gazed up at her, her eyes narrowing ever so slightly. "Maya, how nice to meet you." She held out a small, manicured hand.

Maya hesitated, just a second then shook the other woman's hand, letting go as quickly as possible. "How do you do?"

"Clara," Rajiv interjected to Maya's relief. The woman had been summing her up, taking in her worn, suede jacket, high-street clothes, and scuffed boots in one sweeping glance, leaving Maya feeling awkwardly tall and inadequate. "Maya's a friend of Sanjay's."

She was so polished and so petite. Even with those killer, stiletto boots on, she hardly reached Rajiv's chin, and Maya felt like a frumpy beanstalk beside her.

"Sanjay's had an—accident," he continued, and Maya tried to keep focus on what he was saying. "That's why I completely forgot about our meeting. We were just on our way to the hospital."

"Oh, dear." Clara sounded quite concerned. "Is he going to be all right?"

"Yes, he's going to be fine. He tripped and fell down some stairs, but he's okay now, thank God," he lied smoothly and Maya knew she had to get away. "We'll just have postpone until next week, okay?"

"Can you please excuse me?" Her voice was husky with emotion, but right now, she didn't really care. "I need to go to the loo before we leave."

Before either of them could speak, she made her way down the passage and strode into the bedroom. About to close the bedroom door, she heard Clara's laugh.

"Rajiv, you naughty boy," Clara said.

Maya gripped the doorknob.

"I didn't know you were into cradle snatching, darling. How old is she?"

Quietly Maya closed the door and made her way to the bathroom, seating herself on the closed lid of the toilet and staring down at their mess on the bathroom floor, waiting for him to finish conversing with his mistress. For she *was* his mistress, of that Maya had no doubt.

CHAPTER 15

Bijal had called up while Clara was there. He was waiting downstairs to take them to the hospital. It had been a relief to send Clara on her way, before she could ask anymore, snide questions about Maya. *Christ,* Rajiv was furious with himself for forgetting the damn meeting with her. But could he really blame himself, with all that had happened in the past twenty four hours? It was no wonder he'd forgotten the stupid meeting, which he'd agreed to simply to assuage his guilt for breaking it off with her.

Maya had exited the bathroom after Clara left, looking pale and drawn, and Rajiv could just imagine what was going on in her head. He wondered what dirty deeds her imagination was conjuring up. But that desolate look in her eyes had left him feeling guilty as hell. The meeting with Clara had been exactly what he'd said—assisting and advising her on how to handle her late father's estate. Their relationship had been over the minute he'd set eyes on Maya. But how could he convince her of that?

"I'm sorry about that, Maya," he said, resisting the temptation to touch her. "With all that's happened, I completely forgot she was coming today."

"She's your mistress, isn't she?"

He rubbed the back of his neck. "Ex-mistress. I told you, I haven't touched another woman since we met."

She shrugged, crossing her arms beneath her breasts, avoiding his gaze. "It's really none of my business."

"Maya, look at me, please."

She forced herself to look at him, her eyes telling him nothing.

"It's over with me and her. Even before I met you, it was on its way out," he said. "Today's meeting was completely innocent. I told you, I was just giving her some business advice."

She nodded her head absently, moving back toward the bedroom. "I need to get my bag," she said. "It'll be best if I stay at the house in Knightsbridge tonight and we need to hurry. Jay must be wondering where we are."

"No!" He had to clench his fists to prevent himself from grabbing her. "Please, stay here tonight. I don't want you staying in that big house alone. Besides," he added. "We need to talk—later—after we've seen Sanjay."

She disappeared into the bedroom and returned a few seconds later, her bag slung over her shoulder. "There's nothing to talk about, Rajiv. We need to go to the hospital, now."

He wanted to roar his frustration—at himself, at her, at the world, but she was right about one thing. They needed to leave for the hospital now.

The drive to the hospital was completed in silence, even though the glass partition between them and Bijal was closed. Even though he was desperate to convince her that there was nothing between himself and Clara, desperate to convince her to stay the night with him, now was not the time.

He needed to focus on his brother and the fact that Sanjay had almost lost his life last night. God, was it only last night? It felt like his brother's suicide attempt had happened days ago.

ↄ⁄ↄↄ⁄ↄ

Maya stared out of the window at the darkening London streets. The weather was still dismal, just like her mood, but she shrugged the thought away. It was Sunday evening, so the roads were not that busy and it didn't take them long to reach the private clinic in Holland Park.

The nurse ushered them through to Jay's room. The first thing she noticed was the look of serenity on the younger man's face. It had been many months since Maya had seen him like this and, to her, this was the "old Jay," the easy-going, charismatic young man she remembered from Edinburgh. Then a movement at the window caught her eye.

"Kurt!"

She could hardly believe it, but it was Kurt, with his serious blue eyes, fair hair, and goatee beard, coming toward her, an expression of uncertainty marring his attractive features.

Rajiv stiffened as she hugged the young Swiss man enthusiastically. "When did you arrive in London?" she asked, grinning at him in amazement. "Jay was just trying to phone you earlier today."

"I know, I know." His English was soft and precise with just a hint of an accent. "Jay has been telling me all about it."

He smiled hesitantly at Rajiv and, for the first time, Jay spoke. "Rajiv, I want to introduce you to a very close friend of mine. Kurt, this is my brother Rajiv." There was pride and conviction in his voice.

"How do you do?"

Kurt was exceedingly polite and Maya could see he was apprehensive about this meeting. They shook hands and she noticed a hint of perplexity on Rajiv's face. He moved toward the bed and took his brother's hand in his.

"You look great, Sanjay," he said softly, staring into his brother's shining eyes.

"I know." Jay beamed. "I feel great, Rajiv." He turned to Maya and Kurt, still holding onto his brother's hand. "Maya, could you take Kurt to the canteen for a coffee. He must be parched with all the talking we've been doing. I need to speak to my brother alone."

She caught the look that passed between Jay and Kurt and her heart leapt for them. "Of course. We'll see you guys later."

Rajiv gave her a searching look and Maya smiled at him, the conflicts between them fading into the background now that his brother was finally going to tell him the truth. And, hopefully, put all the agonizing deceit and pretence behind them for good.

After locating the impressive cafeteria and helping themselves to coffee, Maya and Kurt found a quiet table overlooking the gardens, and Kurt relayed to her what had happened when he'd phoned the house the previous evening.

Maya covered her cheeks with her hands once he'd finished talking. "It must have been a terrible shock for you," she said, not wanting to think about what may have happened if he had not phoned.

"Yes, it was." His eyes darkened at the memory. "I feared he was dead when I heard the panic in the housekeeper's voice."

She reached for his hand across the table.

"Such realizations can put a different perspective onto everything," he continued, gaining strength. "Since going back to Bern, I had been waiting and hoping for Jay to contact me. I was missing him badly, but I was also very stubborn. He told you what had happened in Edinburgh, yes?"

She nodded. "I should not have been so hard on him. It was selfish of me. You see, my parents have accepted that I'm gay. It's been easy for me, but, of course it's different for Jay, coming from an Indian family. But I made that stupid ultimatum—" He shut his eyes, squeezing her hand. "Thank God he's all right!"

"Kurt," she said earnestly. "You mustn't blame yourself. Jay has other issues to do with his father. Maybe now he can work through them, especially with you around." She paused. "You are going to be around, aren't you?"

"Of course. We have made many plans during this afternoon and, as you have probably guessed, Jay is going to tell his brother about us." His expression changed. "Do you think he will mind?"

"No." She shook her head. "He's been extremely worried about Jay, so I think he'll be quite relieved."

Kurt smiled broadly, reminding her of their uncomplicated lives in Edinburgh once again. "And maybe also because of you?" He'd had such a wicked sense of humor.

"How do you mean?"

"Well, I notice there is something different about you. I am not sure what it is, but there is definitely a difference."

She flushed at his words. "It's been a very hectic day, Kurt, and don't forget I was in Edinburgh just this morning."

"You misunderstand me, Maya, I did not say that you looked tired, just different." He continued to smile, half apologetically. "Is it because of Rajiv?"

She almost dropped the steaming coffee onto her lap. "I—I don't know what you mean, Kurt?"

He ignored her fumbling avoidance and continued. "He is very attractive, I think, but not like Jay. More...how would you say?...more tough."

She nodded, knowing exactly what he meant.

Kurt's eyes narrowed thoughtfully. "Yes he is quite

opposite to Jay, and I felt something between you and him, I think. So perhaps that is why you look different—more of a woman now, no longer the innocent girl I knew in Edinburgh."

Maya's eyes widened at his last comment, was she more of a woman now? Yes, she suddenly realized. He was right. She did feel more of a woman. The experiences she'd been through in these past weeks—good and bad—had changed her forever.

"Jay told me his family thinks you and him are lovers." He grinned at this. "So perhaps Rajiv will be relieved to know that it is not true?"

Maya stared down at her coffee, much as she hated deceiving people, she couldn't let Kurt know how far her relationship with Rajiv had gone. "Kurt, there's no chance of a relationship between Rajiv and I." There was no deceit in what she was saying now. "He's planning on marrying an Indian woman. It's what he always wanted and, right now, as we speak, his mother is in India looking for a bride for him."

Kurt's blue eyes widened. "His *mother* is looking for a bride for *him*?"

She smiled tightly at the irony of it all. "I know it sounds crazy, but maybe Jay can help you to understand the situation."

"I never knew Jay came from such a…a conventional Indian family."

"I know, Kurt."

Who could have guessed, when they were all living in Edinburgh, that the young and carefree Jay had grown up in such a conservative family, filled with what she saw as old-fashioned, as well as *traditional* customs? Customs that were completely alien to people like her and Kurt.

Kurt frowned, obviously concerned about how this would impact his relationship with Jay. "You say Rajiv will be okay with his brother being gay, but what about his mother?"

Maya had to school her features, not wanting to spoil this happy reunion for Kurt, but she knew in her bones that Anna's reaction to her son's sexuality was going to be very different to Rajiv's.

"I think you should take this one step at a time, Kurt," she said carefully. "Let's see how it goes with Rajiv first, okay?"

He nodded, somewhat reassured by her answer, and Maya smiled warmly, giving his hand another squeeze. "It's so great to have you here and to see Jay so happy, so content. It's wonderful, Kurt."

Their conversation continued on a more positive note, Jay's mother and her reaction put to one side for the moment. Kurt was on a high, but at the same time, he wanted to know all about Jay's depression. He wanted to know what had taken place while Maya was with him, and what happened during her visit to Cranthorp. He was shocked and filled with guilt to hear what Jay had gone through. But Maya reassured him that he could not possibly have known what was going on at the time, and all that anguish was now behind them.

It was over an hour by the time they made their way back up to the waiting room. Maya was aware of a feeling of increasing anxiety tightening like a knot in her stomach, and she was grateful for Kurt's calming presence. A part of her felt like running away from it all, or rather, running away from Rajiv. Would he be angry with her for keeping things from him? Might he see it as a betrayal on her part?

She stared out at the gray London sky, and realized to her surprise that she had become quite fond of this huge metropolis, more than she would ever have imagined, perhaps because Rajiv lived here. Even if she never saw him again, she knew London would always remind her of him. The thought of never seeing him again tore through her, causing actual, physical pain. She breathed deeply, trying to ease the ache in her chest, but she knew that she had to leave as soon as possible. Now that Kurt was here for Jay, she needed to go.

But the pain she was experiencing could not be left behind. It was going to follow her like an unwanted companion, ready to remind her of just what it was she was losing—what might have been.

CHAPTER 16

Rajiv was trying to process what it was his brother was saying. "So, you're telling me that this young man, Kurt, was the reason for your depression, your suicide attempt?"

Jay searched his brother's face, trying to gauge his reaction. "Well, yes—and no. I've been heart-broken, thinking it was over between Kurt and me."

Jay closed his eyes, rubbing his forehead, and Rajiv reached over to hold his brother's other hand, realizing how weak and fragile Jay's body still was. After all, just twenty-four hours ago, he had been fighting for his life.

"I'm sorry, Jay," he said softly. "I guess I'm still trying to get my head round all this. Just take your time and tell me what you can. If you're not up to it, we can always talk tomorrow, or whenever you feel ready"

"No." Sanjay squeezed his hand. "I need you to understand. I need to tell you everything."

Rajiv nodded, reaching out for the chair behind him, not letting go of his brother's hand. "Okay"

"It wasn't just because I was missing—longing for—Kurt." He took a deep breath. "It's the fact that I'm gay, something that's not going to change, Rajiv. And I've been worried, frightened of how you—and especially Ma—would take it. The scandal it will create, plus it's a mortal sin in the eyes of the Catholic Church!"

"Well I don't give a damn, as long as you're happy, as long as we can put this depression—not wanting to carry on living—behind us." He squeezed his brother's slim hand, trying to communicate his unconditional love with his eyes.

"Oh, Rajiv!" Jay's voice was choked with emotion. "I was so afraid you would judge me, maybe even disown me."

"Are you crazy, brother of mine?" He swore softly to himself. "Me judge you? I'm the last person to judge anyone!" His words were torn from him. "Me, with my twisted mind? My perverse lifestyle? I'm the last person to stand in judgment of you. Of anybody!"

Jay smiled, but there was a hint of concern in his eyes. "What about Mother?"

Rajiv sighed, refusing even to think about her reaction. "Let's not worry about her now. Let's just enjoy this moment of you finally sharing with me. We used to share everything when we were kids, remember?"

Jay nodded, and they both became lost in their own thoughts.

Rajiv finally spoke. "So, this Kurt, he's a good guy? Good enough for my brother?"

"Oh, Rajiv, he's a wonderful, kind-hearted person. You will like him. I know you will."

Another silence.

"And, Maya, all this time, there's been nothing between the two of you?"

"Of course not! Maya is my closest friend, besides Kurt, of course. Having her at Cranthorpe, being able to talk to her about Kurt, about my guilt for being gay, lying to my family. She was my life-line to normality."

Rajiv was actually trembling with relief. His brother

was not in love with her! She was free. The realization was almost too good to be true. *She could still be his.* His senses surged at the thought.

"Rajiv, no." Sanjay's voice interrupted his wayward thoughts.

"What?" he asked, keeping his expression blank.

"My being gay changes nothing where Maya is concerned. You have to stay away from her."

Rajiv dragged his hand from his brother's and stood up abruptly, unable to bear Sanjay's piercing gaze. "I don't know what you're talking about."

"Yes, you do. Don't lie to me." The atmosphere was suddenly charged with dissent. "Enough lies! You leave her alone, Rajiv."

Rajiv stared out at the dark, dismal sky, furious with his brother for interfering in something that was now not his business. He forced himself to turn and face Sanjay's accusing stare. "Why?"

"Why? You're asking me why?"

"Isn't it up to her? Surely she can decide for herself."

"While our mother is searching for a suitable wife for you, as we speak. You're going to marry an Indian woman. You can't have your cake and eat it, too." He paused. "Your intentions toward Maya are not honorable."

Rajiv raked his fingers through his hair. "Maybe I'm not in such a hurry to get married, maybe I want to wait another year—or two."

"So that you can have an affair with Maya? And then what? Drop her after *a year or two*, once you're ready to move on, to get married, and leave her broken hearted, ruined by you?"

Rajiv swore beneath his breath, wanting to punch something, anything, rather than having this conversation. Not able to envision letting her go. "You don't know what you're talking about," he said lamely.

"I know exactly what I'm talking about! You can't always get what you want. You're not used to denying yourself. Any woman you've wanted, you've got. But Maya is different. She's special: innocent, not naive, but innocent. You'll break her heart, break her spirit." Sanjay paused, out of breath, staring directly into his brother's eyes. "If you do that, Rajiv, I will never forgive you."

CHAPTER 17

"Here he comes." Kurt's words brought her back to the present, and Maya felt her heart beginning to thump.

She watched him walking along the corridor toward them, his jacket thrown over his shoulder, his expression unreadable. She'd avoided looking at him earlier and realized now that he looked vaguely haggard. His hair was messy, probably from running his fingers through it. There were faint shadows beneath his eyes as well as designer stubble darkening his jawline, but the attraction was stronger than ever and that taut ache began low in her belly. If only he wasn't so devastatingly attractive, she thought desperately, perhaps then she would have more control of herself. Deep down she knew that no matter what he looked like, she could never control her reaction to him.

His eyes skimmed over her and settled on Kurt as he held out his hand to him. "I want to thank you for all you've done for my brother, Kurt," he stated, his expression serious yet warm. "We'll make time to talk properly tomorrow, but right now he's impatient to see you." Kurt nodded eager to be on his way. "Oh, I almost forgot. I've arranged a bed for you in his room for tonight and the two of you can stay at my apartment once Sanjay's discharged. I'll stay in Knightsbridge for a change."

Kurt looked from her to Rajiv, his face beaming. "Thank you."

"You're more than welcome, Kurt."

Rajiv cupped Maya's elbow in a casually possessive manner and eased her toward the exit, as she turned and mouthed goodbye to Kurt.

Kurt gave her an encouraging smile before making his way down the corridor.

"Shall we go?" Rajiv asked impassively, and as they were already walking away, she had little choice. "Bijal's waiting downstairs."

She nodded and they made their way towards the lifts.

She could not stop herself from asking, "Are you okay?"

"Yes." Yet his expression was distracted and Maya was still nervous about keeping the truth from him. "I'm very relieved, Maya. He finally told me the truth."

Then why are you looking so glum? she wanted to shout.

They exited the building and Bijal was there, standing by the Mercedes, concern visible on his face. Maya hung back as Rajiv went over to speak to him.

"He's going to be fine, Bijal," she heard Rajiv say and then suddenly the two men were hugging each other. "It's over."

Maya climbed quietly into the car, not wanting to disturb this moment of intimacy, realizing that Bijal was far more than a driver to this family. What was it Rajiv had said? *I pay him to drive, not to think*. So not true.

Rajiv climbed in the back with her and the car pulled away from the clinic. "I spoke to the doctor after seeing Sanjay," he said. "Apparently he's improved considerably since Kurt arrived and should be discharged tomorrow afternoon, but he has to take it very easy for a while and continue to see his therapist."

Maya resisted the temptation to take his hand in hers. "That's wonderful news, Rajiv. Sanjay must be so happy and relieved."

He nodded his head absently, deep in thought, and she was desperate to know what he was thinking. Surely he didn't mind Jay being gay?"

He glanced at her and then away. "Will you come back to the apartment with me, please?"

She couldn't refuse. They needed to talk now that he knew the truth. His behavior was a puzzle and she needed to know what he was thinking. She also wanted him to understand that she had not wanted to deceive him. No matter what had gone on between them, she could not have revealed Sanjay's sexuality to him.

"Yes," she said softly, even though the partition was closed. "I'll come home with you, if that's what you want."

"Thank you." He closed his eyes and rested his head on the back of the seat.

His cell phone began to ring and with a sigh, he pulled it out of his jacket pocket and stared at it. "It's my mother."

Maya's heart skipped a beat. "From India?"

He nodded and pressed the answer button. "Hi, Ma, how are you?"

Maya could tell he was trying to sound upbeat and she wished she could leave him to talk in private, but that was impossible, so she turned her head and looked out the of the window into the darkness instead, trying futilely not to listen to their conversation.

"He's fine... He's got a friend visiting from Switzerland...He's seems to be much better, Ma, really. I think the worst is over."

There was a pause as his mother spoke.

"He may have switched it off. You know what he's like

with phones. He's probably out sightseeing with Kurt…His Swiss friend. Don't worry, Ma. He's much better, he really is."

Another longer pause.

"That's impossible, Ma. I'm way too busy. I've got meetings back to back for the next few weeks. There's no way I can just drop everything and come to Goa."

Maya felt rather saw him rake his fingers through his hair.

"I'm sorry, Ma. I really can't do that, not next week-end. Besides the board meeting on Friday, Tahir Soma wants to play golf on Sunday, and you know what that means. He's in trouble again."

She heard him sigh heavily.

"Maybe. I'll have to check my diary, but to travel all that way, just for two days…"

Another pause, another sigh.

"Okay, look. Let me check my diary when I get home and I'll call you back later…I understand…Okay, love you too, bye."

Maya continued to look out the window at the lights flickering by. His mother wanted him to come to India, Goa, to meet a prospective bride. It was obvious, and for the best. She was leaving London tomorrow. Jay had Kurt, thank God, and she needed to get on with her life. And forget this man sitting beside her who had turned her, and her world, inside-out.

The Mercedes slowed down. They'd reached his apartment building quickly with the traffic being so light. Had she done the right thing agreeing to spend the night here? Sure, they did need to talk. But did she want to end up in bed with him again?

Her traitorous body kicked up a notch at the thought, but her brain was still functioning. Mistresses, ex-mistresses, prospective brides—it was all too much! *But you'll be leaving tomorrow, just one more night.* That was her body talking.

The car came to a halt and Bijal must have pressed a button, as the partition slid smoothly down.

"Thanks Bijal, for everything," Rajiv said as she grabbed her bag, wondering awkwardly what the older man must think of her. "I'll let you know what time we need to pick him up from the hospital tomorrow, probably in the afternoon."

He squeezed the older man's shoulder and opened the door, climbing out and waiting for her to join him.

"Thank you, Bijal," she said, aware that she probably wouldn't be seeing him again.

This time, as they entered the lobby, Rajiv introduced her to Jackson, and Maya shook his hand, wondering uneasily how many women he had seen coming and going from Rajiv's penthouse.

Of course, Rajiv went straight for the drinks cabinet once they entered the apartment, only pausing to throw his leather jacket onto one of the couches. "What can I offer you?" he asked, pouring himself a stiff whisky.

"Um, I'll have a small whisky with some water, please." She was acquiring a taste for the exclusive single malt whisky, which he drank.

He looked surprised, but poured out a small amount with water, and passed her the tumbler.

"Cheers." He held up his glass to hers and actually smiled. "To Sanjay and Kurt—and seeing my old brother back again."

She clinked his glass and smiled. "To Sanjay and Kurt."

Rajiv took a long pull on his drink, while Maya took a small sip, savoring the taste.

"My mother wants me to visit her in Goa next weekend."

Maya nodded and turned to look out the window at the twinkling lights lining the Thames.

"She's going to be very disappointed."

Maya turned, frowning. "Why? Because of Sanjay?"

"Christ! Don't even go there." He closed his eyes at the notion and then shook his head determinedly. "But I wasn't talking about Sanjay."

Her frown deepened. *Then what?*

He drained the glass, rubbing his mouth with the back of his thumb. "She thinks she's found the perfect wife for me, in Goa."

Maya's stomach hollowed, even though she'd already guessed.

"But I've decided I'm not yet ready for marriage."

His words left Maya dumbfounded.

He grimaced, staring down at the empty tumbler in his hand. "I'll still have to go to Goa though. It would be seen as extremely impolite if I didn't."

Maya drained her whisky as well, needing the sustenance. "Why?" She was not going to get her hopes up because of what he was saying, but she needed to know. "What made you decide that?"

"How can I get married when all I can think about is you?" His expression was bleak and his words squeezed at her heart.

"Rajiv, no. Don't do this. I'm leaving tomorrow. I'm going home to get ready to start my new job and—and move on with my life."

"Tomorrow?" He looked shocked, and then slowly his face changed. He set the glass down and moved towards her. "You've always wanted to go to India, haven't you?"

She stared up at him, perplexed. "Yes, I'm hoping to go next year when I'm entitled to leave from my new job."

"But you're not starting work for another a few weeks, are you?"

"I start working the middle of October."

"Then come to India with me!"

"What!"

"You'll love it. I'll show you places tourists never get to see," he said, excited.

"You want me to go to Goa with you?" Was he losing his mind?

He shook his head. "Not Goa, no." He reached out and put his hands on her shoulders, she could feel his warmth, even though she still had her jacket on. "We'll go to Rajasthan. One of my favourite places in India. There's this beautiful hotel, The Rambagh Palace. It was a maharaja's palace. The architecture's amazing and the décor, a bit over the top, but all original and the atmosphere makes you feel like you've stepped straight back in time. You'll love it, Maya. Please come with me."

It all sounded wonderful, but Maya wasn't convinced. "What about your mother? What about Goa?"

His fingers caressed her shoulders. "I'll fly down to Goa from Jaipur. I won't be gone more than one day, maybe a day and a night, and then I'll fly back to you."

Maya pulled away from him. "You want to take me to some fancy hotel for a dirty weekend and hide me there while you go to Goa to meet a prospective bride?" Her tone was sharp and accusing.

Rajiv face turned to stone. "I thought we could go for a week not a *dirty weekend* and I want to show you India, not just screw you senseless."

"It's never gonna happen, Rajiv," she told him. "When I go to India, I'll pay for myself. I may not be able to stay in five star hotels, but it will be paid for by me. I'll probably be back-packing and staying in budget accommodations, but at least I can hold my head up and not feel like a high-class whore."

"A high-class whore?" His eyes narrowed, whether

with shock or anger she wasn't sure. "God, you really have a low opinion of me, don't you?"

Now she felt terrible. He'd been like an excited child, planning a wonderful outing, and she'd just trashed it.

"I'm sorry, Raj. I shouldn't have said that. It sounded ungrateful, but I need to go back to Edinburgh, start my job, and get on with my life, just as you have to get on with your life."

"And what if I still want you in my life?"

She shook her head. "I can't be your—your part-time mistress." She sounded bitter, yet she wasn't, and she needed him to know that. "And you, you need to get on with your life. Besides, we live in different cities, different worlds. Your life is so totally different from mine. I'm leaving tomorrow, Rajiv. I need to get back to Edinburgh."

He stared at her. Only the pulse beating at his jawline betrayed his emotion. "It sounds like you can't wait to get rid of me."

His beautiful face had taken on a haunted look, and Maya felt awful. "That's not true, Raj."

"I can't say I blame you. I'm not exactly *boyfriend* material, am I?" He paused, veiling his eyes with those thick, blunt lashes, staring down at the floor. "Those anklets I sent you—you haven't even mentioned them."

She swallowed. "Oh God, the silver anklets. They—they are silver, aren't they?"

He returned to the liquor cabinet. After pouring himself a drink, he finally looked across at her. "Does it matter?"

Maya dropped her eyes, unable to bear that haunted look. "Thank you." She didn't know what else to say.

"Do you know why I bought them for you?"

She just managed to stop herself from saying, *As a thank you gift for helping Jay,* shaking her head instead.

"The first time we met at the train station?"

Maya nodded, puzzled.

"You were wearing anklets. You don't remember?"

She thought for a moment. "Yes, of course I remember." They were cheap silver-plated anklets she'd picked up at a market stall, nothing like the intricate, elegant ones he'd sent her. "Did you like them?"

"I liked them on you."

Heat invaded her body at his words. "Oh, Raj, why are you doing this?"

"*You* ask me that?" He drained the second whisky and walked toward her, his beautiful face a tight mask of discontent. "If you don't want me, just say so Maya, don't make excuses."

He was standing right in front of her now, his eyes flat and unreadable, and Maya felt her skin prickle. He looked so disconnected, so detached.

In one of those sudden movements, he slid her jacket off, grabbing her wrists and securing them tightly behind her back, pushing her body up into the heat of his. "Why didn't you tell me Sanjay was gay?"

She stared at him in shock, suddenly hot and out of breath. What was this about? "Because it wasn't my secret to tell!"

"You're lying." He freed one hand, gripping both her wrists painfully in the other, and ran his fingers slowly down from her throat to her heaving breast, gazing at her with a detached curiosity, like an insect under a microscope. "Why didn't you tell me he was gay? That last night in London, after we made love, you could have told me. But you chose not to." He pressed her wrists into her lower back and Maya felt the heated bulge of his erection low against her stomach. The pain in her wrists mingled with the lust suddenly surging through her.

His breath was warm against her cheek and she turned her head, searching his mouth with hers.

Rajiv's hand gripped her jaw, brushing his mouth lightly against hers, forcing her moan of frustration. His eyes were still hard and angry, but she didn't care. Heat was flooding her body and knowing that he wanted it too, wiped all thoughts from her mind.

His kiss, when it finally came was far from tender, his lips bruising hers, the stubble of his beard scraping against her tender skin.

But she didn't care. Even when his fingers fisted into her hair, pulling her head back painfully, Maya ached for him. She would have fallen to the floor if she hadn't been leaning into him—she was that weak with desire. He ground his hips against hers and she felt moisture pool between her thighs.

"I know why you lied to me." He was breathing heavily, but his eyes were still dead cold. "You knew I would leave you alone as long as I believed Sanjay was in love with you. It was *easier* for you."

Her face flushed with guilt as she realized what he was saying was partly true.

"You left me in torment, wanting you, and hating myself for it, because it was an easier way for you to get rid of me!"

"No," she lied desperately. "I told you, I promised Jay I would keep his secret, I couldn't tell you!" His erection rubbing against her sensitized mound was driving her close to the edge.

"Don't lie to me," he growled, forcing her wrists down against her backside, her shoulders pulled back hard and her whole body arched into his.

As he continued to grind himself against her, Maya felt the heat building between her legs, groaning as the first wave of orgasm—

"Oh no you don't." He pulled back and she released a sobbing moan. "Not until you admit the truth. You don't come until I say you can."

Her body aching and confused, she tried to reason with him. "Rajiv, I told you it was not up to me—"

"Liar!"

He let go of her so abruptly that Maya stumbled backward, only the back of the sofa prevented her from falling flat on her ass.

She grabbed onto the soft leather, her head hanging lose as she dragged air into her pumping lungs.

"Let's continue this in the bedroom." He walked back to the drinks cabinet, cool and calm, but Maya noticed his hand trembling as he poured the whisky into the glass. "Come."

She watched him walk down the passage and disappear into the bedroom.

Her heart pounding, her body moist with sweat and arousal, Maya did not know what to do. This was a side of Rajiv she had never seen before, yet it didn't really surprise her. A part of her had always known there was a darker side to him—a sensual, dark side.

She stared around her, in a haze of lust. She could grab her bag and leave—he was not stopping her—but her body was weak with desire, weak with longing to follow him into that bedroom and allow him to finish what he had started. The fact that he had been hard and ready for her pulled her slowly toward the bedroom.

He was sitting in the armchair in the corner, sipping his drink, his shirt unbuttoned, exposing a dark brown strip of muscled torso.

"I thought you were going to do a runner." The ankle of one long leg resting on his bended knee, he took a sip of his drink, gazing at her from above the rim of the glass. "Take off your clothes."

"No." Even though her panties were soaked through, her body throbbing for him, they needed to clear the air first. "We need to talk—"

"Then I'll do it for you." He stood up in one lithe move, dropping the empty glass onto the carpet with a thud, and moved like a feline predator toward her.

"No, please, Rajiv—" She backed away until her legs hit the side of the bed.

"You should have left when you had the chance, Maya." There was regret in his voice, regret and a sensual resignation. He stood right in front of her almost touching her, his hard eyes holding hers like an animal in a trap. Transfixed by his pitiless gaze, she felt rather than saw his hands move to the waistband of her jeans, yanking them open and unzipping them in one jerking move.

She was tempted to push him away but, besides him being much stronger than her, she wanted to see how far he would go with this. And she didn't have long to wait. He crouched down and dragged her jeans and underwear down to her ankles, leaving her crotch naked and exposed within inches of his face.

She was desperate to cover herself with her hands, but clenched her fists to stop herself.

"Beautiful." He breathed in deep and then blew out softly and Maya almost collapsed at the sensation of his warm breath caressing her throbbing flesh. He breathed in again, deeply. "I can smell your need."

Only Maya's fisted hands and some last grains of self-respect prevented her from grabbing his hair and pressing his face between her aching thighs. There was something deeply erotic about being so exposed from the waist down, while she was fully covered above. She reached out to stroke his hair and his fingers circled her wrist in a bruising grip.

"No, you don't get to touch me." He was kneeling in front of her now. "Not unless I say so."

Once again, he imprisoned her wrists behind her back with one hand. The other slid up her thigh, just beside the tiny triangle of auburn silk, where she wanted him. But he wasn't giving her what she wanted.

He lifted his head. "Ask me what I'm going to do to you." His voice was low but mesmerizing in its command.

Maya moistened her parched lips, her legs quivering. "What are you going to do to me?"

"I'm going to torment you with my mouth." And without preamble he ran his tongue up the seam of her sex.

Maya's knees buckled at the intensity of pleasure stabbing her, but he held her wrists tightly and opened his mouth wide between her legs, allowing his tongue to explore her mercilessly. Soft and hard, playful and teasing, bringing her closer and closer to the edge.

He lifted his head, staring into her glazed eyes. "Now you can come for me, baby." The fingers of his free hand joined in the foray and Maya legs gave way as her whole body trembled. She released a strangled moan, an orgasm exploding between her quivering thighs.

He loosened her wrists and she fell backward onto the bed, his head still between her legs, wringing every ounce of shuddering pleasure out of her and then more.

Maya lay back trembling on the bed, one arm covering her eyes, as Rajiv blew softly between her splayed legs. She was gasping for breath, covered in a film of sweat, and too mindless to believe what had just happened. He pulled off her boots, socks, jeans and panties as she lay there with her bottom resting on the edge of the bed, her knees bent and wide apart. She should have felt ashamed, embarrassed. She still had her T-shirt on. It was almost indecent, but she was too wracked with sensation to care.

She heard him move and peeped from beneath her arm as he straightened up, stepping back from the bed and dragging his shirt from his shoulders. His beautifully defined body exposed to her gaze, she peeked at his face to see his eyes fixed fiercely between her legs. Her brain began to function and she closed her legs, scrambling onto the bed, keeping her knees bent to cover herself.

He was shoving his jeans off now, no underwear to be seen, and his erection sprang free, hugely aroused. But it no longer frightened her, rather, she felt her inner muscles clench at the sight of it.

"Open your legs, Maya." His voice still held that cold, commanding tone, and Maya ran wet at the sound of it.

She straightened her legs and opened them, unable to do so with her knees bent. It was just too much. He lowered his naked body onto hers, bracing his arms on either side of her. Immediately she felt his hot erection sliding against the seeping moistness between her legs and instinctively raised her hips to rub herself against him.

"Oh no you don't," he said in that harsh voice. "Not until you've admitted the truth, Maya."

Again, he grabbed her wrists and held them above her head with one hand, bringing his face up close to hers. "Why didn't you tell me, Maya? Why?"

God, she could hardly think, never mind speak. Maya lifted her lids to gaze into his glittering, narrowed eyes, knowing he was not going to let this go, unable to bare the stark accusation staring back at her.

"Okay." She gulped some air. "You're right." Her voice sounded husky and alien. "It was easier if you believed Jay was in love with me."

Rajiv's eyes closed in relief at her admission. "Easier for you, but not for me! Did you ever even think of that?"

She shook her head helplessly, afraid of what he might do now.

He ran his nose up the side of her neck, breathing her in, and then suddenly bit hard on her earlobe. Maya's body jerked as the pain dispersed into a dragging need, her body arching up to meet hard, damp muscle and, finally, he pressed down onto her, covering her mouth with his.

Her body began to undulate beneath him, as he slanted his head, deepening the penetration into her mouth. His free hand coasted up beneath her T-shirt to cup her breast through her bra and capture her nipple, caressing and squeezing in turn. With her hands bound above her, all she could do was kiss him back with desperation.

"Tell me what you want, baby." His voice was still shockingly cool when he finally spoke. Even though covered in a film of sweat, his eyes were glazed, his voice almost lazy, dripping with sex. "Tell me what you want me to do to you."

"Rajiv, please."

"I love it when you beg," he said softly. "But you need to tell me what you want."

"I want you to make love to me," she sobbed softly.

He laughed, rubbing himself suggestively between her pulsing thighs. "Can you be more explicit?"

Maya wanted to slap him, but her need was stronger than her anger. "Rajiv, I need you inside me—now, please."

"That's a bit better." Finally, he released her aching wrists, bracing himself on his arms. Then, with one sudden jerk of his hips, he was deep inside of her.

His groan of agony drowned out her sobbing cry as he rammed himself into her, another orgasm overtaking her immediately.

"Like this?" He ground his body into hers. "Is this what you want, Maya?"

With each thrust, wave after wave of exquisite ecstasy engulfed her. His hips were pounding into her, not holding back, the sounds of moist flesh against flesh mingling with his grunts of satisfaction; sucking her deeper and deeper into an unknown world where nothing mattered, only his body buried inside her, taking her over, and over again.

CHAPTER 18

"A re you all right?" he breathed, hardly able to speak. Rajiv was terrified. The mind-blowing orgasm was dissipating fast and he was hitting the earth hard. He'd gone too far, gotten carried away, and she probably hated him now. *Christ*! How could he have lost control like that? How could he forget how innocent she was?

He looked down at her. God, she was so beautiful. Her T-shirt and bra had finally come off in the aftermath of that unrelenting climax, which seemed to go on, and on, and on. Were men able to experience multiple-orgasms? Well, he just had. The sensation of holding her down, powerless beneath him, telling her what to do, what he was going to do to her, had taken him way beyond anything he'd dreamed of. Perhaps because he'd never imagined, except in his deepest, darkest fantasies, doing that kind of thing to her—to Maya. The kind of sex that turned him on more than anything did, and then left him sickened with himself.

She lifted her lids, her eyes languid. "Oh yes," she murmured breathlessly. "And you? Are you okay?"

He'd expected hatred, cold accusation. Rajiv's anxiety eased a notch. He swallowed hard, heart thumping. "Yeah, why do you ask?"

"Because you were right, Raj." She lifted a trembling hand to his face. "I should have told you the truth about Jay."

"Yeah, you should have," he agreed. "But I shouldn't have reacted the way I did." He closed his eyes, loving it when she caressed him like this.

"Maybe I deserved it." She moved sensuously beneath him. "For all I put you through."

Rajiv's body stirred at her words. '*Maybe I deserved it.*' She wasn't angry. She didn't hate what he'd done to her. God, why was he feeling this rush of excitement?

"I really didn't mean to be so rough." His breathing halted as he waited for her to answer.

"Mmm, you were rather rough, weren't you?" Eyes closed, her fingers trailed down to circle his nipple. "Cold, yet hot at the same time."

His senses surged, unable to believe what he was hearing. "Maya, look at me." He needed to see her eyes, her expression. She opened those cat eyes and looked at him with a sexy, lazy smile, hitting Rajiv low in the groin. "I'm sorry I was so rough and cold."

"It's okay. You didn't stay cold for long. And the rough part—well, it was kind of sexy."

"God, Maya! Don't say things like that. You don't know what you do to me."

She rubbed the instep of her foot leisurely down his leg then up again. "Tell me what I do to you, Raj."

Christ! Rajiv eased himself off her, dragging unsteady fingers through his hair. She lay there, staring at him through heavy-lidded eyes—satiated. She really had enjoyed it, and that only made him want more. And *that* was crazy.

He was convinced she'd hate him for losing control, for taking her so ruthlessly, but he was being given a second chance and he wasn't about to screw it up now. *But what if she likes it*? *What if she wants more*? The demon in him had all the right questions, if not the answers.

"I'm sorry I never thanked you for those anklets, Raj." Her words brought him, mercifully, back down to earth. "They really are beautiful."

"I'd like to see them on you." He paused "Just them and nothing else."

Her eyes opened again, glittering green and curious. "Really?"

"You didn't bring them with you by any chance?" The idea was heating his veins. He was already hard as wood, but he didn't want her to know what a sexual deviant he was.

She shook her head. "No. I was in such a hurry to leave"

He hesitated, wondering if he should tell her. "I bought you another gift besides the anklets." There was no going back now.

She stared at him, her interest piqued. "Why?"

"Why? Because I wanted to." Any other woman would have asked *What?* but she wasn't any other woman. He shifted uncomfortably, nervous. "But I knew you wouldn't accept it."

She frowned. "Why not? Is it something expensive?"

He shrugged, avoiding her gaze. "No, that's not the reason. Anyway you probably wouldn't like it. Forget I mentioned it." Why could he not have kept quiet?

"Do you have it here?" Silence. "Could I at least see it?"

His heart was beginning to pound. "I told you, you won't like it."

She sat up, her long hair hanging deliciously over her breasts, allowing her nipples to peak out as she moved. "I would really like to see it, please?"

He didn't want her to see how aroused he was just by

their conversation. Luckily, the terry-cloth robe was at the bottom of the bed.

He grabbed it and turned aside as he shrugged it on. The gift, which he'd bought on impulse, was at the back of a drawer. He'd regretted buying it, not wanting to see it and be reminded of his perversions.

Rajiv exited the walk-in closet. He carried the long, green velvet box over to where she was sitting with her knees drawn up to her chin, her hair a curtain of copper surrounding her, and dropped it casually onto the bed.

"Open it."

She stared at it, then up at him, moistening her lips as if wary. "No, you open it."

He seated himself on the side of the bed beside her, his mouth dry with tension and excitement. He had never expected her to see it. Quickly, and without hesitation, he flipped it open.

She stared at the rolls of gold chains and frowned. "Is it a necklace?"

"No, not exactly." Rajiv extracted the shorter, thicker chain, made up of chunky gold links, holding it close to the side-lamp he'd switched on earlier. "This is a kind of necklace, a chocker. Do you want to try it on?" He stopped breathing, waiting for her answer.

She hesitated, staring at the gold collar, then back at him and nodded. "Okay, but I'm not keeping it, it looks awfully expensive."

Dear God, the price was the least of his worries. If she allowed him to put the whole thing on her. His heart was pumping, his erection aching at the thought. He slid it gently beneath her hair at the nape of her neck and secured the petite padlock in front at her delicate throat.

"Is it too tight?" His voice sounded hoarse as he slid a shaky, expert finger between the chain and her skin. It was a little too loose for his liking, but then she'd lost weight since he'd bought it. They'd both lost weight. He pushed the thought aside, just wanting to be in the moment.

"No, it feels fine," she said, fingering the little padlock. 'What are the other pieces for?" she asked, looking at the box on the bed.

He pulled out the rest of it, which was long, fine-linked, golden chains all connected to a circular gold disc at the top. "I'll show you, if you'll let me," he said uncertainly. "Can I put it on you?"

She glanced at him, still fingering the little, gold padlock. "Okay," she said, huskily.

He took a deep breath, trying to control his excitement. 'Kneel down on the bed."

Without hesitation, she twisted that sensuous body, folding her long legs beneath her and resting back on her heels.

Seeing her in that position sent the blood flooding to his groin, making it difficult for him to think, to speak. He lifted the shortest chain attached to the top of the disc and snapped the last link to the padlock. The sun-disc immediately rested flat against the pale golden skin of her breastbone. The rest of the chains fell down in different lengths, between her breasts, coming to rest in a small pile of gold between her thighs. Her fingers moved down to the disc and he noticed her nipples had tightened, two hard nubs pointing outward through her silky hair, begging for attention.

Rajiv forced his hands not to shake as his fingers closed over the chains linked to either side of the sun-disc. They curved just beneath her breasts as he pulled them outward.

"Lift your arms," he breathed. "This piece locks at your back.

She lifted her arms and he had to drag his eyes from those high, pouting breasts with their pale rose, hardened nipples. His arms closed around her as he secured the two chains at her back, but he released her quickly, even when he heard her suck in her breath expectantly. Dear God, she looked incredible, her arms above her head, the collar, the sun-disc and the two chains curving outward beneath each perfect breast.

There was one more chain linked to the bottom of the disc, which also had two chains attached to it, just below her navel. She lowered her hands and fingered the fine links beneath her breasts, her breathing uneven, causing her breasts to jump a little with each breath.

Rajiv took hold of the two chains that curved down low on her hips and once again put his arms around her back to secure them together just above her smoothly rounded back-side. For a moment, her breast was pointed right at his face and he couldn't resist taking that tight nipple in his mouth and sucking hard. She gasped, arching into him, but seemed to know not to touch him as he dragged himself away from that tempting nub.

There was only one piece of chain left to secure and it lay curled up like a dozing snake between her thighs.

"Spread your legs, Maya." He spoke with authority, not wanting her to question what he was about to do, desperate to see her wearing it, as he'd imagined when he'd bought it.

She spread her bended knees with divine obedience and he slipped the links between the lips of her sex, wet and slick with their combined juices, sliding his other hand around her back, caressing her cheeks, before drawing the chain between her bottom cheeks, and linking it snugly to the one draping her lower back.

"That's it," he said, struggling to control the rampant desire betrayed in his voice. "That's how it's meant to be worn."

He raised his wary eyes to hers.

"It's beautiful," she said in a breathy, sexy voice, and Rajiv had to close his eyes for a moment to gain some remnant of control. She looked like a pagan goddess. Proud, and yet, shy and submissive at the same time.

"Dear God, you are beautiful," he whispered. "Lift yourself. I want to see it as it should be seen."

She straightened, kneeling as if in prayer, and Rajiv unloosened the belt of his robe, shrugging it off, uncaring that his aching erection was visible now. He stretched out in front of her, leaning on one arm, drinking her in.

The gold was a perfect foil against her pale, golden skin. The collar turned him on big time and the finer chains draped beneath her up-tilted breasts made his mouth water. His gaze followed the chain down to the two chains resting on the flare of her hips and then the last chain looped between her legs, between those moist, pouting lips. He lifted his hand and slid it up one smooth thigh, having the pleasure of feeling her tremble beneath his fingers.

She ran her hands along the chain beneath her breasts, tentatively fingering them, then cupping each breast.

"God, Maya," he groaned. "What you do to me?" He hooked one finger into the chain below her navel and ran it southwards until his knuckle was rubbing against her distended clitoris.

She moaned arching her back as his finger trailed down between the slick flesh beyond. He was breathing hard, and his body was damp, filled with tension.

She might be the one wearing the slave collar, but he knew he was the real slave here, enslaved by this obsession with her.

છ૭૯૭

"Turn over for me, please, baby." Rajiv lifted his upper body off her, running his hand from her breast, to her hip, and then up again.

Maya was floppy with exhaustion. "Raj." Her wrists

were finally free, her arms bent at either side of her head. "I can't move."

They'd been making love for hours with a kind of desperation that was almost scary. He kept holding her down, circling her wrists as if she would run away if he let her go. Kept bringing her to ecstasy and then pulling back. Tormenting her, making her beg and then taking her over that edge, over, and over, again. It was incredibly erotic but slightly disturbing at the same time.

He lifted himself off her and turned her gently over. "I love your back," he whispered. Running both hands from her shoulders down to cup the cheeks of her bottom. "And your backside, of course."

He'd eventually taken the chains off her, but not before he'd driven her mad with them, kissing, licking and sucking her body wherever the chains touched. Rolling them against her nipples with his tongue, then moving down to torment her even more with the chain tugging between her damp thighs. After driving her insane, he'd taken her, furiously, with the body jewellery on, the chain rubbing against him and her as he forced her to come in an orgasm that didn't want to end. But that wasn't enough. He'd taken the chains off, one by one and began to make slow, languorous love to her. Exploring every inch of her body with his mouth, his hands, his tongue, until she was boneless and overdosed on pleasure.

Now he was caressing her lower back, his erection resting against the cheek of her backside, as he kissed the skin of her shoulders. She was limp with exhaustion, but that didn't mean she couldn't feel, and when his hand moved between her legs, exploring her, swollen flesh, Maya moaned helplessly.

"I'm sorry, baby," he whispered against her skin. "I know you're tired and sore, but I just can't get enough." He nudged her legs apart gently and then she felt the hot blunt head of his penis pushing into her again. She heard herself groan. Her body was moist enough for him to ease in without too much effort and then he was thrusting slowly and deeply into her. She cried out as he withdrew, almost completely, and thrust in deep, again, and again, until she was awash with sensation, her inner muscles convulsing around him in spasms that would not end. She was under his erotic spell, totally and utterly his.

CHAPTER 19

Maya lifted her head to the fine spray of water, savoring the luxury of the huge state-of-the-art shower, breathing in the sensual aroma of Rajiv's shampoo, while soaping herself between her sore, tender thighs. Her body was a mass of aches and pains but it was satisfying pain, a reminder of what had transpired between them the night before. She shampooed her hair, thinking about last night rather than the fact that she was leaving today. It had been a revelation to see him so totally out of control after his earlier detachment. The body jewellery had driven him wild. He'd kept fingering the chunky chain around her neck, kissing her skin beneath as he tugged at it with his fingers, even biting her neck gently with his teeth. When she'd reached for him, desperate to explore his aroused flesh he'd grasped her wrist.

"God, Maya, no," he'd choked "You'll make me come." And once again, her hands had been bound behind her back.

She stared at her tender wrists noticing faint bruising on the insides. Heat bloomed within her as she recalled his mindless passion. Would she ever feel such exquisite pleasure again in her life? She doubted it.

He'd woken her gently after showering, telling her he was going to make them breakfast. They were both hungry, not having eaten since earlier the day before. Now Maya could smell the delicious aroma of grilling bacon and she pulled on his terry-cloth bathrobe, trying not to think about saying goodbye to him *again*.

She had to be strong. Just stay in the moment and focus on Jay and Kurt, the one positive thing that uplifted her spirits every time she thought about it.

Making her way to the main room, Maya felt her skin prickle at the thought of facing him after last night. Lord, would she ever be able to be around him without feeling this mixture of anxiety and excitement? No, because she wouldn't be around him after today. *Stop, just be in the moment, and forget about the future,* she told herself firmly.

She could hear his deep, masculine voice as she entered the room. He was talking to someone on the phone and he was bare-chested. Maya swallowed hard. Barefoot, his long, powerful legs clad in white, drawstring, cotton pants, he stretched his legs out, resting his feet on the coffee table, with a laptop sitting on his thighs and the phone at his ear, Rajiv managed to look the image of urbane, masculine perfection. She could just imagine the header in a glossy magazine: *The billionaire relaxing in his penthouse after a night of really hot sex.*

"Is there no way we can move it to tomorrow, or even later today?" he was saying. "Damn…okay, Joseph…it's not your fault," He looked up, saw her standing there, and shrugged impotently. "Thanks, man, bye."

"Is everything okay?"

"Not really, I wanted to go with you to the hospital and the airport." He tugged his long fingers through his hair, impatiently. "But there's a meeting at twelve that I can't get out of."

"That's okay, Rajiv." Blue eyes met hers, his frustration visible. "I'm fine with taking buses. I actually enjoy them."

"Don't be crazy." He threw the phone down on the sofa beside him. "Bijal will take you, of course, but I wanted to do it." He lifted his legs from the coffee-table, snapping the laptop shut and getting up, his gaze not leaving hers. "You had your shower?"

She nodded, fiddling with the belt of the robe, feeling ridiculously flushed and embarrassed. "Yes, thank you."

"Come. I've made us an English breakfast. You must be starving." His sensual gaze roamed her flushed face. "I'm a very bad host. Didn't even feed you last night, just dragged you straight to bed."

She smiled, striving to look relaxed, pushing back her damp hair, and shoving her hands into the deep pockets of the bathrobe. He was obviously used to these morning after scenarios, but for her it was completely new and she wasn't sure how to behave. Did people talk about what had occurred the night before, or did they just pretend it never happened? She had no idea. All she knew was that she wanted to savor every moment left with him. Talking about the airport, and leaving, was looming over her like a dark cloud.

He pulled a stool out from beneath the kitchen counter and invited her to sit, while he went behind the counter into the kitchen and opened the oven. The sight of his dark-skinned, muscled torso drew her gaze and weakened her limbs. There were two place-mats, cutlery, and cotton serviettes set up for them, and even though she had lost most of her appetite, Maya's stomach grumbled as he placed a warm plate filled with bacon, eggs, fried mushrooms, and tomatoes in front of her.

He set the other plate on the mat and made his way back to seat himself on the stool beside her.

Fresh orange juice and a pot of coffee were on the counter besides salt, pepper, and mustard.

"Eat, please," he said. "You've lost enough weight as it is."

She opened her mouth to argue about her weight loss, but popped a grilled mushroom inside instead. Now was not the time to be talking about weight loss. Besides, that lean, brown body and low-waisted Indian pants were making it difficult for her to think, never mind talk.

"I didn't realize you were such a good cook," she said after trying the delicious bacon and egg.

"I'm not." He took a sip of his coffee, eyeing her over the rim of the mug. "English breakfasts and sandwiches are as good as I get in the cooking department."

"Well, you make a mean English breakfast," she said, buttering some warm toast and dipping it into the perfectly fried egg, feeling less nervous now that she had some food in her stomach.

"It's all about timing," he said. "My housekeeper does most of the cooking and shopping for me."

Maya stared at him. "You have a housekeeper?"

"Yeah. Why? Does that surprise you?"

"No." She wiped her mouth with the napkin. "I just didn't realize."

"I don't have time for cooking, cleaning, and shopping, Maya. Sometimes I get home after nine at night. Amira leaves my meal in the warmer."

It sounded quite lonely, but she was sure it wasn't. He could call up Clara or countless other women if he felt in the mood company.

"Can I pour you more coffee?"

"Yes, please." She'd had one cup of the delicious ground coffee and, now that she'd cleaned her plate, she was ready for another. "What time is it, Rajiv?"

"It's just after ten." He pushed his plate away. Unlike

her, he hadn't had much appetite. "Less than two hours left."

Maya sipped her coffee, avoiding his eyes and gazing around the huge apartment "How many bedrooms do you have here?" she asked, changing the subject.

His gaze told her he was aware of what she was doing but, after a long pause, he relented. "There's another two bedrooms, my office, and a TV room." He reached for her hand. "Come, I'll show you around. All you've really seen of my home is the damn bedroom."

"I'm not complaining," she said, smiling, and he smiled ruefully back at her.

His office was situated along the corridor before the main bedroom and almost as big. Dominated by a huge wooden desk set in front of the floor-to-ceiling windows and scattered with documents and files, plus all the impressive computer equipment a high-tech office would require. After she'd walked to the windows and looked out at the view, he took her hand, led her back to the corridor, and opened a door farther along on the opposite side to the main bedroom and his home office.

"The second bedroom," he announced, standing in the doorway while she made her way inside.

The room was easily double the size of hers and still smaller than his. Mainly white—no surprise there—it contained an en-suite bathroom—which she didn't go into, aware that he was getting impatient. But she took a few moments to look at it.

The bed was large, though not as large as his, covered in a beautiful embroidered, orange Indian-silk bedspread.

With the matching curtains, the room gave the impression of being stylish, yet welcoming at the same time.

"Does Jay ever stay here?" she asked.

He sighed, leaning his shoulder against the doorjamb. "He used to stay here, often when we were younger, and then when I was away on business. The other bedroom is his, there's still some of his clothes and stuff in it. He never liked the Knightsbridge house."

She moved past him, back into the corridor, realizing his mind was not with her, and they had so little time left together.

"You can show me the rest another time," she said, knowing there would probably never be "another time."

"There's just Sanjay's room, a TV room, and another bathroom," he pointed to the door facing them at the end of the corridor. "Plus there's the roof terrace and gym upstairs.

Maya tried to keep her expression bland—a roof terrace and gym *upstairs*.

Following her back into the main-room, he moved to-ward the coffee-table, while she retrieved her mug of cof-fee.

"Can we sit on the couch?" He paused, his eyes search-ing her face. "I want to talk to you about something."

Maya's earlier anxiety returned. Were they going to talk about last night? "Yes, of course." She slid off the stool and made her way to one of the sofas, wondering warily what he wanted to talk about.

"Come sit here." He took her hand, the first time they'd touched since she'd entered the room, and that thrill of awareness was still there.

"I want to ask you something," he said, almost tenta-tively, turning to face her. "But I don't want you to say any-thing until I'm done, okay?"

She nodded her head, intrigued. Uncertainty was not his style.

"I want you to think about it while you're back in Ed-inburgh," he said. "Just think about it. I don't want an an-swer now."

"What?" What was *it*?

"I'll come to Edinburgh the weekend after I've sorted

things out in Goa," he told her. "Then you can give me your answer."

She was beginning to see where this was going, but didn't say anything.

"I don't want to stop seeing you, Maya." His gaze locked with hers, imploring. "Please, just think about it?"

"You may fall madly in love with your prospective bride," was all she could think to say, even though the thought made it painful for her to breathe.

"That's never going to happen."

His words shouldn't leave her relieved. There would always be other prospective brides, and this one sounded perfect.

"Will you think about it?" His beautiful, beseeching eyes were almost her undoing.

"Rajiv, I—"

"Maya, please, just think about it!" His gaze held hers, his thumb gently caressing her knuckles.

"But what's—"

"No. No buts, not yet. I want you, need you, in my life. I know I'm all screwed up, my life is all over the place, and yet you're the only thing I can think about." He drew a breath, massaging the back of his neck with his free hand. "As I said, not exactly prime boyfriend material." His smile was cynical. "You could do so much better, but the thought of you with another man, it—it's unbearable to me." The words were torn from him.

She could say it was the same for her, but she didn't. "I'm not interested in other men."

"But they're interested in you, and it's only going to get worse, especially once you start working." He paused, staring down at their entwined fingers. "And sooner or later, you're going to find someone who can offer you so much more than I can." He took a long, deep breath, his face taking on that haunted look that she couldn't bear.

"Okay," she said softly. "I'll think about it."

He closed his eyes in relief, resting his head back against the sofa, their fingers still linked.

"I'm going to go get dressed," she told him after a long silence, trying to untangle her fingers from his. "Raj, it's getting late, I need to dry my hair."

"Yeah, I know." He lifted his eyelids. "Maya, about last night…"

She felt her face flush with heat. "Yes?"

"I don't normally lose it like that." He was working her palm with his thumb, and Maya began to feel that familiar heat blooming deep inside her. "I went a bit crazy. I forgot how new you are to all of this, but that's no excuse." He raked his long fingers through his hair. "It was just—with it being your last night and finding out about Sanjay, as I said—I went a bit crazy." Finally, he lifted his head to stare at her, his blue eyes filled with remorse. "It won't happen again, I'll never be so rough like I was last night."

Her flush subsided at his words. "Why not?" She forced herself to hold his gaze. "Didn't you like it?" Her breath shortened at the memory. "I like it when you lose it—lose control."

"Christ, Maya!" His hands slid beneath the wide sleeves of the bathrobe, caressing her warm skin and her body arched instinctively. Rajiv gripped her bare shoulders under the robe and pulled her toward his naked chest. "You don't know what you're saying."

His mouth covered hers, one hand sliding right up inside the bathrobe to clasp her throat, holding her still while he deepened the kiss, urgently sliding his tongue into the warm interior of her mouth, leaving them both hot and out of breath.

Feeling suddenly audacious and awash with erotic need, Maya pushed his shoulders until he was lying back on the couch.

"Maya, what—"

She covered his lips with her finger. "Hush, just lay back and relax."

She lifted herself and straddled his hips, grabbing his forearms, pushing them above him as he'd done to her last night. Slowly she lowered her head and teased his lips with her tongue until he groaned, lifted his head, and tried to capture her mouth with his, but she was too quick for him.

"Don't move." She drew her hands down against his bunched shoulders and pressed her mouth to his nipple, sucking and then nibbling with her teeth.

His hips lifted off the couch and she widened her legs, allowing the robe to gape open, giving his groin access to her sex. Moisture gathered between her thighs, already hot and pulsing with arousal, and he groaned again, louder and longer. She took pity on him, pressing herself against his groin, liquid heat easing out of her as his hot, hard flesh pushed up urgently against her.

It felt wonderful to be above him, taking control, and Maya pressed hot wet kisses to the smooth skin of his tense, tightened torso, licking and sucking, loving the taste of him.

She lifted herself and arched her back, undoing the knot of the soft belt around her waist. Slowly, watching him, she slid the robe from her shoulders and allowed it to fall around her. His eyes narrowed, roaming her face before settling on her breasts.

She lifted her hands and cupped each breast, squeezing her nipples and gasping with shock at sensations she had not expected.

"Don't stop," he breathed, moving his hips back and forth against her, gripping the arm of the couch with his hands.

His words made her brave. Besides, watching him watch her touch herself was incredibly erotic. She continued to caress her breasts, focusing on her nipples, shocked as throbs of pleasure darted between her legs, where his huge arousal was moving against her.

Eyes heavy with desire, Rajiv lowered his gaze to where their bodies met between her legs. Maya trailed her hands lower down over her taut stomach to settle at the top of her thighs, framing her sex.

"Touch yourself, baby, please" he choked. "Do it for me."

She was trembling, shocked at her own wanton behavior, but his obvious arousal at what she was doing spurred her on. Moving her hands to the apex of her thighs, she went for his erection first, caressing the hard, smooth skin, slick with her juices, fascinated by the hot throbbing power of him. She ran her finger along the tip, finding it oozing with moisture.

His gasp became a long tortured groan. "Maya, God, I need to touch you."

"No!" She was determined to take control this time. "It's my turn, Raj. Don't move."

Fists clenched, he arched his back, jerking his hips between her legs. She knew what this was costing him, but he did as she said.

She lifted her finger, wet with his arousal, and sucked it into her mouth, gazing with sensual knowledge into his burning eyes. His gaze fixated on her mouth, he dragged air into his lungs, obviously on the edge of losing control. It was heady knowing she had this power over him and, for the first time, she was gaining the confidence to use it. The knowledge that this might be their last time, only served to egg her on.

Finally, she pulled her finger from her mouth and did as he'd asked her. She touched herself, closing her eyes, moaning as sweet sensations uncoiled inside her.

"Open your eyes, Maya." His voice broke. "Look at me!"

She lifted her eyelids, captured by the intensity of his burning, blue eyes.

"Now give me your finger."

Her eyes widened, but she did as he said. Lifting her finger from between her legs, Maya pushed it into his waiting mouth. He sucked hard, much harder than she had, in and out, not taking his eyes off hers. The intimacy of the act was almost her undoing.

She moaned, sliding her finger out of his wet mouth. Unable to hold back the powerful surge of need, she leaned both hands against his damp, muscled chest and began to move furtively back and forth, the friction almost too much to bear. Rubbing harder and harder, until that all too familiar ecstasy flooded between her legs to convulse through her whole body, Maya collapsed on top of him with a feral cry. His body was wet and trembling beneath hers. He brought his hands down to caress her bottom, but she wasn't finished with him yet. Grabbing his arms with shaking hands, she pushed them back above his head.

"No you don't," she gasped, awash with pleasure and trembling from the orgasm, but determined to keep control.

"Maya, for pity's sake. I can't do this!"

"Oh yes you can," she breathed. Stretching, weak and languid, she leaned her weight into her arms, pressing down on the rigid muscles of his upper-arms.

He released a strangled groan, continuing to lift and work his hips against the moisture her orgasm had produced, allowing her to hold his arms in place. Maya lifted her thighs away from his groin, hearing him growl as his whole body clench in protest. She ignored his gasping pleas and moved down, pressing hot, wet kisses to his chest, his nipples, his stomach, and finally his huge, straining manhood. God, he was so big. It never failed to amaze her. She licked her lips before running her tongue from the root to the tip of his penis.

"Maya, please. God—"

"I love it when you beg." She repeated what he'd said to her last night, lifting her eyes to gaze straight at him as she took the swollen head in her mouth. She watched his eyes droop closed, his mouth open, dragging air into his lungs.

Maya pleasured him with her mouth, amazed at how hard and yet smooth he was. His hips jerked upward, wanting more, and she gave it to him, taking as much of him into her mouth as she possibly could. She pulled back slowly to see him watching her with glazed eyes, his body tensing and jerking. She kept eye contact as long as she could, but it was difficult when she also wanted to watch what she was doing.

Maya felt his hands in her hair. She wanted to tell him to put arms back up, like he constantly did with her, but decided to let it go. His hands twisted into her hair, pressing down just a little. She knew he was holding back, could hear the urgency in his ragged breathing, and then he pulled her mouth off of him.

"Stop, please, Maya."

He began to comb his fingers through her hair, caressing her scalp, her face, and finally, her mouth, tracing her lips with his thumb, then pushing it inside, where she instinctively sucked on it. He groaned, exploring the warm, soft interior with the pad of his thumb.

"Enough, Maya," he choked, swiftly gripping her upper arms and lifting her effortlessly back onto his groin.

Only this time he settled her a little higher and with a shift of his hips his erection found its target. His hands moved down to grab her hips, pushing her down while he thrust into her.

"Oh God, Raj!" Her body was sore, ultra-sensitive from the night before, but with each stroke, the ache turned into sweet ecstasy.

She released a long, feral cry as their bodies began to move in unison, finding their rhythm. Maya could feel him deep within her, stretching and lengthening his penetration, leaving her gasping and sobbing, while he gripped her hips, lifting and pushing her down hard with each stroke. Ramming himself into her again, and again.

ళ్ళ

Afterward, Rajiv lay motionless, his heart pounding in his chest. Maya was spread out on top of him, her hands threaded into his hair, her face resting on his heaving chest. He could hardly believe what had just happened. He'd never enjoyed a woman taking control before. It was just not his *thing*. But when Maya had sat above him, her beautiful body arched, in rhythm with his, he simply couldn't move. He'd wanted to grab her, to throw her to the floor, and take over mentally as well as physically. But having her above him like that, taking her pleasure in her own sweet time, gazing down at him from a position of power, had thrown him into a new dimension.

Her obvious pleasure, her slow sexy moves, had left him helpless, helpless and *loving* it. Loving the way she looked at him when she was doing what she wanted to do, loving the feeling of opening himself up to her, and allowing her the pleasure of taking total control.

Her fingers trailed lazily from his hair to his damp face and he lifted a hand from her taut backside to press his lips into her palm.

And then he saw the bruises. "What the fuck!"

He jerked onto his side, pressing her into the back of the sofa, holding her hand in his.

"Raj, what is it." Her voice sounded blurred, but she opened her eyes in shock at his crude outburst.

"Let me see the other one." He grabbed her other hand,

forcing himself not to squeeze it, and turned it over to see the inside of her fragile, veined wrist. "Dear God!"

Her eyes followed his gaze to her hands, palms up, bruises visible on her both wrists.

"Raj, it's okay," she murmured, making him feel even more sickened. "I noticed them in the shower. It's nothing. I bruise really easily—"

"*Jesus*. What kind of animal am I?" He lifted his tormented eyes to hers. "Sanjay was right. I will ruin you!"

CHAPTER 20

Maya stared at her reflection in the mirror, wondering if she should wear her hair up or leave it loose. If Josie were around she could have asked her, but Josie was working tonight. Biting into her bottom lip, Maya smoothed her hands over her thighs, gazing back into the mirror. She had on the same black dress she'd first worn to that dreadful dinner-party at Cranthorpe in Wiltshire. The weather was much cooler now than it had been that evening, so she'd teamed it with black tights, boots, and a vintage, burgundy jacket to keep out the cool, damp weather. Autumn was setting in. The days were getting shorter and she'd be starting work at the Bradfield Center on Monday.

First though, she had to get this meeting with Rajiv out of the way. Her stomach lurched at the thought. She would be seeing him in less than an hour, seeing him, and saying goodbye. Putting this affair behind her and getting on with her life, her new job, which she hoped would keep her busy. Keep her mind off the man who had occupied her thoughts constantly these past two weeks.

Since leaving London her mind had been in turmoil. That scene with Rajiv in London, when he'd seen the bruis-

es on her wrists, had disturbed her. She'd felt he was over-
reacting and had told him so, which had only infuriated him
even more. He seemed filled with guilt and a kind of self-
loathing and her heart went out to him. He was not a bad
man, she knew that absolutely. Sure he had his flaws—who
didn't? But he was certainly not the monster he seemed to
believe he was. And her coming into his life had only
served to enhance his troubled mind.

"Are you still coming to Edinburgh?" she'd asked that
morning in London, after he'd seen the bruises and freaked
out.

He'd been sitting on the edge of the sofa with his head
in his hands. He lifted his face to stare starkly at her. "Do
you want me to?"

Maya knew it was crazy. This affair could not continue, but she needed to see him again, just one last time. She
couldn't bear for it to end like this.

"Yes," she breathed, meeting his searching gaze.

"Well, considering what I've done—" he said, talking
about the bruises. "—I'll understand perfectly if your answer is *No* when I come to Edinburgh."

She wanted to continue arguing with him, reassuring
him that she bruised really easily, that there was no reason
for him to feel bad, but she knew that would only make him
angrier than he already was with himself. So she just nodded, relieved that he was still coming up to see her. Even if
she said no, at least she would get to see him one last time.

They'd hardly spoken on the way to the hospital. He'd
been quiet, morose, and she'd decided not to try and lighten
the mood. It would have been a futile effort anyway. They
could talk when he came to Edinburgh. He hadn't even
kissed her goodbye, just informed her in that cool, detached
manner that Bijal would pick her up here at the hospital at
one o'clock to take her to the airport. She'd reached out her
hand and stroked his cheek but he'd pulled it away, staring

at the bruises on her wrist, before pressing his lips to them and gazing at her with bleak, pained eyes.

Watching the Porsche drive away, Maya had experienced a devastating sense of loss. He was going to India next weekend to meet an Indian woman whom his mother believed would make the perfect wife. Jealously sliced through her. There was a good chance that he would see what his mother saw in this prospective bride and fall madly in love with her. Ignoring the physical pain that pierced her chest, making it difficult to breathe, Maya tried telling herself it would be for the best. Their relationship had no future. She was probably going to say no to his proposal anyway. If he decided this woman in Goa was right for him, she should feel pleased for him. After all, he deserved some happiness. Life had not been easy on him. Despite all his millions, he'd had his fair share of hardship and suffering.

When Maya arrived, Jay and Kurt were sharing the hospital bed reading the daily newspapers, looking like a typical Sunday morning couple, despite the fact that it was Monday. Maya smiled indulgently. This was what really mattered. Her angst-ridden morning with Rajiv was forced into the background by the joy that surrounded this couple.

"Maya!" they exclaimed in unison.

"Finally," Jay added, eyebrows raised.

"Hi, you two." She dropped her bag onto a chair and went to hug them both in turn. "Jay you look amazing, positively glowing.

He smiled, glancing at Kurt then back at her. "The power of love."

Kurt folded the newspapers as Jay grabbed her hand and drew her closer to the bed. "How are you? I expected you here earlier."

Maya held her smile, determined to keep the mood positive and light. "Oh, I slept late, had a lovely breakfast." Drawing in a deep breath, she kept her answer vague. "Besides, I wanted to give you two time alone. I'm sure you had a lot of talking and—catching up—to do." Jay actually blushed and Maya laughed. "I'm so happy this is finally sorted out."

Jay's expression changed. "It's not *all* sorted, Maya," he said in that serious voice. "It's far from sorted."

"Jay!" Kurt almost shouted. "Will you stop going on about your mother?"

"Well it's true." Jay glanced at Maya. "He doesn't know my mother."

"True, but we don't have to worry about her right now." Kurt dropped the newspapers onto the floor. "Jay, please put aside your Indian, Catholic, guilt—this shame of yours, and let's just enjoy the moment."

"I know, I know. You're right." Jay rubbed his eyes with his palms. "I spoke to her this morning, Maya."

"You did? From India?"

"Yeah." He nodded. "She seemed relieved. I guess I sounded happy, which I am."

Kurt gave him a reassuring smile. "See?"

"Maybe she'll be okay about it, relieved that you're happy, healthy again." Maya added, not really convinced. "When do you plan on telling her?"

Jay looked at her with worried eyes, not convinced either. "I'll wait till she gets back from India."

"You could give her a chance to get to know Kurt first." As a trained therapist, Maya knew not to give advice, but Jay was her friend not her client. "You don't have to rush into telling her."

"You think?"

Maya shrugged. "It's really up to you and Kurt to decide how you're going to go about it, but you could just take it one day at a time. Play it by ear."

Jay nodded eagerly. "I think you're right, Maya. Once she gets to know Kurt, she may realize how good he is for me, how good we are together." He reached for Kurt's hand, squeezing tight.

The rest of her visit went well. Jay's mood lifted as he put his worries aside. The three of them were served a delicious lunch, which seemed to be the norm if you were being treated in a private clinic like this one. The staff was friendly and helpful, not batting an eyelid at the obviously loving relationship between their patient and Kurt.

It was sad saying goodbye. Jay would be seeing the doctor before being discharged later that day and he and Kurt were both excited at the prospect of spending some quality time together at Rajiv's apartment. Maya felt guilty and uncomfortable, listening to Jay enthuse about how lovely the penthouse was, pretending she'd never seen the place herself. Lying, especially to friends, was not a pleasant feeling.

By the time Bijal arrived, she was ready to leave and, although a little teary eyed, it was generally a happy goodbye. But her flight home came as a shocking surprise. Bijal drove her to London City Airport, where a private jet with the Maddox-Junta logo beaming brightly from its tail, awaited her.

Maya felt uncomfortable, guilty at the thought of all the fuel used just to fly her back to Edinburgh when she could easily have taken a normal domestic flight, or even the train. The luxurious interior and attentive service from the sophisticated stewardess only served to enhance her realisation of how totally different her and Rajiv's worlds were. This was a life-style she could never imagine becoming accustomed to. Jay and Kurt had both emailed her since then and, as Anna was still in India, they sounded happy and content. Jay was taking Kurt to all the museums and galleries in London, as well as the tourist attractions.

They were even planning a weekend in Paris between moving from Rajiv's apartment to the Knightsbridge house.

Rajiv had texted her twice in the past two weeks—even though he had her email address—just two brief texts. The first one was sent soon after he'd returned from Goa, letting her know he was back in London and would inform her when he would be arriving in Edinburgh. The second one was sent a week later, asking if she could meet him for dinner at the Balmoral Hotel where he was staying, and could he send a car to pick her up? Which she'd refused. It was only a twenty minute walk to the hotel, which would give her time to work off some of her anxiety before facing him again.

Turning away from the mirror, she decided to leave her hair as it was. She didn't have the time to put it up now, anyway. Sliding on her burgundy, velvet jacket, she decided her hair looked nicer loose, besides she didn't want to look over-dressed. Nowadays people seemed to dress casually, even in five star hotels. Checking her make-up one last time, she applied a pale pink color to her lips and reached for her small, sling bag, preparing herself mentally to leave the security of her flat and make her way to the hotel where Rajiv awaited her.

CHAPTER 21

Rajiv entered the hotel lobby, spotting Maya immediately. She was talking to the hotel manager at the front desk, her flame-colored hair instantly catching his gaze, setting her apart from everyone else in the vicinity. His eyes ate her up. She was wearing the same sexy, black dress she'd worn at that unfortunate dinner-party at Cranthorpe.

That little black number that had driven him to the brink of losing control. This evening though, she wore it with a plum-colored jacket, black tights, and knee-length, black boots. Possessive desire hit him like a blow to the stomach, particularly when he saw the young hotel manager smiling at her, trying to work his unctuous charm on her—until he noticed Rajiv glaring at him.

"Mr. Maddox." His wary smile was not returned. "There you are."

Rajiv's eyes slid over him to rest on Maya, masking the jealousy that had frosted his gaze.

Her striking, green eyes, shadowed by sooty darkened lashes, appeared to be held captive by the intensity of his stare. He moved in, his eyes still eating her up, and he didn't bother trying to hide it. "Hi." He folded her warm, slender hand in his, caressing her knuckles with his thumb. "Sorry I'm late. I just went out for a walk."

"That's okay." She smiled, nervous. "I only got here a minute ago."

He nodded at the hotel manager and steered her toward one of the marble pillars closer to the elevators.

"I didn't feel like eating in the restaurant." His tone was deliberately casual "So I ordered dinner in my suite. Is that okay with you?" She hesitated, as he knew she would. "Look." He shrugged. "If you want to eat in the restaurant, that's fine. I'll just let the manager know and we can go to the bar for a drink first."

"No." Her body trembled. "You're right. We need to talk in private."

He was still holding her hand and the feel of her delicate skin against his thumb was causing liquid heat to pool in his groin. "Good." He smiled, steering her towards the elevators. "You look beautiful," he said, once the doors had closed.

The dress looked quite different with tights and heeled boots, but just as provocative. With her long, coppery hair spread out against the dark, velvet jacket, she looked like she'd just stepped out of the swinging sixties, and it was sexy as hell. He only hoped he could control the lust that was coursing through him once they were alone in his suite.

"Thank you." Her voice was cool, detached, and he just knew she was going to say no to his proposal. "How are Jay and Kurt doing?" she asked. "Have you seen them lately?"

"Yes." He smiled, recalling his besotted brother with a mixture of cynicism and envy. "They're both really well. In Paris for the weekend. They've moved into the Knightsbridge house while my mother's in India. So I've got my apartment back."

"How do you think she's going to react when Jay tells her the news?" Her look of concern mirrored his own unease. How was his Catholic, Indian mother going to react to the fact that her younger son was gay and very much in love with a man he constantly referred to as his *soul mate*?

He shook his head, distracted by the turn of conversation. "Hell, Maya," he muttered, rubbing the back of his neck. "I can't see her accepting it. They're both living in this bubble at the moment, but I've got a feeling the bubble's going to burst once she gets back to London. I'll do my best to convince her that it's a good thing, and that Jay's happier than he's ever been, but I don't know."

She listened to him, biting into her full, bottom lip, and Rajiv's mind switched, his libido kicking in, and the anxieties about Jay and his mother faded into the ether.

They entered the hotel suite and he made his way to the liquor cabinet. "What can I get you?" he asked, pouring himself a single whisky. He needed his wits about him.

"Oh, can I have a whisky with lots of ice and water, please?"

It looked like he was not the only one wanting to keep his head tonight.

She was staring out of the long windows when he handed her the crystal tumbler. "The view of the castle is beautiful from up here."

"Yes, that's what I like about this hotel." Touching his glass to hers and taking a sip, he watched her over the rim. "I remember you wearing that dress at Cranthorpe," he murmured, his eyes skimming over the stretchy knit, the way it hugged her body in all the right places. "I was crazy that night, believing you were with Sanjay. Crazy with jealousy."

"It all seems like such a long time ago." She stared down at the amber liquid. "How is Kirti, by the way? Do you still keep in contact?"

"Kirti's fine." He sighed, not wanting to talk about her. "I've only seen her once since we broke up. She seems to be quite happy. I don't think she was particularly heart-broken by our splitting up."

"I'm glad," she said. "She deserves to be happy."

He managed to hold her gaze. "And me, do I deserve to be happy?"

Her cat eyes widened at his question, then she nodded. "Yes, Rajiv, you do deserve to be happy. I tried telling you that in London when you were so angry, but you didn't want to listen."

"Christ!" He drained the whisky, all his good intentions evaporating. "Don't remind me. How are the bruises?" He clasped her free hand, turning it palm up, caressing the pale, creamy skin with his thumb. "Thank God, they're gone."

"All gone." She smiled, a real smile, and his senses surged. "You can sleep easy now."

He held onto her hand. "If only…"

She turned back to the window, taking her hand with her, and he went to pour himself another drink, even though he'd promised himself he'd take it easy tonight.

"So how was Goa?" With her back was to him, it was impossible to know what she was thinking. "How's your mother?"

"My mother is not happy, of course." He stalled, knowing they had to get this subject out of the way, but wishing they didn't have to go there.

"And the young woman you went to meet, was she everything you expected?"

Was she jealous? His heart leapt at the idea. "Fatima was lovely, yes." He paused, trying to gauge her reaction, but she kept her gaze fixed outside the window. "Everything my mother would have wanted in a daughter-in-law."

"So do I hear the sound of wedding bells?"

He laughed a harsh, brittle sound. "Not quite. I had a lucky escape."

Finally, she turned to face him. "What do you mean?"

"Her father was a very wise man."

"Her father?"

"Yes." He nodded, recalling the conversation with the girl's father that sultry evening while walking outside, around the family's luscious garden, in one of the older suburbs of Panjim in Goa. "He and I had a man-to-man talk at the end of the day. He told me that he could not accept me as a suitable husband for his only daughter. He wanted to see her married to a man who could love her, adore her, as she deserved to be. And he could see I was not that man."

"I'm sorry, Rajiv."

"You're sorry!" He set the tumbler down with contained violence and went to stand in front of her, where she couldn't avoid his gaze. "Why? Are you that eager to get rid of me?"

His hands moved of their own accord, stroking the wide lapels of the velvet jacket, sliding inside to caress the smooth skin of her shoulders, before slipping the jacket down over her arms to drop to the floor where she stood.

He shook his head, bemused. "I can't believe you're wearing this dress." Running his hands from her creamy, exposed shoulders, carefully to clasp her wrists, Rajiv allowed his gaze to roam over her long, subtle curves, outlined by the stretchy black dress. "Have you any idea what I went through that night, wanting to strip this dress off of you, inch by inch?" He waited for her to ease away, and triumph soured through him when she didn't. He pulled her closer, drawing her arms around his back, bringing their bodies up against each other. Still, she didn't move away. She was staring up at him, her eyes wide, lips parted and inviting.

Lowering his head, Rajiv released her wrists, his spine arching as her fingers spread beneath his jacket, exploring his back, sending shivers of delight through his body, down to his groin.

"Is that why you wore it?" he breathed against her mouth. "Because you knew it would drive me mad?"

"No," she whispered, her eyes glazed and confused. "I didn't know what else to wear to a five star hotel."

His mouth fastened on hers, his hands running from her lower back to cup her buttocks and press her mound against the swelling ridge of his erection. His body was hot and pulsing, as his mouth plundered hers. He tried to control his raging libido, the memory of those bruises still fresh in his mind. Resisting the urge to drag the dress off her and throw her onto the chesterfield behind them, he allowed his mouth free reign, twisting and mating his tongue with hers, hands trembling with the need to slide beneath the dress and caress her until she begged him to take her. But he held back, reminding himself that she was too vulnerable, too innocent for him to forget himself and unleash his carnal needs. Yet she was driving him crazy, dragging his shirt out to explore the taut muscles of his back, raking her fingernails along his hot, damp skin. Rajiv groaned against her mouth, knowing he needed to slow things down.

A knock on the door brought him to his senses.

"That must be the meal I ordered." He dragged some air into his lungs and, circling her wrists, took an unsteady step away from her warm, inviting body.

ფ·ᲒᲔ·Ე

Maya was mortified. Dear God, they hadn't been in his hotel room more than a half hour and she'd been ready to beg him to make love to her! As he went to answer the door, she turned toward the windows again, pressing her hands against her flushed cheeks.

She heard the waiters enter the suite and, taking a deep breath, turned to face them, praying that the low lighting would hide her heightened state of arousal.

The first waiter steered the food-laden, heated trolley close to the dining-room table, ready to be of service. Maya had observed the table on entering the suite. It gleamed with silver and crystal. Curled linen napkins were set in square bone-white plates, a delicate, silver candelabra in the center. A romantic dinner for two. He'd obviously gone to a lot of trouble.

"That's fine, thank you," Rajiv was saying. "We'll see to ourselves. I'm sure the food is perfect."

"The wines, *monsieur,*" the other waiter, whom she guessed to be the sommelier said. He was carrying an ice-bucket with a bottle of white wine inside, as well as a bottle of red, cupped like an object of value, in his free hand.

"Thank you, Pedro." Rajiv's voice was husky and she felt a sense of relief, knowing she was not the only one affected by their crazed behavior. "I'm sure the wines are excellent. If you could just open them, we'll manage."

Both waiters looked disappointed, once the wines were opened and Rajiv held the door ajar for them to leave. But it was an enormous relief for Maya to see the back of them, under the circumstances.

He closed the door, running impatient fingers through his thick hair. "Are you hungry?"

She shook her head, food being the last thing on her mind. "No,"

"Thirsty?" His eyes met hers. "You enjoy white wine, don't you?"

"Not right now."

He'd buttoned the jacket of his suit and Maya felt brave, knowing that he was hard and aroused by her. She'd felt it against her body when he'd cupped her bottom, pulling her tight against him. She went to him, uncaring that this was not how things were meant to go, uncaring that she'd promised herself she'd have her say and leave. Standing right in front of him, almost touching, she unbuttoned his jacket and slowly eased it off his shoulders. He was not wearing a tie and the two top buttons of his white shirt were undone. Lifting her hands, she began to unbutton the rest of his shirt, exposing dark, silky skin defined by hard muscle.

"Maya, we need to talk." He sucked air through his teeth when the palms of her hands made contact with his hot, bare chest. "Please, I don't want to lose control with you."

"Why?" she breathed, pressing her lips to his sternum, hearing his hiss of pleasure. "Why not lose control?"

"Because the last time I ended up hurting you, that's why," he bit out.

Maya drew his hands to her thighs and continued unbuttoning his shirt until it gaped open, exposing his hardened nipples and taut stomach. "I told you," she said and ran her hands over his smooth, muscled torso, brushing her lips against his. "I like it when you lose control."

"No, Maya." He rested his hands gently on her hips, but his mouth betrayed him, searching and capturing hers in a hard, possessive kiss, taking all she had to give. Finally, he dragged his mouth from hers. "I promised myself I'll never lose it, never hurt you like that again."

Maya pushed him away so abruptly that he stumbled back, staring down at her, confused. She turned and walked back to the long windows. "Well, I'm not interested," she said, threading her fingers through her tangled hair, shocked at her own boldness. "If you're planning on giving me some watered-down version of love-making, then I might as well leave."

Suddenly he was right behind her, gripping her naked shoulders and pulling her back against him. "You have no idea what you're saying, Maya." He ran his hands along her smooth bare arms. "But this is a dangerous game you're playing."

His palms slid round to cup her braless breasts, squeezing her tight nipples. Maya moaned, leaning back weakly against him, feeling the heat of his body all the way down her back. His hands sliding along the silky black dress, until his fingers found the top of her thighs where the dress ended and her legs began. "Is this what you want?" His breath was heavy and warm against her ear. "Or maybe this?" He slid one hand beneath the dress, between her thighs, cupping her hot mound in his palm.

Her body sagged into his. His hand tightened between her legs, holding her up against him, her bottom pressed hard against the bulge of his erection.

"Is this what you want, Maya?" he repeated.

"Uhh." She couldn't speak. His middle finger was rubbing against the seam of her sex. And when he fisted his other hand in her hair, pulling her head back hard, exposing her neck, and biting her earlobe, Maya felt her body begin to convulse, heat pulsing between her legs.

His finger continued to work insistently. *God he was so good at this*. The pleasurable pain of her hair pulled tight, the bite of his teeth searing her earlobe, sent her over the edge, plunging her into a shocking, exquisite orgasm. Her hips jerked and thrust against his tormenting hand, until there was nothing but him, his body, his hands, his mouth now sucking the pain away, leaving her trembling, weak, and drenched in pleasure.

"You came to say goodbye, didn't you?" He continued to hold her limp body hard against him, his hand moistened by her pulsing clitoris. "Admit it, go on say it. Say it and put me out of my misery. You want *this*, but you don't want me!"

"Raj, don't—" She was gasping for breath. Her head thrown back against his shoulder, her fingernails digging into his arm, and her legs trembling, unable to hold her up.

He released his hand from between her thighs and hooked his arm beneath her knees. Lifting her off the polished, marble floor, he carried her boneless body through the glass-framed double doors into the luxurious bedroom, lowering her onto the huge bed, straightening himself to stare down at her.

Maya was too drugged with pleasure to care that she was sprawled across the bed, her famous black dress now bunched up around her hips. Rajiv glared down at her with glittering eyes and dragged off his shirt. She stared back at him through heavy lids, uncaring how wanton she might look. This was their last time together and she wanted him more than she could ever have imagined. If he thought she was just after meaningless sex, that all she wanted was *this*, then he was wrong, but perhaps it was better for him to believe that. Easier for both of them really, if he did believe that.

The bedroom had a stately look about it, dark wooden panelling, long windows with views of Edinburgh Castle and the city lights beneath them. Everything was sublimely tasteful and luxurious, including the cool satin bed-spread she was lying on, colored in shades of gold and bronze, reflecting the lights outside, shining through the windows.

"Close the curtains, please, Rajiv?" she asked, wanting to cocoon them in a world of their own.

"Why?"

"Because I want you to, that's why."

He stared at her for a long moment, his lean, bronzed body gleaming in the dim light. She could look at that body forever, but he went to close the curtains, leaving the room in semi-darkness, except for the light reflecting from the room behind them.

"It's too dark." He switched on a side-lamp, casting a soft golden glow over them. "And I want to see you, especially while I take off that dress." He stood at the bottom of the bed, gazing at her through narrowed, searing eyes, naked, except for the black designer trousers hanging low on his hips. He hadn't put on any weight since she last saw him. His hip-bones still protruded, but did not detract one bit from his harsh, sensual masculinity.

She knew she looked wanton, shameless, laying there with her arms and legs spread, the dress pushed high above her crotch, covered only by black panties and semi-transparent tights.

"Don't worry, baby, I'll give you what you want."

He spoke in that insolent tone, which she detested, but she was too helpless to care. Kneeling between her sprawled legs, Rajiv ran his hands up her thighs, smoothing the soft tights against her warm skin, fingers sweeping along her inner legs. Her body was still quivering from the earlier orgasm, and Maya's bottom lifted off the mattress as his fingers brushed against the apex of her thighs.

"Easy," he murmured, but his uneven breathing betrayed his own needs.

Sliding his fingers beneath the dress, he hooked them into the waistband of her tights, pulled them down together with her panties, and over her hips and legs, until they reached the top of her boots and could go no farther. He eased her thighs apart, knees bent, once again leaving only her crotch exposed and Maya was too mindless with need to protest. He ran his hands high up her legs, grazing his thumbs against her bare crevice. Her body jerked at his teasing touch and he smiled a satisfied, masculine smile. Lowering his head, he pressed his open mouth to her welcoming flesh. Maya spasmed. A feral cry tore from her throat as her whole body surged, grabbing his hair to press him down against her.

"Oh no you don't." He circled her wrists gently, removing them from his head and holding them down at her sides. "This time I call the shots. After all, it's a goodbye fuck, isn't it?" His darkened blue eyes were fiery, filled with anger and lust.

Maya hated his crude words, but deep down knew it was the truth. This was goodbye.

He lowered his head again, using his lips and his tongue to tease her into mindless submission. Her hands were pinned at her sides. All she could do was thrust her hips up to meet his teasing ministrations, but he lifted his head easily every time she tried to thrust herself against him.

He kept on and on until she was begging him. "Raj, please stop tormenting me," she moaned, circling her hips. "Why are you doing this to me? It's not fair."

"Fair!" He lifted his head. "You talk to me about fair. Is it fair that you're going to walk away from me tonight?"

A sob escaped her at his accusing words. Collapsing back against the soft spread, she allowed him to continue his torment, because she deserved it. She was going to walk away, so let him torment her as much as he liked. As long as they had this one last night together, let him do what he wanted with her.

And he did. She moaned, she begged, but she didn't demand, allowing him to drive her mad with his sensual expertise. Finally he dragged himself away from her. Unzipping the black trousers, his dark eyes roaming over her semi-naked body, he rose, stripping off completely. After kicking his shoes and trousers away, he stood there naked, his sex jutting straight out of his body, proud and demanding.

He stroked himself with one hand. "This is all you want, isn't it?" His breathing was labored. "You've discovered your sexuality and now you're ready to go out and explore it."

"No!" She raised herself onto her elbows. "Rajiv, are you crazy? I could never do this with anyone else but you."

He wasn't even listening. He just lowered himself onto her, settling himself into the cradle of her thighs and pushing the dress high above her breasts, caressing them with hard, urgent hands, while plundering her mouth with his. The time for talking was over.

Maya could feel his shaft, hot and heavy between her thighs. She was desperate for him to bury himself inside her and satisfy that craving need—for him to pound into her and drive her over the edge, the way only he knew how.

Arching her back, she enticed him with her writhing body until, with an erotic groan of resignation, he grasped his swollen shaft in his fist and drove it into her. A cry of shocked pleasure escaped her, her body exploding around her. There was nothing gentle about their coming together. He didn't wait or allow her inner muscles to stretch and accommodate his huge, rigid length. He just found his rhythm and hammered into her, relentlessly.

Maya, so sensitized from her previous orgasm, splintered into another climax almost immediately, sending her higher and higher with each thrust, until she felt she could not be released from this hold he had over her. He moved with desperate speed and strength. Her legs were trapped by his, the tights pulled taut between her boots. She wanted to wrap her legs around him but it was impossible. All she could do was raise her hips to meet each thrust, digging her nails into his jerking buttocks. He seemed to enjoy the fact that she was so constricted. His legs were a heavy weight against the tights. Gripping her shoulders, he held her down with each thrust, forcing himself deeper inside of her. Maya sobbed, convulsing waves of exquisite pleasure surging through her until, finally, his back arched, taut as a bow. He exploded with a shuddering groan. Hot semen flooded into her and he collapsed heavily on top of her, his flesh still buried deep inside of her.

He lay slumped on top of her, gasping for breath, while she quivered and trembled beneath him. It felt strange. He was completely naked and she was almost completely dressed. She was unable to move her lower body as his powerful legs weighed her down. Eventually he lifted his head, capturing her mouth in a long, languorous kiss, and Maya felt her inner muscles tighten and shudder, another echoing climax overtaking her.

"Are you okay?" he breathed against her mouth.

"I think so." Her voice was blurred, unrecognisable.

His head drooped in defeat. "I'm sorry. God, I was so rough, again."

"Don't." She pressed a finger against his lips. "It was perfect."

He opened his mouth to disabuse her and then closed it. Cupping her face instead, he lowered his head and began kissing her once more. With deep, drugging kisses that left her quivering and clinging to him, he began to make love to her all over again. Maya closed her eyes, sensing everything through a haze of languid lust.

"I think it's time to get you out of these clothes," he murmured huskily, sliding his hand down to the zipper of her boot.

She didn't have the strength to hold her leg up, not that Rajiv needed any assistance. He lifted her boneless leg and slowly unzipped the boot, throwing it to the floor. Then slowly he began massaging her foot, sending shivers of sensual delight through her body.

She groaned, shocked at how sensitive to his touch her feet could be.

"You like this?" he asked, strong fingers doing sinful things to her toes.

"Uhh!" Her body jerked as he pressed his thumb along the arch of her foot.

He laughed a sexy, knowing laugh and unzipped the other boot before sliding her tights and panties off and giving the same attention to her right foot.

By now Maya was naked, except for the dress bunched

above her breasts. Rajiv worked his way up her body, pressing his lips to her inner thighs, skimming over her sodden sex, breathing in the smell of their combined juices, but not touching her there, even when she spread herself invitingly. He was taking it slow and she forced her body to relax, delighting in each caress, each brush of his lips. He reached her breasts, sucking and biting until she began to squirm with impatience. Slowly, as if unwrapping a gift, he peeled the dress over her head. Now she was completely naked against him, her body hot and liquid like molten lava. Her hands began stroking, probing his back, his tight buttocks and finally, her fist closed around his hard, heavy erection.

Rajiv groaned, but he didn't stop her. Instead, he stretched his body, covering hers and captured her mouth again, with hard, consuming kisses, holding her head still with his hands while delving with deep, carnal need into her mouth.

"Sweet Jesus," he chocked, jerking his hips against her tight fist. "I can't get enough of you."

Maya wrapped her legs around him and guided the bulbous head of his manhood to her weeping core, moaning softly as his flesh finally met hers. He made love to her with slow deliberate strokes, savoring each thrust, as he buried himself inside her time, and time again. Maya's body arched and undulated beneath him, her hands caressing his moistened face, lifting her head to bite at his lower lip, feeling voluptuous pleasure as he took her slowly, closer and closer toward the edge, into mindless bliss.

CHAPTER 22

G od this wasn't how I planned for things to go to-night." Rajiv was leaning over her, drawing damp tendrils of hair from her face.

Maya stared at him through drowsy eyes. "Me neither."

He caressed her cheekbones, reverently. "What is it about us, Maya? Why are things always so explosive? I've never experienced this before."

"You haven't?"

"No, not like this."

"What about Clara?" She frowned, not sure she wanted to know, but forcing herself to continue. "Surely she satisfied you in ways that I never could? She seemed so confident, so experienced."

He blinked, shaking his head. "Maya, what I had with Clara was totally different from us."

"In what way?"

"God, in every way." He shook his head, damp, dark hair falling over his face. She stared up at him, needing to know more. He sighed. "What Clara and I had was more of an arrangement than anything else."

"An arrangement?" That sounded so cold-blooded.

He closed his eyes, leaning his forehead against hers.

"We satisfied each other's needs, nothing more than that really."

The thought of him with Clara was like a physical pain, but she needed to understand. "Surely you had feelings for her, for each other?"

There was a long silence, but she waited it out.

"No." He buried his face in the curve of her neck. "There weren't really any feelings involved, just sex."

Maya ran her fingers through his damp, silky hair, forcing herself to persist. "What about the others? Jay told me you had lovers in India as well."

"God, Maya." He threw himself off her, lying on his back, covering his eyes with his arm. "It was different, okay? Just different to how it is with you."

She knew when to let it go. Staring up at the ornate ceiling, she realized she might never understand this complex man and it was pointless trying to anyway.

Afterward, they showered together in the huge, state-of-the-art, marble bathroom. Taking their time, soaping and caressing each other with hot, erotic need, as if they knew it was ending and wanted to drain every ounce of pleasure from their time together.

☙❧☙❧

"Those poor waiters." Rajiv licked the succulent juice of the perfectly baked pheasant off his fingers and smiled. "They'd be devastated if they saw us now."

"Why?" Maya popped a perfectly roasted baby potato into her mouth. "Because we're eating on the floor?"

They'd spread the pristine, white table-cloth onto the Aubusson rug, deposited the different array of dishes onto it, then sat crossed-legged on silken cushions, eating the exceptionally cooked meal as if it were a Thali to be enjoyed all at once, rather than in five different courses.

Rajiv grinned. "That too. They went to so much trouble to serve up the perfect dinner for two."

"Oh, Rajiv, why?"

She was wearing a dark green satin bathrobe, provided by the hotel, and his eyes drawn irresistibly to her shadowed cleavage. "Because I asked them to," he answered.

"Really? Thank you, Raj."

He laughed, shaking his head disparagingly. "I thought I could impress you, maybe seduce you, with the perfect, romantic dinner." Wiping his fingers on the damp hand-towel they'd brought from the bathroom, he threw it onto the table-cloth. "I should have known better, huh?"

Her beautiful face, devoid of all make-up now, became sombre. "I'm sorry, Raj."

Rajiv gazed at her, trying not to think about tomorrow, or the future, or the fact that they never would be like this again, sitting, enjoying just being together. He'd decided earlier, while they were in the shower, that he was going to make the most of their last few hours. It was pointless getting angry and frustrated by the fact that she couldn't, or wouldn't, continue this affair with him. He'd known, deep down, that she would never agree to it. Besides she deserved so much more. She deserved a man who could be there for her all the time, giving her all the love and attention in the world, just like Fatima's father had wanted for his daughter. Not some messed-up degenerate, who could offer her no more than an affair on the side, hiding their relationship from his family, his mother, and his brother. While his long-term plans included marrying an Indian woman, who would not set his blood on fire—a comfortable, traditional Indian woman, who would bear him children, children who would not be messed-up half-breeds, torn between two cultures as he had been—as he still was.

So he was going to value every moment of this last night together and tomorrow—tomorrow, he'd go back to

London and deal with the torment of not seeing her again. They still had tonight and that was all that mattered right now.

"That was absolutely delicious, Raj." She wiped her hands on the damp towel, lifting her arms, stretching, and arching like a satisfied feline. "I'm completely stuffed. And the wine—" she took a sip, closing her eyes and licking her lips. "Mmm, this wine is divine."

Rajiv smiled indulgently. He'd chosen the wines carefully after a long discussion with Paulo. In fact, each course had been carefully chosen, from the quails eggs to the strega crème brulee. And although the dinner hadn't gone as planned, it felt perfect to be sitting here on the floor, Indian style, eating with their hands, enjoying the food and wine, just in a different way from what he'd planned. But then, things seldom went as planned where Maya was concerned.

Her cat eyes were dusky in the soft lighting, giving her a soulful look, her hair damp from their shower, clinging to her bare skin where the robe gaped wide at her breasts. One nipple was peeking out at him, stirring his senses. The blood leaving his brain to flood his groin, his body hardened as always, ready for her. He recalled the last time they'd made love in London, when she'd straddled herself above him, taking control. He'd been thinking about it ever since, besides the bruises, of course. It was something he'd never enjoyed or even indulged in with another woman, but with her it had been incredibly exciting. Even though his instincts had urged him to roll her over and take control, he hadn't. It had just been too good. He wanted her there, above him again, wanted to see if it was just a fluke, a one-time thing. He needed to know, and the idea of it left him throbbing with anticipation.

"Come here," he said.

Her brows lifted, as she sipped her wine. "What?"

"Come over here to me."

She hesitated a moment, then setting the glass down, she smiled, a sexy, feminine smile, and crawled around the mountain of food to his side of the rug. He turned to face her as she reached his side, running his finger from her cheek, down her throat to the exposed nipple peeking at him. She dragged in air as his thumb brushed at the dark rose pebble.

"Beautiful," he said, thickly, pushing the silky robe off her shoulder.

She was kneeling before him. He spread his legs, dragging the towel that covered him off his hips and pulling her between his thighs. Lifting his hand to thread his fingers through her damp hair, he twisted it and held her head tight before covering her mouth in a long, sensual kiss. He leaned back on his free hand, taking her with him.

Lifting her hands, she spread them against his broad shoulders, while he continued to explore her mouth with his tongue, fisting his fingers into her hair.

"Be careful, the wine-glass," she breathed against his lips.

He slid the crystal glass out of their way with sweet anticipation.

The Aubusson rug was soft against his bare skin as he lay back and pulled her, onto his body. Tension tightened deep inside him, his body and mind conflicted, and he wondered if he could again enjoy a woman—*this woman*—above him, taking control. As she slid over him, he realised what an erotic feeling it could be, having her spread above him. It gave his hands free reign over her body, and he took full advantage, easing the robe off her other shoulder, leaving her upper body naked and free to his hungry gaze and hands.

Maya seemed to be enjoying it as much as him. Her warm hands pressed down against him, she lowered her mouth to his, but unlike him, her kisses were light, teasing, and her lips brushed lightly against his, until he couldn't take anymore. Lifting his head, he captured her mouth with his. His hands were at her breasts. He loved the way they fell forward, lush and inviting. He weighed them in his palms, the nipples poking provocatively into his skin.

"Do you like it like this, being on top of me?" he asked thickly.

Blood was pounding through his veins at this new and liberating erotic high. He, who had believed he'd experience everything sexual out there that could him turn him on, was now being sensually subjugated by an innocent, an innocent who was taking him places he'd never imagined.

"I love it," she said, leaning back and trailing her fingers along his tense torso. She lifted her hips and Rajiv groaned as she settled her sex directly against the ridge of his aching shaft. "Do you?"

"I think I do, too," he choked, needing her to know what this meant to him. "With you. You're like a goddess, and I'm your willing slave."

Overloaded by erotic sensations, he let his hands roam from her breast down south, determined to lose the damn robe so that he could watch her, naked in all her glory. Watch her through greedy eyes and touch her, every inch of her. Those tantalizing hip-bones, which he curved his hands around now, were covered by delicate, soft skin, inviting him in between them, where that triangle of coppery, spun silk awaited him.

"Mmm." She threw the robe to one side, lifting her arms and threading them through her hair, just like the goddess he knew she was. Her curved body lengthened and tightened. "To do with as I please?"

He sucked in a breath. Waiting.

"What shall I do with you today?" She sounded a little tipsy from the wine, bolder than usual, but he wasn't about to complain. She rubbed her moist crotch against him, slowly, sinfully, until he felt he would die if he didn't come. "Torture you with pleasure?" she asked.

And she did, beginning with his mouth, teasing her nipples against his suckling, hungry lips, while she held his arms above his head. Rajiv was not sure if this was a punishment or a pleasure too turned inside out to comprehend. He'd hoped he might enjoy it again, but he'd had no inkling of how shattering and overwhelming it could be having her luxuriate in him, taking advantage of her feminine power to seduce him into helpless submission.

He was desperate to get inside her—desperate—but when he tried to enter that wet, inviting core, she simply lifted herself and moved downward until her breasts were brushing, tormenting his erection and her lips were teasing his navel. Gasping for breath, he lurched beneath her, fisting his fingers into her hair. He wanted that warm, tormenting mouth around his flesh, taking him deep, but she grabbed his wrists.

He was too good a teacher and she his avid student. She anchored his wayward hands at his sides. Of course, he could have forcibly taken over, but that was not what he wanted. He had to allow her this power and enjoy the anguish, no matter how tempted he was to grab her, flip her onto her back, and hold her down while, he drove himself into her so long and hard that she wouldn't know where she ended and he began.

"Maya," he said hoarsely. "I can't stand much more of this."

"Oh no." She ran her hot, wet tongue along the ridge of his aching shaft and Rajiv's body wrenched in sweet agony. "You said you were my slave, remember?"

His chest was heaving. He felt like her slave and it was sinful ecstasy.

She gazed up at him while she teased him with that luscious mouth. Rajiv stared into her glazed eyes, erotic intimacy pulling them close together. She seemed fascinated by his manhood, licking, sucking, caressing—fascinated by how it pulsed and jumped in response to her ministrations.

"I love your body," she murmured.

His hips jerked up to her torturing mouth, sweat seeping from every pore as he bucked, on the brink of tumbling into orgasm.

"Please, Maya, "he begged. "I want to come inside you, now!"

She smiled, lifting herself back onto him. Taking him in her hand, she guided his shaft into her body and slowly sank onto him.

Afterward, she lay splayed over him, both of them panting, sweaty and exhausted. Her hair spread out over his chest, sensually tickling his skin, while his hands roamed from her shoulders, down her back and over the sloping rise of her butt. Just another benefit, he realised, of having her on top of him.

"I never enjoyed this position with a woman before," Rajiv confessed, drunk with pleasure.

"Really?" she panted, lifting her heavy head, a blissed-out expression on her face.

"Yeah." He breathed in her scent, caressing her lissom thighs, curled around his hips. "It used to turn me off."

She crossed her hands over his chest, resting her chin on them, searching his face. "Why do you think that was?"

He laughed. "You sound like a therapist. Are you going to psycho-analyse me now?"

CHAPTER 23

Maya sensed an edge of wariness in his tone. "No, Raj." She pressed her lips to his moist skin. "I'm not your therapist. I'm your lover—for tonight anyway."

He released a long sigh, which she felt all along her body. "But I am curious," she said quickly, not wanting to spoil their intimate mood. "I mean, why would you enjoy me being on top and not other women?"

He stared up at the ceiling, his roaming hands sending shivers up her spine. "Do you think I haven't asked myself that question? Since we first did it in London, I've been wondering about it."

"Well, I'm not exactly the voice of experience." She smiled. "But I was under the impression that men loved that this position."

"I think they do." He cupped her bottom and her eyes drooped at the sensation of those strong exploring hands. "And now I understand why." His hips lifted suggestively between her thighs, but she wasn't going to allow him to distract her.

"Maybe you're just too macho and domineering," she said with a laugh, but she wondered if this was true. She knew he wasn't macho, but he did have a very dominant controlling streak. She'd been aware of that from their very first meeting.

"Hey!" He slapped her bottom playfully. "Are you calling me macho?"

She giggled. "No, sorry you're not really macho. I don't think." His eyes twinkled. "But you can be very domineering, even controlling." she ended warily.

He sighed again. She loved the fact that she could actually feel every sensation of his body against hers. How lucky was she that he enjoyed having her sprawled on top of him like this?

"You're right, I am a bit of a control-freak." He hesitated. "In and out of bed."

She kept silent, hoping he'd say more.

"Maybe it's got something to do with my childhood."

That was a no-brainer, but she wasn't about to say so. "Maybe," she agreed cautiously. "Maybe with your father being the person that he was." She chose her words carefully, not wanting to insult his father.

"What do you know about my father? Besides the fact that he was a total bastard." He smiled down at her, taking the edge off his harsh words.

"Raj!" she exclaimed. "Actually Jay spoke quite a lot about your father."

"Yeah, and I'm sure none of it was good." Even though he was looking at her, his mind seemed to be far away.

"So you think he's the reason you need to feel in control?"

She'd brought the subject back to him, wanting to understand him, even if she wasn't going to see him again.

"Yes." His eyes still held that far-away look. "Directly and indirectly."

"Indirectly?" She stroked his brown, masculine throat with her finger. "In what way?"

He blinked suddenly as if now back in the present. "He sent me to boarding school when I was six."

Maya bit back a gasp of shock, forcing her body to remain relaxed against his, though the thought of a six-year-old Rajiv sent off to boarding school left her feeling physically sick.

"My mother begged him not to. Jay wasn't born yet and she was devastated, but he took no notice of her, and I went off to boarding school."

She wanted to shout in outrage, but forced herself not to. This was about him, not her. "Your poor mother." Her heart went out to Anna. No wonder she was so close, so protective of her sons. It must have been hell for her. Never mind what it would have been like for a six-year-old. "How bad was it?"

He laughed, a harsh, unpleasant sound that rumbled from his chest through to her breaking heart.

"Well, I wasn't sexually abused, if that's what you're thinking."

"There are other kinds of abuse besides sexual abuse, Raj." She kept her voice serious, not prepared to trivialise, or gloss over what he was telling her.

"Yeah, well it wasn't that bad, Maya." He lifted his hand to stroke her hair, spreading it against his chest with obvious pleasure. "I wasn't really abused, just a bit of a boarding-school bullying, that's all."

Maya swallowed hard. Her body trembling inside, she kept her breathing slow and even.

"There were quite a few Indian boys in the school, which my mother thought would help." Once again he laughed that humorless, cynical laugh. "But I wasn't fully Indian, nor was I English, so I didn't fit in really. I was a half-breed, neither one nor the other. So I had to stand up for myself, which I learned to do." He must have noticed something in her eyes, for he smiled, a soft reassuring smile. "Hey, what doesn't kill you makes you stronger, right?"

Maya had never agreed with that particular philosophy, but she smiled anyway and cupped his face in her hands, pressing her lips to his. Giving him comfort in the one way she knew he would accept it, she began making love to him all over again.

೮ೞೞ

Eventually they made it back to the bedroom and another shower. Rajiv soaped her sublime body, which was now so familiar to him, he'd come to recognize every curve, every indentation and nuance of her sensual, responsive body. Just when he finally knew her erogenous zones—like the back of her neck, the curve of her spine, her earlobes, which seemed to be a direct hotline to her sex every time he bit them—she was going to leave him. Leave him for another man, eventually, to explore, to possess. Just the thought of it made him want to lash out, to howl at the injustice of it.

He soaped her back, trying to control the agony that was eating into him, each minute bringing them closer to the end. Smoothing the soapy suds off her shoulders and back, he slid his hand between the inviting curve of her buttocks, finding her swollen clitoris, slick and distended, from their prolonged lovemaking. He knew he should stop. Her body was still unaccustomed to so much action, but he couldn't get enough of her. And the thought of not being with her again only left him craving for more.

She pressed her hands against the wall of the shower, arching her spine. The spray of water ran down her long body in rivulets, which he caught with his tongue, licking and sucking at her luscious, wet skin until the urgency of his needs took over and he entered her from behind, pounding into her as if he could make her his with this desperate, compulsive love-making. His hands cupped and squeezed her delicious wet breasts, sliding down between her legs to claim and torment her inflamed flesh, while he drove into her punishingly from behind.

Forgetting all his good intentions, he gripped her sodden hair and pulled her hair back to lick and suck at the water running down her neck. Finally, he bit his teeth into her earlobe, sending her writhing and sobbing over the edge. His own body jerked and bucked, breaking loose and exploding deep inside of her.

Afterward, he sat her on the long marbled counter and dried her limp body, as if she were a child. "Are you okay?" It seemed he was forever asking her that question after sex, always promising himself, he'd go easy on her and then losing control.

"Mmm, wonderful."

He breathed deep, watching her head droop with exhaustion. Being around her seemed to turn him into some kind of animal. He shook his head, water dripping onto the marble tiles. She'd be rid of him soon enough. Carrying her to the bedroom, he lay her gently down on the mattress, covering her with the soft cotton sheet.

Pouring himself a glass of the full-bodied red wine he'd chosen together with Pedro, he went and sat in one of the plush armchairs facing the bed, watching her sleep. It reminded him of the first time they'd been together, when he'd discovered she was a virgin. *God, the shock of it*! How he'd hurt her and then gone into denial, convincing himself that she might still be a virgin, convincing himself that he wouldn't touch her again. He smiled cynically. At least now he'd accepted that he couldn't be anywhere around this woman without losing control and wanting, needing to be inside her. And he couldn't imagine it ever being any other way.

He frowned, recalling what he'd told her about his
childhood. It left him feeling vulnerable and exposed. He'd
never spoken to anyone else about it before, never been in
the least bit tempted to, except his mother. She knew that
he'd suffered, but he'd never told her so, always putting on
a brave front when the holidays were over and it was time to
go back.

But speaking to Maya had given him insight into why
he was the messed-up, disturbed control-freak that he was.
She would make a good psychologist, he realised, feeling a
ridiculous sense of pride. She listened, really listened, and it
became clear to him why he wanted, needed to be the dominant one in the bedroom. It was so obvious. Especially the
fact that he only really enjoyed dominating white, European
woman. The Indian kids at the exclusive boarding-school
had just disdained him, whereas the English ones had really
resented him. They'd resented the fact that he dared to
speak and behave like them. Bigger white, English boys
would throw him to the ground, laughing and humiliating
him, holding him down, while they slapped his face and
punched his body, making sure not to leave any marks. The
pain he could bear. It was the humiliation that had gotten to
him. They'd sat on his small body, holding his hands and
calling him all sorts of names from a half-breed bastard to a
dirty coolie who should never have been allowed into their
prestigious boarding-school. That was when he'd known he
would never be English, never wanted to be English like his
detestable father. He would marry an Indian woman and
have Indian children, who wouldn't even need to know
about their English heritage. It had been just another reason
he'd felt relief when his father had died. Now his children
would never have to face their white, English low-life
grandfather.

Soon after his father's death Rajiv had changed the
company name, much to the distrust and disagreement of

the board-members. He'd changed the name from Maddox Investments to Maddox-Junta Investments.

He drained the wine from the glass, raking his shaky fingers through his hair. The memories evoked unpleasant emotions that left him feeling betrayed and enraged. Sorry for that little boy who'd lost his innocence at the hands of bigger, older bullies who were probably just as miserable and homesick as he was. No wonder he'd never enjoyed the pleasures of a woman taking control. It was there, staring him in the face all this time. Yet, he wanted Maya above him, making him her slave. Just thinking about it made him hard.

ৡৄৡৄ

Rajiv awoke hours later and felt panic rise within him as soon as he realised Maya was not in the bed beside him. He glanced at the ornate bedside clock. Ten-twenty in the morning? Had she left without saying goodbye! He heard noises coming from the other room and jumped out of the bed. Heart racing, he strode through the double doors, almost collapsing with relief.

"What are you doing?" he asked, trying not to reveal the panic pumping through his veins.

ৡৄৡৄ

Maya almost jumped out of her skin. "Rajiv! God, you gave me a fright."

He stared at her for a long moment, then blinked and rubbed his eyes.

Maya recalled their first morning-after, when he'd found her on the phone in his living-room. He'd been so angry. She straightened her spine, ready for another argument. He was naked, just as he'd been that morning, but she was no longer the skittish, innocent, recently de-flowered virgin she'd been then.

"Good morning," she said carefully.

His face was pale beneath his dark, tanned skin. "I thought you'd left."

"Oh, Raj!" She went to him, circling her arms round his waist and pressing her cheek to his thumping chest. "I would never leave without saying goodbye."

He squeezed her tight, stroking her hair as his breathing calmed.

She pressed moist kisses along his strong, brown throat. "You were sleeping so peacefully, and I didn't want to disturb you," she whispered against the scratchy stubble of his jawline.

Her bones melted as she lifted her head to look at him. His eyes were sleepy, hooded, his messy hair falling onto his face where designer stubble darkened his jaw and sur-rounded his sensual mouth. She wanted to press her lips to every inch of that harsh, yet vulnerable face.

He glanced behind her and frowned. "What are you do-ing, Maya?"

She shrugged her slim shoulders. "I was just cleaning up a little."

He shook his head and she lifted her hand to push his hair from his forehead.

"Why on earth—Maya this is a hotel. The staff is paid to clean the rooms. It's their job, not yours."

"I know." She bit her bottom lip. "But they went to so much trouble, and I don't want them to know we ended up eating their gourmet dinner on the floor."

He laughed, a husky, sexy sound that weakened her limbs. "You're crazy, you know that? I'll make sure to tip them generously and I'm sure they won't care where we ate their delicious, gourmet food."

She disagreed with his way of thinking, but kept it to herself and turned in his arms to look at the dishes neatly stacked on the trolley and the table-cloth now covering the oval, antique dining-table. "Well, I'm almost done."

He slid his arms around her from behind, pulling her back against the hard, warm wall of his body. "There's a *Do Not Disturb* sign on the door, so you don't need to worry about any staff coming in and seeing the results of our bad behavior just yet. Well." He buried his face in her hair. "Why don't we go back to bed, hmm?"

"Raj." She leaned into the heat of his masculine torso, sweet, languor invading her body as his bold, erection pressed into her bottom. "You're insatiable, do you know that?"

"I think you may have mentioned it before," he murmured thickly, sliding his hand into the robe she was wearing and cupping her breast. "You feel like heaven and I want some of it. I need it, now."

Maya covered his other hand before it reached its destination, between her legs. "Let me just finish sorting this out."

"Hush." In one swooping move, he lifted her into his arms and carried her into the bedroom.

CHAPTER 24

Maya stared at the bedside clock—almost twelve. The curtains were still drawn, just the bedside-lamp on, leaving her feeling like they were cocooned in their own little universe, but the world outside was still ticking over – and soon she would have to leave.

After carrying her into the bedroom, Rajiv had taken his time, making long, lazy love to her, laying back and allowing her to straddle his thighs and do exactly what she wanted with him. This was as new to him as it was to her, which had given her an extra boost of confidence. And she'd taken full advantage of it, loving the way his eyes glittered with new-found desire as she teased and tormented him. Even going as far as to touch and caress herself like she had in London, revelling in his crazed response. Finally he'd flipped her onto her back and driven into her with uncontrolled passion, leaving her drenched in pleasure and feeling like a wild temptress, just beginning to become aware of her own power to please him and herself.

Rajiv was dozing beside her, one hand resting on her belly, his leg thrown over hers, holding her close between his thighs. She sighed heavily, a hollow feeling, which wasn't hunger, settling beneath his warm hand, deep inside of her. She needed to get up, have a shower, and get ready to leave. Their time in this sweet, sultry little universe was about to come to an end. Shifting herself slowly, she tried not to wake him up.

He lifted his head, eyes blue and alert. "Where are you going?"

Damn, she'd hoped she could have her shower before waking him. "I need to shower, Raj." Hesitant, loathe to bring up the subject, she forced herself to move. His grip tightened. She sighed. "I need to start getting ready. It's getting late."

Her eyes widened as he swore crudely. It still surprised her when he did that, but she knew he only swore when he was really angry or upset.

"Is it because of the bruises, because of the rough sex? Is that why you don't want me anymore?"

"Of course not! You know I love how you make me feel," she said, still too shy to put into words the fact that she loved it when he became wild and lost control during sex.

Desperate eyes searched her face. "It's Jay, isn't it? He's warned you against being with me?"

"Jay?" Maya frowned up at him. "Jay doesn't know about us, does he?"

He shut his eyes, shaking his head. "No."

"Then what are you talking about?"

"It's just—I know he wouldn't approve. My intentions not being honorable and all that."

"How do you mean?"

"You know. The fact that I can't offer you marriage. That eventually I'm going to marry an Indian woman."

Her heart tore. "I told you I don't want marriage!"

"Then why? Why don't you want to be with me?"

Maya dragged herself away from him, got out of bed, pulled on the robe—which was strewn across the bottom of the bed—and tied it with trembling hands. "Because if I stay with you, I'll end up getting my heart broken, that's why." There, she'd said it, to herself and to him, finally.

He sat forward, knees bent, and raked both hands through his hair, pulling at it with tense fingers. He seemed at a loss for words for a change, and Maya walked toward the en-suite bathroom, unable to face him any longer.

"Wait!" She turned round slowly, staring at a point above his head. "You said you didn't want marriage." The words were torn from him. "You said you didn't even believe in marriage. So what is it you want from me? Tell me what to do."

She shook her head in defeat, not knowing the answer herself. "I just want—need—to get on with my life, Rajiv," she said, finally. "This affair was not meant to last. It's been crazy—and wonderful—but its run its course. It needs to end, now, today. We both have to get on with our lives. I start working tomorrow. I've told you this before and you know I'm right. We can't always get what we want. So please—" Finally she lowered her gaze and stared into his despairing, beautiful blue eyes. "Let's not end this badly. I couldn't bear that. Let's behave like sensible, responsible adults and say goodbye without any animosity or recriminations. Let's wish each other well and go our separate ways."

ℰᏡℰᏡ

Rajiv was not in the bedroom when Maya returned from her shower, but she could hear him talking in the main room and wasn't sure if he was on the phone or with someone.

She was drying her hair with the powerful, hotel hairdryer when he entered, closing the door behind him. Maya switched off the hairdryer.

"The cleaning staff is here." There was a guarded, almost formal tone to his voice. "Can I order you some brunch. You must be hungry."

The thought of food left her feeling ill and she felt mean refusing his offer, but she had to prepare for work tomorrow and it was getting late. "Thank you, Rajiv, but I'm really not hungry." She looked into his grave, blue eyes, not wanting any pretence between them. "I'm afraid I couldn't eat anything right now."

He'd put on a pair of faded blue jeans with an Indian collarless shirt open half-way down his dark-skinned chest and Maya's heart melted. He still hadn't shaved, his hair was messy from their love-making, and it was hard to believe she would not be seeing this gorgeous creature, who still wanted her, again.

He raised his dark brows, hopefully. "Coffee?"

Maya smiled, trying to keep things upbeat. "Coffee would be lovely, thank you."

He left the room as if eager for something to do.

By the time she left the bedroom, Maya's hair was dry and she was dressed.

Although she felt over-dressed for daytime, she was simply too numb to care. Her jacket was in the main room, but it was warm and comfortable enough without it.

Gazing longingly at the stately bedroom and tumbled bed for the last time, she entered the main room with as much calm as she could muster. Besides the coffee, there were warm croissants, bowls of curly butter, a selection of cheeses, as well as marmalade and conserves, all set out on the coffee-table. Rajiv stood up, taking her hand, and drew her down to sit beside him on the dark, leather chesterfield. He passed her a large cup of, frothy coffee.

"Please eat something, Maya," he said. "It's after one and you haven't eaten since last night."

"Okay."

She smiled, surprised that the mouth-watering smell of

freshly baked croissants left her feeling like she could eat a little. The coffee was delicious, as was the croissant, which she had with grated cheddar cheese. Somehow her mood had lifted and she wasn't about to question it.

"So you're starting work tomorrow?" he asked, as she bit into the warm, flaky croissant.

"Yes, and I'm a bit nervous about it," she admitted.

"They're lucky to have you, Maya." His eyes were serious. "Believe me, as an employer, I know you'll excel at whatever you put your mind to."

He sounded so earnest that she almost believed him. She was passionate about this job and she would put everything into it. "Thank you, Raj, as someone who employs—" She paused, rolling her eyes. "—thousands of people, your belief in me means a lot."

Rajiv drank three cups of coffee and watched indulgently while she finished off what was on her plate. They spoke of unimportant things, like this hotel that he'd stayed at before, and his previous visits to Edinburgh. He'd visited quite a few times while Jay was studying here, which surprised her.

To think that he'd been here, a twenty minute walk from her home, maybe they'd even passed each other on the streets of Edinburgh. He caressed her with his eyes and pulled her hair back so that he could watch her while she ate, brushing a crumb from the corner of her mouth and licking it off his finger. It was all very intimate, but eventually had to end. She couldn't continue to stall any longer.

"Do you believe in love?" he asked.

Maya almost dropped the coffee cup.

"I mean *being in love,* like Sanjay and Kurt."

She set the cup down, her insides beginning to quake. "I don't know," she lied. "I believe in love—loving my mother, my father, my friends." She took a deep breath. "Do you?"

He scratched his head, frowning. "I don't think so. I never have, really," he answered thoughtfully. "Like you said, I love my mother and my brother, but Sanjay keeps talking about *soul-mates.*" His mouth flattened. He didn't sound convinced. "I don't know."

"So what about Jay and Kurt?" She had to know. "You don't think they're in love."

"Oh, they're *in lust.*" His smile was knowing, suggestive. "Like teenagers. But I think that will eventually fade."

And us, are we in lust? Maya clenched her teeth, he sounded so cynical. "Are you saying you think they'll eventually break-up?"

He seemed to suddenly realise what he was saying, and shook his head. "Who knows? Anything's possible, right?"

She kept quiet, too disturbed to answer.

"I think my grandparents really loved each other," he continued, and Maya stared at him in surprise. He'd never mentioned his grandparents before. "My maternal grandparents," he clarified. "They always seemed so happy, content with other."

"Are they still alive?"

"My grandmother is," he answered. "My grandfather died not long after my father. She was devastated, my grandmother, when he died. And yet theirs was an arranged marriage. They hardly knew each other, and they were so young. I think she was about fifteen when they married."

"Fifteen!" Maya knew this must have been a long time ago, but still—*fifteen*?

He smiled at her shocked outburst. "That was the norm in those days, and it's still quite common today. Not that I agree with it." He reached out and stroked her stocking-clad leg, just below the hem of her dress. "But they were the happiest couple I've ever seen and they were married for about fifty years."

She covered his hand when his fingers began making their way beneath the dress. "So where is she now?"

He smiled at her diverting tactics. "She lives in Delhi, a beautiful, colonial house in Old Delhi. I try to see her whenever I travel to India." His expression changed. "You'd really like her. She's a very specially lady."

☙❧☙

It was after two by the time she was ready to leave. Their conversation about love and his grandmother had disturbed her, but she didn't want to go there. She would process it once she was home alone, she decided, locating her small, sling bag while Rajiv spoke in another language to someone on his phone in the bedroom. It sounded like business and, eventually, he ended the call and exited the bedroom, barefoot, but wearing the same jeans and shirt, now buttoned almost to the top.

He looked stunned at the sight of her standing there with her jacket on and her bag over her shoulder. "You need to leave now?"

She was twitchy, filled with anxiety, needing to get this over and done as quickly as possible. "I'm starting a new job tomorrow, Raj. I need to go home and get my head together."

His look of defeat was almost too much to bear. "Okay, let me just get my jacket."

"You don't have to come down with me." She'd been expecting him to say goodbye here at the door and now he was prolonging it. Maya breathed deeply, desperate to get away. "Really, Raj, let's just say goodbye here."

He turned at the bedroom door. "I'm walking you home, Maya." His eyes were shuttered. "Don't worry. I'm not asking you to invite me in. I just want to walk with you."

Maya forced herself to control the agitation of wanting to escape, taking long deep breaths, while he went to get his jacket.

By the time he returned, wearing a leather jacket, unzipped, and looking ruggedly sexy, all she could do was gaze at this gorgeous male, and wonder if she was crazy to refuse him.

"What?" He grabbed his phone and slid it into his pocket. "You don't want me to walk you? Well, tough, 'cause I'm going to."

She swallowed, suddenly relieved that she didn't have to say goodbye right now. She wanted to look at him a little more. "No." She shook her head. "I want you to walk me home."

He eyed her suspiciously then nodded, opening the door. "You sure you have everything?"

"Yes."

The walk from the hotel was mainly in silence. It was a dreary day, but when Rajiv put his arm around her shoulders, and she slid hers beneath his jacket, the warmth of his body made her feel like the sun was shining, but it was a poignant pleasure.

He asked her how long she'd lived in the area. She told him, she'd lived there most of her life, pointing out the park where she played as a child and the house where the scary old man lived, amazed that he was interested in such trivialities of her life. But he was, gazing around him with real curiosity and interest.

Finally, they reached the bottom-floor, the red door leading up to her flat. She pulled her keys out, turning to face him. "Thank you for a really special evening, Rajiv."

He cupped the back of her neck, beneath her hair, and, breathing her in, brought his mouth down to hers in a deep, longing kiss. Maya clung to his jacket, forcing herself to let go as soon as the kiss ended.

"Goodbye, Maya," he said, waiting for her to open the door.

She managed, despite her shaking fingers. "Goodbye, Raj." She tried to smile, closing the door too quickly, as tears filled her eyes.

By the time, she reached her bedroom the tears were streaming down her face and she threw herself onto her bed, thanking God that Josie wasn't there. She thought about what Rajiv had said about love, reminding herself that the man did not believe in love.

And if what she was feeling now had anything to do with love, she wanted none of it. Curling up like a wounded animal, Maya sobbed, the pain eating into her stomach and chest, making it difficult to breathe.

A long time later, she found some tissues, clearing her blocked nose and rubbing her swollen eyes.

Taking a deep breath, she turned over and stared up at the ceiling. She had to decide what to wear to work tomorrow.

ଔଓଔଓ

Rajiv walked away from her building, looking up at the overcast sky, trying to imagine his life without Maya in it. He searched for something good, positive, to hold onto, but there was nothing. Not even the reminder of his brother's new-found happiness could lift his mood.

He clenched his fists in his pockets, recalling the first time he'd met her at the train station, when he'd believed nothing could make him happier than seeing his brother recovered from that dark, depression, but he'd been wrong. Right now, nothing seemed to matter.

Just like the gray sky above him, there was no sign of sunlight to be seen.

But there would be. Rajiv was determined not to let her

go. He had to find a way to convince her to keep seeing him. And he would. One way or another.

End of Book One

If you enjoyed

PASSION & DECEIT

By Leela Atherton

Turn the page for a
Preview of Book Two

PASSION & DENIAL

Six weeks later:

Can you get that, Maya," Josie shouted from her bedroom. "It's probably Mags. She's working the same shift as me today."

Maya left the assessment forms she'd brought home from work on the coffee-table and went to answer the door. Josie worked as a barmaid-cum-waitress at The Pool Lounge just off Princes Street, which brought in an extra income, while she built up her jewellery-design business.

Thinking about the assessments she was working on, Maya opened the door, but it wasn't Mags on the other side. It was the last person in the world she would have expected to see.

"Hi," Rajiv said

Maya was dumbfounded. He was standing in the doorway staring at her through tired, red-rimmed eyes.

"Rajiv? What—what are you doing here?"

"I'm sorry, have I come at a bad time?" he asked, leaning one arm against the door-frame.

He'd cut his hair, she noticed. His beautiful, silky hair was now buzz-cut, military style short, giving his beautiful face an almost brutal edge.

"No," she said automatically. "I was just—um—going over some stuff from work. Please, come in."

She stepped aside, heart racing, and allowed him to enter the large, main room of the flat. Rajiv looked around with enquiring eyes, leaving Maya feeling relieved that the place looked reasonably tidy. It was Saturday, so she and Josie had done some cleaning this morning.

She closed the door as he turned around to face her. His white shirt was creased and unbuttoned half-way down to his chest, hanging out over tailored black trousers. She couldn't help staring. She'd never seen the urbane, sophisticated Rajiv looking so much the worse for wear before.

There was a bruised split near the middle of his sensual bottom lip. "What happened to your lip, Rajiv?"

"Maya, what—" Josie entered the room, dressed all in black, staring from her to Rajiv then back again with puzzled concern visible on her appealing face.

"Sorry, Josie, it wasn't Mags." Maya just managed to keep her voice steady. "Rajiv, this is my flatmate Josie, Josie this is Jay's brother, Rajiv."

"Oh, really." Josie's expression cooled as she looked him up and down. She moved forward, reluctantly holding out her hand. "How do you do?"

Rajiv's mouth twisted into a semblance of a smile, the cut on his lip looking sore and swollen. "It's nice to finally meet you, Josie." His tone was formal as he shook her hand and Josie frowned, obviously having noticed the creased shirt and the split lip. "I do apologize for turning up here unannounced."

Josie still looked perplexed at his scruffy appearance, which contrasted with his formal Indian manners. "That's okay," she mumbled, giving Maya a loaded look from the corner of her eye. "I'm just on my way out to work, anyway."

"I see," Rajiv said, and Maya's stomach knotted. "Maya, could I use your bathroom, please." He ran his fingers over his short hair. "We just drove up from London and I need to freshen up."

"Of course." She was tempted to take him to her en-suite bathroom, but Josie's watchful gaze deterred her. "It's just through that door at the end of the passage."

He excused himself and made his way down the hallway.

"What the hell is he doing here?" Josie fumed as soon as the bathroom door closed.

"Shh, Josie, please. This is hard enough as it is."

"I can imagine. The bastard just oozes sex doesn't he?"

"Josie, don't—don't call him that!"

"Maya." Her friend clasped both her hands. "Get him out of here. I don't know what the hell he's doing here—actually I know exactly what he's doing here." She had that look on her face that Maya knew too well. "Maybe I should phone in sick. I don't like the idea of you here alone with him. The man's dangerous. You can see it from a mile away. You're gonna need back-up."

"No!" It was crazy, but she didn't want Josie here with them. "It's Saturday, they'll fire you if you take another a sickie."

"Damn! You're right. Gordon will not be happy." Josie dragged her fingers through her spiky black hair. "You have to get rid of him, Maya, or the shit's gonna hit the fan!"

"Josie, he'll hear you!"

"I don't give a damn." Josie stared at Maya defiantly and they both jumped as someone knocked hard at the door, again.

It was Mags, leaning against the door-frame, out of breath. "Your bloody intercom's not working," she gasped. "God I'm so unfit."

"Sorry, Mags." Maya tried not to let the relief she was feeling show. "We reported it over a week ago."

"S'okay." She straightened up, catching her breath. "Come on, Josie, we're gonna be late."

Josie stared at Maya, frustration oozing from every pore.

"What?" Mags sounded impatient.

"Nothing. Just let me grab my bag and we'll get going."

Maya breathed a sigh of relief as the door finally closed behind them. Having Josie around exuding her disapproval would just make things more difficult than they already were.

Hearing the bathroom door close and Rajiv returning, Maya made her way around the counter into the kitchen, needing to put some space between them.

"Would you like a coffee?" she asked, busying herself with the kettle and avoiding his eyes. "I'm afraid I don't have anything alcoholic to offer you."

"Coffee would be great, thanks." He walked toward the long windows, which looked out onto the rooftops and the ocean in the distance. "The view is beautiful from up here. It's a lovely apartment, Maya. Different from what I imagined."

She wanted to ask what he'd imagined, but decided to let it go.

Locating some ground coffee at the back of the cupboard, she breathed a sigh of relief. Jose and she seldom bothered with anything other than instant, which should be good enough for him seeing as he'd turned up unannounced. *Like a bad penny*, Josie would have said, but Maya had the ground coffee so she may as well use it.

He had turned to gaze at her, his eyes taking in her faded, black yoga pants, long-sleeved white T-shirt, and slipper-socks. "You look nice."

Nice? Without a scrap of make-up on and her hair tied back in a pony-tail, she would hardly describe the way she looked as *nice*.

She spooned the coffee into the cafetier, then gazed back at him with all the confidence she could muster. "And you look pretty rough yourself." Crossing her arms over her braless breasts where his eyes were resting, she continued. "What's going on, Rajiv? What are you doing here in Edinburgh? And what happened to your lip? Did you get into a fight or something?"

There, it was out. Now would he tell her what the hell was going on? Then she noticed his left hand. His knuckles and fingers were bandaged. Dear God. Maya felt ill in her stomach. What had happened to him? His beautiful hands, those long, sensual fingers were they permanently damaged?

She stared at him with wide, anxious eyes. "What's going on, Rajiv?"

His gaze followed hers. Drawing in a deep breath, he ran his good hand over his brush-cut, before shoving them both into the pockets of his trousers. "Sanjay and I got into an argument, which turned into a bit of a scuffle."

"Oh God, is he all right?" Jay was, like the least violent person she knew. "Your hand! Don't tell me you hit him?"

His tongue snaked out to explore his tender bottom lip. "No, I did not hit him. He hit me, hence the cut lip."

"But your hand—"

"I punched the door." He released a long sigh. "I'd never hit my little brother, no matter how tempted I was."

"Oh God." Her arms moved from her breasts to circle her hollowed stomach. The thought of Rajiv and Jay resorting to violence left her feeling sick. "What on earth brought that on?"

"You. What else?"

"Me?"

He nodded. His hands still in his pockets, he made his way toward the kitchen sink and rested his hips against it. Too close for comfort. "He found out that you'd stayed at my apartment while he was 'in hospital.'" Hooded eyes watched her rock slowly back and forth, her arms still wrapped around her. "Don't distress yourself, Maya. It's me his furious with, not you."

She swallowed, trying to take it all in. "How—how did he find out?"

He shrugged, dismissively. "I think it was Mrs Travis. It must have slipped out in conversation. She's not the type to deliberately cause trouble." He looked so tired, so worn out that Maya was tempted to go over and put her arms around him, but she stopped herself. "It's no big deal. I assured him it was over between us."

It was a big deal. She would never want to come between Rajiv and Jay. They'd been doing so well since Rajiv had found out about Kurt. She'd been so happy for all of them. And now this. "Is that why you came here, to Edinburgh? To explain what happened?"

Rajiv shook his head, silent for a long moment. "After the argument last night in Knightsbridge, I proceeded to get 'motherless,' while Kurt listened to me wallowing in pathetic self-pity." He stared down at the floor, pulling his hands from his pockets and fingering the bandage with his good hand. "Bijal was supposed to take me back to my apartment, but in my drunken state, I insisted he drive me up here to see you." He lifted his head to stare at the ceiling. "He's not very happy with me either. I passed out in the back of the car—only woke up when we reached the outskirts of Edinburgh."

"So where is he now? Bijal?"

"I told him to drop me here and book us into Balmoral. Hopefully, he's sleeping off some of his resentment right now."

Maya did not know what to say. Her mind was spinning with thoughts of Jay. What he must think of her? And Mrs Travis? Dear God! Shame suffused her body and she turned her back on him—her nemesis, her weakness. She gripped the edge of the counter, staring down at her pale knuckles.

She heard him move, then his arms were around her, and he was burying his face in the curve of her neck. And pathetic as she was, she felt that familiar longing pulse through her body. Why did she feel safe in his arms? This sensual weakness was making her forget that he was the cause of all her shame, all her troubles.

About the Author

Leela Atherton loves reading and writing "romantica" (romance/erotica). Born in Johannesburg, South Africa, when apartheid was at its peak, she moved to London at the age of twenty, where she eventually met her Italian husband. They traveled extensively throughout Asia, falling in love with India in particular, before their daughter was born in London. Atherton now lives in the beautiful city of Cape Town with her husband and teenage daughter. Before she started writing full-time, she worked with former-offenders and young-offenders in Cape Town's notorious Pollsmoor Prison. Working in Pollsmoor underlined her belief that if you treat people like animals they will behave like animals, but if you treat them with kindness and respect, they will reciprocate.

Passion & Deceit was written with her love for India and all things Indian in mind—especially the food! Apart from reading and writing, Atherton loves making up stories and characters in her head, spending quality time with her husband and daughter, and swimming at night under the African sky. Her favorite romance author is Anne Mather, particularly her earlier novels: '60s, '70s and '80s.